To Stand

on

Solid Ground

To Stand

on

Solid Ground

A Civil War Novel

Based on Real People and Events

By G. Keith Parker and Leslie Parker Borhaug

ISBN: 978-1-7352642-0-2
Published in the United States of America

Whether you turn to the right or to the left,

your ears will hear a voice behind you, saying,

"This is the way; walk in it."

DEDICATION

We affectionately dedicate this work to Mary Galyon, whose passion for history and genealogy is an inspiration for all who wish to keep alive the memories of ancestors. Her decades of research provided a treasure trove of information, and her excitement about learning from the past is contagious. We honor her as she continues to honor our ancestors.

TABLE OF CONTENTS

Authors' Note

This is a work of fiction, although we have worked diligently to portray a sense of the life and times of the historical figures portrayed as well as the historical events around Transylvania County, North Carolina during the Civil War and Reconstruction. Many early settlers played key roles in the county during these troubled times; to cover or list all of them and their important contributions is beyond the scope of this work.

A note about language is in order. For purposes of readability, a few characters are depicted as using simplified forms of the local dialect even though many, or most, of the persons would have spoken the older, common English from that time, carried over from the British Isles and the times of Shakespeare, Chaucer and Wyclif. A glossary of such archaic folk words is not included, but hopefully the reader can follow the few used. Many studies have been made into the remnant language and music of Appalachia. Very few still speak it today except in remote, isolated areas. As Tyndale would have said, "Them words is right scase nowadays." In the early documents and maps, different spellings of names and places are used. We have chosen to use Deavor, rather than Deaver, Dever or Devore. Likewise, we use earlier common terms such as Lambs Creek and Dunns Rock rather than Lamb's Creek, Lamb Creek, Dunn's Rock or Dunn Rock.

We have carefully sought a realistic balance between authenticity and readability. It is our hope that the reader effortlessly finds themselves drawn into an era very different from their own, yet one that feels simultaneously timely.

CHARACTER CONNECTIONS & MAP

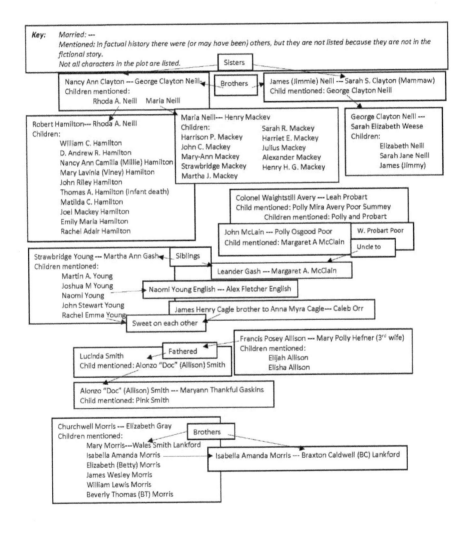

Key: Married: ---
        Mentioned: In factual history there were (or may have been) others, but they are not listed because they are not in the fictional story.
        Not all characters in the plot are listed.

Sisters

Nancy Ann Clayton --- George Clayton Neill
Children mentioned:
        Rhoda A. Neill   Maria Neill

Brothers

James (Jimmie) Neill --- Sarah S. Clayton (Mammaw)
Child mentioned: George Clayton Neill

Robert Hamilton--- Rhoda A. Neill
Children:
        William C. Hamilton
        D. Andrew R. Hamilton
        Nancy Ann Camilla (Millie) Hamilton
        Mary Lavinia (Viney) Hamilton
        John Riley Hamilton
        Thomas A. Hamilton (infant death)
        Matilda C. Hamilton
        Joel Mackey Hamilton
        Emily Maria Hamilton
        Rachel Adair Hamilton

Maria Neill--- Henry Mackev
Children:
        Harrison P. Mackey   Sarah R. Mackey
        John C. Mackey   Harriet E. Mackey
        Mary-Ann Mackey   Julius Mackey
        Strawbridge Mackey   Alexander Mackey
        Martha J. Mackey   Henry H. G. Mackey

George Clayton Neill ---
Sarah Elizabeth Weese
Children:
        Elizabeth Neill
        Sarah Jane Neill
        James (Jimmy)

Colonel Waightstill Avery --- Leah Probart
Child mentioned: Polly Mira Avery Poor Summey
        Children mentioned: Polly and Probart

John McLain --- Polly Osgood Poor
Child mentioned: Margaret A McClain

W. Probart Poor

Uncle to

Strawbridge Young --- Martha Ann Gash
Children mentioned:
        Martin A. Young
        Joshua M Young
        Naomi Young
        John Stewart Young
        Rachel Emma Young

Siblings

Leander Gash --- Margaret A. McClain

Naomi Young English --- Alex Fletcher English

James Henry Cagle brother to Anna Myra Cagle--- Caleb Orr

Sweet on each other

Francis Posey Allison --- Mary Polly Hefner (3rd wife)
Children mentioned:
        Elijah Allison
        Elisha Allison

Fathered

Lucinda Smith
Child mentioned: Alonzo "Doc" (Allison) Smith

Alonzo "Doc" (Allison) Smith --- Maryann Thankful Gaskins
Child mentioned: Pink Smith

Churchwell Morris --- Elizabeth Gray
Children mentioned:
        Mary Morris---Wales Smith Lankford
        Isabella Amanda Morris
        Elizabeth (Betty) Morris
        James Wesley Morris
        William Lewis Morris
        Beverly Thomas (BT) Morris

Brothers

Isabella Amanda Morris --- Braxton Caldwell (BC) Lankford

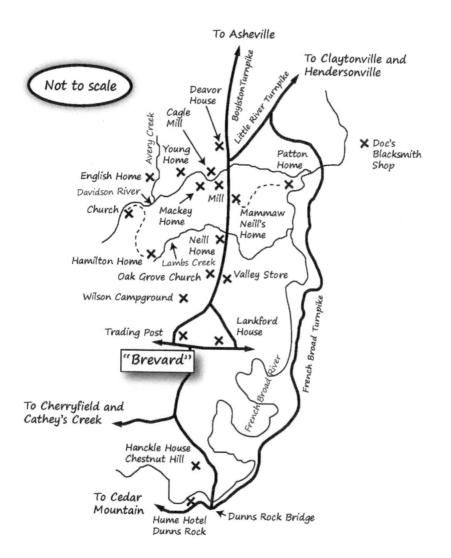

Not to scale

To Asheville

To Claytonville and
Hendersonville

Deavor
House

Cagle
Mill

Boylston Turnpike

Little River Turnpike

Avery Creek

Young
Home

Patton
Home

Doc's
Blacksmith
Shop

English Home

Davidson River

Church

Mackey
Home

Mill

Mammaw
Neill's
Home

Neill
Home

Hamilton Home

Lambs Creek

Oak Grove Church

Valley Store

Wilson Campground

Lankford
House

Trading Post

French Broad Turnpike

"Brevard"

French Broad River

To Cherryfield and
Cathey's Creek

Hanckle House
Chestnut Hill

To Cedar
Mountain

Dunns Rock Bridge

Hume Hotel
Dunns Rock

xiii

PROLOGUE

The Scots-Irishman, Robert Hamilton, was one of the early pioneer European settlers in Western North Carolina, one whose literary skills and ongoing interests in revolutionary thought and writing impacted his engagement in education and local government. When he arrived in Charleston, South Carolina in 1791, the Revolutionary War had ended only eight years before and revolutionary thinking was still in the air. His crates carried not only Latin and Greek books, but also those of French revolutionary thinkers like Voltaire, Condorcet and Volney, names he passed on to his children and future generations, abbreviated as "V.C.V."

Like many European immigrants, his search for freedom and justice in the new world was not only an escape from the violence and unrest in the old country, but also a chance to put into practice some of the ideas filling minds and hearts of hopeful settlers and their families. Although he appears to have arrived from Dublin, recent DNA studies underline that he was closely related to the Hamiltons of Scotland, many of whom had been part of the mass migration from Scotland to Northern Ireland in the seventeenth century. Later, the "great migration" of Scots-Irish to the North American colonies took place in the 1700s as they became a dominant group on the frontier, bringing a dedication to education and literacy. Though Presbyterian in heritage, many became Methodists or Baptists in the religious revivals of the frontier.

By 1799 Robert Hamilton had bought about five hundred acres in the Little River/ Crab Creek area of Western North Carolina that would become Buncombe, then Henderson and, finally, Transylvania County. Several treaties had pushed most of the native Cherokee further west and the land was rich for farming, hunting, gardening, fishing and harvesting timber. More than a dozen children were born into the Hamilton family, but at great cost to the lives of his three wives, a common occurrence on the wild frontier. Lydia Altum, Ann Finley and Anne Orr produced thirteen children, some of whom were key players in the formation of Buncombe County, Henderson County and Transylvania County.

Robert, the dedicated scholar who corresponded with others in Charleston, South Carolina about revolutionary French thinkers, eventually became the teacher for a subscription school in Cane Creek, Buncombe County. He later became Clerk of Court for that County, serving until he died in 1822 at age 52. He was buried at the Central Methodist Church in Asheville where he had been active.

The name "Robert" was passed on to generations of Hamilton descendants, some with additional names. His grandson and namesake, Robert Hamilton, became the first Sheriff of Transylvania County, and a most unique local leader during the Civil War and Reconstruction Era. That powerful image of the original Robert Hamilton cast a long shadow over those formative years of Transylvania County and Sheriff Robert Hamilton.

This fictional story is based on accounts of Sheriff Robert Hamilton's life during those tumultuous years while weaving in other real people, families, colleagues, friends or local folk, who managed to build community in the midst of divided loyalties and Civil War secrets.

CHAPTER 1

Robert Hamilton, January 25, 1861

"George," Robert carefully hands his closest neighbor and friend a cup of coffee as they sit in the wicker rockers on the porch. Wisps of heat curl around Robert's whiskers as he carefully takes a sip before all the heat escapes. He welcomes the tranquility that the warm liquid and the presence of family offers. Although George is Robert's wife's cousin, he feels more like kin than his own flesh and blood, a sentiment both families share and is easily recognized in their children's endearing use of *uncle* and *aunt*.

"Thanks, Bob!" George has already enjoyed his first sip and is deliberately embracing the cup with both hands. Robert nods, but George can see his friend already has his mind somewhere else as he gently rocks. They are strategically overlooking the stretch of valley gently cradling not only the remains of a generous summer garden, but a large pasture dotted with several dozen sheep, all surrounded by thick forest. Most of the flock are grazing a little up the valley, staying close to the hollowed out-log that feeds their trough with fresh creek water. George doesn't question why Robert asked to sit outside in the cold, rather than sit by the fire inside. Instead, he savors another sip of coffee before he breaks the peaceful silence. "Seems the winter-wool will be a reward come spring-time."

"True." Robert smiles briefly, but his eyes are drawn to the far corner of the field. He watches his son, Andrew, throw a bucket of corn husks over the wooden fence, showering one sheep that retaliates with a loud baaah, but doesn't run very far before turning around to consume a few husks. The family's two hounds bark at the sheep a moment before they quickly follow Andrew into the barn.

"Andrew seems to be helpin' you more lately." George realizes that at eighteen Andrew still struggles with not being William, Robert's oldest son. Since he was already twenty, William had convinced his father that it was time to build his own place, especially with ten children crowding their two-story wooden home. There is talk of land directly east of the homestead, still along the Lambs Creek road, right before the bend that opens to the Hamilton's small private valley, land that William could easily develop into his own homestead and still be there for the extended family.

"Yes, Andrew is tryin' to show me he can hold his own, but it's more than that." Robert looks at George and starts to rock a little more intensely. "It's all this talk of secession. The tensions between the North and the South may be at a breaking point, one I fear will only churn up more trouble." He pauses only a moment to look at George, hoping he will understand. "I have kept nothin' from my children. The oldest seven children understand somethin' serious is happenin'." The serious frown on Robert's face gives way to a soft chuckle. "Of course, the youngest three have no worries."

George realizes how Robert is very different in his approach to raising children. George's own three children, Elizabeth, Sarah-Jane and Jimmy are mostly worried about who gets to sleep in the middle of the bed during long cold nights, a coveted spot. For a moment George wonders if he has been too protective, but telling even Elizabeth, his oldest, doesn't seem right. Not when the reality of seceding seems almost unreal. Yet, Robert has even let Matilda, at age ten, share in the woes of the nation. "Is Andrew strugglin' with the possibility of North Carolina seceding?"

"We're all strugglin' with this possibility," Robert pauses. He stands, leaving the rocker to settle itself, "But Andrew has let me know he will not support me." Robert places his empty mug on a bench up against the wall and reaches into his coat pocket, retrieving his pipe, along with his flint and steel striker, and begins to prepare his pipe.

2

George frowns, "What do you mean?" He slowly stands to join Robert on the edge of the porch.

Both men watch Andrew and the hounds emerge from the barn to throw another bucket of husks onto the existing pile. "I have made it clear that I do not support North Carolina seceding and will do what I can to stop it." George waits for Robert to take his first slow-long mouth-filling draw from his pipe. George's silence brings Robert to face his friend. He knows this is a topic George would rather avoid, but also knows he needs to encourage his friend to deal with the reality they are all facing. Finally, Robert speaks as he exhales the warm smoke. "We are meetin' at Lankford's store on the 30th if you would like to be there. Gash, Wilson, Hamblin, Erwin, Morgan and I are pushin' to send Raleigh a document statin' our position."

George raises an eyebrow, "You think it will make a difference?"

"We won't know unless we try." He smiles, but it doesn't reach his eyes. He takes another long draw, followed by several short puffs, making sure his tobacco is burning well enough.

"So, what does Andrew have to say in all this?" After a moment he adds with as much affirmation as he can muster, "It seems like a fine approach." George wishes the coffee was still warm.

"He said that if we secede, he would side with the South." Robert sighs, but is pleased George is talking. "He knows I don't feel the same way, especially if war comes a knockin'."

George's heart races, the reality of the situation hits home quickly. He can pretend there will be no war and that life along Lambs Creek will remain routine and familiar. The creek will rise during summer freshets leaving the afternoon air thick with moisture. Winters will continue to harden the muddy roads that web out from his own home at the foot of Lambs Creek, the bees will continue to fill his hives in the spring and summer with honey and, most of all, the greeting of many strangers and acquaintances, who pass his homestead on the Boylston Turnpike, should never be filled with trepidation. But already he knows something is changing. He can't pin it down quite yet, but fear is already claiming the holler he knows as home.

Robert is saddened as he watches George battle the turmoil within. He moves his head quickly and takes another draw from his pipe, as George turns to face him.

But George sees him and knows Robert pities him. But he must start taking a stand. He feels the unbearable, yet unavoidable push. Choose a side. Choose it now! "I feel the same way as you do, Bob." He finally states emphatically, assuring his cousin's husband that they will be on the same side. Robert nods, not surprised by the statement. He knows where George stands, always has, but guilt of pulling him down to face the facts, weighs heavily on Robert.

When he finally looks at George, he is slightly surprised; he doesn't see the same sadness, but some form of determination or even hope seems to be pulling at the back of George's mind. He slowly asks Robert, "But what does this mean? How can we take such a stand?"

Robert stretches his legs. The cold reminds him that being in his forties does not allow him to push his body to the same limits as in his younger years. "We will take it a day at a time." He smiles weakly, "First things first. Let's see if we can convince Raleigh to remain in the Union."

Tiring of the cold mug in his hands, George moves to place his coffee cup on the window-sill closest the door and returns to stand next to Robert and the lingering tobacco smoke. Both men look out towards Andrew who is finally heading back toward the house while calling out to the dogs who are still barking at the sheep. "Blue! Grady! Hush up!" Suddenly, Andrew catches the men watching him and waves at his uncle with a big smile plastered across his ruddy face. George waves back and his heart sinks. He thinks of Elizabeth, hoping she is too young to make any choice; continuing to keep her focused on being a child may still work.

Elizabeth Neill, January 25, 1861

"Elizabeth!" Ma's voice felt like a faint whisper through the cluster of trees that I liked to call my own. The roots twisted and curved into a saddle just for me before they reached down deep into the creek to drink their fill. Wearing my winter-jacket I straddled my personal wooden saddle as un-ladylike as possible, hiking my dress up as close to my drawers as possible, and dared to thrust one foot into the icy mountain water. I always dreaded winter. No more walking barefoot until blister-birthed callused feet were ready to climb the roughest trees. Doing chores and helping Ma and Pa came with rewards of drawn out evenings spent up Lambs Creek visiting with my Hamilton cousins. The mile walk was nothing. But winter's shorter days always left a dread in me. I suddenly swung my foot as hard as I could to sling water across the creek. Pa had made me angry, because he had not taken me with him this morning when he headed up the valley to talk to Uncle Bob. The two of them were always talking and planning something. I couldn't understand why I had to stay behind to help Ma rather than see my cousins.

"Elizabeth!" Ma's irritation broke through my wishful thinking that maybe I was just imagining her call for me to do yet another chore. My apron was still wrapped around my waist; the sour smell, from milking Nellie this morning, was strong. I had accidently squirted the warm liquid across my apron and needed to remember to target that spot next time I washed it, which would be soon. I sighed and quickly thrust my wet foot into the fold of my already dirt-stained skirt. My attempt to dry off helped a bit before I shoved my slightly numb toes back into the warm sock and leather boot, quickly lacing it up to hide all the evidence. Ma would kill me if she knew I was playing in the creek this time of year, but what she didn't know wouldn't hurt her.

I decided to take off into a run, only to show Ma I was listening. I emerged from the bustle of trees into the small field that gently sloped around to the right and dead-ended at a carefully laid rock wall, wrapping along the side of the hill like a thick ribbon, keeping the soil from loosening. Our two-story wood framed house was perched above the wall, but was set a little back, enough room to drive a wagon around with a load of corn to shuck on an early August morning. I could see Ma standing on the front porch wrapped tightly in her woolen shawl. "I'm here Ma!" I waved with a big smile plastered on my face. In hindsight, I may have been over-reacting, thus guilt was the only message that was sent. I scrambled up the side of the wall, not bothering to walk around it properly. Getting closer, Ma hadn't said a word, so I started to slow down. No need to hurry to my death. Dramatic, maybe, but Ma was all business and had little room for my "idle ways".

"Been playin' in the creek again?" Ma's eyes went straight to the wet spot on the lower half of my skirt, barely revealing a few dirty toe imprints. I rolled my eyes, realizing my mistake too late and wished I had used my already soiled milking-apron instead.

"Yes'm!" was all I could manage as I walked up the porch steps with my best head-hung-low look. The yelling was coming. Soon.

The wait seemed longer than usual, but I didn't dare lift my head. "Elizabeth!" Ma's voice was different. She lifted my chin up to look into her blue eyes. Like my own, they were full of deep longing for answers. But unlike mine, hers were full of fear. Her round face with full cheeks, rosy from yelling for me, seemed to quiver ever so slightly. "You're fourteen. You should be concerned with doin' your part to help me in the household, like your cousins Millie and Viney. They don't give their Ma near as much a fret as you do." She let go of my chin, and reached up to my dark auburn hair, gently combing through it with her fingers, pulling at knots that I hadn't successfully dislodged the night before. "Don't you see you are a young woman now?" I stood there with my mouth slightly open. I was used to arguing and giving Ma a fit with excuses and promises. It had worked for years with Pa's voice always assuring Ma in the still of the night that I was only a child and to let me be. Suddenly, Sarah-Jane and Jimmy came running around from out back, hollering at each other. Even they were helping with the chickens, the sheep, and sometimes the beehives, even if they sometimes got in the way. I wished one of them had been the oldest, then maybe I wouldn't feel so awful.

"Don't you like to wade in the creek, Ma?" I reached up to pull her hand off my hair but didn't let go, holding it tight in front of me, hoping that at least my touch could soften her better than my weak words.

A little sigh escaped her lips and I saw a hint of a smile. "I used to." She looked down toward the hidden creek. "But sometimes it is time to grow up, Elizabeth." She started to say something, but she stopped. What was she not telling me?

"Is Elizabeth in trouble?" I could see Sarah-Jane's head peak over the far end of the porch where it reached the corner of the house. Her rosy red nose stood out against her green eyes and brown hair.

"I hope so!" Jimmy joined in as his six-year old arms reached the edge of the porch, heaving himself up before reaching back down for Sarah-Jane to pass him the basket of eggs. Once her arms were free, she jumped up to sit on the edge with her legs still dangling. She was only nine, but I knew she was better at helping raise our little brother than I was.

"Bite your tongue!" was all I could spit out before Mom's look reminded me once again that even speaking those words marked me as a child.

"Stop your fussin' and get those eggs inside." Ma ruffled Jimmy's hair and one look at Sarah-Jane was all my sister needed to hop up and head in the house.

"I'm sorry, Ma." I meant it.

"Well, get your hair pulled back and head to Lankford's Valley Store." Ma, remembering why she called me in the first place, tucked her hand into her apron, pulled out a scrap piece of paper and handed it to me. "I'm runnin' low on some key staples. Put some saddle bags on Jack and take him with you." She paused a minute and touched my cheek. "Make sure you take your head scarf! Don't go gettin' sick on me!" She glanced at my apron, "And give me that. Don't go wearin' that smelly apron into the store."

"Yes'm," was all I managed as I followed my mother into the house, untied and handed her my apron and headed up the steps to the room I shared with Sarah-Jane and Jimmy. I reached under our bed for a small wooden box Pa made for me last year that held some of my personal belongings. I grabbed my comb and did my best to pull out the tangles without losing too much hair. After I plaited my hair in two braids, I grabbed small strips of cloth made from an old flour sack that Ma had sewn into dresses, leaving left-over material for hair ties.

I hurried downstairs, grabbed my wool scarf and was heading out the back door through the kitchen when Ma stopped me. "Take this to Mr. Lankford." She handed me the basket of the newly gathered eggs and then turned to finish peeling potatoes with Sarah-Jane already picking up the scraps to throw in the slop bucket.

Jack, our mule, was my favorite of our animals. He let me put the bags on him with no fuss and was happy to let me lead him down the dirt road. With my basket of eggs dangling from one arm and leading Jack with my other I was finally feeling like myself again. Walking the mile to the store was the one chore I really looked forward to, that is when I got to go alone without Ma or Pa. They preferred to go along to catch up on the latest news or simply sit a spell with other folk, but I was thankful for those times they were too tied up to make the short journey. I knew Pa was up Lambs Creek talking with Uncle Bob and suddenly being left behind didn't seem so awful.

I pulled the scarf up over my ears when a sudden wind hit me as I rounded the bend that revealed the two-story Valley Store strategically placed across the road from the Oak Grove Church. The wooden church nestled up on a hill overlooking the country store, making the little valley seem like a real community. I loved the sight. Made me think there might be a world outside mine that could be a little more exciting. If I was lucky enough, I would occasionally arrive on a day when the drovers were coming through with a slew of hogs, sheep, cattle or horses and stopping for supplies or selling freshly slaughtered meat. I wasn't disappointed though, that, on that particular day, all seemed quiet, because heading into the store always offered new surprises. I wondered what new items Mr. Lankford might have betted on as a sure sell to the ladies in the community who could actually afford to pay for an item deemed fashionable.

Lost in thought, I was tying up Jack to the hitching post when I heard footsteps scurry along the wooden porch, coming to an abrupt halt. "Miss Neill!" The familiar young voice made me smile.

"Pink!" I squealed and, with Ma's basket in my hand, ran up onto the porch to face the only black boy that I knew that seemed to run around as free as any white boy. He had told me his grandpa was Francis Allison, a well-known white settler over along the Little River, so I guessed that made him one of us. It seemed good enough reason to me. "What're you fetchin' today?" Pink's empty basket was slung around one shoulder. He was always running errands for his Pa, Doc. Pa and Uncle Bob always said Doc was one of the best blacksmiths around and that the Allison family would sometimes hire him out when necessary. Pink was about a year older than Sarah-Jane, which meant that when he came to our house, we would holler at him to come down to the creek with us for a bit to build a dam or hunt for lizards under slimy rocks. He always did. There were times he'd disappear up Lambs Creek to spend time with Uncle Bob's oldest boy, William, who, as Pink explained, secretly taught him the ins and outs of trapping small game. I would roll my eyes when Pink would boast, but then he'd throw a couple of mink pelts at me and I'd shut up.

Pink's smile reached his striking blue-gray eyes, a unique feature that I reckoned baffled some whites he encountered. "Well, Miss Neill, I'm a gittin' the extra scrap metal from Mister Lankford."

"Well that's kind of him." I started walking next to Pink as we headed to the front door of the store.

Pink laughed as he came to a stop and put the basket on the dusty planks, "Pa said Mister Lankford gets his fair share. Ain't nothin' about bein' kind."

"Pink!" A loud voice broke our seemingly harmless conversation and before I knew it a strong black arm swung in front of my face and swept Pink away from me as fast as lighting. Tony, the Lankfords' slave, had the poor boy by the ear and was hauling him back to the other end of the porch. "Boy! You better be careful runnin' off Master Lankford's customers!"

"We're just talkin'!" Pink's voice held a little more sass than Tony appreciated, and I wondered if I should say something, but Ma told me a long time to stay out of colored folk's business. They have their ways and we have ours, not that I quite understood it, since Pink seemed like any other boy I knew, but even I knew my place, especially since Tony was a grown man and was sure to know something I didn't know.

"Your daddy's gonna hear how you was actin'!" Tony let go of Pink and moved towards me slowly, leaving Pink fuming at the other end of the porch. Tony lowered his eyes as he came closer to me and I noticed his voice's sudden change to a soft whisper, "So sorry, Miss Neill. Pink don't know it's not fitten to speak so familiar." Before I could respond, he reached down and grabbed Pink's basket. He turned from me and faced Pink, who had already sat himself on the edge of the porch with his legs dangling. Tony flung the basket at Pink. "Wait, boy, until I'm ready to deal wid you!" Pink scrambled to his knees to catch the basket, but as Tony turned towards me, I saw Pink stick his tongue out at Tony's back. My eyes grew wide and I couldn't help giggle. Tony turned quickly to see what Pink was doing, but the boy was already sitting again with the basket slung over his shoulder and pretending to pick dirt from under his nails.

Tony turned to me again and spoke softly, "Miss Neill, Missus Lankford wishes to see you before you head inside."

"Oh." I was surprised by the sudden change of topic, but then again, I was supposed to pretend that nothing was happening. "Okay, that'll be fine."

Tony pointed away from the porch back towards the Oak Grove Church. I hadn't noticed the small figure sitting under one of the many oak trees that gave the church its name. One hand waved at me, while the other hand held a bundle tightly. I carefully placed Ma's basket on the porch before I hustled down the porch steps and made my way across to see what Mrs. Amanda Lankford could possibly need from me. She had young girls of her own that could help her, although her oldest, Susan, was only eight. As I got closer, I noticed that Mrs. Lankford was rocking the bundle of what looked like blankets.

"Ma'm," was all I could say when I was close enough to realize that their baby, Amanda -Thomas was wrapped in the blankets and looked as pale as milk. She was at least ten months old because I remember it was last spring when Ma and my cousin Mille went to help deliver the little girl.

"Hello, sweet Betty." I wasn't sure why she thought I went by Betty, but it seemed rude to correct her now. "My little Amanda-Thomas aint' fairin' so well and I was wonderin' if your Ma had any honey left over? I know it's not the season yet, but didn't know if you could spare some. I heard honey has some mighty-fine healin' powers." She looked at her baby and then snuggled the blankets around her a little more tightly before pulling up her own coat collar against the sudden gust of cold that made me shiver. "I was hopin' some fresh air and some sun would do her some good. All that heavy bad-air inside this winter is sure to keep my baby sick." Mrs. Lankford smiled as sweetly as she could, but it looked more like a strain, "Do you think your Ma has some extra honey?"

My smile mirrored hers, "I will be happy to ask her. I do believe we have at least some still in the kitchen for our biscuits." I suddenly felt stupid talking about biscuits when she was talking about her baby's life, so I quickly added, "So, I'm sure even if there is nothin' else, we can at least give you that."

Her smile was genuine this time. "Thank you, Betty. You give me hope." She looked down at Amanda-Thomas and started humming Amazing Graze as her rocking took on a slow, almost trance-like motion. Realizing that she had dismissed me, I quietly headed back to the store. I briefly glanced at Pink who was now sprawled out on the porch balancing the basket on one finger, and then headed up the steps, grabbed Ma's basket and walked, relieved, into the Valley Store.

"Hello Miss Neill. Got some fresh eggs for me?" Mr. Lankford came out from behind the wooden countertop as I walked through the door. It took a minute for my eyes to adjust to the dark room. The

11

cast-iron stove was working hard to keep the cold out, but left a sooty smell mixed in with an odd combination of tobacco and wet dog.

"Yes, sir." I smiled handing him Ma's basket, genuinely happy to see the man. He was a large man with dark eyebrows and straight nose that stood out against his graying hair that turned whiter as it cascaded down the side of his face to merge with the most magnificent white beard I had ever seen. Although his beard was clearly combed into obedient straight lines, several tuffs closer to his prominent ears would occasionally have a mind of their own and curl up like small ringlets. That was my favorite part of his beard. If he were my Pappaw I would probably reach out and ask to stick my fingers through the tiny loops. But since he wasn't kin, I settled for his genuine kindness.

"Lookin' forward to your Pa's jars of honey!" Mr. Lankford smiled as he pulled Ma's eggs out of the basket.

"Me too!" I said, remembering my conversation with his wife. But I didn't want to bring that up with him, since he seemed to be focused on Ma's basket, so I backed away from the counter towards the shelves. As Mr. Lankford looked at Ma's list and gathered the items together, he would always let me take my time wandering around the room examining the items on each shelf and in each crate. I suspected he strategically slowed down the process of fulfilling Ma's order so I would have time to see the newest remedy to cure a cough or, on that particular day, touch a small box full of colorful ribbons.

"Ain't no ribbon as pretty as the ones already in your hair." A deep voice startled me. I turned around to look up at a young man who wasn't much taller than me. His red hair was slicked back some with one long light-red strand falling almost into his face. I quickly looked away from his hazel eyes, but then felt stupid because he had spoken to me.

So, I turned toward him again, feeling my face flush, thankful my cheeks were already red from the cold. "Excuse me, Sir?"

A grin spread across his face, "I don't think you've been out much."

I frowned and quickly placed the box back down on the shelf. I was suddenly aware of my filthy dress that wasn't quite hidden by the length of my coat, with the remnants of my dirty feet still smeared across the bottom. "I don't know you and sure don't like your citified attitude!" I huffed and started walking back to the front of the store where Mr. Lankford had placed a large flour sack on the counter, along with a small sack of coffee and one of salt. I sighed realizing it wasn't going to be a quick exit.

"Everything okay, Miss Neill?" Mr. Lankford could see I was startled, and his wonderful beard was closer to me than it had ever been as his eyes focused in on mine. "You look awful upset."

"I think I scared her, B.C." The redhead came up next to me, but looked slightly upset himself.

Mr. Lankford smiled, "Miss Neill, this is my wife's brother, James Wesley Morris." I quickly turned my head toward James and nodded briefly before placing my hand on the large sack of flour. Mr. Lankford continued, "He's come to stay with us for a while and will be helpin' me in the store. My Amanda has got her hands full with the children right now." I could see a glimpse of worry cross his eyes, but he quickly shook it off and roughly slapped the younger man's slighter frame. "Got to earn your keep, right?" Then he squeezed James' shoulder a little too hard making the younger man wince, "And you cain't do that scarin' off my customers!"

James shook off Lankford's grip and laughed, "No worries! She seems to think it is okay to call a country boy like me citified." James winked at me to which I simply huffed and crossed my arms. Like the child I was.

Mr. Lankford shook his head chuckling, "Well, if Polk county farmin' is the city then I'll be damned."

"I only meant. . ." I started, but realized the two men weren't going to listen to me, so I sighed and started to pull at the flour. I felt a tug on the sack from the opposite direction and realized James had also reached for the flour sack. I moved my hand away and looked James straight in the eyes and whispered, "What are you doin'?"

13

He leaned in slightly and whispered back, "Helpin' you." He then threw the sack over his shoulder and headed out the door.

Mr. Lankford laughed. "You'll get used to him." Then he handed me Ma's basket with a slip of paper inside with the newest tally of what was bartered for and what was still held on account. I grabbed the basket and the smaller sack of coffee, took a deep breath and headed out the door.

"I assume this is your mule," James secured the flour in the one saddle bag and then shoved his one strand of light-red hair back out of his face.

I looked around at the empty store front and saw that Pink was no longer waiting on the porch, Mrs. Lankford was still rocking her baby across the way and Tony was nowhere to be seen. I couldn't help myself as a small mischievous smile formed. "What other mule were you considerin'? Unless you were plannin' on haulin' the staples on your back?"

There was a moment in which I wondered if I'd gone too far, after all he was only trying to be nice and I still needed him to carry my salt sack. His hazel eyes locked with mine and I did not budge. Suddenly he broke out into such a guffaw I thought the whole valley heard his laughter. After he wiped his eyes, he walked right up to me, "You sure are somethin' else Miss Neill." He bowed his head slightly, "So pleased to make your acquaintance."

Chapter 2

Robert Hamilton, January 30, 1861

The Lankford Store appears as a strange sight to anyone who might journey along the road this winter day, with horses and buggies tied up and taking every free hitching post space, as well as random trees acting as make-shift posts. The oddity is not the amount of people gathered, but the *Closed* sign clearly hung across the front door.

Inside, Robert and George stand with several men against the shelves while others straddle empty crates that Lankford has provided. Robert scoots in next to Henry Mackey, his brother-in law. Robert nods as he whispers, "Hi, Henry, glad you could make it."

Henry, who is only a few years older than Robert, snickers quietly. "Not much of a choice, I reckon. With your Rhoda tellin' my Maria all about the commotion goin' on, I figured I better get on over here or I might never hear the end of it." Stroking his beard, Henry glances at Robert and smiles mischievously, "If I had my druthers, I'd be tendin' to my pigs and cattle."

Robert chuckles, knowing that Rhoda's little sister can be equally persuasive, clearly a family trait. "I hear you. But I think this will be a meetin' you'll be happy you didn't miss." Although Rhoda and Maria are sisters, the two families do not spend much time together, unlike the close bond the Hamilton family share with George and his family. Sometimes Robert regrets the distance, especially at times like this when he wasn't the one to inform Henry about the meeting, instead the news reached him through his wife. Still, farms require attention and children raising, so it is no different than most farmers in the mountains. Everyone does what they have to do and everyone knows that friends and family won't let time or distance come between them.

Suddenly a strong attention-seeking cough draws the locals to all stare at the man behind the store's wooden counter. Major Samuel Wilson has some documents spread out before him and he shuffles them around nervously before he calls the meeting to order. "Thank you for coming. Sorry we are so crowded, but it is too cold for the campground over the hill, so huddle up to each other and get closer in here." A few snickers and shoves ripple through the store, since the room is already feeling stuffy from the wood burning stove and the many bodies blocking the front door's promise of fresh air. However, a few laughs cannot break the tension felt about the meeting. Wilson continues, "Rev. Duckworth has agreed to be the secretary and I have been asked to chair this meeting. Hopefully we can put together some of our concerns for folks in Raleigh."

An older farmer stands up from his crate and calls out, "Will we git sucked into this war like them others?" As he sits down, others in the room murmur in agreed concern. South Carolina's clear stand against the North only makes the situation worse, with so many of the community used to the Charleston folk spending their summers in the mountains.

A younger voice angrily responds, "Sometimes ye got to fight fer what is right!" Both nods and shaking heads cause Robert to wonder if the meeting was such a good idea. He feels Henry shift awkwardly next to him, still stroking his beard.

Wilson raises both hands to calm the group. "We already got a lot of input from our folks here and are trying to spread the word. We have created a committee made of men you all know and respect. They are trying to formulate some resolutions and a preamble and hopefully, by this afternoon, will come back to read them for our approval." The room is still. Robert is not sure if it is because people are hopeful or skeptical. But the looks on his neighbors' faces reveal both sentiments abound.

Major Wilson clears his throat to further clarify, "The committee is made of Leander Gash, Robert Hamilton, James Hamblin, Overton

Erwin and Squire Morgan. We can assume we call ourselves 'Transylvania County' since they are about to approve us as a new county with that name." Some nod, pleased to hear a name settled on since it has taken several years of debate, including consideration of the name 'Ruffin County'. Wilson continues, "Anyway, formed or not formed yet, we need to express our feelings about the dark clouds hanging over us." Robert feels some relief to find agreement in standing together as a county, even before it is official.

Once questions have been addressed and opinions stated, Wilson dismisses the gathering, and sets a time for the small committee to meet again after lunch. A few people cross the road to Oak Grove Church to eat their prepared picnics and to offer up prayer about the decisions. George encourages Henry to walk with him to join some neighbors as they climb the bank to the church, leaving Robert to walk with Leander Gash, as they follow others back towards the store to finish their preparations for the afternoon meeting.

Although the committee arrived that morning with key parts written, they begin to climb the steps, rather than enter the store, so they can retreat upstairs to Lankford's living quarters to take time to review their resolutions. They want to stand confident when the document is presented clearly. Robert is thankful that Leander Gash is a part of this process, since he is a prominent business man and landowner. His trading post up the hill, has been used as a key location for most official business for years and is not only one of the largest buildings in the valley, but is rumored to be the first one built. Since Gash lives further east, closer to Hendersonville, his wife's Uncle, Probart Poor, manages his trading post. Robert, though pleased with Gash's support for this current undertaking, is also somewhat baffled, since Gash has over a dozen slaves, a curious and seemingly incompatible detail when considering arguing against secession. Robert shakes off his concern since a few others present are also slave owners, mostly business owners and larger land-holders. The reality is that the majority of the local folk work their lands and crops themselves and they rely on large families to provide the needed help.

Robert, still pondering the curious circumstances, has chosen to take up the rear, and is slightly startled when he comes face to face with a red-headed young man, who is eagerly waiting to make his exit from the upper level of the store. Robert smiles and extends his hand when he realizes that this must be B.C.'s brother-in law. "You must be James. Welcome to our valley."

James, thankful for some acknowledgement, among what he assumes are important folk, eagerly returns the hand-shake. "Yes sir!" He looks at the men as they begin to move the benches from the table to the side of the room, allowing them to stand and look down on the already open documents. "Pardon me, Sirs. I'll leave you to your business!" James nods to Robert, who realizes that time to acquaint himself with the young man will need to wait for another day. By the time the door closes, the sound of James' boots clattering down the stairs is not heard by the men inside, already engulfed in intense discussions.

In the early afternoon, a cowbell rings and folks gather anxiously. This time Leander Gash stands at the counter and addresses the group on behalf of the committee. His clean-shaven face and distinguished posture, draws attention from those gathered. "We have a rough draft of a preamble and six resolutions. I've asked Bob Hamilton to give the essence of the Preamble. Bob please do so."

Robert, preferring not to look more official than he needs to, does not move from his spot near the door, well aware all within the room can hear him. Henry and George once again flank his sides, but both men shift awkwardly, eager to avoid drawing attention to themselves. Robert sighs and shifts one step in front of them, allowing them to be at ease as they partially fade into his background. "Well, we try to underline our rights to gather and do this appeal, and to call for peace as well as stick to our Constitution. We go on to mention how dreadful and devastatin' a civil war will be and how we could face starvation and ruin up here in the mountains without railroads and steamboats like other parts of the state."

Robert stops a moment and the silence is only broken by a cough. He sees worry grip the faces. Saying what is already in their minds is not easy, but he forces himself to continue, "We underline that taxing the people heavily and takin' out loans to pay for fightin' as well as conscription of our men to fight is heavy upon us. To remove protections of the *writ of habeas corpus* as proposed by several states really scares us." Robert pauses and sees some confusion in the eyes of a few and decides to clarify. "It means we believe no one should be held or imprisoned without a real legal reason." Once he sees some acknowledgement he adds, "We want to remain free and not suffer a military despotism." A few shouts of approval rise with some men standing up as Bob steps back to once again lean against the wall between George and Henry.

Wilson, still behind the counter, draws attention back to himself. "Thank you, Bob. This is heavy work for us all. I will summarize briefly the six resolutions now being refined by Brother Duckworth." The chairman waves his hand to the end of the counter where a tall, slender man lifts and waves one of his documents, with as much ceremonial air that he can muster, acknowledging the gravity of his role, before quickly returning his attention to scrutinizing the parchment in front of him.

Wilson, drawing attention back to himself, begins, "First, we call for a Convention of the State in its sovereign capacity, along with other sovereign states, to seek a treaty of peace with the federal government or with other states." The gathering is struck silent on hearing the plea for seeking peace first.

No comments arise as Wilson continues. "Secondly, we realize other Southern states may not want to do this, so the Sovereign State of North Carolina will pursue on her own to make such overtures for peace in her sovereign capacity and as a convention approves, also subject to a vote of the people." The room remains silent as he pauses for a moment.

Suddenly they hear the momentary racket of benches overhead clearly being returned to their correct placement. The rise of a woman's voice seeps through the ceilings boards, "Jimmy! Stop that! You'll disturb them talking' downstairs! Ain't you heard of respectin' official meetings?"

"Ain't they heard of respectin' tables and benches?" James' voice isn't as loud as his sister's, but any more conversation between them is muffled by some snickering from the men who need something easier to digest. Robert glances at B.C. who is covering his face with one large hand, while shaking his head. Robert smiles thinking that James at least cares for some order.

Wilson clears his throat, obviously trying to regain the crowd's focus, and once he is assured that all are listening, he continues listing the resolutions, "Thirdly, we ask Governor Vance to call for such a convention or have the people vote for a convention. Fourthly, if there are enough votes for such a convention, that the Governor be directed to call for representatives to it as soon as possible. Fifthly, we ask that the Senate and House members from our areas vote for such." He takes a breath, as do several in the room. "Finally, we ask that newspapers all over the state publish these proceedings, but especially the *Standard* there in Raleigh and the *Times*. That is pretty much the essence. Brother Duckworth thinks he can have it in final form within the hour for anyone who wants to sign." Duckworth does not look up at the mention of his name but continues pressing on with the final wording of the resolutions.

"Sam?" B.C.'s familiar voice is a welcome change.

"Yes?" Wilson is open to questions from the floor.

B.C. takes a moment to run his fingers through his beard once before he sets his eyes on Wilson. "Are you sayin' that we are askin' North Carolina to stand alone, without our southern neighbors when it comes to takin' a stand for peace?" B.C.'s words are simple, but the reality is far more complicated than most can handle.

The tangle of emotions ranging from fear, anger and disbelief to hope, begins to transform the small store. Robert feels Henry lean into him. "Bob, you are right. I can't quite say I believe any of this will do any good, but I reckon we got to do somethin'." Robert begins to respond, but is cut short as Wilson quickly raises his voice to restore order.

"Neighbors! Friends!" He pulls them all back to attention. "We are only stating that we wish to avoid war at all cost. But we know that this is a long shot. We only speak on behalf of those who wish to sign the resolution. Those of you who do not, can walk away from here informed and aware of the challenges we face." He looks at each man in the room. "This is not a call to divide our community. We are simply trying to preserve it!"

Elizabeth Neill, February 20, 1861

"Elizabeth, it ain't so cold if you tuck your fangers under your arm pits!" At first, I couldn't tell who was talking to me. I was sitting on an old wooden cart that had no wheels but made for a perfect bench in the Hamilton's barn, away from all the commotion in the house. I was sharing my hide-away and seat with my favorite cousin, Lavinia Hamilton, but we all called her Viney, which was a perfect nickname. She would wrap her wiry arms around my own, so we could get as close as possible without anyone hearing us.

"Shut your mouth, John-Riley! Elizabeth don't want to hear your yackin'," Viney yelled through the empty barn and then leaned in so her breath was warm on my ear. "He's only a year younger than me, but he acts like a lamb that ain't found its legs."

"I heard that!" A head popped out above us, looking down from the loft. Pieces of straw stuck out of his brown hair like horns. Viney and I started to laugh so hard at John-Riley that we barely even noticed him jump down and stomp out of the barn, causing a low *moo* from the corner where their one cow was happily devouring fresh hay.

We finally took some deep breaths and Viney leaned into me, "So glad you came for a visit." She glanced toward the barn door for a moment before she added, "It's been so depressin' here with all that talk of war."

I frowned a minute and then laughed. "What are you talkin' about?" I looked into her eyes reflecting equal confusion. I shoved her lightly, "You're just joshin'."

Viney pulled away from me quite dramatically and grabbed my two shoulders. "Elizabeth! Are you serious?" When I didn't answer she dropped my shoulders and was suddenly wondering if she was the one who should to be telling me. The sudden flash in her eyes told me she was going to tell me and all others be damned for keeping me in the dark. "South Carolina is already breakin' away from the United States and there's rumors that they're fixin' to fight if they have to. A bunch of other states are thinkin' about breakin' away, even North Carolina. It's awful scary!"

I couldn't really understand much of what she was saying. Although we were the same age, I suddenly felt very young and ignorant. "That is scary," was all I could say. Then I sighed because Ma and Pa were clearly keeping something from me, maybe they really did see me as a child.

"Let's talk about somethin' fun!" Viney jerked me out of my self-pity stupor. I smiled best I could. "Did you hear Mr. Lankford's brother-in law has moved here?"

My smile suddenly became genuine as I remembered the red-headed young man who had been pleased to meet me. "In fact, I did talk to him. Twice!" I smiled.

"Well go on!"

"He helped me load up the staples I bought for Ma and then when I took some honey for poor Mrs. Lankford's baby, he answered the door." I suddenly wasn't as chipper remembering that moment, about two days after she asked for the honey; I brought it by hoping to talk with James again, although I wasn't sure why exactly. Maybe his laugh had thrown me off a bit, thinking he might not be so awful. But when I knocked on the door, he had been quick to thank me and shut it again. Was the baby really that sick?

A tug of my arm and a tiny giggle brought me back from the melancholy thoughts that were beginning to engulf me. "Well, Pa talked to him!" Viney turned into my giddy equal again. "I overheard him talk to Ma about how he would be a perfect young man to meet Millie."

"What do you mean?" I was a little confused with where Viney was going. Camilla, who was called Millie, was her oldest sister and at age eighteen she was practically rearing the three youngest Hamilton children.

"Well, it seems a perfect match since . . . oh, what is that man's name?" Viney touched her head, almost looking like her father for a moment.

"James Wesley Morris." I said without hesitation.

Viney looked at me in shock. "Well, Elizabeth! How come you know his name so well?"

I laughed at her. "I just told you that I met him last month."

"That's right!" Viney wrapped her arm through mine again. "Go on. Tell me all the details!" So, I did, feeling like maybe her impression of this encounter was not the same as what I was trying to tell. But I wasn't sure why I even cared.

"Well, he seems nice and funny." She leaned her head on my shoulder and sighed. "I can see it now. Millie and James married with little red-headed babies!" She laughed so I laughed, but it never reached the core of me.

"What makes you think Millie is the perfect person for James?" I asked as calmly as possible, but realized too late that it was the second time I had asked her for clarification.

Viney looked in my eyes with a sudden curiosity, "You're not sweet on him, are you?"

I shook my head awkwardly, "I don't know."

Suddenly she knocked the top of my head with the back of her hand. "Well, get that notion out of that gourd of yours!"

"Ouch!" I rubbed the sore spot on my head. "What did you do that for?"

"For your own good." Viney started to laugh. "You're only fourteen!"

"So?" I didn't see her point.

"James is twenty-eight!" She started to roll on the ground in hysterical laughter after she saw the shock on my face.

Robert Hamilton, February 20, 1861

"It's good to have you and Sarah visitin' again." Rhoda shoos the little ones out of the chairs in front of the fireplace. Robert welcomes his wife's gentle, but firm command of the room as she places George and Sarah in the "guest rockers", a term the children tease their ma about, being the newest furniture in the room, while he obediently takes his seat in the one that is clearly missing strands from the carefully woven split river cane. Robert knows Millie will tend to re-weaving when she can. Robert smiles at Rhoda as she finally settles in her straight back chair that she pulled from the table's end, and without taking a breath she continues, "Lookin' forward to the spring thaw and more time together."

Robert is thankful that the whole Neill family came to sit a spell. Earlier, Andrew whistled for the dogs to join him and said he'd keep an eye on the sheep outside while Robert enjoyed guests inside, but Robert knows Andrew prefers to avoid any potential political arguments in front of friends. Robert had agreed that the sheep would probably be better company for him. Although Robert had tried to keep it light and Andrew had obligingly laughed, Robert saw a streak of anger flash through his son's eyes quickly suppressed. As Robert reflects on the moment, he can't but help worry about his son's lack of levelheadedness.

The laughter and the warmth of the fire bring Robert back to his friends and the moment at hand. The talk of weather and sheep herding in front of the fire soon turns into delightful thank-yous as Millie serves them coffee, while ten-year-old Matilda follows her older sister with a pan of warm cornbread, carefully dividing up and placing the golden treat into out-stretched hands.

After the cornbread is finished, Sarah looks around the living room until she is satisfied that the children are occupied. Jimmy and Sarah-Jane have joined their cousins on the floor at the back of the room. Millie has already gathered the girls in front of her spinning wheel, which is currently pushed far up against the wall, next to a basket of raw wool ready to be spun. She is clearly enjoying taking time to teach the younger girls how to make corn-husk dolls. Jimmy has joined Joel, who is the same age, and they appear to be tossing pebbles into a coffee cup shoved in a corner. Sarah leans into Robert, "Do you think there is any chance for this gettin' a hearin'?" Sarah speaks what is on her mind, trying to keep her voice low. A month has passed since the petition was sent and there has been no word from Raleigh.

Robert, however, does not lower his voice, "Well, I'm not too sure. As I understand it, back in November, not long after Lincoln was elected- maybe a couple of weeks- our Governor Ellis did ask the Legislators to call for a convention to discuss secession which he badly wanted then. But those two influential friends, Zebulon Vance and the *Standard* Editor, William Holden, both Unionists, said 'absolutely not.' We must 'wait and see' what this new president will do."

George, who has begun to rock a little more quickly than the others can't help but keep his voice lowered, not used to having children nearby when discussing serious matters. "So, do you think we have any chance of not bein' drawn into war, now that at least five other states have joined the Confederacy? Is our Buncombe County neighbor Vance such a strong Unionist that he will really fight for peace and push this proposal we are sendin'?"

Robert thinks a moment, thankful Andrew is not present to give his opinion, but is interrupted when the front door opens, and John-Riley comes pounding through the room without looking at anyone. "I hate those girls!"

"John-Riley!" Rhoda is up and grabs her son by the back of the shirt. "You don't come in here talkin' like that!"

John-Riley looks at George and Sarah. "I'm sorry Uncle George, Aunt Sarah." He swallows. "I'm sorry Viney and Elizabeth are so mean and cantankerous!" He slips out of his mother's grip, being almost as tall as her, and escapes up the steps, slamming a door. As Rhoda starts up the stairs, she sees Robert shake his head encouraging her to let it be. Rhoda notices all three adults are trying to muffle their laughter, so she returns giving no more thought of her thirteen-year-old son's outburst.

Finally, Robert answers, "Hard to say. As you know, Zeb does not like the conservative Democrats and still calls himself a 'Whig' although few others do. He even tried the 'Know Nothing Party' a while. When he took his seat in the House of Representatives back in

25

'58 he fought hard to keep the Union intact and proclaimed that secession was unwise and dangerous. I'm not sure if he is among those pragmatists who want to keep the Union because they believe only the Union can keep slavery intact. So many Southern representatives thought those early federal agreements to respect each state's laws would be kept until new states out west came in and all hell broke loose about slavery." Robert, suddenly reflecting on his own statement, wonders if Gash is one of those men as well, pushing for peace with hopes of still striking some deal to keep their way of life intact. Robert shakes of his thoughts off doubt over his friend and respected member of the community, feeling guilty for doubting Gash's intentions.

"All the waitin' is worrisome." Sarah looks behind her at the children who are contently playing with each other.

"The honest truth is that we may never get a response from Raleigh." Robert follows Sarah's gaze.

Sarah doesn't move her eyes from Jimmy who has just let out a joyful guffaw having landed a pebble in the coffee cup from across the room. She sighs and looks back at Robert. "That's what I'm afraid of. No answer will mean war."

CHAPTER 3

Elizabeth Neill, February 27, 1861

"Elizabeth?" Ma's voice whispered as she managed to finally climb into my bed, as much as I tried to push her away. I couldn't ignore her anymore, especially when she snuggled up next to me. Jimmy and Sarah-Jane where already dressed and busy with their chores leaving me to clean up the mess they made with the bed, so stealing another five minutes seemed okay, or at least until Ma's gentle morning beckoning turned into the scream of a hungry panther. I didn't move away when I could feel her breath on my face. Her morning cup of coffee must have been strong. "Elizabeth, what's wrong?"

I frowned slightly, not really sure what she was talking about. "Nothin'," was all I could whisper, although deep down somewhere I knew that was a lie.

"Baby," Ma pushed a strand of my auburn hair behind my ears. She hadn't called me baby in a long time. "Somethin' is wrong. You've been mopin' ever since we were at your cousin's house a week ago. What happened? Are you upset about fightin' with John-Riley?"

I suddenly laughed. "I didn't fight with him! His sister was teasin' him. He'll get over it!" I giggled at the memory of my cousin with hay-horn hair. I suddenly realized that I hadn't laughed since that day, maybe moping was a good word.

Ma smiled a little, "Then what is it?"

I looked at Ma and spoke words I didn't know were caught deep inside of me. Words I believed would shatter everything, but holding them in might keep everything normal. Yet, the more I swallowed the words, the harder it was to keep them down. "Are we goin' to be in a war?"

Ma didn't say no. She didn't say anything at first. The more she looked at me, her eyes searching for the right words, the faster I started breathing. "I don't know." Ma finally said as she wiped the first of my tears away. She pulled me close as she finally told me everything she knew. Everything. "No more keepin' secrets." She promised.

I nodded not really believing it, but I could tell she was relieved. I could have shared with her the one other worry on my mind that week. I should have told her about Viney teasing me about James. But liking someone, so much older than me, was nothing I wanted to share with Ma. Keeping secrets was something I was also good at. I had learned from the best. Ma didn't need to worry any more about me anyway. I had to get over James Wesley Morris quickly. After all, I was used to liking handsome men, like that James-Henry Cagle. Everyone talked about those Cagle-blue eyes, even Ma. Anytime Pa needed to head down to the Cagle Gristmill on the Davidson River, I would ask to go along and help, but I was only hoping to look in those eyes. But James-Henry was sweet on Rachel-Emma Young and he, being ten years older than me, quickly squashed any notion of romance. So, clearly, James Wesley Morris was another silly notion. Another childish behavior that I needed to snap out of. No need to bother Ma with silly childlike notions.

Robert Hamilton, May 2, 1861

"Wait up! I'm goin' with you today." Andrew yells at Robert as he and Rhoda follow behind Viney, John-Riley, Matilda and Joel heading up the path leading away from the back of their home. Millie is still in the house to care for Emily and Rachel, still too young to head to school. Rhoda knows that once Emily starts school, they will have to use Mae to carry Emily. Although Emily never makes a fuss over her club foot, walking to school will be too much. Rhoda doesn't say anything, though, since Mae is only one of two horses they own. The other mare, Nell, foaled Mae five years ago and was not as keen on the children climbing her. She preferred the plow and occasionally pulling the wagon. It was Mae that took to the children, but Robert was also beginning to ride her exclusively when he left the farm. Rhoda tells herself that it is not yet time to worry about Mae being tied up with traversing up and down the mountain carrying Emily to school, rather than working the farm or being accessible to Robert's needs. Still, Rhoda knows it's a worry she can't let go. Andrew suddenly yells at the two hounds eagerly following at his heels, "Grady! Blue! Go home!" He points his finger back towards the house and the dogs immediately stop and begin whining as Andrew continues up the path without them.

"Why are you comin' along?" Robert stops to face his son. "You're done with school. You got work to do."

Andrew walks right past his father, and then glances briefly at him, "Why are you goin'? You're done with school, too." He tries to smile at his father, "It's Thursday and last I heard there ain't no sermons on Thursday neither." Andrew picks up a rock and tosses it into the creek on his right, which follows the path for a short while. "And don't worry about the farm. I asked William if he could take a day away from building his new home to tend to the sheep at feedin' time. He seemed more than happy to jump back into his old job that he dumped on me. I guess he figured he owes me," He picks up another rock and throws it with a little more force.

Robert speeds up to walk next to his son, ignoring Andrew's anger towards his brother, he now tries to sound official, "Well, I got some business with Reverend Young."

Andrew looks at his father straight in the eye, all lightness gone, "And I got business with his boys." Robert frowns, not sure what Andrew means, but guesses that they both are seeking out news. Robert lets Andrew move ahead of him to catch up with the others. As Andrew shoves Joel into a Rhododendron bush and then takes off up the path with Joel screaming and chasing after him, Robert can't laugh, not even smile.

Rhoda, chuckling at the banter, slows down and puts her arm through Robert's, "What's wrong?"

"Andrew is pretendin' to be part of this family." Robert sighs.

The words hurt, but Rhoda shoves her husband gently, "Oh, come now! A little dramatic!" She moves from her husband's arm and takes his hand as they continue around a bend where the children have all climbed up onto Andrew as he pretends to carry them like a bear. Rhoda has a brief sigh of relief when Robert can't help but smile at the unfolding scene.

The well-worn path between Lambs Creek and the little Methodist church on Davidson River reflects not only the families of worshipers, but also the many children who traverse it to attend school during the limited teaching months. Sometimes the Neill children, who live closer to the Boylston Turnpike, cross over to the school with their cousins during the spring and fall, but otherwise they reach the school by walking along Boylston Turnpike to the mills powered by the Davidson River, then up the river road itself. Simple enough since it is a shorter distance for them in that direction. But on beautiful days they will often join their cousins trekking over the mountain, from behind the Hamilton home, not minding the extra mile.

Strawbridge Young began the missionary work along the Davidson River and his son-in-law, Reverend Fletcher English, was continuing the calling. Fletcher also provided the lumber for the little Methodist church and Oak Grove Methodist Episcopal Church from his sawmill up Avery's Creek nearby.

After about an hour, the Hamilton family walks into a clearing that boasts a well-worn path prompting them to turn left and continue to head towards the river. The clearing is one of the favorite parts of the journey because Strawbridge and his family had planted rows of apple seeds that were now small saplings, with the hopes that one day a beautiful apple orchard would define the valley. As anticipated, within minutes Robert hears the babbling Davidson River on their right as their trail stops and they continue their journey walking along the dirt road. Only a few more minutes pass before they reach the church.

Viney and Matilda quickly find Elizabeth as she waves at them from the front door. The two boys drag their feet as they follow their sisters. Andrew flicks John-Riley on the head, "Go on, boy!" Joel laughs, happy to not be the victim this time. John Riley, in turn, pops him across the head.

"That's enough!" Rhoda fusses at Andrew. "Seems like *you* need to get in that school and learn some manners!" Rhoda sighs and can't wait to cross over the small foot bridge and head up Avery Creek to sit for a spell at the English home. Rhoda delights at the thought that she will take some time alone to enjoy a visit with Naomi, Reverend English's wife, one of Strawbridge Young's daughters. Rhoda smiles to herself as she thinks of holding Naomi's first baby, only eight months old. She looks at Andrew, "I'm goin' to go hold a baby who don't know yet how to be so cantankerous!"

Andrew kisses his ma on the cheek and quickly heads after his father who is already crossing a wooden foot bridge to head to Strawbridge Young's house. Once Andrew catches up with his father, the two men walk in silence for about five minutes through the forest until a clearing reveals a two-story frame house. As the two emerge from the forest into the clearing they see John Stewart Young, the youngest of Strawbridge's three sons, wave at them as he stops swinging a large ax at an old stump.

"Looks like the stump is losin'?" Andrew teases. "Can't you pick on somethin' your own size?"

John laughs. "Like you?" He grabs Andrew's arm. "You ain't no boy no-more." Andrew smiles, thankful that he finally holds the same status as John, who, at age twenty-three, is somewhat of a hero to Andrew. After all, it was John who chose to befriend Andrew, rather than William, although William is older. John told Andrew that William was just a sheep farmer like his father, not quite as exciting or dangerous as cutting lumber.

"Where's your father?" Robert interrupts the young men in their banter.

John looks at Robert and as seriously as he possibly can he answers, "Sir, Pa is out back behind the house. You will find him there doin' his business."

Robert nods his head in thanks as he moves towards the back of the house, but frowns slightly when Andrew and John break into uncontrollable snickering. Robert shakes his head and thinks there are some things he will never understand until he finds himself face to face with the family outhouse. Suddenly, Strawbridge Young steps out with half pulled up coveralls. After a moment of shock and awkward silence he immediately says, "To what do I owe this honor, Brother Bob?"

Robert, taking Strawbridge's lead, moves on, "Straub, do you have a few minutes to spare to help me think through a couple of things?" Strawbridge nods and they walk to the front of the house and the reverend points to the log bench under an oak tree. They are positioned well away from the two young men who have now settled onto the front porch steps and are in their own deep discussion. "What's ailin' you, Brother Bob?"

"Just about everything that is goin' on in our land, but we cannot deal with all that." Robert begins to pour out some of the heavy burdens on his mind. "Mostly local stuff and tryin' to figure out where we fit into it. My young'uns, the tensions, all that. I'll get to the point. We are but a few who do not want to secede from the Union and we have to lie low and be quiet."

Strawbridge replies before Robert is finished, "Yep. As you know I get regular threats because I speak out against the Union splitting and was very outspoken against the Methodist Church split back in '44, just before the Baptists did in '45." Roberts remembers how Strawbridge Young has always spoken his mind. And to receive threats about a split in the church seems minor to what will happen when he speaks out against a split from the Union.

Robert asks, "Then are you unhappy with those churches who are now 'Methodist Episcopal South'?"

Strawbridge runs his hand through his short dark hair, and then combs back through it with his fingers like he is trying to tame the unruly curls, a motion Robert has seen many times when Strawbridge tries to pick his words carefully. He finally points his finger in the

32

direction of the little church where Robert dropped off their children only moments ago, "As long as I am alive, this little church will never have 'South' attached because it means we approve and support slavery. Besides, as long as I own the land, it will be registered in the official United States documents."

Robert nods and then hesitates a moment. He is not sure if he should speak what is really on his mind.

Strawbridge settles his hands in his lap. "I believe something else is ailin' you. Speak up Brother Bob."

Robert responds quickly, "Well, to get to the point, I think you, like many of us, are opposed to slavery. Your sermons clearly say it. Help me to understand that you have a couple of slaves yourself. I am not judgin' you at all, only tryin' to understand." Hamilton takes a breath hoping he has not offended his friend. He sticks his slightly shaking hands into is pockets.

Strawbridge takes a moment to focus on a squirrel scurrying underneath their log bench, only concerned with burrowing into the thick brush to escape a second squirrel's angry chatter. Robert hopes he has not pushed too far, but suddenly Strawbridge draws his attention away from the critters back to Robert. "Bob, you are kind in the way you ask, and I know you well enough that you do not judge anybody." Strawbridge raises his eyebrows for a moment and chuckles, "Although you clearly have strong opinions of your own." Robert is surprised at his friend's levity and offers a gentle smile of acknowledgement. Strawbridge takes a deep breath, clearly trying to find a way to explain. "The short answer is two-fold. First, we try to love and include our slaves as family, even providing an education which is forbidden in this state. They would not make it in the North as the mother is quite insane, so the father is caring for her and the little girl." He leans in for a moment to Robert and winks one of his heavy eyebrows, "It is our little secret."

Robert nods showing that he acknowledges his friend's explanation, although it only makes sense to a certain extent. To Robert slavery is slavery, regardless of well-meaning thought processes that seem to justify one person owning another. Yet, in spite of his doubts, Robert does his best to support his friend. "Well, Straub, that makes some sense and appears you feel you are carin' for these people. I reckon it aligns well enough with your preachin' about Christian care for those unable to fend for themselves." Robert shifts and, hoping for deeper clarity, he leans in to ask, "And what might be the other reason?"

"Don't laugh, Bob, but it is very practical and offers some crazy defense against those who attack me for my stance for the Unionist cause. As you know, we get regular notes and warnings in public. But several critics seem confused that we still have slaves, so they figure we must not be all that bad. Some have even said that keeping slaves has kept us from being burned out." Strawbridge shakes his head at the ridiculous seriousness of his own words.

Robert shakes his head not sure how he should respond. "Strawbridge Young, I could never laugh at you." Robert does not feel this is a laughing matter, but does not indicate that this is why he does not join the chuckling preacher's levity. However, Robert appreciates the honesty of his friend's last statement. It appears men will do anything to keep their families safe and he understands this notion. "I think I am beginnin' to understand what you are tryin' to do and how you and Fletcher are educatin' our families and tryin' to protect them." Robert reflects on how Fletcher, on Sundays when he is addressed as Reverend English, does not hold back preaching anti-slavery and his stand against secession. Robert suddenly smiles thinking that Fletcher and his father-in-law must have some very heated discussions. Robert glances in the direction of the path that will lead him back to the school. Then his eyes focus on Andrew and John who are still dialoguing, glancing over at the two older men occasionally. Robert finally adds, "Most of all, during the weeks our children are able to attend school and Fletcher turns into their teacher, he does not appear to indoctrinate them but gives them tools to think for themselves. I reckon he learned something from you and you teachin' your children." Robert knows his own son has a mind of his own. Yet, it is hard to celebrate, knowing it differs from his own.

Strawbridge watches Robert's face and joins him in observing the young men for a few moments before he sighs, "I need to tell you one more piece of news." Robert frowns as Strawbridge's hands reach for his hair once more. "War is only a matter of time now with the attack on Fort Sumter last month. If, or when it comes to war, our three boys plan to serve in the Confederate Army."

Robert stands suddenly, shocked, "After what you just said? After all you have preached! All you stand for! All you fought for when it comes to keepin' the church anti-slavery?" Robert begins to pace, but he quickly sits down again when he draws Andrew's attention.

"It's not that simple Brother Bob," Strawbridge flattens down his curls. "And you know it. Our family is like most in these parts- split apart in trying to figure what is right or best. For a lot of folks, loyalty to community is vital. Even a lot of young fellers will one day be conscripted and will reckon they got to fight for home and family." When Robert is silent Strawbridge continues. "Then there is the rising fear that each state will no longer have the rights they feel are theirs according to the Constitution. My boys feel strongly about each state's rights, whether what they choose is right or wrong, it is still a right of the State." Robert remains still, staring at the kicked-up dirt at his feet. Finally, after a long silence Strawbridge adds, "This is not an easy time. Slavery is wrong. But do we let northern States dictate our choices, as flawed as they might be?"

Robert does not know what to say, but he manages to look up and shake his head. He looks one more time at Andrew and John who suddenly shake hands, promising something only they know. "I reckon your boys will pull Andrew to their side."

Young speaks softly, but his words hit like a hammer, "Andrew will choose what Andrew chooses. The question is, how will you respond?"

Elizabeth Neill, May 2, 1861

The small wooden church, transformed into a small one room school, was one of my favorite places to spend time with my cousins and my friends. That spring day was particularly beautiful with the sun finally warm enough to dip our feet in the river, but only if Reverend English would let us take a moment to go down to the bank to gossip and play. I kept looking over my shoulder at the church door, hoping that he would soon open them, his only indication that we could stop writing down the sentences he was dictating.

I finally leaned back in my chair and glanced up at the rafters above me. My heart stopped. Something was moving. Actually, there were many movements. I raised my hand slowly.

"Yes, Elizabeth?" Reverend English stopped dictating. I didn't answer him, but my raised hand suddenly displayed a pointed finger. All the children looked up and a collective gasp filled the room. "Okay, children, stay calm." English spoke softly, but I could tell he was irritated. "We've had snakes before!"

"Yes, Sir," John-Riley whistled, "But that's a whole den of them!"

Reverend English began to usher us out of the little church frantically waving his sinewy arms, leaving our papers abandoned. "I'm not sure why they keep coming back!"

"Must be your teachin'," John-Riley laughed, being his silly usual self. I always thought he was trying to be like his older brother Andrew.

"Or your preachin'," Joel added. We all couldn't help laughing.

"Very funny!" the Reverend attempted to scold us, but he couldn't hide the chuckle that escaped. "Why don't you have a short recess while I remove the snakes?" He glanced towards the open door and muttered, "Lankford promised me he had something that could help."

While sitting alongside the others with our feet in the river, I could hear some cursing coming from the inside of the church. It seemed our holy man thought such language okay as he battled snakes rather than quoting scripture. I tucked that knowledge away for later. Cursing okay when fighting snakes, and maybe other evil creatures? I wondered if Sarah-Jane and Jimmy counted as evil creatures when they bothered me.

The thudding of a horse-hooves coming from down the dirt road along the river suddenly pulled me out of my thoughts. In fact, we all ran up the riverbank with britches and skirts hiked up revealing wet pink toes and calves, hoping to see further down the road. But there was no need since the rider was already upon us.

"Well, hello!" James' voice surprised me. I hadn't seen him since January; I'd been avoiding the Lankford store, much to my parent's frustration. They wondered why I suddenly abandoned my favorite chore and had even punished me on one occasion for refusing to go.

I quickly dropped my skirt and smoothed it out nervously. I hoped my cheeks weren't red and especially hoped that Viney wasn't watching. I didn't run up to James, like the rest of the students, but stayed back busy searching for my pair of worn-leather booties somewhere hiding in the carelessly discarded pile of shoes and socks.

"Hi. Who you lookin' for?" It was John-Riley who decided to be the acting grown-up, at the moment.

"Reverend English is expectin' me. Have you seen him?" James looked towards the open door of the church and watched as Reverend English walked out with a lifeless snake in each hand. His face was all red and sweat soaked through his white shirt. "I think I found him." James laughed. He jumped off his horse, grabbed his pistol from one of the saddle bags and ran up the steps to Reverend English who towered over the redheaded young man by at least a foot. English said something and swung the dead snake in his left hand obviously pointing to the rafters within, enough direction for James to slip into the church. Suddenly, I heard four shots. We were all silent for a moment and then James appeared with the last four snakes slung over his shoulder. I thought he was such a show-off and decided to lace up my booties, rather than run to him and touch the dead snakes, like everyone else.

English, still holding his own two snakes, hollered at James, "Why'd you shoot them? Now we will have holes in the roof. Got to get those patched up now!"

James started to laugh, "I'm sorry Reverend, but I ain't as good at wranglin' snakes as you are. Seems it takes a holy man to kill snakes with his bare hands!" He glanced my way for a moment before he added. "I don't mind comin' back and patchin' up any holes I might have made."

English sighed and nodded. "I'm sorry, James. Thanks for helping me clear them out. But I'm afraid they will come back. We got good carpentry help from neighbors like the Neills, Cagles, Hollingsworths and others. But snakes are a problem that even the best carpenters can't take care of."

James tossed the snakes on a wooden bench for later, knowing the meat and skin would not go to waste. "I have somethin' that B.C. sent over here for you to try." He walked back to his horse and pulled a mason jar out of the other saddle bag. He walked up to Reverend English who was placing his two snakes on the snake pile. "Here."

The Reverend took the jar and opened the lid and briefly stuck his nose into the jar. "Cinnamon sticks?"

James shrugged his shoulders, "B.C says snakes don't like strong smells and some people swear cinnamon keeps the snakes away. I really don't know, though. But worth a try!"

English looked at the pile of snakes and then at all the students who were standing around James and him, wishing every day would be this exciting. "I guess it will be worth a try." He looked at the bare feet of the students surrounding him reminding him of the quickly fading school day. "Thanks James! Okay girls, boys, go get your shoes on and let us get back to learning." Moans and objections were quickly silenced with a stern look from the snake-wrestling holy man.

As the class began to run to the shoe pile, I was already heading back toward the church. I tried to keep my head down as James passed me, but he stopped and turned to me instead of heading to his horse. Everyone was busy, and English had already headed inside. "Miss Neill?" His voice was soft, but formal.

"Yes, Mr. Morris?" I stopped moving and looked at him as formal and courteous as possible. I had no plans to be rude.

"Thank you for bringin' the honey. Seems Amanda-Thomas is feelin' better. Her color is comin' back." He shuffled awkwardly.

"Well, that is good news." I smiled genuinely and could see him beam at my response, causing me to suddenly feel awkward.

"It's a shame you don't come 'round the store no more." He dropped his eyes briefly and then looked back up at me. "Ain't much good goin' on now-a-days."

"Sir?" I am confused.

"When I saw you and your ribbons." He paused, knowing he was being forward. I suddenly felt my heart race, but I didn't look around to see if Viney was watching. I was listening to this man. He was telling me something. By holding his gaze, he took my own daring to be forward as a sign to continue. "You made me have hope. Then you made me laugh, Miss Neill." He smiled and shoved his red hair out of his face, smoothing it down, only for it to fall right back almost into his eyes, bringing attention to their hazel color, almost green at that moment. "I will always remember that day." He stepped away from me abruptly as he observed Viney starting to head our way.

I didn't care who was coming. I suddenly smiled. And before James completely turned to go, I whispered, "Me too."

At that moment James grinned. It was the silliest thing I had ever seen. Like a little boy who caught his first fish. "I'm goin' to be goin' home to Polk County, but only for a few months to check on family. But I will be back as soon as I can."

"I guess I'll be seein' you then?" My cheeks blushed, but I didn't really care.

"Yes, Ma'm!" James almost shouted. I couldn't help but laugh as the red-haired man jumped on his horse and took off at a gallop.

"What got into him?" Viney asked as we both watched him disappear into the thick forest. "He didn't even take the snakes he killed."

"I guess he has more important things to care about." I held my head high. I loved Viney, but I didn't tell her. She wasn't going to take that moment away from me too.

Robert Hamilton, May 9, 1861

Robert feels Viney's arms squeezing him tightly from behind as they both straddle Mae who is moving slowly under the added weight. The Valley Store looks solemn in the early morning light with wisps of fog weaving in and out of its shadows. Oak Grove Church is barely visible at first, but as the fog slithers around each gravestone it soon seems to lose interest and move on, slowly unveiling the small church, as it makes its way up the valley.

"Pa, it's not fair!" Viney sobs and presses her face to his back trying to muffle the groan that escapes.

With one hand Robert grasps her clinching fingers that are clasped around his waist, "I know Viney. But we cannot understand God's ways."

"But Amanda-Thomas was a baby!" Viney's sobs continue. Robert wonders if it had been wise to let Viney accompany Millie to help Amanda and B.C. But since James had not returned yet, he knew that both parents were thankful that Viney could help watch their other children while the adults took turns staying up all night with the baby. It was Viney, though, that ran all the way home to fetch him only an hour ago.

"It hits all of us at some time in our lives when we grieve the loss of a child. You were only three when we lost our three-month-old son, Thomas." Robert remembers burying his baby boy in the cold of winter.

"Confound it Pa! That don't help any!" Viney's words are angry now. "So, God just kills off babies! That don't make a lick of sense."

Robert sighs and takes a moment before he answers, "God doesn't kill off babies. It is a part of life and death, and we can't understand the ways of God." As Mae comes to a stop at the hitching post, Robert jumps down first and turns to look up at Viney before he helps her down. He intentionally changes his tone to make sure she understands her place. "You need to pull yourself together and ask no more questions 'til we are home. It does this poor family no good to have you so upset when they are the ones needin' to grieve. They need our support! If you can't do this then you need to wait out here. Do you understand?"

He holds her in place up on the horse as she contemplates what he has said. Her face changes from anger to understanding and she finally nods, "Yes, Sir." He quickly helps her off the horse and they proceed to make their way to the stairs that lead to the second floor of the store. Once Robert knocks, he hears footsteps behind him as Viney scrambles back down the stairs to wait with Mae after all.

Millie answers the door and Robert notices her face is not only blotchy from crying, but the deep circles under her usually cheery eyes reveal sleepless hours. She only nods at her father as he silently follows her to the small bedroom where B.C. is leaning against the door frame. His white beard is all disheveled and his eyes are blood shot. Millie leaves them to head over to the other three little Lankford girls who are quietly sleeping on a bed in the far corner.

Robert finds his voice and almost whispers, "I'm so sorry B.C." B.C. doesn't say anything but allows Robert to embrace him as he sobs. Once the storekeeper pulls himself together, he signals for Robert to come into the small room where Amanda is sitting on the edge of a bed with her baby in her arms.

B.C. finally finds his voice, "She won't let her go. The baby's been dead two hours now. I tried to take her, but Amanda screams and fights me." He looks past Robert towards the door, "I can't let the litt'l uns see their ma this way."

Robert nods and walks towards Amanda and kneels beside her. The grieving mother is rocking slowly and when she finally looks at Robert she whispers, "I'll never get to hold her again." There were no tears, only a deep emptiness.

"Will you let me hold your baby?" Robert holds out his hands, but does not touch the infant.

Amanda clutches the child tighter, "But you'll take her from me. I cain't let that happen." Her eyes begin to take on a wild look.

"Yes, I will." Robert speaks truth hoping to pull Amanda back to reality. "But only if you let me."

Amanda frowns, "And why would I let you?"

Robert keeps his hands open, "Because you know that you've been the best mother and Amanda-Thomas knows it too, but now heaven is waitin' for her."

41

Amanda looks at the pale life-less infant in her arms and a glimpse of something spreads to her eyes, "She does look like an angel already, don't she?"

"She sure does!" Robert moves closer.

"I guess I better let her go so she can be my angel." Amanda looks at Robert who only nods. Slowly she kisses her baby one last time and hands her to Robert who carefully carries the almost weightless body out of the room.

Elizabeth Neill, May 10, 1861

The sound of blades hitting hard dirt pulled my attention away from the figure-eight I was scratching into the dirt in front of me with the toe of my boot. I had reluctantly agreed to help Ma carry some food to the Lankford family since she would have me wait outside, once I paid my respects to Mr. and Mrs. Lankford. With the already limited living space, there was no room for a curious onlooker. As Ma was busy talking with Mrs. Lankford in the small bedroom, I did glimpse the small wooden box on the middle of the table. Millie, who was watching me, nodded to me that it was okay for me to go closer. I only walked close enough to see Amanda-Thomas' pale face appear to be no more than a sleeping baby-doll. "Don't touch," Millie whispered, "Just in case she got some sickness. Got to be careful of that bad air!" That was all I needed to hear to step back quickly and make my way outside, with fresh air, to wait until Ma finished paying her respects.

Two figures, to the right of the little church, caught my eye. It looked like Tony and someone that looked like Pink, but I wasn't entirely sure since it didn't make sense that he would be helping Tony, so I decided to investigate. As I climbed the small hill, both figures stopped to look at me. I waved and yelled, "Hello. It's me, Elizabeth Neill."

Sweat glistened off their dark skin and I could see it was Pink after all as soon as his smile spread from ear to ear at the sight of me. "Hi,

Miss Neill." He quickly looked at Tony and his smile disappeared as if suddenly remembering his place.

"Good afternoon, Miss Neill." Tony was less excited to see me, but he seemed somewhat grateful to take a break. I moved closer to see what they were digging and as Tony moved out of my way, a small rectangular hole appeared reaching several feet into the earth. My smile disappeared and Tony quickly added, "It's for Missus' dead baby."

I nodded, not sure what to say, so I awkwardly mumbled, "It's a fine hole."

"TONY!" Mr. Lankford's booming voice startled me, but Tony quickly turned and hustled down the slope towards Mr. Lankford leaving Pink and me and a hole in the ground.

"Why are you here?" I asked Pink, curious how he came to work alongside Tony.

Pink's mischievous smile returned as soon as he saw Tony wasn't running back up to us, but instead following Mr. Lankford into the house. "Well, Pa wasn't too happy none about my back-talk and told me he'd tan my hide if I ever had a notion to sass Tony again. Pa has always preached we better be respectin' others. Don't ever eat nothin' from nobody we don't know, but should always respect 'em." I smiled at the strange combination of advice, but it seemed reasonable enough. He sat down on the side of the grave and let his legs dangle into the darkness below. "So, I came to make it right with Tony and he said I could work off my sass." He shook his head, "I ain't gonna sass Tony no more. Shore don't like diggin' graves for babies."

I shook my head not sure how to respond, but suddenly Pink jumped up and moved himself a few feet from the grave, holding the shovel in one hand and straightening up his shirt with the other. I looked behind me and saw Mr. Lankford followed by Tony who was carrying the small wooden box towards us. Ma, Mrs. Lankford, Millie and the little ones were not far behind, all making their way up the gentle hill.

I knew it wasn't the funeral. That would come when family could gather, but they needed to get the baby in the ground. There was always fear that sickness would strike others if the dead were left in wake too long, especially those who died like Amanda-Thomas did. I took a step back as Tony placed the small box in the grave. I didn't say a word to the grieving family. Nothing seemed fitting, so I bowed my head instead.

Chapter 4

Robert Hamilton, May 18, 1861

The warm spring day, following a night of heavy rain showers, boasts green fields and sheep greedily enjoying the new growth. Robert, standing in the shade of the large pine tree at the bend in the road, watches as his Uncle Joe Hamilton canters away, heading back toward the Boylston Turnpike, busy as always laying the groundwork to establish Transylvania County. Robert remains standing long after the sound of hooves slinging mud has faded. Rhoda calls to him three times before her voice, the barking dogs and the growl in his stomach tear him away from his thoughts.

Rhoda has lunch ready for him and has sent the children outside to give them some privacy. "Well, my love, what did you learn from Uncle Joe about tomorrow's planning meeting?" Robert takes a bite of the warm beans before he looks at her with worried eyes. Rhoda plops herself down on the bench next to him rather than settle in at the place setting across the table. "What is wrong?" Rhoda's cheeks begin to color when her husband hesitates, "You better be quicker than two shakes of a lamb's tail answerin' me before I shove all that food on your plate back into the pot!"

Robert, taken aback by his wife's reaction, almost chokes on the mouthful of beans he is swallowing. After some hearty coughs he finally reaches for his wife's hand and speaks, "I'm sorry. Uncle Joe said some serious things that have me ponderin', rather than listenin'."

When Rhoda doesn't respond he continues. "He and the others are pushing for me to be sheriff."

Rhoda is confused. "This is nothin' new, Bob. You know they have been pushin' you to consider this, and you even said yourself that it would be an honor."

"But that was months ago, when there was first talk."

"What difference does that make?" Rhoda squeezes her husband's hand. "You are the same man today as you were then!"

Robert sighs and shakes his head, "But North Carolina is not the same place it was with war on our heels."

"Nonsense!" Rhoda speaks firmly. "You know that up here mountain folk are mountain folk first, through feast or famine and now through possible war."

Robert smiles gently and wishes his wife's simple statement of fact were true. He hears more than she does and knows families are already torn apart in South Carolina. "Okay, let's say that we hold that statement to be true. I am still not like my uncle. He is a natural leader. I fear I can never measure up to him or my own Pa." Robert's own father, John Hamilton, and his uncle Colonel Joseph Hamilton were well known politicians throughout Henderson County. He does not say it, but the comparison to the original Robert Hamilton, his grandfather, also weighs heavy on him. Robert was only five when his grandfather died, but it seems to the sheep-farmer that his name sake is slowly becoming a legend. Robert once glanced at his Grandfather's collection of books including the writings of French revolutionary thinkers and texts in Greek and Latin. Not only was his grandfather a teacher at Cane Creek, but he was active in Buncombe County politics and was their Clerk of Court for a while. Robert doesn't know if he should laugh or cry at the realization that the Hamilton family would, as soon as Transylvania County is founded, be a key political player in multiple counties. He is simply not sure if that is an expectation he can live up to.

"Robert Hamilton do not put yourself down! You have as much talent as any man in these parts. Why do you think so many people come to you for help or advice?" Rhoda finally gets up and heads to her own seat, dishing herself up her own pile of green beans.

Robert smiles at his wife's mindset and takes a few minutes to enjoy some cornbread before stating, "Well, Rhoda, it looks like I will be asked to be the sheriff of our new county. Am I not too old for all that?" Now he eagerly awaits her adulation of his qualifications.

Without swallowing the half-chewed beans and accompanied by a swinging fork to punctuate each point, Rhoda educates her husband. "With your years comes a lot of wisdom and experience. That is undoubtedly why they want you. Lord knows, if we end up in war, those two things alone are crucial. Then there is the fact that you know everyone in this neck of the woods already. They know that has value, *and* you are a good listener!" Rhoda pauses and puts down her fork and finally swallows. "But I get the feelin' there is more behind your hesitancy."

Robert, having thoroughly enjoyed his wife's oration, and wondering if *good listener* is on his grandfather's list of legendary traits, hates to strike a solemn tone. "You know me well, my lovely wife. You know my faith convictions about slavery and my real opposition to this secession idea. If those folks in Raleigh decide North Carolina must join the Confederates, our county will have to follow, gather and send troops."

Rhoda nods. "Yes, dear Bob. I have overheard your agonizin' talks over the past several months with your Uncle Joseph and know of your faith talks with Pastor English as well as Strawbridge Young. If I recollect correctly, each of them said you have to follow your own conscience and follow what your faith tells you." Rhoda smiles, "Besides, so many folks are tryin' to build this new Transylvania County. It's kind of like tryin' to build a movin' horse-drawn-wagon while you are in it. You do the best you can, when you can."

"Well, Rhoda. Never heard that image before, but it fits, I reckon. Must be a Neill saying from your family." Robert forces a smile. "I just don't want to fall under that wagon!"

Elizabeth Neill, May 19, 1861

I couldn't wait to see James again and was hoping he had maybe returned recently since the baby died, but I didn't divulge this key piece of information to my father on why I wanted to join him going to the Lankford's store. I mumbled something about wanting to understand what was going on in forming the county and, since he still carried some guilt of his own for leaving me out of the whole talk of war, my father agreed. As soon as we started walking, I regretted my overenthusiastic display of curiosity since Pa then proceeded to lecture me on, I'm sure, *everything* he knew about starting a county. It was a long mile.

Once we arrived, I was thankful that Pa quickly abandoned his daughter to mingle with the growing crowd of country folk. Since the crowd was lingering in front of the store, I quickly slipped inside to look for James. It took only a moment for my eyes to adjust to the dark room, but I was surprised to find almost as many men and women in the store as were standing outside. Several folks were taking a moment to purchase goods before the meeting began.

"Miss Neill," Mr. Lankford's voice took me by surprise as two women carrying baskets almost knocked into me. "Would you kindly wait outside, if you aren't here on your Ma's behalf?" My cheeks warmed realizing I was not carrying a basket full of eggs or jars of honey. I quickly nodded and scurried out the door and kept walking.

"Where you runnin' off to?" Mrs. Lankfords' voice broke what must have looked like a full-on gallop.

Within moments, I was almost at the foot of the hill that rose to meet the Oak Grove Church perched on top. Mrs. Lankford was sitting in the same spot where I last saw her rocking her baby, but this time she had a small wooden box that was open and revealed some paper and ink. "I'm not runnin' *to* anywhere." I looked at her for only a moment before turning away, and then, suddenly embarrassed to be perceived as rude, I turned back around to explain. "I'm runnin' away *from*." I said as matter of fact. Then I smiled and shook my head, still looking up towards the white church. "I guess I was not in the right place to begin with."

"How's that?" Mrs. Lankford asks gently as she begins to pull out a piece of paper.

I finally turned my head to look at her, not sure if speaking the truth to her was wise. She seemed harmless enough, so I explained, "Well, James wasn't in the store, so, when I went lookin' for him, I was shooed out like a dog in a chicken pen." I cocked my head as if figuring out the answer to a complicated question. "So, I reckon it's really his fault I was fussed at!"

Mrs. Lankford laughed so loud that, for a minute, she seemed to be crying. "Well, I sure needed a good laugh. I think it's fair enough to blame my brother... he never seems to be at the right place at the right time." Her eyes turned sorrowful in an instant. I figured she was sick at heart that James hadn't been here when she needed him most.

"I'm so sorry." Was all I could say, feeling foolish to even share a glimpse of my frustration with James, when hers was knit from real pain, mine only a child's wishful whim.

The grieving mother smiled gently, "Well, I'm fixin' to write him now." She started to pull out the ink and looked up at the sky, "Hope it won't rain anymore today. Last night's dreary drizzle near made me feel heaven was cryin' with me."

"You're writin' James?" I moved a little closer, curious of her small makeshift writing table. She was pulling out a steel pen and dipped it in the small inkwell.

I could see her scribble what looked like *Dear brother* before she answered me, "I am." Then she had a gentle smile that was almost a smirk, "Do you want me to tell Jimmy that you was lookin' for him today? I could tell him he's got a youngin' that is sweet on him."

To my dismay, my cheeks burst forth with color, "Oh, no! Please don't." She started laughing and shook her head. I wasn't sure if she thought me to be silly or what, but I wasn't going to find out. "I better go, I think the meetin' is startin'."

"I can hear fine from where I'm sittin'." Mrs. Lankford dipped her pen one more time and was busy writing James, not really concerned of my whereabouts.

Relieved, I walked back to the store as Lankford's clanging bell drew everyone's attention. I was thankful for the distraction, hoping that no-one would notice my red cheeks. Reality was that no one really cared, after all a county was being formed. However, my father did look at me and wave before turning to listen to official business.

I quickly found myself standing next to some unfamiliar women. But I was relieved to find that most of the women folk were standing together, allowing me to hear bits and pieces of news that drew my thoughts into other people's business. Soon a very large woman shushed us and told us to pay attention to the meeting at hand. So, I obliged, after all I would need to know what Pa was talking about on our walk home.

Joseph Hamilton was the first to speak to the gathering crowd. I knew he was somehow related to Uncle Bob, but I hadn't seen him much myself. When he spoke, he sounded like he was a man at home there, standing in front of that crowd. "Friends, thanks for coming. Most of you know why we are gathered. I want to assure you all that I am not in charge, just trying to help us get ready." I chuckled slightly, since he clearly was in charge, but no one else thought it funny so I bit my lip and focused. Joseph Hamilton continued, "Got a lot to do. As you know I was already asked back in April to help locate a site for the county seat."

I couldn't tell where it came from, but someone yelled, "What's the hurry?"

Without a feather ruffled Hamilton continued, "Well, to meet some state requirements, we got to elect a county clerk, a sheriff, a coroner, a registrar, an entry taker, a surveyor, a constable and several others, as well as justices for our new court of pleas. A lot to do in a short time." He paused to punctuate the seriousness of the business at hand. I glanced around to see if anyone else dared to yell at the man, but when no one did he continued while pointing at a large paper already tacked to the front of the building. "I've posted these here on the wall and ask you to give some thought, so we can get right into it. Don't really know if we can do it all in one day anyway!"

An older man I vaguely remember living somewhere lower in the Little River community, asked, "Will we have a chance to discuss the folks to be elected, or will they be just shoved down our throats?"

Hamilton responded less officially this time. I guessed this man was someone he knew and respected, "No shoving, but we do need to make some decisions very soon in these troubled times. As you know, Raleigh failed to respond to our appeal to vote on a convention to appeal for peace. We know not what is coming." There were several nods and murmurs that spread through the crowd. I tried to make out what was being said, but could only catch words like *war*, *split* and several cuss words Ma would not approve of, although I did tuck them away with Reverend English's unintended lesson, for a day I might need such blasphemous language. Hamilton raised his voice only to draw attention back to him, "What is your concern? Do you want to speak to any possible candidate?"

The sudden shifting of bodies and murmuring between individuals made me think that the crowd was a little surprised at first to be asked for their input. A voice finally called out, "They's talk of George Orr a-bein' county clerk and I reckon that is good."

Hamilton scribbled on a sheet only he could see, "Let us add him to our possibilities." He looked around, "Any others?"

"I heard some talk about your nephew as possible sheriff." Another voice spoke, and my heart beat a little faster. Were they talking about Uncle Bob?

Hamilton asked as officially as he possibly could, but I could hear the slightest waver in his voice. "You have a problem with that, if Robert is elected?" This was obviously no new piece of information. He wanted Uncle Bob to be Sheriff.

The man was clearly wearing his Sunday best with a top hat keeping the sun from burning his head. Although I thought it might soon be protecting him from rain since the sun was peaking in and out from behind dark clouds, I wondered for a moment if it was one of my Papaw's hats, a Jimmie Neill. In fact, there were several top hats spotting the crowd, along with the usual leather short and wide brimmed hats. But Papaw's hats were a favorite as people came from all over to buy a "Jimmie Neill," or at least that's what I was told. He'd died back in '53, but people still wore his hats and were upset Pa hadn't learned to be a hatter. I guess Pa thought naming my brother Jimmy was enough to pass down. I was pulled out of my daydreaming when the man with the Jimmie Neill hat answered, "Not really, seein' that you Hamiltons have so much experience in government in Buncombe and Henderson County. But ought we not find a younger, more powerful man who can keep them outlaws and Yankees away?"

I looked around the crowd for Uncle Bob and found him leaning against the pole at the other end of the porch. His face was serious as he scanned the crowd with an expression I couldn't make out. He didn't look like he was really excited about the possibility, but he wasn't discouraging further dialogue either. Hamilton continued patiently, but firmly with his neighbor, finally placing a name with the face. "Well, Howard, if we are, in fact, drawn into this war, all our young, able-bodied men will be drawn in as well. The sheriff is not part of some army to keep away any other troops, from anywhere. His job is to try to keep local law and order, collect taxes, and do many chores assigned by the new court to be set up."

Howard, dramatically waving his hand in the direction of my home, responded, "How can he, from way up on Lambs Creek, keep us safe down Little River or up in Cedar Mountain or up in Gloucester?" Several nods made way for some grumblings. I had lived my whole life on Lambs Creek and had never set foot in some of these small mountain communities, so it seemed a logical concern to me. I kept my eye on Uncle Bob who didn't move and might as well have been a second post holding up that corner of the porch.

Hamilton didn't hesitate, and I could tell he'd already thought the whole thing through, "Well, he will find a deputy shortly and the new court will authorize either deputies or community rangers to watch each community. So, you will have a local guard or group to help watch each area. We hope this war does not sweep us up and take most of our men away."

I watched Uncle Bob slowly slip away, leaving Hamilton to answer any more questions. But I didn't hear anything else. One phrase repeated itself in my head until panic griped me. *We hope this war does not sweep us up and take most of our men away . . . war does not sweep us up and take most of our men away. . . take most of our men away.*

"Elizabeth!" Pa's voice tore me out of my spiraling thoughts. "It's time to head home!" I looked around and found the crowd dispersing. Droplets of rain finally demanded to be taken seriously. How long had I been lost in my thoughts? "Are you okay?" Pa grabbed my shoulders trying to pick me up off the dirt. When had I sat down?

"I don't know what's got into you Elizabeth! You know better than to sit like a child in the dirt." He took my hand and pulled me along, "Let's head home, Ma's bound to have lunch ready." When he pulled me away from the store, I glanced one last time toward the small church and was relieved that Mrs. Lankford was already gone, hopefully missing the spectacle of me sprawled in the dirt.

As we walked home, I was thankful for the rain that demanded our attention, allowing me to sadly contemplate that I was a silly child to both Mrs. Lankford and Pa.

CHAPTER 5

Robert Hamilton, May 20, 1861

Robert already feels sticky and wonders if it is the beginning of the relentless sun that promised a cloudless day, or if his nerves are getting the best of him. He arrives at The Valley Store and settles in, leaning against the same post as he did yesterday, not only because there is some shade and it offers a good view of the people gathering, but it also grants him the perfect position to hear the official reports. He removes his hat for a moment to fan himself, but quickly replaces it when he notices others are clearly embracing the sun's rays for warmth. He tries not to laugh at his unfortunate regression to his school-boy days and realizes that the more he tries not to draw attention, the more head-nods and hand-waves he receives. A bench, one Robert recognizes from B.C.'s kitchen, has been placed on some higher ground a few feet from the porch, in hopes that more people can see the proceedings. The bench sits behind an oak podium; the simply carved cross on the front panel boldly declares it has been borrowed from the Oak Grove Methodist Church from across the dirt road. Several men begin to sit on the bench, trying to look as official as possible in their woolen suits. Robert smiles at the undesirable drops of sweat that begin to form on the brow of these men, who, as inconspicuously as possible, try to dab their foreheads. Robert chuckles, feeling a little more at ease.

The sudden stomping of some boots and shuffling across the porch draws Robert's attention behind him where he finds his old friend Craf McGaha on the porch positioning himself against the other post, obviously relieved to find a spot in the shade. Craf's hospitality and leadership in Cedar Mountain are well known throughout the county and all the way down into South Carolina. Drover's drive their livestock through the mountains, both up from and down into South Carolina and are relieved to find his home and farm open to rest and nourishment. The two men smile and nod at each other, knowing that there will be time to catch-up after the meeting.

Within moments all eyes turn to focus on Leander Gash who rings B.C.'s bell, bringing the large gathering to order. He quickly draws the crowd's attention, presenting an official air in the form of a clean-shaven face, a perfectly tailored jacket, and his white shirt's collar stiffly pulled up and held in place with a tightly wrapped cravat. "Thank you for comin'. As you know the State of North Carolina on February 15th approved our new county."

There is some applause which is quickly broken by a loud voice calling from somewhere amid the crowd, "Yeah, after turnin' us down several times."

Although a few murmurs rise, Gash responds quickly, "Hold on brother. This is not simply another community meetin' but an official court of law, our own court of law. Regardless of how long it has taken. We are a county now." Cheers burst forth, reminding the crowd this is a joyful occasion. So, when no other words of dissension are offered, Gash continues. "Charles Patton, James W. Killian and I make up the Select Court of Pleas and Quarters. We have chosen brother Killian as Chair and now will proceed with business without interruption." He pauses for effect and once he is fully satisfied with the silence of the crowd he proceeds, "After today's business we can open the meetin' for questions and comments." He turns to another smartly dressed man who is clearly willing to play his part, "Mr. Killian, the floor is yours."

James Killian rises off the bench and, with one final dab to the forehead, begins, "Before we read the official bill that establishes our new county, let me have a personal word. This is a formidable job in very uncertain times. I am honored to be asked to set this up and am thankful for the many folks who worked so long and hard to bring us here to the Valley Storehouse of B. C. Lankford. We met many times

55

early in the planning process down at the James Neill's Hattery on Davidson River to work these matters out, God rest his soul." Robert glances over to where George is standing at the back of the crowd. A few friendly pats followed with several nods seem to please George as the court honors the memory of his father. Killian, glancing out at the still growing crowd, continues, "I note that several others are arriving as we speak. As I read the official act, I will try to speak as loudly as I can."

The reading takes significant time as the crowd listens carefully, waiting for the business of electing officers. The justices take turns diligently explaining every legal and procedural detail carefully. Robert looks at Craf and they both shake their heads at the complexities, finding themselves and others overwhelmed at times. As a result, the justices repeat often in order to assure clarity. Finally, after some justices, as well as many locals have excused themselves to run to the outhouses or into the grove to relieve themselves, key offices are finally announced. George Orr is elected court clerk, James Clayton appointed as coroner and Robert Hamilton sheriff, without any dissention. The appointment of other officers, including, registrar, entry taker, surveyor, and constable transpired as well. Robert is thankful when he observes that there are mostly agreeable nods.

Robert takes a deep breath realizing that the process may not be as contested as he anticipated. After the reading and election, the Chairman announces that a supplemental act was added calling for a county seat to be set up by several commissioners. "Senator Erwin appointed George Orr, James L. Siniard, Joshua Bryant, F. W, Johnstone, Joseph Hamilton and a Mr. Henry from Henderson County."

A sudden rise in voices breaks the growing lull of the crowd, "Why Henderson County?" a female voice yells out. "We are a-making our own."

James Killian nods acknowledging the question, but quickly raises his hand when other voices begin to shout out the same concern, within moments the crowd is quiet again, eager to hear the explanation. "Simple. We are being formed mostly from Henderson County, and some part of Jackson County, so the changes of taxes, Superior Court action, and other matters must be worked out together." The sun is finally causing real discomfort as many folks, who were warming themselves earlier, are now seeking any available shade. Killian raises his voice so all who are beginning to move away from the immediate area can still hear him. "It is time for us to have a recess. The commissioners on the committee to determine the county seat, please gather inside The Valley Store. We have been given some non-negotiable directives, but we must make some more decisions today." Johnstone is the first to move towards the store with Siniard close behind him. Robert notices his Uncle Joe, being the only committee member to be standing with the justices, waiting for Killian to finish before he joins the others. "As for when we will resume, that will depend on the committee meeting. We will sound the bell when it is time." Killian looks to Joseph Hamilton who nods that he understands the task set before them. He reaches the store's entrance at the same time as George Orr, Joshua Bryant and Mr. Henry.

As Robert sits down on the edge of the porch to rest a moment, he quickly feels a strong pat on his shoulder as Craf joins him. "Sheriff Hamilton!" Robert hears his new title for the first time. Craf smiles and continues, "Thank the Lord it's you!"

Robert, who suddenly receives several handshakes and congratulations, is curious about Craf's statement. As the novelty of congratulating the new sheriff settles down, and resting under some trees or chewing the fat with old friends is more compelling, Robert turns to Craf. "What do you mean? Thankin' the Lord is good, but it seems maybe you are a little too thankful."

Craf raises an eyebrow and chuckles, "Yes, thankin' the Lord is good." With one glance, Craf studies the porch they are sitting on, alone, before he continues. "You're a good man, and I reckon if the time comes for hard decisions to be made, you'll make 'em with the Lord's help." Craf notices Robert's brow furrow slightly, but he has no words to help ease the burden.

Robert pulls out his pipe and begins to prepare his tobacco as he contemplates Craf's words. He glances at his friend and whispers, "Not sure how we will weather our divisions if it comes to war." Craf nods, watching Robert begin to light his pipe. The well-respected mountain

57

man clears his throat, causing Robert to turn and face him. Robert frowns, unsure why Craf is staring at him, clearly contemplating if he should share what is on his mind. Robert draws three short puffs from his pipe before he addresses Craf. "What is it? What aren't you askin'?"

Craf takes a moment to glance around again to make sure they are still out of ear shot of any curious folk. Once he is confident that it is safe to speak, he leans in to Robert. "It's my brother's wife I'm concerned about. My brother, Eph, has been dead over a year now and Nancy is fairin' well enough with the rest of the McGaha family watchin' out for her. But we all reckon that the war may bring folk into these mountains that won't take too kindly to her kind." Robert locks eyes with Craf, aware that his friend is asking for protection for Nancy. Known for years as Nancy Guice, before she married Eph McGaha, she was rumored to be Cherokee, or at least in part. Still, it has only been a few decades since the Cherokee Nation was removed, and the memory remains fresh for those who managed to escape into the mountains, some even marrying white mountain folk. Most families do not speak of their Cherokee family members, still fearing they will be taken from them.

"I hope that if war comes a-knockin' we keep protectin' our own. That is my intention." Robert takes another long draw from his pipe. Robert slaps his friend on the back before gracefully shifting the conversation to news of wives, children and the famous McGaha waystation for drovers and their livestock.

As the oak trees begin to cast longer shadows, the bell finally rings bringing the meeting to attention. Gash and Patton return to the bench while Killian resumes his responsibility at the podium. Robert notices the chairman receive a piece of paper from Uncle Joe, and the two speak briefly, clarifying what the paper says. Killian nods and then looks to the reassembled crowd. "Thanks to the committee, we have made some steps in picking the county seat. However, how to divide up specific places for needed buildings will need several more meetings, and they hope to provide those proposals in a week."

There are some nods of understanding, but since it appears to most, having relaxed and visited for the afternoon, that an open forum has been informally declared, several questions arise loudly. "Will the county seat be in Davidson River?" A voice calls out.

Before it can be addressed, another interrupts, "No, what about Cathey's Creek?"

An old man adds to what he thinks is clear negotiations, "No, Crabtree Creek!"

"Well, how about out in Dunns Rock?" A large woman with arms crossed stands her ground with an even larger strapping-young man next to her, clearly her son in stance and manner.

"Sorry," Killian sincerely responds, aware that each community has its reasons for wanting to be the county seat. He regrets they assumed that there was much public input in the matter. "The state orders are clear that it is not to be one of the established communities, but a new one, laid out with public space, a courthouse and streets for homes and businesses. There are so many investors in land hereabouts we hope some can be donors to help start our own little county seat. We need to start fresh with a clear plan." Robert observes how surprisingly agreeable the folk are, especially since no one community is being favorably designated.

Robert watches as his Uncle Joe steps close to the podium for a moment to be recognized by the speaker. With a clear approving nod from Killian, Joseph Hamilton raises his voice, "Also, the Act gives an order that it is not to be more than five miles from Probart Poor's house and store and must be about fifty acres for a start." He nods at Killian and turns to sit down.

The seemingly placated crowd begins to murmur again realizing a place has already been chosen. The murmurs continue as Killian continues, "Thanks, Colonel Hamilton." Ignoring the private discussions disrupting the crowd he tries to raise his already strained voice, "Further, we are to name this new town 'Brevard' after the Revolutionary War hero, Doctor Brevard. Some of you are more familiar with his daughter, Nancy Brevard, who married Lambert Clayton, another Revolutionary War hero. But there's already a Claytonville, so Brevard seems fitting."

Suddenly, out of the private conversations, a voice raises up revealing the key concern, one the locals will not let the officials smooth over with the ongoing proceedings. "Hey Lee, ain't thet store he talked about yourn?" Leander Gash, who is sitting quietly on the bench, is taken by surprise. Seeing that Killian does not know how to address this question, he stands and walks to the podium.

By the time he reaches the podium and straightens his cravat around his neck, the crowd is attentive again. Killian steps out of the way and Gash steps right behind the beautiful oak pulpit. He gently caresses the wood as if in deep thought. After enough of a dramatic pause he speaks with a deep commanding tone, "Well, yes, but Probart Poor is my wife's uncle and he does a great job takin' care of the store. I reckon since many official meetings have taken place there over the years, it seems like a place the government already recognizes as somewhat official." There are some nods, realizing that the store had been around longer than any and was already very central to the county. However, Gash runs his fingers through his hair and then speaks with all seriousness. "Although, Lord knows, most official decrees I receive are from my wife! Maybe she got ahold of the senator's ear."

A ripple of laughter relaxes the crowd and Robert smiles at Gash's ability to command the crowd not only with seriousness, but with his masterful use of a little humor. With all hostility aside, a curious question arises this time from an older gentleman who has perched himself on a stump right at the foot of the podium, "How come we got thet name, Transylvania?"

Gash looks at Killian who is already taking Gash's seat on the bench. The two men give each other quick nods, unofficially passing the torch. Gash, comfortable at the borrowed pulpit responds, affirming the gentleman. "Good question." He is quite aware that the new county name has been discussed on several occasions, but a thorough discussion at this time would be prudent. "Several have asked about that. It means simply 'across the woods'. For the early discussion they considered the name 'Ruffin' after a retired Chief Justice of the State Supreme Court. Our own Senator Erwin put forth the name 'Transylvania' probably because he graduated from Transylvania University in Kentucky. By the way, that part of Kentucky was also called 'Transylvania' by Daniel Boone, our own North Carolina fellow who opened up that wilderness. The name is pretty descriptive of our area and has some historical ties to the state!" Gash smiles, pleased that he can excite others about the name.

Robert watches as Gash walks back to the bench to confer with Killian and his Uncle Joseph Hamilton. They look at the crowd and nod to each other before Killian returns to the podium. "A few more words of business." He looks down at a paper and reads, "We have elected many County officers and the Select Court of Joseph Hamilton, Charles Patton and Lee Gash has been elected." Applause finally brings a smile to Killian's face, knowing that Gash's presence made the final reading a success. "It has been a long afternoon, and I note that we do not have much water available for the horses or enough outhouses for so many people. "Please come back tomorrow for the rest of our work. We must decide on schools, roads, bridges, taxes and one other vital item. And we'll need to meet over in Wilson's Campground across the way, beyond the Oak Grove Methodist Church. We'll find more water and facilities there."

There are murmurs of agreement as the crowd begins to move towards their horses and wagons, even before Killian finishes. Robert laughs as Killian makes a joke about Methodists being good at providing for necessities, but most miss it, or don't understand it; although it's a Methodist campground, it is used by most churches in the community. So Killian raises his voice one last time. "So be it. Court dismissed until 10 a.m. tomorrow, May 21, 1861." Killian seems relieved.

As Robert heads home, pleased the cloudless day is transforming into a clear night, allowing for some natural light to guide him home, he is thankful that the first day as sheriff was a memorable one. As he rounds the final bend before he reaches home, it sinks in that he is the first sheriff of the county. He is suddenly determined to bring his whole family tomorrow. This must be a time of celebration.

Elizabeth Neill, May 21, 1861

I couldn't believe that Pa had Sarah-Jane, Jimmy and me jump into the back of the wagon, while he and Ma sat on the bench at the front.

61

It seemed like ages since the last time we packed for a potluck at the campground with the whole community turning out. The most recent church revival, always a draw for locals to flock together, was last fall. All I knew was this was not a preaching that we were headed to, but the founding of our county. "Get your nose out of that basket!" Ma fussed at Jimmy who was already hungry for Ma's apple pie. He quickly settled down, but not for long. We all tried to hold ourselves up on our knees to get a better view of all the wagons headed into town. The back and forth rattling was sure to wear a hole in my dress where my knees pinned it to the rough wooden boards, so I gave up and settled on top of the large quilt Ma only used for picnics. The musty smell hinted that it had been a while since it had benefitted from the fresh air.

As the wagon pulled past the Lankford store, I shifted slightly to get a better look at the porch, hoping that James had come home and might happen to be heading towards the campground, but I suddenly felt like a foolish child and turned my head quickly to look at my sister who was also looking at the front porch. "What ya lookin' for?" Sarah-Jane asked not wanting to miss out on anything that might be important.

"Nobody!" I said a little too quickly.

My little sister looked at me with wide eyes, "I didn't say *who*!" A betraying blush began to emerge, so I tried to hide it by pulling my shawl up around my cheeks as if chasing away the cool morning air. Suddenly, my sister giggled and as loudly as possible teased me. "OOOooooh! Elizabeth's got a boyfriend!"

"I do not!" I tried to sound calm.

Sarah-Jane couldn't let it go. "Who ya been seein'? Who ya been neckin'?" I took my shawl and flung it over her head to shove her down, trying to get her to stop yelling.

"Elizabeth, let your sister go!" Ma was glancing back at us from the front of the wagon with a look of horror across her face. "And you stop that talk, Sarah-Jane!" Ma fussed at my sister. "Your sister ain't courtn' anybody. So, hush up and act more lady-like!"

"I was just joshin' Ma." Sarah-Jane tried to defend herself.

Ma wasn't accepting any explanations. "You want all these folks to think I didn't raise ladies?" Ma was really embarrassed and was pointing at some of the people already looking at us and shaking their heads as Pa pulled the wagon up next to at least two dozen other ones outside of the campground. "You act like that then neither of you will ever be a courtin'!" Ma was looking at both of us at this point. "Do you understand?"

Sarah-Jane and I, both confused at Ma getting her dander up so quickly, spoke in unison, "Yes, Ma'am!"

Pa jumped down from the wagon first and helped all of us down, although we could do it ourselves. Suddenly allies again, my sister and I wanted to show Mom that we could act like ladies.

Walking into the campground was always enjoyable. It was what I imagined a fort might feel like, but, instead of wood or rocks, the walls were made of twenty-eight canvas tents all formed into one large rectangle. Each corner, and in the middle of each of the longer sides, there was space to come and go, but it was clear that the main entrance was marked by two eight-foot wide passageways traveling along each side of the preacher's tent located in the center of one of the shorter sides of the campground "wall". This was always my favorite way to walk into this special place, because right in front of the preacher's tent was the large platform, which was often used for the sermons. It was covered by a beautiful arbor that offered shade, especially in the spring and summer when the trees were in full bloom. But my favorite was when several fiddlers joined together with guitars and voices on that platform to share sacred mountain music. That morning, however, I was quickly disappointed to find no one pulling out instruments, but instead, several wooden benches where already occupied by what I could only describe as official-looking men all tightly buttoned up, some in woolen jackets they might have slightly outgrown ten years earlier. My family and I followed others as they headed around the platform to the open area on the other side.

"Get off that!" Pa fussed at Jimmy who hopped up on some old weather-beaten church benches that had been set up in front of the podium. "That's for older people who need to rest their bones."

Jimmy, without missing a beat, jumped off the bench and asked, "Like you, Pa?"

Sarah-Jane and I giggled as Pa mussed Jimmy's hair, "Very funny!" Pa walked us past several tents whose flaps were open wide revealing families that clearly had spent the night. Sometimes I wished we didn't live so close so we could spend the night, but I was thankful that most of the families that claimed permanent tents were happy to let anyone share the shade with them.

To me the whole day seemed somewhat chaotic. I tried to pay attention to the boring business that the officials were discussing. At one point I waved at Pink when he emerged from the Allison's tent, but he didn't see me as he quickly ran across the open area to disappear through the other wall of tents. He was clearly headed to the other children who gathered to play games as the adults droned on. Along the perimeter of one tent several black faces raised an eyebrow at Pink's behavior, but no one said anything. I had not spent much time with any slaves, and I only really knew Pink and Tony, but, still, I swallowed as the faces of some of the slaves turned to stone as they stood beside the tent waiting to be told what to do. It was as if they weren't even there.

Pa, on the other hand, was pretty engaged with the proceedings and sometimes would explain it to Ma, who was as confused as I was, mostly due to keeping an eye on Jimmy. What I did gather was that several officers were elected, or appointed, and necessary surveyors were set out to clarify the lines with Henderson and Jackson Counties.

Pa leaned into Ma at one point and explained, "The court ordered a committee of William Deavor, Francis W. Johnstone and Overton Leander Erwin to develop a plan for the county seat in the town of Brevard includin' a brick courthouse and jail. And they also appointed a school board." He squeezed Ma's hand.

64

"I know George! I can't believe it either." Ma smiled and then looked at me, "Elizabeth, can you take my pie over to that table?" It wasn't quite what I expected to come out of her mouth, since she and Pa were having a moment, but it was typical. All the women were already hustling around to prepare the largest potluck I'd ever seen. We had just formed our own county and established the town of Brevard, but folks still had to be fed. I nodded and happily walked the apple pie over to the table, hoping to find my cousins. As I walked by one of the passageways that led to the back of the tents, I saw my cousins and other children screaming and chasing each other, clearly happy to be away from the stuffy seriousness of the meeting. Viney was with them and when she saw me, she waved for me to join them. I nodded, but then quickly held up the pie. She shrugged and then tucked behind the tent out of my sight. I walked with a little more haste to deposit the pie next to a beautiful apple cobbler. It took all of my will power not to shove my pinky into the soft desert for an undetectable sample.

Suddenly a finger came from behind me dipping quicker than lighting. When I turned around in shock, James stood before me with his finger in his mouth, but for only a second. "What? You know it was callin' to be tasted?"

"James! Shame on you!" I couldn't help but smile as I pretended to fuss at the man in front of me with his hair pouring out like flames from under a short-brimmed hat. Then I was suddenly embarrassed, "I mean, Mr. Morris." I looked around at the ladies busy around us and was thankful no one observed my forward behavior.

James grinned and whispered, "That's okay, Miss Neill."

I gathered myself together and thought I'd put him in his place. "Well, I guess if you act like a boy, then you get fussed at like a boy!" James laughed out-loud drawing attention to the two of us. "Can you please be a little quieter, Mr. Morris." I whispered quickly pretending to straighten the several deserts in front of me, the desire to taste the cobbler was long gone, I was too excited that James had returned.

"I'm back one day and already bein' fussed at!" He teased, and I dared to look straight at him, soaking up his boyish banter and smile.

"You got home yesterday?" I asked, but then sobered up realizing Mrs. Lankford had just sent him a letter. "But your sister just sent you a letter."

James frowned ever so slightly, obviously surprised at the knowledge I had of his sister's letter and obviously not wanting to discuss the melancholy happenings of the last month. "Yes, I heard she sent word. I'm sure my Ma will hold the letter for me until I visit her and Pa again." He paused and as his eyes dropped to his fingers that were fiddling with his belt, "I hate it that I wasn't here for Amanda and B.C." He eyes were guilt stricken. "Honest. I thought the baby was on the mend or I'd never have left."

I smiled and nodded, "I know you would have been here. No one is blamin' you for anything." Of course, just two days ago I was blaming him for making me look like a fool in the store, but I wasn't going to tell him that.

"Thank you for your kind words, Miss Neill." His voice was almost a whisper. I looked away again, and we were both quiet for some time, simply standing over the bread-pudding that I had needlessly adjusted two inches to the left. Finally, James took a deep breath as if drawing strength to move on. "What do you figure to be the most interestin' part the meetin' so far?" I swallowed as I looked at James realizing I didn't have anything to say. Should I tell him the justices looked like they needed to lose a few pounds or that the children's game outside the confines of the campground looked enticing. I glanced at the platform at the other end of the open space where continued discussions were taking place and realized I knew very little. "Miss Neill?" James broke my silence.

"I reckon I like that we are called Transylvania County?" I asked more than stated.

James smiled, "I promise this ain't a test question. It's hard for me to follow everything as well." I let out a sigh of relief. "If you want," James continued, "You can join me for the first court case they are getting' ready to announce. We can see if we can understand it together."

"Will that be okay?" I asked suddenly aware that we were in a very public place and he was practically asking me to spend time with him. At least that was my interpretation.

James frowned a little, "I'm not sure what you mean, Miss Neill. Cain't we join the rest of the crowd and take part in this historic day with everyone else?"

"I'm sorry, Mr. Morris," I stuttered, "I thought . . . I mean . . ." I suddenly cleared my throat. "Yes, let's join the others." I could have sworn that a smirk on that man's face appeared before we turned to walk toward the platform. I glanced for a moment down the passageway as a serious game of Blind-man's bluff was underway. I hoped Viney would understand. I wasn't sure if I was learning about the business of the county or if I was learning what courtin' really looked like.

As we stood with many others, I smiled as Uncle Bob stood up with the justices on the platform; he was trying to play the role of the new sheriff. I couldn't help but feel proud.

The chairman, a Mr. Killian, addressed Uncle Bob, "Sheriff Hamilton, we do have one legal matter before the court. Can you present this since you have been consulting with the two parties involved?" It seemed to me that the court dealing with the business of setting up the county was transforming for a time into a court of law.

I watched with fascination as the first court case was being presented. I noticed Uncle Bob was shaking and wondered if this was his first time to talk in front of so many people at once. "Yes sir. The State has this case of Bastardy against this young man, but the child has died. The defendant has agreed to pay all related costs." The Justices very quickly dismiss the first case in the Transylvania Court. I was a little disappointed that there wasn't more to it, not that I understood it at all, strange to have a bastard child be our county's inaugural court case, but since the justices seemed satisfied, everyone was looking to the next order of business. To my relief it was lunch.

I hesitantly left James to join my family and other kin to enjoy a spread of food that I could only imagine would be fit for a king. A few times I spotted James talking with others as his uncle walked around the campground introducing his brother-in law to folks who had not met him yet, even a few young women smiled and nodded politely. I turned my head away feeling foolish to even care.

The noon sun was quickly chasing people into the shade and under the arbor. I could see some folks begin to head towards their wagons or horses to begin the journey back to their communities and leave any unfinished business to those left behind. A sudden gunshot brought everyone to a standstill. I looked to the platform where Uncle Bob was standing with his flintlock pistol held above his head. It wasn't the gun shot that worried me, since gun shots were a common way to get everyone's attention, it was the look of despair on Uncle Bob's face. He slowly lowered the smoking gun and as loudly as possible announced, "Now hear up all you citizens of Transylvania County, North Carolina!" Uncle Bob's shaky voice drew everyone to him. "Let us hear from Mr. Francis Johnstone, a member of our honorable court here. He has important news for us."

We all looked at one of the justices as he stood. He was the only one, other than Mr. Gash, with a suit more fittingly tailored to his form. I figured that he must be the well-respected Mr. Johnstone, who, I once heard Ma once whisper about with women at Lankford's store, had a beautiful home. I remembered that day vividly because I found it funny at the time, that the Johnstone family gave their homestead a name: Montclove. Montclove was then a name I wove into my imagination when Viney and I would pretend to be high-falutin. But Ma caught us once and strictly informed us they were regular good-Christian-folk like us since they let the Episcopalians meet at Montclove while a church across the river in Dunns Rock was being built. I figured we weren't doing any harm, but Ma thought otherwise. So, suddenly seeing Mr. Johnstone in real flesh and blood before us, made me instantly embarrassed that I had ever pretended to be his family. My childish dismay quickly vanished as I realized something crucial was taking place. A powerful man stood before me with a full beard that covered most of his face, but an additional thickly distinguished mustache cascaded down drawing attention to his serious frown. I could see from the hesitation in his step and the long stare he gave the crowd, that the news was not one he was proud to share. His Charleston drawl dramatically drew us in, "My fellah Carolinians, fellah patriots of this God-given land. News has reached us over these days that the Yankee troops in Fort Sumter have surrendered to our side. Seven states have seceded from the Union and others are following in the next days. The Yankees want to take away our rights, our homes and businesses, our way of life. They are aggressors, denying us what God has given us." My heart started racing. Was this what we had all been dreading would happen? I found myself growing irritated with Johnstone who was taking much longer than he needed to pull out a piece of paper, a telegram, which he then waved before all of us. Finally, he proclaimed loudly, "Just now our mail courier rode in from Hendersonville with a telegram from our Honorable North Carolina Governor Ellis! Just yesterday, May 20, in the year of our Lord one thousand eight hundred sixty-one, as we were giving birth to this county, our leaders in Raleigh voted to join our sister states and secede!! Welcome to the Confederate States of America!"

Suddenly, I was overwhelmed by the conflicting rise of outbursts that turned the campground upside down. I watched as my mother and father gasped in horror and Uncle Bob, still standing on the podium, looked like the blood had drained from his face, while others were patting each other on the back and heads were held high. Moving from one extreme to another, I realized that neighbors, who had just shared the best cobbler ever, were now swiftly divided. It wasn't as if neighbors were suddenly fighting each other, but it was the subtle movement of bodies towards those who shared their sentiments. In the midst of the chaos I couldn't find James. I didn't dare move away from my parents, but I hoped I could at least see him. Before I could scan the whole campground, Uncle Bob's gun went off again.

The crowd became quiet, and Johnstone continued, "There is more. Governor Ellis has called for 30,000 volunteers to stand against this invasion from the North. We could form a company of militia from right here in Transylvania." Some cheers rose up, and I watched as Johnstone turned to huddle with others behind the podium, while Uncle Bob stood like a statue. His eyes seemed to be scanning everyone, and I could tell he was aware of every movement and every reaction.

Suddenly a man Pa described as the clerk, came to the podium and announced, "This court hereby orders that each man who volunteers will receive $15 and will be subject to orders from the Governor." This announcement seemed to sober the cheering band of men gathered closest to the podium.

Johnstone returned to the podium and was frowning at the lull in the crowd. "What is wrong?" he asked. "Are we missing something?"

I wasn't sure what was going on either, but I could see Uncle Bob, with the sun hitting his new Sheriff's badge for a moment. He was gently shaking his head. Johnstone looked at Uncle Bob for an answer. Uncle Bob took a deep breath, cautiously explaining, "They are worried about their families. Many will fight but they are hard-workin' farmers for the most part and have no one to care for their families."

Johnstone seemed slightly confused. "Can't their slaves do most of the farming?" I couldn't believe he had asked that question. Several men started whispering, and women began to slowly clean up the potluck tables, quietly shaking their heads. Only one female slave was helping pack up the baskets along-side her owner. I then looked at the slaves who had stood stone-faced earlier and realized they must have been Johnstone's slaves. Their faces remained unreadable.

Uncle Bob stood and couldn't help but sound a little sarcastic, "Mister, you don't seem to understand. There are very few slaves in

Transylvania, and most of them belong to you South Carolina folks who bring your household servants."

Several disgruntled shouts rose from the crowd which caused Johnstone, not sure if he should be offended, to begin to unbutton his vest. The clerk started dialoguing with the other official-looking people on the platform, obviously trying to come up with a new proposal. They agreed and he then faced the crowd, cleared his throat, and announced, "Upon further deliberation, the Court should supply support for the families of volunteers who may be in want of necessities."

Although there were some nods in the crowd, it was my Pa who spoke up. "Where are you going to get that money?" I looked at him and was shocked as he continued, "We haven't collected any taxes yet and are only settin' up the county. . ." he paused then raised his voice, "Today . . . if you haven't forgotten!" Pa was more worried than angry.

The clerk smiled, but his lips were so tight that it looked like a very thin wire being forced to bend in the wrong direction. "Of course we remember what momentous day today is." He said, putting on airs, which I knew ate into Pa. He didn't like anyone talking down to him. The clerk then looked at the whole crowd, probably avoiding Pa's death stare. "We have authorized the Chairman to go to a bank in Asheville to borrow $1500 to pay the Transylvania volunteers."

I watched as Johnstone walked to the podium again and figured he was going to try to say something to reconcile with the crowd. This time he looked a little less highfalutin. "Of course, we know it will take some time to get your affairs in order." He stood as tall as he could and re-buttoned his vest, "I myself will lead the Transylvania Volunteers." There were some cheers seeing that this man was going to put his life on the line and not only expect it of others. Even I was impressed. "I will collect my orders and hope to gather together our regiment by July." I could see more nods and some relief from others who felt that maybe there was a little time to make sure homesteads were in good hands and plant some crops that would hopefully not out-live them.

I didn't pay attention to any more of the official adjourning of the court session and neither did many other people. Most families were somberly gathering their belongings and heading toward wagons. Ma's voice pulled my attention away from the unfolding scene. "Elizabeth, can you go find your sister and brother?"

"Yes'm." I walk toward the closest side pathway between two tents to head out of the campground to find at least a dozen youth still playing and squealing.

"Are you heading home?" James' voice was matter of fact, having lost all lightness. I wasn't even surprised finding him walking next to me as I headed towards Jimmy, who disappeared behind a tree.

"Yeah." I answered, glancing at him. He seemed older; or maybe he just looked his age for the first time. "I guess you are headed back to the store?" I nodded in the direction of the gentle hill that hid the church and the Valley Store just beyond.

He nodded, but then ran his fingers through his hair. "I'm goin' to join."

"I know." I swallowed hard and looked at him. His red hair fell back around his hazel eyes. I couldn't quite read him, but his eyes looked like they held a question. I felt my eyes blur as I failed to push down the stinging knot in my throat creeping up my jaw asking me to let go a flood of tears. I held it as long as possible before my lips trembled as a sniffle and a few tears escaped. I quickly wiped them away hoping Sarah-Jane was still playing, ignoring the unfolding scene nearby.

James dropped his eyes to the ground and kicked a clump of dirt, his youthful side pushing its way to the surface. He then looked at me with a slight smile, "I'll be seeing you Miss Neill." Before I could answer he was headed up the hill towards the Oak Grove Church.

Robert Hamilton, May 21, 1861

Sitting at the edge of the preacher's tent, Robert watches as the campground begins to slowly empty. There are still many families who are clearly staying another night in the tents, but for the most part dishes have been gathered from the communal lunch table and benches on the podium have been carried off the platform to be returned to their original locations. The only evidences of the past few hours are lingering discussions scattered around the campground.

"Hard to believe only a few minutes ago we were pulled into war!" A deep familiar voice pulls Robert to his feet.

"Pa, thank you for bein' here today." Robert embraces John Hamilton, Sr. former Henderson County Justice and Court of Pleas member. He had traveled to be present on this historical day. After he emerges from the embrace, Robert doesn't pull away from his father, but keeps both hands planted on his Pa's shoulders. Looking directly at his father, he solemnly states, "I'm sorry this was not more of a celebration. You came all this way to support me and the foundin' of the county."

John Hamilton chuckles, "Son, the apology is not accepted since there is no need for one! I am proud to have been here today and watch the foundin' of the county as well as watch you as sheriff. You belong here, son, not in Alabama where most of us have gone or are fixin' to go." Robert drops his arms and is relieved with his father's response. "However," John begins using a concerned tone, "there is one order of business you need to work on if you plan on holdin' yourself as a respectable sheriff."

Robert frowns at his father's statement but then notices a cloth in his father's hands, wrapped around an object. "Pa, what are you talkin' about? What do you have there?"

The former justice gently holds the cloth up to Robert, "Now a little fatherly advice. You do quite well with that Gillespie rifle and, now that you had them adapt it from flintlock to ball and cap firing, you are fine. Likewise, you are a fair shot with that flintlock pistol you got attention with today. Here is a gift from your ma and me, a more modern pistol for a new sheriff." Robert's father removes the cloth from the pistol, "It's an 1851 Navy Colt and just what a lawman needs in these times. We sure hope you don't have to use it against somebody, but if you do, it may save your life."

Robert takes the Colt into his hand. The new heavier weight of the gun will take a little getting used to, but the natural fit of the contour of the handle to his palm will be a welcome adjustment. Robert is suddenly aware of the flintlock pistol shoved into the side of his belt. He pulls it out holding the two weapons side by side, "But Pa, this beautiful Ketland pistol was brought over from the old country by Grandpa Robert! I am a pretty good shot with it as well. It's been in the family for many years!"

"That's right, son, but times are changin' and havin' only one shot versus having six ready to shoot is what others are gettin'. You have a large family to protect. For the sake of all our grandchildren and this new county please carry this modern Colt."

"Thanks, Pa," Robert carefully places a gun on each side of his belt, realizing purchasing a holster at this point might be wise. He hopes that he never has to use either weapon against another human.

"Pa?" Viney pulls Robert out of his thoughts. "Uncle John wants to talk to you?"

Robert had almost forgotten that he had brought four of his children along for this historical day. Of course, they seem more eager to gather with the other children, oblivious to the significance of these moments. The sheriff is pleasantly surprised at Viney's words. He looks at his father who takes a deep breath and becomes sincerely solemn this time. Robert quickly frowns as he scans the vicinity, "Where is he? I can't see him anywhere?"

Viney shifts nervously. She looks at her grandpa who nods for her to tell her father what is going on.

"What is it, Viney?" Robert kneels to look his daughter straight in the eyes.

"Uncle John told me to come fetch you. He didn't want to be seen. He's in a wagon over behind Lankford's store where you met yesterday."

Robert nods and musses up Viney's hair. "You done good." He stands and then smiles, "You best stay here and keep an eye on your sister and brothers." Viney smiles and runs to Matilda, John-Riley and

Joel, who are still engaging in a game of Blindman's Bluff with the other children gathered. Viney is happy that Robert thinks she can watch her siblings, but knows darn well they only listen to Millie. Accepting that fact, she joins the children and screams louder than any one of them when Joel, with a cloth tied around his eyes, grabs her.

Robert smiles at his daughter, but frowns when he sees his father still looks serious. "Pa what is it?"

John Hamilton grabs his son's shoulder for a moment, "I already said my goodbyes. You go on." And he shoves Robert gently in the direction of the store.

Robert doesn't understand what his Pa means about goodbyes, but he is anxious to see his brother, even though they are not legally brothers, they have always called themselves family. He quickly leaves the campground behind him and rounds the bend with the church to his left and soon crosses the road to Lankford's store, quiet at the moment. He quickly walks behind the store to find John Wesley Hamilton seated on a wagon loaded with blacksmith equipment and a few clothing items. The tall black man jumps down from the wagon with a wide smile as Robert emerges. The two men embrace firmly, and Robert asks, "What are you up to, my brother?"

"I wanted to say goodbye and head out." John Wesley tries to sound factual, but there is a notable strain in his voice.

Robert steps back and looks John Wesley straight in the eyes. "Why?" Robert feels some frustration towards his Pa for not warning him.

John Wesley looks away trying to keep his composure. "Well, I did turn twenty-one and it is harder and harder to be a blacksmith in these parts."

Robert shakes his head and can't simply agree with this vague reason. "But you have learned your trade well. The folks in both Henderson and now Transylvania County love your skilled work. You are a member of the family. We grew up as brothers." Robert remembers the day his father brought John Wesley home, not as a slave, but as a child bound to the Hamilton family to be taught a trade and given his independence at age twenty-one. Never did Robert think John Wesley would actually leave as soon as he came of age. Was Robert wrong all of these years to think that John Wesley was family? Robert can't hide his anger, "I thought we were brothers. How can you just up and leave?"

John Wesley takes a deep breath and walks straight up to Robert. He gently places his arm on the sheriff's shoulder and softly explains, "Well, Bobby, in case you did not notice all these years, my skin is black and many folks cannot understand that I was only bound to the Hamilton family and not a slave. Recently, some slavers have been riding up from South Carolina and capturing freed blacks calling them escaped slaves and hoping to sell them in another state. My legal papers are lookin' weaker these days." He smiles, "Even a sheriff brother won't be able to protect me!"

Robert sighs and realizes that John Wesley is right. Just yesterday when debate was in full swing the Hamilton family loyalty was questioned. For some, Robert realizes, it will not be easy having a sheriff that came from a family that raised a black boy and spoke of French Revolutionary thinkers. But John Wesley interrupts his brother's thoughts, "Bobby, another problem is the Hamilton family belief in education. With a risk to yourselves, you all taught me to read, write and figure with numbers."

"Of course. How can you work as a blacksmith without such basics?" Robert shakes his head trying to come to grips with the anger he is feeling towards ignorance.

"Well, you know as well as I do that in the wisdom of our State legislators, slaves are forbidden to learn readin' and writin'. Figures are okay. I guess that they fear slaves might learn to want freedom. It's a real fear they have about all of us black folks. And my fear of them is even greater if I want to live! I'd best head on out while I can." John Wesley shakes his head knowing this is not what he wants, but what he has to do.

Robert nods hesitantly. "But what will you do, where will you go?"

"When your folks took me in and promised me a trade and equipment, they really blessed me with a great name." Robert knows that the original John Wesley was that great leader of Methodists and his name was known everywhere. It is a relief to know that his brother draws strength from his name. John Wesley continues, "So your folks gave me some contact names up North. I need to head up before this war really heats up." The blacksmith begins to head back towards the wagon. He checks to make sure the equipment is secure.

Robert follows him and helps him tighten a strap. "But which state, where?"

John Wesley sighs. "For your sake, I'd best not say. I fear some fanatics might put you in a spot. The need for blacksmiths is high in both the North and South. I'd ruther not make hardware for Confederate wagons or guns."

"Understood, but hard news to swallow." Tears flow down the sheriff's face, realizing this may be a final goodbye. As John Wesley smiles at Robert, the new sheriff can only nod, hug his "little brother" and watch the simple wagon head toward the North.

CHAPTER 6

Elizabeth Neill, May 31, 1861

"Elizabeth, go help your Pa!" Ma's voice reached me as I stacked the last of the breakfast dishes neatly in the cupboard and hung the dish towel over a wooden dowel Pa had attached across the window and over the sink. It was a good idea when the window was open, letting the fresh air quickly dry the towel, but I didn't like the way it blocked the light, usually taking it down as soon as it was dry. By the feel of the warm breeze already coming through the window I thought I might get to tuck the dry towel away sooner than later.

"Yes, Ma!" I yelled back through the house. She didn't have to explain why, since we were in the middle of collecting honey from Pa's hives. The spring had been a strong season and summer was coming soon with the blooming of the sourwood trees. Sourwood honey was everyone's favorite, and I couldn't wait for the first spoonful of clear-as-water honey sweetness dripping onto my morning biscuit. The Valley Store was always eager to keep their shelves stocked with Pa's honey, although we mostly bartered with family and neighbors.

I ran upstairs first to quickly brush through my hair and make sure my dress was still dry after doing the dishes. Once satisfied, I ran outside and up the slope behind our house to the beehives neatly lined up in rows. People would often tell us how they could see Pa's hives up on the hill as they came around the corner heading toward the Valley Store, a clear sign they were getting close. The visibility of the hives would sometimes cause strangers to stop and ask if we had any honey for sale. Ma didn't like those times, but they weren't very often.

I ran past the hives to Pa's work area. It wasn't a barn because there were only three walls and a roof made of roughly cut strips of lumber, sturdy enough to keep out the rain and provide some shade in the heat of the summer. I smiled as I reached the lean-to because Pa turned towards me with two baskets full of honey jars. "Good, you're here." Pa handed one basket to me. "I'll walk with you back down to the barn to load the jars onto Jack's back."

"I can carry them both myself, Pa." I started to reach for the second basket, but Pa didn't hand it to me, so I quickly dropped my hand and looked at my father. I hadn't paid attention to anything really, other than my own fancy of getting those jars to the Valley Store. His beard was graying, and his hair hung over his ears, a little longer than he usually liked it to grow.

Recently, Ma and Pa were holding their conversations late into the nights, but in quiet tones. I knew, if I asked, that they would say they were being quiet so as not to wake us up, but it was obvious they didn't want us to hear. I didn't ask, though, because Ma might keep her promise and not keep secrets from me anymore, and I didn't want to know more than I had already seen. It had almost been two weeks since the campground meeting announced we were drawn into the war, but it felt like nothing had really changed. With each day, hope grew inside of me that maybe the war wouldn't really reach us. I had seen James once already last week when I delivered Ma's eggs and a few jars of honey. He only nodded at me as he helped Mr. Fowler load some grains on the back of his wagon. But the nod was good enough. He hadn't enlisted in any regiment and he hadn't left Brevard. It felt strange calling this place Brevard or Transylvania County, but it was also exciting to have our own county seat so close to home. One day the actual town of Brevard would be built from the land, but I had no idea how long it would take for streets and buildings and some form of courthouse to transform Brevard from a name into an actual town. I figured it couldn't take too long since a town's name couldn't last without actual structures.

Suddenly a wagon rambled along Lambs Creek, passing our house. A tall black man was at the reigns and what looked to me like Mr. Gash sitting next to him, only because I thought I recognized the dignified way he sat. They were quickly followed by a cantering horse with a portly man trying to come alongside the wagon. I recognized Mr. Poor, which confirmed my first guess that the man in the wagon had to be Mr. Gash, since Mr. Poor managed Mr. Gash's trading post, located at least another mile on the other side of the Valley Store. I hadn't been there in a while, but it was much larger than the Valley Store and boasted crates of goods that lined the walls from floor to ceiling. The men did not see us, but neither did Pa try to wave to get their attention. Instead, he looked at me and continued, "I just want to make sure the jars are secure when you place them in the saddlebags, so they don't knock into each other." Pa smiled weakly since he knew as well as I did that I always made sure the jars were secure, but I didn't challenge him.

"Okay, Pa." I took his empty hand in mine as we walked toward the barn, trying to remember the last time I had held Pa's hand. "Are you frettin' about somethin'?"

He squeezed my hand, "I guess I'm not too good at foolin' you." He smiled but then didn't hesitate to explain. "I worry about what this war will mean to our family?"

"Pa, maybe nothin' will happen. It's been two weeks and everything is like war isn't even takin' place. You're still gatherin' honey, and the chickens are still a-layin' eggs." I dropped Pa's hand and pointed at the dirt road beyond our home where it met Lambs Creek. "People still haul their supplies and livestock up and down Boylston Turnpike. And every time I am at the Valley Store people are still talkin' about the weather and whose heifer is expectin'."

Pa laughed out loud as we reached the barn. "You sure make a good point! I wish it were that easy." Pa pulled Jack out of his stall to secure the saddlebags. Nellie scolded us for not paying her attention by mooing twice, until Pa went back into the barn and threw her a handful of fresh hay. Within a minute he returned and finished securing the saddlebags.

"What is it, Pa?" I asked as I handed him my basket of honey.

He took his time thinking and, once all the jars were carefully packed, he looked at me very seriously. "You need to be careful what you say Elizabeth."

"What do you mean?" I frowned, but still held his gaze. "Am I sayin' somethin' wrong?"

Pa touched my cheek for a second and his eyes softened, "No, baby, you need to understand that everything you say will be heard by others around you. Everyone is lookin' for loyalties right now and it's only goin' to get worse." I was really confused, and Pa could tell. He glanced down at the road where the kicked-up dust from the wagon had finished settling. "This means when you take our goods to the store," he paused and patted the saddlebags, "you only listen and do not give any hint of what we may be discussin' or doin' at home." He paused for a minute, "or with family."

"Okay, Pa, but I don't know what we are sayin' or doin' that would bother other people?" I shook my head and was trying really hard to understand what Pa was telling me.

"Nothin' yet." He smiled. "But as the war hits us we may be forced to say or do things that others won't agree with and I don't want harm to come to you, or any of us, if our loyalties are questioned."

I was trying not to get all flustered, but was struggling. "But I'm not sure what you mean by our loyalties. Aren't we all loyal to Transylvania County? The name may be new, but our mountain communities aren't."

Pa smiled again. "Yes, we are." He pinched my cheek. "Let's hope everyone feels the same way you do!" Then he became serious again. "Promise me you speak to me first if anything should be brought up that you don't understand. And never share with anyone what you hear at home."

His eyes were scaring me. I saw a desperation I had never seen before. This seemed like a simple enough promise to make. "Of course, Pa, I swear it!"

Relief swept across his face, and he handed me Jack's reins. He didn't say anything, but a continuous nod seemed to possess him as he headed back up towards the hives. He was clearly assuring himself he could trust me. I shook off the whole conversation as a bit over-intense, as I resumed my initial focus of heading to the Valley Store. I would need help unloading the jars since Pa didn't send the baskets with me. Clearly, a promising predicament.

Robert Hamilton, May 31, 1861

Robert is already standing on the porch as the wagon pulls around the final bend before reaching the Hamilton homestead. Several minutes earlier Grady and Blue had announced their approach with deep bellows which bought Robert enough time to contemplate the meaning of this unexpected visit. As the wagon pulls around, it reveals the presence of Leander Gash and his Uncle Probart Poor, accompanied by a man that Robert recognizes as Ben, one of Leander's slaves that often helps Probart at the Trading Post. The sheriff is suddenly grateful that the majority of the Hamilton children have already disappeared into the forest behind him to attend school. Andrew is busy with the sheep and Millie and Rhoda are occupied with the two youngest girls. Any other day, the sound of the wagon and the dogs barking would have drawn the children like flies to honey.

"What brings you men out on this fine mornin'?" Robert descends his porch steps to meet the wagon as it comes to a stop. Ben keeps the reigns drawn tight as Leander jumps down to join Robert.

The well-respected landowner grins, putting Robert somewhat at ease, since a visit like this is quite unusual. "Probart and I would be much obliged if we could have a word with our new sheriff." Probart dismounts and ties his horse to the back of the wagon. With a quick nod, Leander indicates to Ben to pull the wagon on up towards the barn.

"I reckon that will be just fine. Why don't you two gentlemen join me on the porch? I'll see if I can't get Rhoda to put on another pot of coffee." Robert turns to head inside, but Leander's gentle, but firm pat on his shoulder stops him.

"No need, Sheriff." The businessman walks over to one of the rockers and plops down without invitation. "We aren't goin' to stay long, seein' we have other business to attend to and all."

"That's right Sheriff. But thank you for your hospitality." Probart chimes in as he ascends the stairs and chooses to sit on the flat wooden bench against the wall, only a few feet from Leander. Robert nods and is relieved he doesn't have to burden Rhoda into brewing another pot of coffee.

As Robert reaches to turn his own rocker to face the two men he asks, "Well then, let's get right to business." Robert doesn't flinch at by-passing the usual familiar talk about family or the fine weather, a common and most expected custom to easing into serious topics. He acknowledges that as sheriff certain pleasantries would have to be abandoned, at least occasionally. He settles into his rocker and address both men directly. "What brings you here today?"

Leander looks at Probart for a moment as if confirming one last time that they will move forward with their personal petition to their sheriff. Robert is immediately intrigued that *the* confident Leander Gash hesitates and finds himself leaning in towards the men. Probart Poor may be Leander's wife's uncle, but the fact is that he is only a few years older than Leander. He grew up near Morganton on his grandfather Waightstill Avery's plantation after his mother, Polly, divorced her husband, a Caleb Poor; quite the scandal at the time. Probart often tells how his grandfather was the first North Carolina Attorney General and how he practically raised him and his six siblings, giving them the best education. Captain Avery, as Polly's father was called due to his fighting in the Revolutionary War, deeded his daughter Horse Shoe farm; it consisted of several acres along the French Broad River in Henderson County. It was there where Probart's older sister, Polly Osgood, married a McClain and they had a daughter named Margret, who eventually married Leander. The complexity of their history and its weight on both men only draws Robert to wonder how two men who appear to be educated and well-connected find themselves sitting before a mountain sheep-farmer and novice sheriff, needing something from him.

Leander takes a deep breath and finally speaks. "Well, it appears we are taking a chance in sharing our views with you and beseech you to keep our concerns in utmost confidence."

Robert nods and leans back in his rocker. "Of course, I will honor your request. As long as you are not askin' me to look the other way for some law-breakin' crimes you are comittin'." Robert laughs hoping to break the tension.

Leander smiles, but only to acknowledge Robert's attempt at levity. "We have no intention of committin' any crimes, but to some our loyalties may be considered an act of treason."

Robert scratches his beard and nods. "Well, it seems the letter we sent to Raleigh could be considered such if folk seek out those of us who petitioned the state to avoid secedin'. If that is the case, then I am as guilty as you."

Probart clears his throat. "Leander and I have a slight predicament, setting us apart from others who opposed seceding. We don't quite fall into the same category. Many folk around here may not understand." Robert turns his head and watches Ben, who has climbed off the wagon and is now patting the nose of one horse, clearly out of earshot of the men on the porch. Before his guest say the words, Robert knows what is coming next. "We both own slaves."

Robert turns his head again to face the men in front of him. "Yes, and what does this have to do with me?"

It is Leander's turn to lean in. "Here's where it gets confounded."

Robert frowns. "Seems it has always confounded me. Was peculiar you signin' the petition alongside us askin' to avoid secedin' . . . with a dozen or so slaves of your own." The sheriff hopes his statement is perceived as a matter of fact rather than a confrontation and is relieved to find Leander nodding, clearly accepting the observation.

Leander leans back in his chair and begins to rock. "Some of us have slaves and large farms or businesses where slaves are a real advantage to the needed labor."

Robert can't help but chuckle, "Around here we call the extra farm help our children."

Leander smiles and nods, "Yes, I am aware that most mountain fork are blessed with large families to work their lands." Robert decides not to argue the notion of "blessings" weighed against the reality of hardships. Leander continues, "We had hoped, and still do hope that even with the war underway that our leaders will continue to negotiate with the North and find ways to come to an agreement where slavery can experience a gradual extinction rather than a sudden severing. It seems it would behoove a smoother transition to abolishin' the undesirable and no longer acceptable institution of slavery."

Robert finds himself struggling to understand this completely new thought process that he has never heard before. He drops his eyes to the floorboards to study the packed-in dirt, so as to buy him some time to react appropriately. He finally looks up at the men who are patiently waiting for his response. "So, am I to understand that you are for and against slavery at the same time? I am sorry, but this is difficult for me to follow."

Leander contemplates his next words carefully. "Both Probart and I were born into a time where slavery was considered an acceptable institution." Robert watches Probart nod, remembering his years on his grandfather's plantation. Last Robert counted, Probart had three slaves, not counting the times Ben comes to help at the trading post. The small slave house near the building is well kept and often you can see the slaves, a husband, wife and child, busy minding the store's business. Still, to Robert, they are slaves. He waits for Leander to help him understand. "As the country has grappled with slavery, so have we." Leander pauses and looks for the first time at Ben who is now gently patting the second horse. "There must be a way to support the Union in their efforts and still keep hope that we may be compensated for our financial loss if the North were to win."

Robert scratches his beard and longs for a draw on his pipe, but unfortunately it is inside laying on the mantle above the fireplace. "So, am I to understand you support the abolishing of slavery, but you do not want to bear the financial loss they represent."

Leander and Probart both nod, although somewhat hesitantly, since the notion is still somewhat befuddling. Robert sighs and asks, "And what does this have to do with me?"

Leander does not hesitate. "We hope that you will continue to support protecting our businesses and our property."

"I'm assuming you mean your land and slaves?" Robert asks trying not to shake his head.

Leander suddenly stands, his clean-shaven cheeks are suddenly flushed. He moves to the top of the porch steps and looks out at Ben. "Confound it, Bob!" It is the first time that morning he does not address him as Sheriff. "You make it sound so awful. I care deeply for my slaves, a notion widely scoffed. And I can't find any way to justify why I should not free them all and let them make their own way. Except it would be the ruin of me and my farm. Ben over there is great friends with my son, and he seems satisfied with his life."

Robert can't help himself and sarcastically states. "But it's the only life he knows. Right?"

Leander turns abruptly and is furious. "What is that supposed to mean?" Probart tries to reach out and calm him, but Leander brushes off the gesture.

Robert does not let up and adds, "Have you ever asked Ben what he wants? Or any of your other slaves?" Leander, momentarily puzzled by the question, runs his hand through his hair, disrupting his stately appearance. Probart sits silently, reluctant to add to the building tension. Robert pauses a moment before he adds, "You see Leander, the slaves do know better! They see what they don't have every day. How can they not?"

Leander shakes his head, and, unable to come up with a dignified rebuttal, he settles on his only justifiable answer. "I sure as hell did NOT create slavery. And I am trying my damnedest to find a peaceful way to resolve this so we are not all left destitute."

Robert stands and faces the towering man as best he can. He has never seen Leander Gash, the ever-smooth and tactful politician, so out-of-sorts. Robert's voice is calm. "Not sure there is a way." This time Robert is the one to place a firm hand on his friend's arm. "But as Sheriff I will protect you and yours from any outside threat to the best of my ability and will keep your confusin' Union-sympathizin' thoughts confidential." Robert looks at Ben one last time, "Just as you will continue to do your part to protect this community." Leander's political aspirations are well known and he has connections to powerful men like Zeb Vance, who is already vying for the governor's seat. Knowing that Leander is in deep inner turmoil on how to peacefully resolve a conflict that is in full swing, brings Robert a glimmer of hope, even if he doesn't completely understand the somewhat peculiar reasoning.

Elizabeth Neill, May 31, 1861

"Hello, Miss Neill," Mr. Lankford was delighted to see me holding two jars of honey as I approached the counter. "I see you have some precious supplies."

"Yes, sir and there are several more jars in the saddle bags. I need help unloadin' them." I suddenly felt myself blush at the last comment, hoping I didn't sound too eager. So, I quickly added, "Or I can do it, if you have a crate I could use to carry them."

Lankford, who thankfully was more preoccupied with opening a jar and sampling the sweet golden liquid, didn't seem to notice my awkwardness. "JAMES!" he yelled. But when he heard no answer, he took a broom and, using the wooden end, slammed it into the ceiling several times until the scurry of footsteps above allowed him to replace the broom against the wall behind him. "He will be right down, Miss Neill." Mr. Lankford smiled as if causing such a ruckus was as normal as waking up in the morning.

Suddenly James burst through the front door, still buttoning up his vest and flattening down his hair. "B.C.! You know I hate it when you do that!" James said before he noticed me standing near the counter.

He turned slightly red, and I was thankful it was him for a change. "Miss Neill." He nodded.

"Well if you'd come down here when I called, instead of nappin', then I'd haven't the need." Lankford fussed back, but a small grin revealed how much he enjoyed joshing with his brother-in law.

James took a breath and then tried to contain how much fussing he wanted to do in front of me, but he couldn't help himself. "If you hadn't had me re-shelvin' your entire store last night until late I wouldn't need to be sleepin'!" I looked around at the shelves and noticed it had been reorganized, or more cleaned up than anything.

"It looks real nice," I smiled and touched a shelf that usually left a finger print in the dust.

"See!" Mr. Lankford teased, "The customer likes the spring-cleanin' you did!"

James rolled his eyes, "More like never-been-touched cleanin'!" At that we all three laughed because we knew James was right. With the constant outside dust mixed in with the room heated by the wood stove, it was no surprise that dust was a given nuisance, so much so that Mr. Lankford never bothered keeping up with it.

"Well it does look nice," I repeated, "Maybe Mr. Lankford will find a need for a spring cleanin' every week."

As Mr. Lankford laughed, James scowled at me, but his green eyes couldn't keep away the grin, "Now don't you go puttin' any notions in B.C.'s head!" He paused and looked at the open lid of the honey sitting on the counter and Mr. Lankford taking another sample. "Did you come here to harass me, or did you need me for somethin'?"

This time it was my turn to blush, but before I could answer Mr. Lankford, licking his finger with much concentration, jumped in, "Help Miss Neill bring in the rest of this delicious honey. You'll need a crate!"

James held the door for me as I stepped back out into the sunlight. The day was warming up, and I could feel the heat of summer would soon make me long for days like this. I walked to Jack and started to open one saddle bag while James retrieved a crate stacked on the porch with other crates, most empty, but some were full of odd and end items, from discarded horseshoes to bent horseshoe nails. I figured the blacksmith next door was collecting scrap metal or Pink was coming soon to take some to his pa.

"Good to see you, Miss Neill." James' tone had clearly changed now that Mr. Lankford was no longer a spectator.

I smiled, enjoying his playful glance. "I'm thankful you see me, Mr. Morris." I teased.

He laughed and started helping me place the jars into the crate. At one point I thought my heart would be heard when he accidentally touched my hand reaching for a jar. Neither one of us flinched away, but the moment still felt too short.

"Well, that is all the honey there is." I said once the last jar was unpacked.

James lifted the crate and grunted slightly at the weight. "Wait here a minute, and I'll be right back." I nodded, excited that he wanted to visit some more but was quickly disappointed when he returned with the final tally-of-goods-exchanged between Lankford and my family. I felt stupid that I had actually forgotten to get that myself. I sighed and took the paper from him and tucked it into one of the saddle bags.

"Thank you, Mr. Morris," I nodded awkwardly but then added. "I am glad you haven't left yet."

I instantly regretted my words when James' face darkened. He started to stroke Jack's mane. Without looking at me he said, "I'm waiting to hear from my brothers. I will follow their lead." He turned to look at me, hoping I would understand what he was about to say, "I will protect the South and all of those I care about." He was suddenly very serious.

I nodded, but dropped my eyes, not able to bare his intensity. I moved around James and took a hold of Jack's reins. "I think we better head home." I could see that James was disappointed in my response, but it was the second conversation I had had that day that was beyond my understanding. As I started to lead Jack away, I turned and found James still looking at me. His intensity had been replaced with a visible sadness. I suddenly smiled, "Come now, Mr. Morris. I'm sure the war will be over before you ever get all that cleanin' done!"

He tried to smile at my childlike banter that had worked only a few moments ago. "Let's hope you are right, Miss Neill." He dropped his head and walked inside, leaving me alone with Jack. I knew at that moment that my hope for war to not touch us, was a child's dream and, clearly, I was still a child.

Robert Hamilton, June 18, 1861

"Pa, I don't think that is what the Colt pistol is supposed to be used for!" Andrew shakes his head as Robert slams the butt of the Colt for the final time against the head of a nail, now flat against the fence post.

Robert, sweating from the muggy heat that only the mid-afternoon thunderstorm could usher in, smiles at his son, "Who knew the Colt would come in so handy! Don't always have a hammer around when I need one." He gently touches the small nail indention left on the handle, "But I reckon I better watch it, looks like the wood can't take too many blows."

Robert and Andrew walk over to the bustling stream still overflowing from the afternoon downpour. Grady and Blue lap up water from its overflowing banks and then scurry off to settle in the shade under the back-porch. Robert and Andrew reach the hollowed-out log nearby, carrying the underground spring water into the house. Robert opens a small duct and watches freshwater flow into a bucket as a wooden-hewn ladle floats to the top. After both men drink their fill, Andrew takes the bucket and pours the rest of the water over his head, enjoying the cool relief from the stifling muggy heat. Robert laughs at his son and realizes that there has been little turmoil between the two of them for several weeks now.

Robert enjoys watching Andrew respond with a huge grin. "Andrew, I've been meanin' to tell you that you really are a great help to me. You've also been helpin' William out a great deal with his home down the road and I'm really proud of you!" Andrew's boyish grin disappears, and Robert frowns at his son's response. "I know we don't always see eye-to eye, but you need to know what your Ma and I really feel." Robert pulls his pipe out of his back pocket and preps it for a smoke.

Andrew pulls out a flint and steel striker of his own and lights his Pa's pipe. Robert thanks him with a nod. "Pa, I need to talk to you about joinin' up with Captain Johnstone when he calls for volunteers." Robert frowns and pulls in a long draw from his pipe. "Pa, John Stewart told me yesterday that we won the battle at Bethel Church in Virginia over a week ago."

Robert slowly blows out the smoke, "When you say we, you mean. . ."

"The South, Pa!" Andrew's voice was louder, but still controlled, "It's where we live! I want to be on a side. I want to say that when the South wins the war that I had a part in it, that I protected my people."

Robert's fears of Strawbridge Young's son influencing Andrew had been real. "Are you goin' to listen to John Stewart Young more than your own Pa?" Robert tries to hold his temper.

"Listen to what, Pa?" Andrew peels off his wet shirt up over his head and uses it as a towel to dry off his hair. "You said I should wait and see what happens. You said I should not let this war divide us." He flings the shirt over a protruding tree branch then turns to look right at his father, "You said I should not pick sides!" Robert inhales another mouth full of smoke, calming his nerves and waiting for his son to finish. "But not picking sides *is* picking sides. As far as I'm concerned, with all your talk, you're just a damn Yankee!"

"How dare you!" Robert can feel the heat rise. "I am proud to be a Southerner. Don't you dare take that from me. You know it's not that simple!"

"Ain't it, Pa?" Andrew has tears begin to spill down his ruddy cheeks. "You'd think you'd be proud of me for wantin' to volunteer to fight." He starts shaking his head. "No, you're proud 'cause I'm helpin' my brother build his house. A house he hopes doesn't get burned down by some Yanks!" Andrew's hand is pointing down Lambs Creek and his fingers are tightly drawn. "Who you gonna let protect your son's house? Who you gonna let protect you and Ma and

John-Riley and Millie and . . .?" A guttural gasp brakes through with such force that Robert takes a step backward not sure what demon is suddenly possessing his son. The look of horror on Robert's face stops Andrew and causes him to take a deep breath.

Robert looks down at the Colt he has carelessly thrown next to the water bucket, the small nail dent fresh on his mind. He walks to the gun and lifts it, wipes off the dirt and shoves it into the holster he procured the week before from B.C. "I hope I can keep everyone safe. But I'll need help."

Andrew takes in his aging father adjusting the gun holster that hasn't molded to his body or mannerism and starts laughing. But he is laughing at his father, no longer with him. "You're an old man! What're you gonna do?"

Robert straightens his shoulders and will not have his son mock him, "I will tell you what I will not do. I will not go against what I believe!" Robert takes in a deep breath and lifts his chin. "And, I will not let a boy barely off the teat tell me who I am or what I can and can't do."

Andrew shakes his head and spits at his father's feet, "I'm not gonna let a man with a foot halfway in the grave determine my future!" With that Andrew turns his back to his father and walks toward the house.

Robert stumbles to the ground and buries his face in his hands. His pipe slowly goes out as it lays next to him. Robert doesn't know how long it is before he hears the front porch door slam and boots pound down the steps. Rhoda's screaming at her son to not leave only paralyzes Robert longer as he sits near the empty bucket. He only moves to open his arms when his wife's grief-stricken face finds him, and together they weep with Andrew's shirt still dripping from the nearby branch.

Elizabeth Neill, June 20, 1861

I could feel sweat trickle down my back as I walked along the dirt road with the Davidson River on my left tempting me to enjoy its cool liquid manna. But I had to push on since Ma needed me at home. I had finished delivering a jar of honey to Mrs. Young across the river and one to Mrs. English, a little on up Avery Creek. It was strange walking by my school without heading in for more learning, but summer was here and there was too much work to be done. Thankful that my basket was lighter, I kept walking back towards the Cagle Grist Mill before turning right towards home again. Although I had already delivered honey to the Mackey's on my way up the river, I was seriously considering a possible second stop by their home for a second glass of cold cider, a refreshing treat I had enjoyed an hour ago, and intensely longed for more. It seemed logical since their house was set back off the river on my way. Although Henry and Maria Mackey were not as close kin to us as they were to Viney, I still knew they were kin and hoped they would not turn away a sweating relative. But reality took a grip and I sighed, since Ma would be mortified if I took advantage of their kindness, and, besides, she would reprimand me for wasting more time instead of helping her. She was right, of course.

"Hi Elizabeth." A sweet voice made me look down the riverbank at a young woman who was dangling her feet in the river.

"Hi Rachel-Emma." I stared at her feet gently moving back and forth. I had wondered why she hadn't come out to greet me at the Young's home when I delivered the honey to her ma.

"Can you come sit with me a minute?" Before Rachel-Emma had finished talking, I had already put down my basket and was scurrying down the dirt towards her. "I guess you can!" Rachel-Emma laughed at my overly-eager speed of taking off my shoes with one hand while hiking up my skirt with the other.

"Can't be rude now, can I?" I said while I flung my last sock on top of my shoes. The cold water felt like the sweetest relief against my hot and sweaty feet. "Ohhhhhhhhhh, soooo nice!" I moaned. Of course, that made Rachel-Emma fall into hysterical laughter.

After she pulled herself together, she asked, "Where're you headed?"

I didn't want to think about getting out, but Rachel-Emma was older than me, I thought maybe about twenty, and, being more lady like than me, I thought I better learn all I could from her, so grunting-that-I-wasn't-going-anywhere wouldn't have been in my favor. So, I moved over to sit next to her and began to mimic her gentle weaving of her feet in and out of the refreshing water. "Well, it seems I am headin' home, since I finished deliverin' honey."

Rachel-Emma perked up, "So are you goin' to pass the grist mill?"

"I always do." I said as a matter of fact.

"May I come?" Rachel-Emma was the one who looked like a child now.

"Well of course." I was confused, "Why, you can do what you want can't you?"

Rachel-Emma dropped her eyes. "Well, Ma fusses at me if I go to the mill by myself, sayin' I will give folk the wrong idea and all."

"I go there all the time. Should I not be doin' that?" I was worried I had missed some rule about being a young woman.

"Well," Rachel-Emma swung her shoulders in towards me and whispered, "You ain't got a sweet-heart there."

"Oh," I finally understood. She and James-Henry Cagle, and his Cagle-blue eyes, were sweet on each other and she wanted to see him. "Well let's go then!" Her smile was worth cutting my time at the river short.

After we had managed to put on our shoes and make sure neither of us looked like a mess, we walked about ten more minutes before we heard the churning of the waterwheel. Soon, a large three-story wooden building rose before us as we began to emerge from the forest. Across the river a little way down I could glimpse the Linsey-woolsey Plant, where most sheep farmers in the area sold their wool to be transformed into fabric. I was used to this walk and didn't think much of it until we saw several horses tied up to hitching posts and voices soon overpowered the sound of the river. Rachel-Emma and I looked at each other and frowned, "Is that someone yellin'?" She whispered. I shrugged and nodded at the same time, so we slowed down as we approached since we weren't sure what we were getting ourselves into.

"I'm going to fight for the South and not stay here and hide in these mountains!" A voice boomed.

Rachel-Emma went white stopping me before we came around the corner of the mill. "That's my brother, John!" I didn't know what to say so, with Rachel-Emma on my heels, I pulled myself around the corner enough to see who he was talking to.

"What's that supposed to mean?" James-Henry barked back. We could see Uncle Bob's son, Andrew, standing next to John with his shoulders pulled back and the ugliest snarl on his lips I'd ever seen. At that moment he was not the fun-lovin' cousin I had grown up with. On the other side of James-Henry stood an older man, Caleb Orr, who had married James-Henry's sister, Anna-Myra, several years earlier. I didn't know he was helping out at the mill.

"Boys, let it go," Mr. Orr's voice sounded steady. I could see him set down a bag of freshly ground cornmeal on the ground next to another one. "Let them take their cornmeal and go."

"No, Caleb!" James-Henry wasn't going to let John get away with anything. "John, what do you mean?" He was all up in John's face now.

"I mean you and yours! You ain't gonna fight for the South. I hear you talkin' about the North and how it ain't right for the South to secede... fillin' my sister's head with all sorts of notions." Rachel-Emma turned pale as John spit on the ground and finished, "Go hide in these Mountains. Andrew and I ain't gonna be cowards." Andrew's age showed as he nodded his head like a young boy. I felt my stomach lurch. Aunt Rhoda would be upset if she knew her boy was taking a stand in public alongside John Young.

"Now wait just a minute." It was Mr. Orr that jumped in and was trying to keep calm. "You know your daddy ain't as clear cut as you seem to be! So, don't throw around your general statement about us! Now take your cornmeal and go on!"

John and James-Henry still stood face to face. John couldn't stop, "My Pa believes we boys can fight for what we believe in. And no Yank is going to make decisions for me!"

95

"You do what you gotta do, and you ain't got no say in what I do and don't do." James-Henry started to turn and head towards two people I hadn't seen until that moment. My jaw dropped. James and Tony were each loading several sacks of flour and corn-meal on to a wagon. They were pretending to mind their own business, but their silence, quick movements and James' constantly shoving his light red strand of hair out of his face told me they were trying to get out of there as soon as possible.

"Don't you walk away from me!" John's voice was louder. James-Henry didn't look at him, but kept walking towards James who nodded to Tony to help him lift a heavy barrel onto the wagon. John didn't let up, "You coward! You stay away from my sister!" Suddenly, Rachel-Emma grabbed my shoulder to steady herself.

James-Henry slowly turned around. His Cagle-blue eyes narrowed, "What did you say?"

"You heard me!" An ugly smirk emerged. "Don't want you turnin' her into a Yankee's bitch!"

James-Henry pounced on John, madder than a wet hen. The first punch landed square upside John's lip and blood splattered across Andrew's face, while John tumbled to the ground with James-Henry on him. A moment of shock froze Andrew, but for only a minute, before he pounced on James-Henry's back landing a fist into the side of his ribs. James-Henry's fury turned to Andrew quickly knocking the breath out of my cousin by flinging himself straight back slamming Andrew to the ground with James-Henry's back on top of Andrew, pinning him down. At that point John had found his feet and jumped on top of James-Henry. A strange sort of sandwich emerged with James-Henry squished between the two. Mr. Orr was yelling at James and Tony to come help him break them up although neither of the men seemed eager to engage.

I felt Rachel-Emma leave my side and run to the scuffle, reaching them before James and Tony could make a decision to help or not. "Stop it!" She screamed now pounding her brother's back. "Stop it! NOW!" I dropped my basket and ran to grab the young woman around her waist, trying to pull her off. Her dark hair was sticking to her tear-streaked face and her perfect white cheeks were blotchy.

In the midst of it all I felt some strong arms reach around my middle, trying to pull me off of Rachel-Emma, "Elizabeth!" James' voice broke my concentration. "Let go!" I could feel my fingers slip. "This is not your fight!" His voice was firm, so I obeyed. As soon as I let go, a gun fired and suddenly the three men jumped up from the ground and Rachel-Emma ran to James-Henry, who held her tightly.

"That's enough!" Anna Myra Orr, who was Caleb's wife and James-Henry's sister, was standing with a shotgun in her hand, close to Tony, who had not strayed from the wagon. He was moving slowly to the other side of the wagon to put distance between him and the mess-at-hand. "Grown men fightin' like schoolboys!" The dirt and blood streaked faces didn't say a word but stared at the woman who was now in command. "Shame on you! Shame on you all!" She looked at her husband, who only dropped his eyes. He had tried to break it up, but he knew he hadn't tried hard enough. "You are all neighbors. You are all from these mountains! Shame on you for lettin' this God-forsaken war break you before you even face the blood-stained battle grounds." The silence was only broken by the heavy breathing of the men. I was suddenly aware how close James was to me and although he was no longer holding my waist, his closeness was intentional and protective. Finally, Mrs. Orr placed her gun by her side, "If I were you, I would thank God for every day you wake up and can breathe this mountain air and drink this mountain water. Don't any of us know how long we will be able to!" When she saw no-one was moving, she yelled, "Now git!"

At that point Andrew and John grabbed the sacks they had come for and started heading up the river, but before he disappeared behind the rhododendron bush that marked the beginning of the road, John looked at his sister. His eyes were full of anger and at the same time he was looking to her for forgiveness. She turned her head and buried it in James-Henry's blood covered shirt, so John shook his head and moved on.

"Are you okay, Miss Neill?" James' voice was suddenly formal again.

I smiled gently. "Yes, Mr. Morris. I think so." I wasn't really, though, because I wasn't so sure what had just happened.

"May I offer you a ride home?" James picked up my empty basket. "Tony and I are haulin' the sacks and barrels back to the store, and if I am correct, we will pass by your home."

I glanced at Rachel-Emma who was fussing over James-Henry at this point and was no longer concerned with being alone at the mill in case it looked bad. Nothing could look worse than what I just witnessed. Along with my mind trying to make sense of it all, the muggy air suddenly became unbearable, leaving me very tired. I sighed, "Yes, that would be kind of you. But maybe you can drop me at my Mammaw's. She's along the way as well." I felt like a child asking to go to my Mammaw's, but I didn't care. I needed her.

James smiled, but a heaviness was still weighing on him. He helped me onto the bench of the wagon while Tony jumped into the back, securing the flour and cornmeal sacks and barrels a little better, since they had hastily thrown the supplies in the back. No one spoke; we were all not okay.

Halfway between the grist mill and my house the road came to a small crest in the hill where my Mammaw Neill still lived in the home she and her husband built. As a hatter, Pappaw had made a good living and the two of them always welcomed friends and family to stop and sit a spell. I considered offering James to come in for a cup of cold cider, but I couldn't bring myself to share Mammaw with anyone at that moment. I thanked James for the ride and hopped down. As soon as I hit the ground, I stared running and yelling, "Mammaw?" Before I even got to the door, Mammaw was standing there with a big-old grin on her face and her arms open wide. I fell right into those arms and began to sob. I didn't care if James was watching or not, all I heard was the gentle slap of the reins and the wagon's creaking back into motion.

Mammaw stroked my hair, "Nothin' a cold glass of cider and a good hug cain't fix."

I smiled and spent the next hour sharing everything with her. Everything. She would sigh and whisper, "Is that so" once in a while, but as the hours waned, I eventually had to head down the other side of the hill to our house and get on with life, even if it meant Ma would be fussing at me for taking my time and "playing" along the way. But I knew her fussing would turn to fear when she heard the whole story.

Robert Hamilton, June 23, 1861

Word of the fight at the grist mill reaches all the homes up the Davidson River and makes for perfect preaching material for Reverend English to build his sermon around forgiveness. From those involved in the incident, only James-Henry and Rachel-Emma are present in the front pews while, closer to the back door, Elizabeth squirms in her seat through the part on individuals' roles as by-standers. Robert grabs Rhoda's hand and squeezes it. He knows the topic is just as painful for Strawbridge and his wife, Martha-Ann, who are sitting on the other side of the church.

"I can't bear it." Rhoda whispers to Robert as they leave the little church along the Davidson River. "I'm going to talk to her." Without waiting for Robert's response Rhoda heads over to Martha-Ann and Strawbridge who are slowly making their way to the wooden foot bridge to cross over the river and head home. After instructing Millie to watch the rest of the children for a few minutes, Robert is right behind his wife, knowing that Strawbridge will surely have a few words of his own.

"Martha-Ann?" Rhoda's voice carries over the noisy river. "Can we talk a moment?"

The Youngs wait for Rhoda and Robert to join them on the other side of the river, "Of course, Rhoda." Martha-Ann holds out her hand and then, when their hands clasp, she pulls Rhoda into her.

"Why don't we sit here." Strawbridge points to some benches that he and his boys crafted and positioned years ago along the bank facing the church. Robert catches Rhoda shoot a glance at him, knowing their suspicions are now confirmed. In all the years they have been neighbors, the Young family has never simply sat along the river to talk. They have always asked others to retire with them to the Young's homestead, only a few minutes away.

Rhoda gets right to it, "You have Andrew, don't you?"

Martha-Ann does not let go of her friend's hand, but squeezes it. "Sweet Rhoda, your son *is* stayin' with us, but only until he can sort out what he is doin' next."

Robert watches as Rhoda is at a loss for words, so he speaks, "It is kind of you to take him in. It has been hard on his mother that he and I don't see eye to eye." Robert tries to hide his own anger at Andrew for pulling their friends into the midst of their own predicament and is ashamed that Andrew has embarrassed his family. "I figure we are beholden to you." Robert swallows and adds, "I'd ask a favor that you use your discretion in these matters. I wouldn't want word to spread that the Sheriff's own son wasn't bein' taken care of by his own." Of course, Robert wants to, more importantly, not let others know why Andrew and he are at odds.

He looks straight at Strawbridge who is aware of the tension and is relieved when Strawbridge nods, "Of course, discretion is of utmost importance." His eyes drop for a moment and, as he looks up again, he moves his attention to Rhoda who is still in the clutches of Martha-Ann. "What's ailin you is already poisoning our family too! That night Rachel-Emma did not come home 'til after dark worrying her Ma to death, and when she is home she doesn't speak to any of her brothers."

Martha-Ann and Rhoda move in closer to the men until their circle looks like four children huddled in secrecy. Martha-Ann adds, "And my boys are talking of joinin' the Confederate army." Her voice is almost a whisper, "As much as it grieves my heart, how can I not be proud of their willingness to stand for what they believe?" This is not what Robert expected to hear and his shock is visible in his silence. Support was one thing, but to be proud was beyond Robert's grasp. Robert can only make sense of the fact that Martha-Ann is Leander

Gash's sister and he has to somehow reconcile himself with the certainty that he will never understand their way of thinking.

Rhoda scowls at Robert and then turns her face, at this point almost nose to nose, to her friend, "I'm so sorry that you are torn. You receive no judgement from me as you support your boys as a mother." Rhoda turns her attention to Robert with intensity. "We all have to remember we are family first and foremost. I'll be damned if I let this war take my boy away without knowin' his Ma is behind him." Robert frowns and is aware that Rhoda's words are not only about their son, but her prayers of late are for her sister Maria and brother-in law Henry Mackey who have chosen to support the Confederacy. Robert and Rhoda stare at each other for a moment longer before she takes a deep breath. He knows Rhoda has no intention of heading home at that moment. Before she turns her head away, she adds, "You take the littluns and head on home. I'll be there after a while."

Robert watches Rhoda and Martha-Ann head towards the Young's home, leaving the two men alone. Strawbridge moves to stand shoulder to shoulder with Robert as they watch their wives disappear into the forest. "Sometimes it's better to let women-folk have it their way."

"I reckon so." Robert tries to smile but settles for a nod and turns to cross over the bridge to his waiting children. There is no usual playing or running around, the usual aftermath of a long sermon. Instead, with the exception of three-year-old Rachel who is asleep in Millie's arms, the other six of them are staring at Robert with eyes wide open. It is the first time they will walk home from church without their ma.

CHAPTER 7

Elizabeth Neill, July 4, 1861

I could feel the sweat trickle down my back as I attempted to ease into the shade of one of the tents. But the lack of a breeze propelled me forward again to stand in the alley way leading out of the campground towards the Oak Grove Church. At least, occasionally, a forgiving warm breeze would bring some relief. I had begged Ma to leave me behind since the last time we were at the campground, the celebration of founding Transylvania had turned upside down causing everyone to fret. Ma told me that coming together as a county on our day of liberation from England would be a good way to bring healing. But when I rolled my eyes and my sister groaned, she looked at us with a stern look and, in essence, told us we better not make a spectacle of ourselves as we did last time on the way to the campground. She stared at me longer than my sister and, as she fixed her eyes on me, her look softened, knowing that what I witnessed at the grist mill was more than child's play. She was worried.

I pretended to listen to Reverend English as he stood on the platform, behind him a bench with a few official looking men as well as Uncle Bob, all fanning themselves with hats or accepting sips of water from a leather pouch passing between them.

"So, God has placed on us a great responsibility to love one another and take care of the least of these..." Reverend English's sermon droned on like his school lessons so I was having a hard time following him. Once in a while I glanced at the branches, carefully molded into the arbor that offered him shade, wondering if there were any snakes he could kill instead. It seemed that most folk gathered were preoccupied with the heat, but a token "amen" thrown in every few minutes encouraged the sermon to needlessly drag on. It was vividly clear that the usual merriment was missing as several women quietly prepared the table of dishes, without the usual giggling and hugging. The only real signs of celebrating the Fourth of July was the American flag hanging from the preacher's tent and the occasional whiff of skewed pig still slow roasting in a fire pit outside the fortress of tents. I saw Viney wave at me. She was sitting with Aunt Rhoda and the rest of her family on some old quilts only a stone's throw away. I had wanted to sit with them earlier, but Ma had told me she didn't want any of the children playing during the sermon.

Ma quietly asked me if I had noticed the flag. I said, "Of course, red, white and blue."

She gently said, "Yes, but it is the new Confederate flag, also red, white and blue, the 'Stars and Bars' of the Confederacy with nine stars. Likely more will be added soon. One of our neighbors made this one." She whispered it like it was a secret, which it clearly wasn't.

"But hangin' down like that sure looks like the U.S. flag." I sighed. But when Ma didn't respond I realized she was staring at the flag so hard like an answer to some question would suddenly pop out of the folds that occasionally stirred.

Feeling uncomfortable, I changed the subject. "Are we goin' to eat soon?" My stomach began to growl, and I was tired of being quiet, so when Ma and Pa ignored me, I grabbed my plate and slipped away toward the table, so I could be first in line, hoping Ma wouldn't see this as me making a spectacle of myself. I signaled to Viney to join me and she nodded then turned to Aunt Rhoda to find a way to escape. In the last two hours, I had seen James sitting with B.C. and other men who were pretending to listen to Reverend English, but the constant leaning in to each other and nodding at odd times during the sermon revealed discussions beyond God's call to love-one-another. We hadn't spoken since the grist mill after James dropped me off at Mammaw's, but I had resigned myself to the fact that I was a child and that he could take his-old-man-self and do what-ever he wanted. I didn't care.

"Hi Elizabeth." Viney's voice made me feel a spark of joy that I hadn't felt all day.

"Viney!" With a big grin we hugged, defying the dark mood. "So glad you got away. I'm starved!"

Viney giggled, drawing the attention of the two women closest to us. But instead of fussing, they found their smiles, and, as if waking up, reached out and embraced each other. Viney kept her voice quiet, hoping we wouldn't be shooed back to our family quilts. "I'm goin' crazy up the creek without you. John-Riley has been angry with Pa since Andrew left and there ain't much fun goin' on. Except Rachel was able to use the outhouse on her own for the first time." Viney sighed, "Yes, sad times when a three-year old's life is the best news I have."

"Maybe Ma will let me come up soon." I smiled, but wondered what had changed. Summer was always about the long days and late nights spent up at Uncle Bob's, but since he became sheriff it seemed everyone was too busy. "I don't know why I haven't been allowed."

"I know!" Viney leaned in and whispered, excited to feed me the newest gossip. "It's the war." That tid-bit was a disappointing explanation, but instead of fussing at her I nodded as if I was intrigued. "Pa has had William come up and they been working in the cellar. . . not sure why? They cleared out the boxes stored in the fireplace and made sure it is still a workin' fireplace. I can't imagine why we need a fire in the basement with all this heat!" Viney wiped the sweat off her forehead with a soft blue apron she had tied around her light gray dress.

I rolled my eyes at her story. I loved their cool cellar, which stored most of their potatoes, apples and other staples. "That don't make a lick of sense." I leaned into her and added, "But men don't ever make a lick of sense to me!" We both giggled, and, at that moment, I embraced the fact that being a girl was exactly the best thing to be.

As the platter of pulled pork reached the communal table, I heard Reverend English say grace and finish with a loud "Amen" which was followed by a chorus of "amens". Just as I thought the official discussions were over, Mr. Johnstone traded places with Reverend English. My heart dropped, not because I remembered much about his promise to return, or because he represented the war in all its solemnity, but because I was hungry and waiting any longer was not acceptable.

As Mr. Johnstone began to speak, I began to fill my plate. "What are you doin'?" Viney asked as her eyes skirted from me to the women standing round us.

"Did he, or did he not just say grace?" I asked as a matter of fact, with a piece of cornbread already balancing on the plate.

"He shore did!" An older lady came up next to me with her plate and was reaching for her own piece of cornbread. "I cain't listen to them no more. So, we might as well fix our plates." Her partially toothless grin made me smile and Viney felt, since an adult had condoned my behavior, it was okay to follow. To her relief, she wasn't the only one. Several women had gathered their children together and were already filling plates of their own.

I looked at my family and was expecting them to head my way, but the crowd of people closest to the platform were clearly very drawn to what the man was saying. I noticed several men were standing one at a time and the hush that had fallen over the crowd was finally reaching us, silencing the clattering dishes.

"Captain Johnstone, sign me up!" Leonard Cagle's voice carried through the crowd. He turned to face us with strong arms raised triumphantly. "I am in good form! I might as well use it to defend our rights!" A cheer rose from the men beside him. I couldn't believe there was more than one Leonard Cagle, but I knew for sure that young whipper-snapper wasn't James-Henry's Pa.

"Thank you, Leonard," Captain Johnstone's voice boomed with confidence. "It is an honor that you choose to make this statement publicly, but it is not necessary to do so publicly." The captain pointed to the Allison tent only a few feet from where I was standing. A serious looking man was sitting on the edge of the tent's platform with a paper spread out in front of him. "Those of you who would like to sign up as volunteers with my regiment, please sign up with Alexander Allison behind you." It was as if the entire crowd turned and looked at me, holding my plate filled with food. I froze as several men stood and walked towards me, but they walked right past me. I slowly stepped sideways to avoid the sweaty men eager to place their names on a sheet of paper. The Orrs and the McCalls were first in line and I was shocked to watch seven Raines men brush past me. How could so many from one family decide it was the right thing to do?

"Watch out with that food, Elizabeth!" Uncle Bob's cousin, Robert F. Hamilton, grabbed what was left of my half-eaten cornbread as he fell in line behind Nathaniel Scruggs. Another same-name- relative! I never understood why so many men in the Hamilton family were called Robert. I didn't fuss at him as he swallowed the bread with one mouthful.

"Andrew!" Viney's cry tore me out of my daze. I turned to see Viney walk towards me, shove her plate at me and rush to her brother, who was close to the end of the slow-moving line of volunteers. I walked carefully towards her, awkwardly holding two plates of delicious fixings. His voice was barely audible through her cries, "Please don't sign up, Andrew! I'm sure you and Pa can see eye to eye again."

"Hush up Viney!" Andrew's voice was stern. "Don't you bring more attention to this than your cryin' is already doin'." Her sobs were suddenly replaced by a look of fear. I followed her look as she looked through the crowd to her Pa who was standing on the platform with a face of stone. I couldn't tell if Uncle Bob was angry or afraid, but it was enough to shut Viney down. "Sorry, Andrew." I noticed Aunt

Rhoda, who, by raising a single finger into the air, kept the other children from running to their brother.

Andrew's voice changed as he grabbed Viney's chin with his hand, "You take care of your little brothers and sisters for me. You hear me!"

Viney nodded pitifully, turned her back on her brother and walked up to me. She looked at me and my stomach turned as I saw a fear I had never seen before in her eyes. It wasn't only a fear of her brother's death, it also was something else. When I questioned her, she gently took her plate from my hand and walked to Aunt Rhoda to join them sitting as calmly as possible, letting her plate of fixings be devoured by a stray dog.

Suddenly, Uncle Bob started walking towards me, and I thought for sure he was getting ready to talk to Andrew, but instead he stopped next to an older man who looked small against the strapping, young men in line. I could barely hear Uncle Bob, so I stepped a little closer. His voice was shaky, "Craf. What are you doin'? You got young'uns and your farm."

The older man named Craf, someone I had never met before, nodded and answered, "Well Bob, I figured I better make a decision before one is made for me." He winked at my Uncle and whispered just loud enough for me to hear. "Can't draw too much attention to my family." I frowned at what he might be hiding that caused him to sign up so quickly.

"This is not the way!" Uncle Bob was trying to stay calm and not show too much disappointment in this man's choice. Heads finally turned to look at Uncle Bob, which caused him to stand up straight and clearly back track on his last statement, at least publically. He stated maybe a little too loudly, "I . . . I will find a way . . . to help your family, and . . . I will be sure to check in on them while you are gone." Craf's eyes understood Uncle Bob's bumbling statement more than I did and nodded at him. Uncle Bob awkwardly backed away, almost running into me, and then headed towards his family, still huddled on their quilt.

I shook my head in disbelief at the scene and had to get out of the campground. I quickly walked through an alley way and found myself scurrying up towards the church as fast as possible. I didn't stop until I couldn't see the campground anymore and settled halfway down the slope between the church and the Valley Store. I plopped down on the grass, thankful that it hadn't rained, even though the distant thunder promised an afternoon shower. The sun was still relentless, so I scooted closer to a dogwood tree, beautiful in its full white blossoms a few weeks ago, but it had already shed its coat of white and full green leaves provided shade from the sun. I looked at the pork and pile of beans that still hadn't been touched. I felt silly thinking that my hunger was the most important thing only thirty minutes earlier and wondered how the deep growl was so easily replaced by a sick, hollow feeling.

"Can I join you, Miss Neill?" James' voice didn't change the sick feeling, not like it would have a few months ago.

I didn't know what to say, so I nodded. He sat down and stretched out his legs while he leaned back on his elbows. "This is an awful pretty view." I looked out at the tops of the small rolling hills and had never really thought it was pretty, not compared to the majestic mountains that, when we hiked high enough, would take our breath away. Pa always told us there wasn't any prettier place on earth. I believed him.

"I guess it is pretty, but nothin' like some of the views higher up, or go down the valley to the Little River area . . . they got some real pretty mountain views."

"Is that right?" James smiled at me. I hadn't seen his smile in some time and something I thought was gone stirred in me. "Maybe you can show me sometime."

I flushed and then started to pick at the food on my plate, not knowing what else to say. I handed him a piece of the pork and he eagerly devoured it. After a few minutes, I dared whisper, "Did you sign up?" My heart began to race.

James sat up and crossed his legs. He took in the view one more time before he looked at me, pushing the hair out of his eyes, "No, I didn't." I could feel my body sigh, but he kept looking at me. "But I'm goin' back down to Polk County to see what my brothers are doin'. I want to join up with them." My initial relief was gone. He looked away almost ashamed to have made me feel this way. "I'll miss the mountains. But I have to be with my family right now."

I could feel a tear escape before I choked out, "Well, the mountains will miss you."

James chuckled gently. "If I could, I'd sit here on the side of this slope with you forever, Miss Neill."

I smiled and wiped away the tear. "Well that could have been mighty nice."

James suddenly stood up and reached into the dogwood tree and grabbed at something a few feet away. When he sat back up, he opened his hand, "Here. I know it's not much." A white dogwood blossom was laying in his hand. I couldn't believe there was still one left. He took my hand and gently placed it in my palm, "If I live through this war, I'll come a courtin' you, Miss Neill."

I looked at the small flower, four blooms forming a perfect white cross, and then looked up at James as his eyes were asking me a question. I laughed out loud as I held the small dogwood blossom in my palm, "Well, James Morris, I'll be curious to see what courtin' looks like to you, if that ain't been what we been doin'!"

Robert Hamilton, August 3, 1861

"Bob," Rhoda's voice yelling from inside the house, is all business, "Make sure you and George don't mess up my pile of corn husks on the porch! I wouldn't want the sheep upset if they didn't get their treats!" Robert looks at George who is rocking in the rocking chair next to him. Rhoda's pile of corn husks sits at their feet, left over from the early-morning corn-shucking.

Robert shakes his head and stands up, "Why don't we take the husks up to the field?" His voice is loud enough for Rhoda to hear him and his sarcasm.

"That's a mighty fine idea!" Rhoda's voice answers, but then trails off, barking orders out the back door at Joel and Jimmy who have decided it best to splash the little girls and the dogs with water from the stream. George wonders for a minute if he needs to deal with Jimmy, but an audible *Yes'm*, quickly tells him Rhoda has it all under control.

"It almost feels like any other summer." George stands up and grabs a basket to join Robert, filling them with the corn husks. "Elizabeth was worried that these days were over, with the war on us."

Robert fills his basket first and stands to look out over his farm. "Standin' from my porch, it almost seems like there is no war at all." His eyes scan the fields of sheep to his right and the large spread of a vegetable garden to his left with a manageable corn field just beyond. "B.C. has begun building his house up on the hill, close to the land that he donated to create the city of Brevard. Seems once the city is finally built, his home will be close to all the comings and goings."

George chuckles, "Seems he likes to stay in the middle of it all, like he is right now."

"Seems so!" Robert nods and smiles, but it fades quickly as he heads down the steps with George close behind. "But it's not true for everyone in the county."

George quickly catches up to walk next to Robert, remembering that, as Sheriff, he sees more than Lambs Creek. "I figured as much, but I hadn't heard. Most people are keepin' to themselves." The soft thumping of hooves hurrying to the fence and the bleating of hungry ewes bring his focus for a moment back to dumping the husks over the wooden fence, a few feet away from Robert's pile. George thumps the bottom of the upside-down bucket to loosen up a stuck corn husk. Once it dislodges, George turns to Robert who is lost in thought. "Seems you are keepin' to yourself too!"

Robert leans on one of the wooden posts and looks at George, sorting out his thoughts. George raises an eyebrow, wondering if he really wants to know what Robert is thinking, so instead of asking, he looks at the feeding frenzy only a few feet away. "They sure like those husks!" At that moment Blue and Grady appear and shake their stream-drenched coats vigorously, causing George to step back in surprise.

"Grady! Blue! Stop that! Go home!" Robert fusses at the dogs and points his finger towards the house. The dogs reluctantly obey, but as soon as they see the girls are still playing in the stream, they take off again to continue frolicking with people who want their attention. George smiles at the scene and then looks at Robert who takes a deep breath. "Will you be my deputy?" Robert suddenly asks the question that has been weighing on him. George studies Robert and runs a hand through his beard slowly. Robert pulls out his pipe and lights it, giving George a minute to process the request. "You are one of the few people I can trust." He waves his pipe around pointing at everything and nothing at the same time, "It's not only about keepin' all our own families safe, but it's the families I am already seein' who have sons and husbands off to war. Crops that have been set before the men-folk left are bein' harvested as best as possible, but by children and neighbors comin' together. Some families are only beginnin' to see the effects of missin' husbands and sons." Robert takes a long draw from his pipe. "I'm afraid I need you to help me make sure we are takin' care of our own, so we don't have to turn on each other one day."

"How will we take care of each other with so many split loyalties?" George slowly puts the empty bucket on the ground and then leans on the fence, facing the hills that protectively guard the Hamilton homestead. "It seems most live up hollers like yours, and you never know what you're goin' to face."

Robert takes another puff and then slowly lets the smoke spill out from between his lips. "We have to trust that our loyalty is with the mountain people and that they share that same notion."

"That seems like an awful lot of trust to put into folk who may or may not share our view." George shakes his head as he focuses on the children innocently playing.

Robert takes a minute to find words to help convince his friend that theirs is not a lost cause. "The way I see it, we need to always make it about the task at hand. Never about views. Never talk about views. Only feed people. Make sure women folk on both sides aren't alone fendin' for themselves." Robert knows he is making a very complicated situation sound simple.

Robert turns to see John-Riley chase the girls into the bubbling creek and smiles when Elizabeth and Viney, in turn, splash him relentlessly. The sheriff's face then turns dark, "Many of us have families that have split." George knows Robert is thinking of Andrew. "Even Staub, whose sons are eager to fight for the Confederacy, while their neighbor, James-Henry, is clearly a Union supporter and has no fear talkin' and encouragin' others to consider fightin' for the North." Robert shakes his head, "And nothin' has happened to him yet, except a few words and a scuffle." Robert shakes his head and turns back towards the sheep. "If we can keep the battle here at home to scuffles and harsh words, I will consider that quite a feat."

George doesn't know what being in law-enforcement is going to exactly entail, but he isn't going to let the sheriff do it alone. "Okay Robert, I'll be your deputy. For what it's worth, I hope we can at least protect our families."

Robert nods, and George can hear the sheriff let out a deep breath, "I'll talk to the court about gettin' you bonded as soon as possible."

"Then it will be official?" George asks having forgotten that being a deputy was an actual paid job.

"No, as far as I'm concerned it's official now, but you won't get paid until you're bonded!" Robert grins mischievously and slaps George on the back, "But you don't mind a few weeks workin' for free, do you?"

George laughs, "Well I'm used to it! Been feedin' your sheep here for free, haven't I?"

CHAPTER 8

Elizabeth Neill, August 31, 1861

"I really don't think there will be any left-over ears!" I whined as my mother shoved me out the door with a wicker basket. She was busy putting-up apple-butter from the three bushels of apples Naomi English traded with us for some honey. I would have preferred to help her stir the slow-cooking apples, mixed with cinnamon and cloves, over fighting off gnats in the wilting cornfield. "Any ears left are probably just as dried up as the stalks! I think Jack would love to finish off any remaining ears!" I was half-way down the steps when I turned around to look at Ma with one last plea. "You've never made me look this hard for the slim pickin's! Am I being punished?" As soon as the last word left my scrunched-up lips, I regretted it.

"Elizabeth Ann Neill! Don't you make your Ma ashamed!" Red heat was crawling up Ma's neck lighting her round cheeks on fire. "You think you can go puttin' on airs like you're better than everyone else pullin' their weight to survive?" Ma's eyes were aflame, and she took one step down off the porch towards me as I quickly jumped off the bottom step. "Don't you think for a minute that you are too grown up for a lickin'." My face turned white. Last time Ma took a switch to my rear was when I was six and had decided it was a good idea to throw eggs at my sister. I hadn't needed a lickin' since, and I treated eggs like each one was a gold nugget, which they were, according to Ma.

I quickly lost my whine and stood up straight as possible with the basket firmly gripped by both of my hands. "Sorry, Ma. I didn't mean no disrespect. Honest!" I saw Ma take a breath as she became aware of her own fury. I held my voice as steady as possible, but it began to crack into the beginnings of a desperate cry. "I'll search every stalk, I swear!"

Ma slowly patted down her apron as her much calmer voice eased my growing fear. "No need to swear." She tried to smile, like she was apologizing for her anger. She climbed down the rest of the steps and by the time she reached me, still gripping the basket, I had tears pouring down my cheeks. She took my chin in one of her hands and lifted it to look me square in the eyes, "Not knowin' what the war is going to bring has got us all on edge. Got to make sure we got all the food we can get. Do you understand?" I nodded as best I could with my chin still cradled in her hand, which smelled like apple-butter. The familiar scent soothed my nerves. A quick peck on my forehead and a final squeeze of my chin told me the discussion was over, much to my relief. A lickin' would have marked me a child again, which would simply not have been acceptable for a young lady that James was planning on courting when he returned.

I walked with my head held high to the edge of the field and, once hidden within folds of dried stalks and withering silts still dangling from abandoned worm-eaten ears, I let myself have a good cry. I hated the war. It had taken away James, and it had turned everyday life upside down. Even Pa had been bonded as Deputy Sheriff, which meant I had to carry more of the responsibility for minding the livestock and assisting him with his honey business. I stopped sobbing for a moment when I realized that the only good that came from the current circumstances was that Sarah-Jane and Jimmy had to mind me more. I wiped my nose on my apron and decided that I had had a good-enough-cry. As I shoved my way through the rows, picking ears that we would have easily left as fodder for the chickens, I pictured James coming home soon, or at least getting a letter from him. The simple thought helped me realize that I could endure whatever the war had to bring. At that point, the war seemed a far-off event that was quite the nuisance.

Robert Hamilton, November 6, 1861

The morning frost on the grass doesn't keep the sheep from eagerly scavenging for their cold morning meal, but Robert is not paying attention to the resourcefulness of his flock. He is standing on his porch pulling on his left suspender, facing John C. Duckworth, the younger brother of James H. Duckworth, a friend and fellow participant in helping found the county. After Robert manages to get Grady and Blue to hush-up with their incessant barking, he finally addresses his early morning guest. "Hello John," Robert's breath appears before him reminding him to quickly finish dressing. "What a surprise to find you here so early this morn. Is there a problem?" Robert quickly buttons up his wool jacket and nods to John to follow him off the porch so as not to disturb Emily and Rachel, still too young to be of much help with early morning chores. Always easiest to let them sleep while the house prepares for the day.

"Sheriff, I'm sorry to disrupt your mornin' but this is a matter of great urgency!" John walks with Robert to the mare standing only a few feet from the porch. Robert notices two rifles tied to the saddle bag as well as John's holster around his waist, boasting a Colt ready for action. Robert, furious that he is standing without his own Colt in front of a fully armed man, takes a slow deep breath to calm himself, knowing the holster with his Colt is carelessly hanging on a nail in the barn next to his saddle.

"Do tell!" Robert speaks as calmly as possible as he leads John away from the mare up towards the barn. Blue and Grady follow eagerly wagging their tails.

"I got word that Thomas Filmore has returned to the mountains." John takes a moment to see how Robert responds, but only receives one raised eyebrow with a questioning look. "He signed up with the Confederacy only four months ago. Can't believe he already deserted!"

"Is that so?" Robert remains calm and is thankful they have reached the barn. He knows Thomas well only because he asked Rhoda to watch out for his wife Annie since she was expecting their second child. A little boy was born to Annie only two weeks ago and the neighbors were doing their best to keep Annie and her two boys fed and warm.

"He's a deserter, and you're the sheriff. Somethin' has got to be done!" Robert sees relief on John's face as the sheriff reaches for the holster and securely buckles it around his waist. Robert, of course, feels some relief that he is no longer without his Colt at his side, facing an armed man. He makes a mental note that he needs to find a better place to store his gun.

"Yes, I reckon you're right, John. I'll look into it." Robert moves over to Mae, his mare, eager for attention, and grabs the brush off the barn floor where it has been carelessly discarded. He is trying to remember whose job it was to brush Mae so he can bring the matter up at dinner. He then begins firm downward strokes over the chestnut coat that is already thicker, ready for the cold winter. The hounds jump up onto the closest hay bail and settle in for a possible nap.

When Duckworth realizes that the sheriff is not saddling his own horse he frowns. "Sheriff, I'm ready to assist you now, and I have three men saddled and armed waitin' for us around the bend." When he sees the surprise in Robert's eyes, Duckworth continues, "I didn't want to cause a frightenin' sight for your children, so I asked them to wait for us." John then stands as straight as possible. "Sir, we are here to assist you because we can't do this without the law. But we are here to follow your orders, Sir."

Robert stands still for a moment weighing his options, but he knows he must do something to enforce the law and he can see that John Duckworth is eager to show him the respect that his office deserves. "Yes, John you are right." Robert places the brush in its designated spot on a roughly hewn wooden shelf precariously jutting out of the barn wall. He moves to retrieve his saddle, thrown over the closest stall door. "Since you have already gathered men, then there is no need to wait in dealin' with the matter. Well done, John!" Robert gives the slightly younger man a respectful nod to which John responds with an even straighter stance and a grin that he quickly removes to show he understands the gravity of the situation.

* * *

Robert feels strange leading armed men up the holler that only leads to a small log cabin with Annie most likely still asleep under the covers with a child warmly tucked under each arm. Robert is quite aware that he is not sure what he will do if he finds Thomas tucked in under the quilt as well. This is his first encounter with a deserter, and he can't jeopardize his position as sheriff, not when the war has only begun.

As he leads the silent procession around the final bend, the already fragile dirt road is washed out and two flat boards straddle the gaping hole, offering a make-shift bridge. Robert is filled with a moment of hope as he guides Mae over the planks. The morning silence is broken with the clippity-clop of hooves clearly reaching the ears of the small home's inhabitants. Only moments pass before little Otto presses his pale face to a small opening in the shutter. Robert hopes he is the only one who saw the brief look of shock on the five-year old's face as it disappears behind the heavy canvas covering the opening once again.

"I reckon they know we're a comin' now!" One of John's men snickers. Robert doesn't say anything but feels foolish to think that this search party would be made of ignorant non-observant men.

Another man snickers, "Don't matter none! We got 'em now!" The four horses that had remained behind him up to this point begin to fan out as if the final approach on this small homestead would be best achieved as a moving wall. Robert breathes deeply once again trying to mask his sense of urgency to reclaim the lead quickly. No blood will be shed on his watch.

He pulls his horse in front of the three men again and turns Mae to face the men. "Gentlemen," Robert speaks with as much authority as possible. "I want you to wait here while I knock on the door and check the house. We are not going to force ourselves into Annie's home with a newborn on the teat." The men bring their horses to a stop and look to Duckworth for their next move. Robert feels the heat rise and is thankful his coat collar is pulled up over his neck. "I remind you all that I'm the High Sheriff here and any move on your part without my okay is unlawful."

The men still look to Duckworth who quickly nods to them so that they will obey Robert's orders, "Sheriff, we are here under your charge." His voice is honest, and Robert remembers the years of friendship with the Duckworths. He trusts John, at least he is trying to, but he worries why he has allied himself with a seemingly blood-thirsty search-party.

Robert acknowledges the reluctant submission of authority with a nod and dismounts, "Wait here while I speak with Annie." The Sheriff doesn't look behind him as he ascends a small dirt pathway leading up to the door, only pausing for a second when he notices freshly laid river rock beneath his boot. Robert quickly moves on hoping not to draw attention to his discovery and avoids looking around the property for other freshly completed evidence of physical work that might indicate guilt.

"Hello, Annie?" Robert yells as he knocks on the door. "It's Sheriff Hamilton." He hesitates a moment and then as forcefully as possible yells, "Open the door now, we are lookin' for Tommy." He hears footstep and hushing sounds. Suddenly boots hit the ground behind him and Robert turns to find all four men have dismounted and are walking slowly toward him. Robert waves at them to wait a moment as he yells, "Annie, open the door now." This time his urgency is not masked.

Finally, the door cracks enough to see a young woman, with matted dark hair pressed up against the left side of her head; a new-born in her arms, still asleep. A thread bare quilt awkwardly wrapped around her shoulders acts as the only protection from the cold. "Hello, Sheriff, what braings you to our little holler?" Annie's voice is too sweet, and her eyes keep shifting between Robert and the armed men behind him.

"Look at me, Annie." Robert whispers so only she can hear. "Only talk when I tell you to." Annie frowns but shows she understands with a slight nod. Her eyes grow wide and Robert is confused at first until he notices John suddenly appear at his side, rifle slung over his shoulder, trying to seem aloof, but the hostility elicits a small cry from deep within Annie.

"John, please, for the love of God, put that gun away!" It is not a plea. Robert locks eyes with John until the younger man backs up and returns to his horse, only shifting the weapon to his other shoulder. Robert speaks softly, "Annie, I'm sorry. But desertin' is a serious crime."

Annie nods shifting the baby to nestle it more snuggly within the folds of the quilt. "I knowd that Sheriff! I promise you my Tommy ain't here." Annie quickly flinches at Robert's look; she has already broken his one rule not to talk.

Robert watches little Otto scurry to his Momma and whimper, "They takin' Pa away?"

"Hush up Otto! You go back to bed!" She shoves Otto towards the back of the room, where Robert can barely make out the bed all disheveled, a second quilt awkwardly cascading over the side of the bed covering the dark space underneath.

Louder than necessary Robert asks, "So you say you haven't seem Tommy anywhere in these parts?" Annie knew she hadn't said that, but she nods. Robert continues with his official business, "So you won't mind if we take a look around?" Annie doesn't have time to answer before Robert turns to the search party and barks, "John, you take a man and head out to the barn. He could be hidin' in the loft, and they have a small chicken shed. Be careful." Robert turns and points at the two who had already shown him an eagerness to hunt, "You two! There is a small abandoned panther cave up through those trees where Tommy used to play as a boy. Would make a good hide out. Move out quickly and quietly." As he sees the men responding quickly to his orders, he takes a deep breath and adds as if an afterthought, "I'll check the small house and meet you back at the horses." When he looks back at Annie, her face is white.

"Sheriff, but. . ." She begins.

"I said for you only to talk when I tell you to." His voice is firm, so Annie nods. "Now close the door behind me." When Robert has moved into the small one room home, Annie closes out the light from the outside with a small shove of the wooden door. "I don't have much time, so listen up." Annie nods. "Tommy, I know you're under that damned bed! And you better plan on stayin' there for a few hours, at least 'til I clear us out of here. Then you better come up with a better plan if you want a chance in hell to keep you and your family safe." When there is no answer, Robert lifts the quilt and looks straight under the bed at a half-naked man shivering, "Do you understand?" Tommy nods as Annie's guttural cries draw Robert's attention. He throws the quilt back over the opening. "Annie you stop that cryin' and pull yourself together. I'm not takin' Tommy, but if you draw those men in here with your cryin', I can't promise anything."

"Yes, Sir." Annie takes a deep breath. "How'd you know he was here?"

"I saw the covers." Robert starts, "I also reckoned I'd ruther be in the arms of my Rhoda and my babes than in a chicken coop or an abandoned panther cave." Robert smiles, "It is abandoned isn't it?"

CHAPTER 9

Elizabeth Neill, December 14, 1861

Chores finished, and I was eager to steal away a little moment at the creek before it was time to help Ma with dinner. Sarah-Jane and Jimmy followed me over the rock wall, climbing down key footholds that landed us quickly at the bottom without a tear in our skirts or britches. Ma shook her head at us, but I could see her fail at trying to hide a smile. Over the past few months, Jimmy and Sarah-Jane were following me around more, which kept my mind on them and not James. My longing to hear word from him was slowly fading into a dull gnawing that would only surface when I let it, so keeping my mind and days busy was my only weapon. I smiled at my sister and brother as they each proudly grabbed one of my hands so I could show them my favorite spot to break the ice. I promised Ma I would keep them from falling in the creek and catching their death.

The afternoon sun was warm enough to let us dig around the bank for the largest stones we could carry. We giggled as we heaved the rocks over our heads and dropped them onto the frozen creek below us. The broken ice revealed the trickle of moving water which drew us to examine the secret workings of a hidden stream below the magical icy layer. We dared to lay on our bellies across the frozen surface, which was only as wide as a grown man's chest. Still, once we tired of watching the trickle of fresh water, our sense of daring and adventure pushed us to seek out small strips of ice we had not yet broken. Slipping and sliding and pushing and laughing commanded all our attention until we heard a horse galloping. We all became still at once. We never heard a horse galloping, especially not coming from the Hamilton's up Lambs Creek. The galloping suddenly stopped, and we heard Uncle Bob yell, "George!" The urgency in his voice was unexpected.

Jimmy and Sarah-Jane looked to me and I simply held my finger to my lips. Suddenly, a new adventure was emerging and the momentary fear and confusion in my brother's and sister's eyes quickly turned into excitement.

Slowly, we climbed up the creek bank and scurried across the dirt road to the foot of the rock wall, plastering our backs to the stones. We were all breathing heavily and, when I looked at Sarah-Jane, I could hardly keep from giggling. Her hair was sticking straight up and dirt smudged her nose. Jimmy didn't look much better with his knees covered in dirt and wet splotches. "Ma's going to kill me!" I whispered. "You both look like I threw you in the creek!"

"Shhh," Jimmy frowned. "I thought we were spymasters!" He whispered as loudly as possible. I was obviously ruining the game.

I quickly resumed my role, "Yes, Sir!" Jimmy smiled, and the game was back on. "Which way, Sir?"

Jimmy glanced both ways around the wall, but then looked up. Of course he would choose our favorite path up the footholds we knew so well. We giggled and climbed. Since I was quicker and, of course, simply larger than they were (though not by much), I reached the top first. As I swung my leg over the ledge, I could suddenly hear Pa's voice. "Not out here, Bob! Let's go into the barn." By the time Jimmy and Sarah-Jane's head emerged, Pa spotted us and, leaving Uncle Bob to slip behind the house towards the barn, Pa came walking straight at me with a fierceness I had never seen. By the time he reached us we were all standing up and flattening down our garments as if nothing was out of sorts. "Elizabeth!"

"Yes, Pa?" I said, possibly too sweetly.

He glanced at the three of us in our wild unkempt state. "What have you been doin'?" His breath was strained, which was strange since we hadn't really been doing anything that we might not do any other Saturday. When I began to explain he quickly stopped me, "Never mind." He took my hand, a little too hard. "Elizabeth, promise me you take Jimmy and Sarah-Jane inside and get cleaned up to help your Ma."

I frowned a little, "Of course, Pa."

But he didn't let go of my hand and pulled me in to him. "Promise me you all stay in the house till I tell you can come back out."

"Pa, did we do somethin' wrong?" Sarah-Jane's voice broke my father's fierce look as she started to cry.

"No," Pa let go of my hand and leaned down to lift Sarah-Jane into his arms. "No, my sweet honey-bee," he kissed my sister's head. "You didn't do anything wrong, but you need to listen to Pa now." Since she was ten, I was surprised to see him hold her, but her legs wrapped around him securely and once she nodded her understanding, he put Sarah-Jane on the ground again and ruffled Jimmy's hair. I started to follow my siblings as they went running up the steps into the house, but Pa stopped me.

He was frowning again, a seriousness I was beginning to believe he saved for his oldest child. I suddenly realized he needed me. Why, I wasn't sure. Before he could speak, I whispered, "I understand, Pa! No one will leave the house 'til you tell us!"

We looked at each other for a moment, and I saw something shift in Pa. He knew I would keep my word, he knew in spite of my grimy clothes, I understood that this moment was not part of a game.

Robert Hamilton, December 14, 1861

Robert meets George at the barn door as it swings open, but doesn't speak until George has carefully made sure it is closed by flipping down a small piece of wood, his home-made turn-buckle attached to the frame. Before Robert can say a word, George faces him, visibly irritated, "Confound it, Bob! With all the commotion you made, I wouldn't be surprised my young'uns aren't trying to listen in on us!" Robert knows that George is still trying to protect his children from any notion that the country is at war. Robert sighs; he really doesn't have time to worry about the children, a luxury he abandoned long ago in his own home.

"George, we need to do somethin'!" Robert watches as George's thoughts move from his children to the issue at hand.

"What do you mean?" George swallows, but his eyes remain focused, irritation visibly yielding to worry.

"Duckworth came by this afternoon and said he and some men would take another look up the holler for Tommy Filmore." Robert pauses for only a moment, lowering his voice, but George knows it isn't for his children's sake. "I told him I thought it would be a fine idea but strongly urged him to do it tomorrow, bein' Sunday." Robert shakes his head clearly questioning his own instructions, "I even said that bein' Sunday tomorrow, the Filmore's may think people would be in church rather than out and about lookin' for the likes of a deserter."

"Did he think you were pullin' the wool over his eyes?" George asks, expecting the worst.

Robert keeps shaking his head, as if somehow the motion would make the whole situation better. "I really don't know. But it may buy us time to get Tommy and Annie out of there." Robert moves to George's wagon and touches the side of it as if he were inspecting the depth of the wooden board.

George's eyes widen, "Are you wantin' me to fetch them with my wagon?" When Robert nods George runs a shaking hand through his hair. "Now?"

Robert knows he needs to remain calm, although he feels nausea begin to work its way to the core of him. "Now is best. I figured you use your wagon and fill it with an old quilt and a few baskets of staples, cover them with your canvas and then head up the holler." Robert pauses briefly. "This way, if you run into Duckworth, then you can simply say you are bringin' Annie some things. All their neighbors have been helpin' her since Tommy left, so it wouldn't be questioned."

"Then what?" George interrupts, "Sling Annie, and her children into the back of the wagon and cover them and, oh-by-the-way, a deserter tucked in there with them?" Robert doesn't answer, but watches his good friend begin to pace, "Then what if I run into anyone on my way back?" George catches himself raising his voice, so he moves in closer and forces an angry whisper, "And what if I get them back here? What then? I have no place for them!"

"I do." Robert's voice is calm, but his answer shocks George into silence. "I have a place ready to take them until I can figure a better way to hide them." Robert can see George searching his brain, but he doesn't make him think too long, "In the cellar."

"The root cellar?" George asks, baffled.

"It's more than that. The back of a fireplace looks like a wall when you walk into the cellar, but a small room is on the other side, facing an open fireplace."

"All under your house?" When Robert nods, George walks up to the wagon and begins shuffling the canvas to the side.

Robert knew a time would come when he would have to stand on one side of the war or the other. "I'm sorry, George." Robert walks over to help Robert prepare the wagon. "I wish I could do this without you. But I can't."

George moves towards Jack's stall silently and Robert wonders if he has made a mistake. Once he properly tacks the horse, George leads Jack towards Robert and hands him the reins. "Here, you can at least hold him while I get the wagon ready." Robert nods and rubs Jack's nose with his free hand.

The silence between the two men is almost unbearable for Robert as George prepares the horse and wagon. The two face a moment of inactivity once there is nothing else to do with Jack or the wagon. Clearly, they cannot proceed until Sarah knows. After the awkward silence stretches longer than either man can bear, George does not even look at Robert as he unlatches the door and disappears into the house. Robert has to remember to breathe while George retrieves a basket or two filled with staples; it seems to be taking more time than it should. Only when he returns to the barn and places a single basket under the canvas, does George finally look at Robert, but George no longer seems as angry. In fact, George's voice is almost soft. "Sarah just said somethin' interestin'."

Robert is taken aback by an apparent change of topic, as if they were about to talk about the weather. "Is that so?"

"Yes," George awkwardly chuckles to himself, "She asked me, what if it were the other way around? What if it wasn't Annie? What if it was her, and our babies?" George opens up the barn door and Robert leads Jack out with the wagon obediently following. After George hops up onto the seat and leans down for Robert to hand him the reins he whispers, "She's right, you know!" Robert smiles, relieved that George is siding with him, although he can tell his friend is not really at peace. "But I'll tell you this! Don't you ever play me for ignorant again. I need to know everything if I'm all in. Do you understand?"

Robert nods and is a little ashamed he hasn't shared the information about the root-cellar earlier. "I understand. All in. No secrets."

Robert watches George throw back his shoulders and turn to face his friend with a sly look on his face, "Sarah may be right, but I'm not so sure I'd fancy livin' in your root cellar!" Robert's guffaw brings the children to the windows, and they only see two old friends laughing on a cold winter's afternoon.

Elizabeth Neill, December 25, 1861

It was cold, but it was Christmas, so I tightened my shawl around my neck, covered up half my face and drew the basket of warm biscuits as close to my body as possible as we walked the easy mile up to Uncle Bob's farm. It was tradition. Laughter, fireplace warming us all, crowded in around a table of fixin's, more than you might think God would ever intend for us to eat. I pushed away any pining for a letter from James that might dare to surface. Not on Christmas. This day would not be touched by war and its vexations.

Before we even rounded the final bend, I felt the familiar joy dare to rise within me as the smell of a wood-burning fire greeted us. I could already feel it begin to warm my innards. Suddenly, Blue and

Grady began barking and Joel screamed, "They're here!" Jumping from a small look-out perch tucked away in a tall pine tree, he ran for the house still screaming instead of heading towards us. Jimmy took it as a cue to start running too, so he took off after Joel until Ma stopped him, reminding him he was carrying a precious jar of Neill honey that he better not drop. Jimmy obliged, but not without suggesting I could add the honey to my basket. I began to agree with him, after all it was Christmas, but both Ma and Pa gave me a very serious look which seemed out of place for such a small request. The final few yards up the small incline to the towering two-story home with the welcoming front porch, seemed to take forever. But by the time we reached the porch, most of the Hamilton Family was gathered, waving at us, swallowing up not only the size of the porch, but my growing sense of unease.

Aunt Rhoda took my basket, and, to Jimmy's delight, she relieved him of his jar of honey, leaving us with freedom to seek out our cousins while Ma, Millie and she continued to prepare the meal. Viney waved at me to come sit with her near the fireplace. She had a basket of corn husks and was busy taking a single husk and twisting it into the arms. "Hi Elizabeth, you want to make a doll too?"

I smiled and sat down next to her, picking up the already folded over husks where she had carefully tied a piece of twine around the top to create the head. "Sure, Viney. I could make an angel. Got any husks already soaked?"

"Sure do." Viney pointed to a few husks that were spread out flat on the floor. "They should be soft enough to bend." I handed the doll she had started back to her, so she could weave the arms through the center before she continued to tie off more body parts. I began to select the lightest husks that I envisioned best for angel's wings. I looked up from my first bend in the husks to see Viney carefully creating the legs. "Are you making a boy or a girl?" I asked more to chat with my favorite cousin than really caring one way or another.

"A boy for sure!" Viney smiled and grabbed a piece of almost worn-through green cloth from a smaller basket full of old rags and left-over quilt pieces. She began to wrap the cloth around the husk, "I want it to be soft as possible, so the baby can hold it."

I smiled watching Viney gently wrap the rough husks as if they were fragile. "What baby do you have in mind?" I was curious on what news I had missed.

Suddenly Viney's eyes widened as if I'd asked her an unforgivable question. She quickly glanced around and had some relief when she saw Aunt Rhoda busy talking to Ma. "No baby." She lied and quickly shoved the soft green cloth back into the rag basket.

"Viney? What's wrong? You just said a baby boy for sure." I tried to reach for the green cloth, so she could continue.

She smacked my hand, "Don't you touch that, missy."

I stood up abruptly. I don't know if my hand or my cheeks were burning worse. "Don't you call me missy!"

"Shhhhhh!" Viney quickly pulled me down as close to her as possible, wrapping her wiry arms around me. The familiar closeness calmed me some, but I was confused by her strange contradicting actions. "Please say nothin' about the baby doll."

I frowned, but her eyes were welling up and I could feel her breath hit my cheek in shorter bursts. "But Viney. . ."

"Swear it!" her voice was desperate now. We'd only ever sworn to something when we accidently broke Uncle Bob's fence and blamed it on a poor rambunctious lamb, or the time we skipped school and waded in the river instead, although we both received a whooping from that one since she had some tattling brothers. But those times we had both been in on it. She was asking me to swear to something I didn't understand. She gripped my arms more tightly, "Swear it! Please."

"Viney?" Aunt Rhoda's voice broke Viney's hold on my arm. "What's all the fuss about? Are you and Elizabeth havin' a quarrel?"

"No Ma'am." Viney's eyes dropped, and I noted that I needed to tell her she needed to work on her lying skills.

"No problem, Aunt Rhoda," I jumped right in with the best smile I could fake. "We were arguing over who has the best way to twist the

128

husks and make the best angel." I lifted up my loose husks and flung one husk out to the side. I spoke a little louder than I intended, "I think this would make a pretty angel, don't you?"

Suddenly John-Riley laughed and hollered from across the room, "Only if the angel was tryin' to look like a scare-crow!" The rest of the boys hooted for a minute before they ran outside, slamming the door.

"Don't you worry about your angel," Aunt Rhoda assured me as I dropped my head in mock disappointment, "all angels are special to God. Now you and Viney don't take this so seriously!" She gave Viney one last questioning look before returning to the kitchen.

"Thanks, Elizabeth," Viney's head was on my shoulder.

"Well, you better tell me what is going on, so I can at least be in on whatever I swore I'd keep secret." I smiled and expected Viney to pour out her heart to me.

"I can't." She whispered. "Not now." She sighed. "But I promise you, I will one day."

I wasn't too happy about the answer, but I wanted to stop this arguing and enjoy Christmas. "You swear it?"

"I swear it!" She whispered.

A few angels later, my hands were thankful when dinner was called. We all sat around the table that had been extended with a work-bench from the barn. Even though we all settled eagerly onto our seats, it was clear that the whole family was pretending that Andrew wasn't missing. The boys spread out a little more where Andrew would usually crowd in between them to steal bits and pieces of food off of their plates. I could see Aunt Rhoda quickly excuse herself to bring something from the back room that she'd forgotten. We all waited for her and when she returned no-one asked her why she had returned empty-handed. Ma raised her voice up to draw attention away from my aunt and started singing *Silent Night*, with each of us joining in helping us focus back on the birth of baby Jesus. Once grace was offered, the table came alive with arms elbowing each other and hands reaching for slow-cooked mutton, greens, potatoes, biscuits with ham and cornbread slathered in Pa's honey. I noticed though, the grown-up's plates weren't filled as full as last Christmas and even Millie and Viney seemed to be only taking one serving of the fixin's.

I began to reach for one of the last two biscuits when Ma cleared her throat and shook her head, so I returned my hand to my lap hoping no one had noticed the exchange between my mother and me. The busy chatter came to a lull for only a moment, but that moment was quiet enough that I thought I heard the cry of a baby. "What was that?" The words were out before I had taken a moment to see fear appear in my cousins' eyes. Even Ma and Pa shifted awkwardly. I looked at Viney who was suddenly looking at her plate, shoving a piece of ham from one side of the plate to the other. Only the hounds outside acknowledged something wasn't right because they began scratching the door and barking.

Uncle Bob cleared his throat and shoved back his chair. "Sounds like a baby lamb bleating for its ma. I'll go and check on it." He nodded at me and winked. "You don't worry about anything, Elizabeth. I'm sure it's nothin' serious." Suddenly all the cousins at the table were nodding and agreeing a little too eagerly. I sighed and continued to finish my food, hoping for the first time ever that Christmas dinner would be over soon.

As we headed back home down Lambs Creek that evening, I carried an empty basket in one arm and snuggled my way into the crook of Pa's arm with the other. He leaned into me and kissed the top of my head, "Merry Christmas, Elizabeth."

I smiled, "Merry Christmas, Pa." I waited a few minutes before I added. "Strangest Christmas ever, though!"

Pa kept his voice steady, but I could tell he was a little worried about what I was going to say. "Is that so?"

I sighed and said as matter of fact as possible, "Well, Pa, it seems everyone is tryin' to keep a secret from me and maybe Jimmy and Sarah-Jane too." Pa only grunted at my observation, which I took for an invitation for me to continue. "I'll tell you one thing. I'll figure it out one day. I ain't ignorant. Even I know Uncle Bob didn't put his ram out to breed until late October. There won't be any ewes lambing 'til spring."

Robert Hamilton, December 25, 1861

The cold damp root cellar is usually a place Robert likes to escape to on a hot summer day as he stores the summer bounty for cold days like this one. With a small pail in one hand and a larger basket in the other, he carefully makes his way down the wooden stairs hidden underneath a simple trapdoor above. He takes notice of the dirt wall to his left lined with shelves packed with jars of green beans, pickled cucumbers, home-made apple butter and enough okra to feed his family through the harsh winter. Several bushels of apples and potatoes line the opposite wall and, as he moves carefully to the back of the room, he carefully dodges slabs of dried meats. When he reaches the backside of the chimney that stretches above him two stories to warm his home, he breathes deeply, places the large basket on the ground, and makes his way around the solid rock to a hidden room with embers of its own burning in a fireplace. Robert never imagined he would be thankful for this extra fireplace he thought originally would offer extra work space for putting up summer foods for winter storage. Empty jars, reminding him of the original purpose of the space, sit in a large basket to his right as he enters the small room. Three quilts lay folded neatly on three wide benches that line the edge of the room, offering dry but hard sleeping spaces. In two chairs near the fire place with a small roughly constructed table between them sit Annie and Tommy Filmore. They are wide-eyed, and Annie has the baby nestled in her arms, while Tommy's lap is occupied by Otto.

Tommy scurries to his feet when he sees Robert, "Sheriff?" he barely whispers as he places Otto in his empty chair.

"So sorry fer the cryin'," Annie can hardly breathe.

Robert places the small pail, holding left-over mutton, potatoes and biscuits with ham on the table and then walks over to the small pile of wood and adds two logs to the embers. "You need to keep the fire goin' or it will get too cold." Robert fusses. "I'll tell John-Riley to bring you some more." He turns to face the sickly thin couple with Otto no longer bustling about like a child of five should. "Don't worry any about the cryin'. We were makin' so much noise ourselves." Annie drops her shoulders, but with guarded relief and slowly reaches for a biscuit.

"We cain't thank you 'nough Sheriff." Tommy lifts Otto off the chair and puts him as close as possible to the pail of food. Ruffling his toe-head, streaked with dirt and soot, he nods to him to take some food. "I'd not git a chance to be with my family if'n it weren't for . . ."

"No thanks needed." Robert stops the unnecessary talk. "You need to move on come mornin'." Tommy nods and Annie stops chewing and begins to shake a little. "I know it's hard, but you can't stay here. I told you it would only be a place to move on from." Robert wishes he could do more, but today's incident with Elizabeth hearing the baby's cry was a harsh reminder of the danger his family is in. No, the danger *he* is putting his family in. He knows Elizabeth is not a real threat and thanks God it was only her, but it could have been Duckworth on another early morning visit. No more babies, he tells himself. No more children.

"That's right, Sheriff," Tommy keeps nodding, "It's time to see if we cain't reach Annie's Great-Aunt's place over near Knoxville." Annie nods as eagerly at Tommy, while Otto settles himself next to the fire gnawing on a large potato.

"That is a good plan." Robert disappears back behind the chimney for a moment and reappears with the basket before he moves in closer to the anxious couple. "Rhoda has put together some staples to help you on your journey for a few days. There are many homes along the way that will be friendly if you simply tell them you are journeying through. But first you need to avoid the Boylston Turnpike and head up our holler and travel as best you can through the Pink-Beds over the mountains. Once you head into Tennessee you will find homes willin' to help. I can't promise it will be easy."

Tommy holds the basket while Annie pulls out dried meats, cornbread and other food Robert is sure will be helpful for a short while. But two small warm wool lined jackets bring the couple to tears. "This is too much." Annie whispers.

"Maybe," Robert doesn't argue. "But I have several children of my own and the little ones have out-grown their winter coats. The baby will be swallowed in the one jacket, but this will be best to keep him warm." Robert points at a small corn-husk doll swaddled in a soft green rag sitting at the bottom of the basket. "My Viney made this for your baby." Annie awkwardly holds it in her already leathering hands, not sure what to say. Robert chuckles, "Not a necessity, I know, but Viney insisted. You do what you want with it." He reaches one last time into the basket and pulls out what looks like an angel and tosses it at Tommy. "Or, at least this angel may make the best kindlin' when you need it most." Robert chuckles, but then swallows hard when he looks at Tommy awkwardly holding a poorly-crafted angel with growing dread enveloping his whole being. Robert realizes too late that there is too much truth in his statement.

CHAPTER 10

Elizabeth Neill, March 31, 1862

It had been almost nine months since I last saw James, so leading Jack towards Lankford's Valley Store to retrieve staples, no longer kindled any spark of hope. I imagined it best if James found himself a girl back home to see him through this war. Besides, at fifteen I would seem scrawny to most. Although I'd fully met womanhood, I was afraid I'd already reached my full height which still only reached Pa's shoulders. But then I pushed away that silly thought and almost laughed out loud, remembering that James was really not much taller than I was, and *he* was a grown man.

I unbuttoned my jacket to let the warm spring breeze breathe new life into my stuffy winter clothes. It wouldn't be long before I could abandon the shoes and enjoy warm dirt between my toes. As I approached the store, wagons were coming and going, some children were playing tag and an old couple was up Oak Grove Church's small hill, sitting under the still-bare dogwood tree, enjoying the promise of warmer weather. I realized that Transylvania was doing its best to move on with daily life, in spite of the constant news of growing tensions. Ma and Pa had finally decided to share with me all the news they heard. Even Sarah-Jane and Jimmy were allowed to listen in. I wasn't sure what had happened to make my parents decide we should know what they knew, but, for me, it was another sign that they thought I could handle the news. More importantly, though, I could talk with Viney without feeling ignorant. Sometimes I'd even know something she didn't, so I ate up every bit of information I could get. At times I heard the latest report before Ma and Pa if I dared to linger at the store.

"Hello Miss Neill," Mr. Lankford's greeting always made me smile. "Hope your family is faring well in these times."

Handing Mr. Lankford Ma's list, I nodded, "Can't complain." We were doing better than several in the county since Pa had left a couple of times with baskets of food to take to hungry folk around the county.

"That's good to hear." Mr. Lankford smiled.

"How is Mrs. Lankford?" I asked sincerely hoping her spirits were up since she was expecting another baby within the next few months. Dinner prayers had been, for months, full of praying for a healthy Lankford baby, so I was eager to see how God would respond.

"Doin' fine." Mr. Lankford stroked his beard and then smiled. "She's pleased to be movin' into our new house soon. It's taken some years to complete it, but now that Brevard is in the planning process, I figured it best to complete it properly. I have an order of some fine furniture from South Carolina that I'm waitin' on. It will be good to finally move, especially with the growin' family."

"That's wonderful!" I replied, sincerely happy for them. I wanted to ask more about their new home that was built up the small hill and would be close to all the happenings in Brevard. The building of the city would soon need to catch up with the new homes that were beginning to claim it as our county seat. But he was already sorting the staples into piles, so I didn't ask any more questions, instead I slipped away to take inventory of the new items that had arrived.

A stack of at least ten linsey-woolsey shirts were folded neatly next to some woolen socks. I started to frown when I saw several canvas bags of something called hardtack, "What is this for?" I held a bag up so Mr. Lankford could see what I was talking about.

He walked over to me and took a bag in his hand and opened it. He pulled out a small piece of something that looked like a cracker and handed it to me, "Here try it!"

I was curious so I tried to bite down. It took several tries before I managed to break off a small piece to chew it. The taste was almost unbearable, so I swallowed it as quickly as possible, although I wanted to spit it out, which would not have met my family's approval. Mr. Lankford chuckled a little as he closed the bag back up and placed it back on the shelf, "Yes, it's not especially tasty, but if you're starvin', you'd eat anything!" I frowned, so he continued, "Our soldiers need somethin' that won't spoil while they are fightin' the Yanks, so I'm makin' sure either our boys or any troops comin' through have supplies they may need."

"Oh, that makes sense!" I smiled, realizing the shirts and socks were also a part of those supplies, along with other items I had yet to discover.

Before I could explore anymore, Mr. Lankford stopped me, "Miss Neill, I almost forgot. I have somethin' for you." I wasn't sure I wanted anything else after that hardtack, but I followed him back up to the counter. He reached under the counter and brought forth a small letter. It was stamped with a round circle and *Miss Elizabeth Neill, the Valley Store, Brevard*, was written on it. "Miss Neill?" Mr. Lankford's voice pulled me out of my shock, "Are you goin' to take it or do you need me to read it to you?"

"Oh no, Mr. Lankford," I quickly reached for the letter. "I can read. But I've never had a letter sent to me. That's all."

The store owner pulled away to talk to an older gentleman who walked in, and I was grateful. I tucked the letter into a small pocket on my skirt, then buttoned up my jacket, reducing the odds for the letter to fall out before I got a chance to read it. With my heart racing, I almost forgot the sack of flour and the salt, along with some other items he had already placed in my basket. I tried to wait patiently for Mr. Lankford to finish, but the rhythm of his new conversation led me to believe it would be a while. I finally cleared my throat and was thankful Mr. Lankford saw my urgency. "Miss Neill, I'll have Tony help you." He opened the door and hollered for his slave, who appeared after a few moments. Mr. Lankford nodded in my direction, and Tony knew immediately what he needed to do.

I was thankful Tony was helping me and was curious about how Pink was doing, but I didn't dare ask. Tony would not approve. But I still had one question I thought I could dare to utter. So, as Tony made sure all the saddle bags were fastened down, I dared to whisper, "Do you miss Mr. Morris?"

Tony suddenly smiled, "Yes'm. I miss that ole' Master Morris." He pointed at my saddle bags. "I got double the work doin' his work and mine!" We both laughed at the truth.

"I miss him too." I smiled.

"Don't you worry none, Miss. He'll find his way back." Tony quickly turned, eager to be on his way, leaving me with an opportunity to read the letter.

I forced myself to at least wait until we were moving along the road, but I wanted to read it before Sarah-Jane would make a fuss over it and ruin it for me.

Dearest Elizabeth,

It is with great sadness that I write you to tell you that I will not be with you this spring. The war expects much of me, and I must request your patience in this matter. My grandfather, Thomas Morris, during the war for independence fought against his own brother, John, at the battle of Kings Mountain, at which time John died fighting for what he thought would protect his family. He had been a Liberty Man, but for fear of endangering his family, he sided with the Tories. It was a grievous decision, one that cost his life. This tragedy cannot be repeated in my family. I must stand by my brothers as we fight together when we are called up. News of Lincoln drawing a draft earlier this month, conscripting thousands of men, leads me to believe the war is only beginning. When the South calls, we will go.

As we stand as brothers, so we stand together with my parents and sisters to make sure there is food and grain for the winters ahead.

It is with great hope I write you, hoping you have the fortitude to wait for me.

With greatest sincerity,

James

And just like that, my hope returned. I could wait. I knew I could, because he was waiting for me.

Robert Hamilton, July 30, 1862

It's only mid-morning and Sheriff Robert Hamilton is already following Lambs Creek home rather than continue making his rounds throughout the county, checking on those who may be in need. As soon as Rhoda hears the dogs barking and sees him coming, she will know something is not right, so he rides as slowly and as calmly as possible, although he can't remove the ache he feels from the letter tucked into his vest pocket.

As Robert had anticipated, Rhoda sees him from afar and, following Blue and Grady who eagerly wag their tails, runs to meet him. "What is it? Are you sick? Is someone sick?" He hasn't reached the house yet, but since his wife is already grabbing Mae by the reins, he jumps down stirring up the dry dirt road. He pulls out the letter and hands it to her. Searching his face and only finding a deep sadness, she doesn't reach for the envelope, but instead cries and pleads, "Is it our boy? Is it bad news?" Her eyes grow wide as she searches all possibilities. "Or is it word about Harrison or John Mackey? Are they hurt?" The reminder that everyone is facing worry, including Rhoda's sister, startles Robert for a moment. He has not spoken with Henry for a while about his two oldest boys enlisting in the Confederate army, but he is sure they, too, spend their nights on their knees in prayer. Robert realizes he better answer his wife quickly before Rhoda lists all of her relatives fighting in the war.

Robert sighs and opens the letter, not because he needs to remember what is written, but because he draws strength from at least seeing

Andrew's hand-writing. "No and yes. He is alive but was captured over at Carter's Depot, Tennessee. The letter is from him and says he was paroled for a little bit, but we don't know what that means. It appears he is still a prisoner of war."

Rhoda drops Mae's reins and begins to weep, but, before she can fall to the ground, Robert grabs her arm and gently leads her to the bustling stream nearby to sit on a strategically placed log. Mae obediently follows them and does not hesitate to drink her fill and graze a little unconcerned with Rhoda's weeping as Robert wraps his arm around her shoulders. Blue and Grady, oblivious to the turmoil surrounding them, decide to chase a rabbit they spot in the large vegetable garden; their barking fades as they disappear into the brush on the other side. After some time, Robert speaks, "In many ways this is good news, we know he is alive and able to write."

Rhoda nods her head, and her weeping ebbs into sniffles. "I guess you're right. I guess I should really be thankful." She sighs and then abruptly stands up and carefully spreads out her apron. "I need to stop this fussin' and get back to work." Rhoda realizes her husband has not stood up yet and so she sits down again. "What is it? Did you leave somethin' out?"

Robert shakes his head. "Nothin' serious. And only somethin' Andrew knew would bother me." Robert hands the letter to Rhoda once again, this time she does not hesitate to fold it into her own hands, but she still looks up at her husband as he adds, "Best you read it yourself. At least his devilment means he must be doin' fine and has too much time on his hands."

Rhoda slowly stands up again and watches as her husband begins to head down Lambs Creek. Too curious to wait any longer, she quickly unfolds the paper. "Oh, my!" She whispers as she reads the letter which is addressed *Dear Ma*, and every one of Andrew's sibling's names are carefully written as well, all the way down to the toddler. But there is no mention of Robert. "Bob!" Rhoda's voice reaches Robert before he makes the final turn around the bend. He looks back at his wife who waves at him to turn around. The sheriff sighs, but obediently returns to his wife who is walking towards him, shoving the letter into her apron. As soon as he is close enough, she reaches up and rests her hand on his knee waiting for his calloused hand to clasp her own. Robert obliges and is thankful for his wife's touch, but he assures her. "I'm fine Rhoda. I really am."

"Andrew is angry and hurt. He really is not thinkin' straight." She squeezes his hand. "I reckon one day we will all laugh about this." Rhoda forces a chuckle. "Grown men hurtin' each other's feeling in the midst of war." She immediately regrets her words as she sees Robert frown.

"You know it's more than hurtin' feelings." Robert squeezes her hand and then releases it. "I better be off."

"I know, Bob." Rhoda lets her hand linger on his knee. "But he's also your boy. Please don't forget that blood is thicker than water." Rhoda quickly shoves away the tears with her free hand while she tightens the one on Robert's knee.

Robert is trying to be patient with his wife who is always trying to make him remember how family always comes first. "I know, Rhoda. But it sure is hard to live it when your own boy can't remember it."

Rhoda's eyes suddenly widen with an epiphany and a gentle smile crosses her face. "I know what you should do!" Robert rolls his eyes knowing some wise words are about to roll out of her mouth with the expectation of him following through. She slaps his knee, "Don't you roll your eyes at me."

Thankful for the slight banter, he clasps his wife's hand again. "What is it dear?"

Ignoring his mocking tone, she answers, "You should head over the mountain and visit the Young Family. Bring them news of Andrew." She grabs the letter out of her pocket and shoves it into his hand that is clasped over hers. "You have held your distance from them ever since they took in Andrew. I'm sure they are eager for some news. It is a good reason for a visit. This would allow some healin'." Rhoda finally removes her hand from Robert's knee, stepping back from Mae and giving her husband a moment to think.

Robert sighs loud enough for his wife to hear his vexation with the whole situation, but it only takes a moment of watching his wife patiently standing in front of him waiting for him to make the "right"

140

decision. Her head is slightly bowed. "Damn it Rhoda! Are you prayin'?"

Rhoda lifts her head and sheepishly answers, "Maybe?"

Robert shakes his head and can't help but let out a laugh. "I swear you'll be the death of me!" After shoving the letter into his vest pocket, he gently swings Mae around to face the path leading up the mountain behind their house. Before he disappears, he glances at his wife one last time as she wipes her nose with her apron, and somberly climbs up the porch steps. Suddenly, Blue and Grady come tearing through the vegetable garden still chasing the rabbit.

* * *

Riding over the hill between Lambs Creek to the little wooden Davidson River church, mid-week and without his family in-tow, feels odd. He is pleased the ride is quick and he soon guides Mae to wade across the Davidson River, not bothering with seeking out the closest ford, where carefully cleared shallow sections of the river allow for a friendlier crossing of the river for wagons. Guilt floods through his thoughts as he realizes he has neglected his friends along the Davidson River. Rhoda had told him that Fletcher and Naomi had delivered a baby girl only days ago. Have his own worries caused him to forget to check in on his friends? He rests in the thought that Rhoda will surely insist on a visit to the English homestead this coming Sunday filling a basket with some biscuits and apple-butter while Millie will likely present Naomi the infant-sized quilt she has been working on as a gift.

Momentarily, Robert arrives at the Young household, announcing his coming some distance away with a "hoot", not only the mountain custom but also the only safe way in such trying and troubled times.

Robert is not surprised to find Martin Young emerge from the barn to greet him with one wave of his hand while wiping his other one on his sweaty shirt. Almost ten years older than John Young, Martin still has the strong wiry build of the Young boys. Martin, seemingly busy, quickly informs him that his pa is in the garden with his mother. As Martin is about to return to the barn he notices the letter sticking out from Robert's vest and can hardly restrain himself. "Is there news from our Confederate war soldiers? Have they won some battles recently?"

141

Surprised by the volley of random questions Robert answers directly, "No, nothing about specific battles... well one incident... but... I really need to see your pa."

The sheriff tries to leave Martin, but the agile man simply moves in closer to follow him around the barn. "Or maybe you have heard from my brothers Joshua and John? I know it's only been two weeks since they enlisted." Robert shakes his head regrettably, realizing that it must be hard for Martin that his younger brothers left for war without him. Yet, Robert is confident that, being in his early thirties, it seemed fitting that Martin remain home to care for his aging parents and younger sisters.

The heat of the day is finally breaking through the thick forest canopy and clearly the reason why Robert finds Martha-Ann and Strawbridge sitting along a small stream eagerly working its way to join the nearby river.

"Well what a pleasant surprise!" Strawbridge stands and comes to greet Robert with a hearty handshake and pat on the back while Martha-Ann remains seated with a basket of string beans in her lap. She rhythmically removes the strings and snaps the beans as she leans her head to listen to the men.

Robert, with Martin on his heels, moves in closer for Martha-Ann to be included. "Hey, Straub and Martha-Ann. Wanted to bring you up to date with news from Andrew as we just got a letter from him." Robert pulls out the letter from his vest, noticing Martin's intensity waning some, although, instead of leaving, he chooses to sit next to his ma and grab a handful of beans.

Martha-Ann perks up and quickly lifts her voice for the first time. "It must be good news if he wrote a letter."

Robert returns the letter to his vest, knowing the content well enough to share. "Yes, in a way. But he was captured over in Tennessee, at Carter's Depot. He is a prisoner of war now."

Strawbridge, settling himself back down next to his wife, speaks. "Some good news inside the bad, I guess. Is he wounded?"

"Apparently not. He was able to get this letter approved and sent." Strawbridge clears his throat and pulls out his pipe, to which Robert happily responds by pulling out his own pipe from his lower vest pocket. After Strawbridge lights his pipe, he leans in to help Robert ignite his own tobacco. Once both men have settled into chewing on the end of their pipes, Strawbridge finally shares. "I reckon you already heard our Joshua and John have joined the Confederates?"

Robert nods and feels somewhat regretful he did not come to speak with his friend weeks ago when he first heard the news. But showing compassion or excitement for those joining to fight for the South is not a strong quality of his. "I'm sorry I did not come earlier. I'm sure it is hard for you to have both boys gone." With his empty hand, he gently pats his upper vest pocket where the letter still reminds him of his own dilemma, "It sure is a heavy burden for me."

Martin, throwing a handful of snapped beans in the bowl, interrupts, "But I bet Andrew is a glorious burden to those Yanks! Did he tell about any bloody battles? Did he shoot any Yankee invaders?"

"Martin! Bite your tongue!" Martha-Ann's voice silences her son.

Strawbridge, with a red flush creeping up his neck into his cheeks, adds, "What sort of devil-talk is that!" He clears his throat and continues, "You boys know how I feel about this here war. And I have allowed you to form your own judgement, but how dare you revel in shedding the blood of another American!"

Both parents are horrified and stare him down with hostile scowls, to which Martin speaks, "Yeah, yeah, I know Christians are not to say such or want to kill others. I've heard your sermons in church." He stands and tosses the remaining beans back onto his ma's lap. "But I will tell you one thing. If war gets worse, I ain't sittin' around here puttin' up beans. I may not be as young as my brothers, but I shore as hell can fight beside them!" As Robert watches Martin stomp off towards the barn, he has to suppress his desire to smile, because at that moment he realizes that even respectable Strawbridge Young has predicaments of his own.

CHAPTER 11

Elizabeth Neill, August 2, 1862

The summer felt like most summers in the mountains. The wet thick morning fog would slowly lift as single white wisps woke up and danced, each as they pleased, before they slowly reached up towards the sun to finally burn off around mid-morning, leaving me feeling sticky the rest of the day. I was thankful for the reliability of the fog that would faithfully follow the same dance well into autumn. I'm not sure if it was because it was a heaviness I understood, one where the promise of the sun and blue skies appearing was more often than not fulfilled. Even gloomy days would rarely last more than a day or two. This I understood. I could count on. As I stretched out on the edge of our rock wall, I watched the final wisp burn off that morning, and I lifted a small prayer to God that maybe this war could lift as easily.

I wondered often about James who was "down-the mountain" in Polk county and couldn't much understand what down-the mountain meant since all I'd ever known was the blue-ridged mountains and life at the foot of their majesty. I couldn't imagine that I was still *up*, up somewhere above a valley below me. I figured James would take me one day to see what down-the mountain meant. At least I hoped so.

I had received one more letter from him since last March and had sent him at least three of my own. I was always relieved that the letters were about farming and news of war, but never an announcement of him, nor his brothers, enlisting. I counted this as one of my many blessings. In the letter I sent James only yesterday, I told him how well his new niece, Hattie, was doing and that his sister, Mrs. Lankford, looked well. I also told him that Reverend English had a new girl that they named Martha Louella. I quickly ended the letter feeling my cheeks flush with all the talk of babies.

"Hi, Miss Neill!" Pink's voice jarred me out of my thoughts and made me jump to my feet, almost falling off the wall, but he grabbed my arm just in time and then was quick to let it go as soon as he saw I was stable.

"Pink! Confound it! You almost got me killed!" My cheeks turned red, more out of embarrassment from my mind wandering, than anything. But I could tell Pink didn't understand my reaction so he quickly backed away, looking around to see if Ma was watching or not.

"Real sorry, Miss Neill." His eyes dropped and he started to head down the path that winds around to the bottom of the wall. It was really the correct way to get to the front door of the house, one my siblings and I rarely used.

"Where are you goin'?" Pink's lanky body scurried away from me with his arms clasping a basket filled with some honey awkwardly weighing him down to one side. "Pink! I asked you a question!"

He stopped and turned to face me, placing the basket on the ground. Shifting his weight to his other side he lifted his chin as best he could. "I'm headin' home." I had never seen Pink be so meek. Last year he would have told me I deserved to die.

"Can't you stay a spell and head to the creek with us?" I smiled hoping he'd forgive my earlier meanness.

He looked confused. "Ain't shore you want me to," he stated with a little more spunk.

I started walking towards him and nodded. "I reckon you are right for thinkin' that." He didn't move as I reached for his basket. "I didn't mean to upset you so. But you did scare me!" He followed me as I placed his basket on the porch, in the shade.

I was relieved to see Pink's old wide smile return. "I reckon I did."

145

A squeal erupted from the direction of the chicken coop. "Pink!" Sarah-Jane came running right up to us with Jimmy on her heels. "Ya comin' with us to the creek?" She didn't wait for an answer as she ran up the porch steps carefully balancing a bowl full of eggs, opening the already cracked door with her foot, disappearing for only a few moments before dashing back out letting the door slam behind her.

"My ma would of tanned my hide for makin' such ruckus!" Pink teased Sarah-Jane, but she just stuck out her tongue and started to climb down the wall with Jimmy already in the lead.

By the time all four of us had reached the creek, Pink had settled into his familiar old self. He threw several rocks within inches of our toes, drenching us with cool goodness.

Soon Jimmy and Sarah-Jane were working on building a rock wall while Pink and I were searching for the best stones to fortify the structure, so easily swept away with any summer down-pour.

"This will be a mighty fine wall!" Sarah-Jane announced.

"Ain't no structure as fine as what Mister Lankford built!" Pink was holding a large stone with both hands moving it carefully to the gap in the wall where Sarah-Jane was pointing. "Tony told me the new house got the fanciest chairs he's ever seen."

"I've seen them." I announced as I hauled my own rock to the growing structure.

"Do tell!" Pink stopped and looked at me, putting his hands on his hips. His gray-green eyes eager for the latest news.

I felt a little silly since I realized I was bragging, but I had delivered Pa's honey to Mrs. Lankford several times and she had let me come and sit a spell in her new home. "Well, it's got a wonderful back porch that you can see as you walk up, but I didn't go to her back door. No, I climbed some carefully laid stone steps to reach the front door. It feels like a two-story house with a large chimney climbing up the middle, but when you stand on those front steps, you can look down to your right and you realize there's more. You see a cellar has been dug into the hill, but it has its own entrance as well. So, it makes the house feel like it's three stories high. It's a glorious house with fancy wooden steps that climb to the upstairs rooms, but also wind downstairs into the cool cellar where Mrs. Lankford had me set down the honey. It's the most beautiful kitchen cellar I've ever seen." I scratched my head like I was trying to remember. "But she had me stay for some tea, which we carried back upstairs to sip as we sat in their large living area. The chairs are soft and made with fine material and I felt strange sittin' on them because I thought I'd get them dirty." Pink laughed and then we both started looking for rocks again.

Pink, went on about his vast knowledge of rocks, and then suddenly changed the tone of his voice causing me to look at him so I could hear what he was saying. "I heard Sheriff Hamilton's cousin, Robert F. Hamilton, got discharged from the Confederate army because he was bleedin' from his insides out."

"What are you talkin' about?" I was confused. I remembered last summer when Uncle Bob's cousin had snagged a half-eaten piece of my corn-bread off of my plate and swallowed it in one mouthful as he signed up to follow Captain Johnstone.

Pink dropped the rock he was holding and sauntered over to where I was standing. Then all suspicious-like he looked up and down the stream before a mischievous grin spread across his face and he answered, "Well, the word is that he was bleedin' like a stuck hog when they brung him home. Said his insides was bleedin' to the outside so he couldn't fight no more. So they discharged him." He crossed his arms like he was trying to be like a grown up, pausing for effect.

I put my hands on my hips and fussed, "Dog-gone-it, Pink! Get on with it will you!"

"No need to git your dander up!" Pink dropped his arms and came in closer with a gleam in his eyes, "It seems that Mister Hamilton got home and everyone says the Lord healed him quick."

"Well that is good, right?" I asked, not sure where Pink was going.

"It is mighty fine!" But Pink almost whispered, "and the Lord may git all the credit, but all the neighbors know he was pullin' the wool over them Confederates' eyes."

I was dumbfounded. "How did he do that? That can't be an easy thing to do."

Pink's dramatic voice melted into his boyish giggle. "Heck if I know. But I'll let you know when I hear." He headed back across the stream to retrieve the last rock he dropped.

"Well that is somethin' else. I never heard such a thing before." I started to look for a rock of my own.

"I guess there's lots we're still gonna hear." Pink started moving towards Jimmy and Sarah who were now yelling at us to hurry up. Pinks voice was almost swallowed by their fussing, but I did manage to hear him utter, "I reckon war will make some people do crazy things."

Robert Hamilton, August 6, 1862

Despite the summer heat, Robert plans to meet George at the Cagle Mill so he can help divide the barrels of grains into manageable sacks for distribution. Although George had insisted that he could handle the task on his own, Robert is already in the area after sitting a spell with Strawbridge just up the Davidson River. Robert is spending more time with his old friend, hoping to mend the distance he has unnecessarily created. News of the Confederate campaign helps Robert hear the truths of their struggles and he, for the first time, feels he can understand his friend's woes. Yet, he makes sure he draws a clear line between compassion and support, a differentiation Strawbridge never calls upon for clarification.

Following the path along the Davidson River, Robert lets the familiar sound of the bustling river ease his thoughts and forget, if only for a moment, the bloody war raging beyond the county. He soon rounds the back of the Cagle Mill to find George already heaving a barrel onto the back of his wagon with the help of Reverend Fletcher English. Robert smiles at the site of the preacher doing his part to help them feed families. One other wagon is pulled up closer to the front door with a solitary young black boy sitting up high on the wagon bench and manning the goods already piled in the back. His eyes widden at Robert's sudden approach, and quickly stammers, "My grandpa's got my papers, sir. But he's inside with Mister Orr and Mister Cagle. He'll be along shortly."

"Not a problem, son." The sheriff smiles and nods as he eases around the wagon and heads towards his friends. He has never checked slave papers and isn't about to start, especially with Fletcher and George witnessing his approach. With an audible sigh, the boy relaxes and loosens his grip on the reins.

"Hi, Bob!" Fletcher waves at Robert with one hand while wiping his forehead with the back of his other hand. "Glad you could finally join us," he teases.

"Someone's got to keep the peace!" Robert's rebuttal is only met with a laugh from both Fletcher and George.

"So, what's so dangerous up Davidson River that you need to protect us from? Some giant fish about to attack?" Fletcher laughs.

Robert dismounts and ties Mae up at the closest post. He saunters over to George's wagon and rolls up his sleeves to help. "You never know what might lurk in the depths of the forest!"

The banter subsides as the truth of the sheriff's words sets in. Panthers have been spotted and Fletcher worries at times for the safety of his own young'uns. George throws Robert a sack and a large wooden scoop as he declares, "Well, you might as well get to work!" Without instruction, Robert begins to scoop cornmeal into a sack and hands it to Fletcher who ties it off to then throw it to George who, unknowing to any spectator, begins to create piles divided into supplies for needy families and one inconspicuous pile for Robert's root cellar. Fletcher, a long-time abolitionist and an openly Northern sympathizer, is aware of Robert's root cellar and has been cooperating with Robert for some time, a fact that George has only recently discovered.

"Well hello, Sheriff!" James Deavor's military voice stops the men's efficient assembly line. Robert is not surprised to see the young Deavor whose large farm fans out from the entrance of the forest with numerous acres and boasts a beautiful two-story wooden frame house up on a knoll within hollering distance. Currently, as a Lieutenant in the Confederate army, Deavor was mustered out in July and explained he will return in September once the farm is in good order. His father, Captain William Deavor, a Captain in the former Buncombe County Militia, owns the homestead, but his son clearly takes pride in the upkeep and managing of what will one day be his responsibility.

"Hello, James," Robert genuinely smiles at the well-respected young community member. His dark hair is cut short and his seemingly child-like face is attempting to grow a respectable mustache, which barely covers his upper lip. Still, in spite of his appearance and having recently turned eighteen, this young man is not a child. He has been a part of the Confederate's 25th Regiment, facing the battlefield and has already earned the title of Lieutenant. Robert smiles at the young whippersnapper and asks, "How are you and yours faring these days?"

Deavor takes a moment to eye Fletcher, who does not spare a glance at the man, a clear insult not soothed by George's quick nod and smile. Deavor finally answers Robert, all the while staring a hole into Fletcher's back, "We are faring better than most, I reckon." Moving in closer to the wagon, he glances at the sacks that have begun to create defined mounds. "Gatherin' up goods for the unfortunate again, Sheriff?"

Robert smiles and pats a tightly sealed sack, "Yes sir. Thankful we can provide some relief. Afraid it will only get worse if this war carries on, keepin' our men on the battle field and not in the corn field."

At this point, Deavor leans against the wagon, with one arm casually leaning on the open single wide-board tailgate of the wagon. "If certain people in the county weren't workin' aginst us then we might have a fightin' chance. In fact," Deavor waves his free hand towards the wagon with the boy, "I wondered for a minute whose slave that was, and knew without a doubt he couldn't be yourn."

Fletcher stops for a moment before he ties the final sack in his hands with vicious intensity and finally looks at Deavor. "If you have something to say to me then say it like a man and not a coward hiding behind vague insults!"

"Now Fletcher, no need to get your dander up," Robert uses his best calming voice. He is aware of the stiffness that has set into the young slave sitting patiently waiting for someone to appear, eager to be gone from this hostility. The sheriff addresses both men when he adds, "Don't say anything you will regret!"

"Oh, no regrets Sheriff! This here preacher's been on the wrong side for a long time!" Deavor spits on Fletcher's boots, "Been hiding Negroes and helpin' em escape for as long as I can remember!"

A slamming door interrupts the combative exchange as James-Henry Cagle and Caleb Orr walk out of the mill followed by a black man. Robert immediately recognizes Jesse, the Patton's slave, and knows him well. He frequents businesses who accept his educated-slave's signature on behalf of the Patton family. Not all appreciate Mrs. Patton teaching a slave to read and write, but Robert is aware that many white-folk don't dare to confront the slave about breaking the slave code, since the Pattons are one of the wealthier landowners and leaders, alongside the Deavors. The three men stop and stare at the hostile scene unfolding in front of the store. Jesse quickly nods to Caleb who acknowledges the slave's need to hurry on down the road. Robert realizes that the young black boy who has taken in the whole scene must be Jesse's grandson, Riley. Jesse acknowledges Robert with a short, but confident, "Sheriff."

Roberts nods and acknowledges him in return, "Jesse." The aging slave doesn't even mention the papers, causing the boy to glance at Robert, panic visible in the widening white of his eyes, and his mouth suddenly opens ready to challenge his elder. However, Robert simply winks at the boy, who quickly closes his mouth and faces his grandfather.

Jesse quickly jumps onto the Patton's wagon to sit next to Riley. But when his grandson hesitates, Robert hears, "Move it Riley! Aint no time to tarry." With a sudden jolt, the Patton's wagon lurches forward and disappears around the bend.

"Well, they were sure in a hurry!" Deavor's boyish surprise startles Robert and Fletcher who struggle to muffle their laughter. Deavor looks at the two men, "What's so funny?"

Fletcher doesn't try to hide his astonishment, "You really are surprised the two took off with all your aggravating talk?"

Deavor shifts awkwardly, "Well, I wasn't talking about them?" He nods assuring himself that it all makes sense, "We take care of our own here, slaves or not." His eyes darken again and he points at Fletcher. "But you, you helpin' escape slaves comin' up through here from God knows where, endangerin' the whole county!" At this point, Caleb is visibly holding James-Henry from heading toward the unfolding scene.

"That's the damndest thing I've ever heard! Are you so ignorant to think there's a difference between slaves here and slaves anywhere else?" Fletcher stands as close to Deavor's finger as he can get.

"Some talk for a preacher man!" Deavor sneers, "Hope you burn in hell for your high and mighty opinion of your self doin' what you reckon is right without regards to the law!"

"James! Fletcher! Stop it now!" Robert interrupts, hoping he can restore some sense of reason, "Let's focus on our county right now." He pats the sack of grain closest to him. "Can we agree on the fact that we must focus on our people?" Robert looks back at Caleb and James-Henry who look like they're holding off from berating Deavor because the sheriff and deputy sheriff are present. Robert stares at the two of them and adds, "Can we *all* agree to focus on our people?" James-Henry and Caleb nod and take a step back.

Deavor looks at the sacks of grain and then back at Fletcher, "That's all *I'm* ever thinkin' about!" Robert appreciates that Deavor is well known to take care of many of the people in the county in need. "In fact," Deavor adds, "Caleb?"

"Yes, James?" Caleb's voice is louder than expected since he isn't used to holding his tongue. "What do you need?"

"Add two more barrels of grain for these men to distribute." Deavor pats the one barrel already sitting on the wagon, half-way divided into sacks. "One barrel ain't gonna feed the hungry!"

"James-Henry and I will bring them out shortly!" Caleb grabs James-Henry's collar to break him away from the strangely unfolding scene.

"Well thank you, James," Robert steals a glimpse at George who is standing with his mouth wide open in disbelief. The sheriff quickly makes eye contact with Deavor, "We are much obliged."

Even Fletcher is surprised by the sudden change of events and drops his head to focus his attention on grabbing another empty cloth sack to fill; he simply can't bring himself to utter any words of thanks.

Deavor lets out a sudden guffaw and slaps Fletcher on the back, bringing the preacher up ready to take down the prosperous farmer, but the look of ecstatic boyish triumph written across Deavor's face stuns the preacher into inaction. Deavor points to the two large barrels being rolled in their direction by Caleb and James-Henry. "Have fun dividin' up all that grain into your sacks!" Deavor quickly turns to head home and continues laughing and looking back at the grain that will take triple the time to prepare before the men can leave.

Within a few minutes, Caleb and James-Henry leave the three men alone and the rippling of the Davidson River begins to be the only familiar sound outside of the soft swoosh of grain filling each sack to the brim. It is Fletcher who begins to chuckle first with George and Robert quickly joining in. They are careful not to say a word, and as they all eye each other, they simultaneously glance at the growing "Robert's root-cellar" pile.

Elizabeth Neill, October 10, 1862

"Elizabeth," Reverend English's voice broke my concentration as I was helping Viney's brother, Joel, with his spelling. It was only the beginning of the school year, but I was already thankful for the few times I was able to walk to school with Jimmy and Sarah-Jane, and wasn't kept home to work the farm while Pa was off with Uncle Bob keeping the peace, whatever that meant. When I *was* at school the reverend always had me working with the younger children, a task I enjoyed, unless it was my own siblings.

"Yes, Sir?" I turned in the direction of the reverend's voice, expecting him to guide me to the next child he wanted me to work with, but instead he waved me to follow him out the front door. Stepping outside the church, I pulled my sweater up to cover my bare neck, but still welcomed the fresh cool breeze. "Is everything okay?"

Reverend English smiled and patted my shoulders as if I was having a peaceful conversation with him on a Sunday morning, "Yes, Elizabeth, no worries. It's been mighty fine having your help this beautiful day. I was hoping you would be alright with minding the class while I speak a moment with your Pa?"

I frowned and glanced at the colorful leaves dancing over the empty spread of partially dried dirt and clods of grass trying to reclaim the earth, with no sign of anyone, and especially not my Pa. "I'm not sure what you mean? I don't see Pa anywhere."

The reverend shifted awkwardly for a moment before explaining, "Oh, he told me he would be by to pick you, Jimmy and Sarah up," he cleared his throat and looked at my confused expression before he continued, "That is. . . he told me this when he came by yesterday and needed some advice on some matters." When I didn't respond he added, "So, I had some thoughts I wanted to still share with him about those matters." As if satisfied with his explanation, he finished with a nod, a punctuation mark of sorts.

"Of course, Reverend, whatever you need." I smiled awkwardly. Suddenly, my attention was drawn to the sound of a wagon, but it wasn't coming from the road in the direction of the mill. Instead, it was moving towards us from across the river. I soon recognized Pa as he maneuvered Jack to ease the wagon down the dirt road that disappeared into the river and then reappeared on our side of the water. Jack wasn't too happy getting his legs all wet, but he obediently pulled our wagon through the river. The wooden wheels, half-way submerged, churned the water like four water wheels. "What was he doing on the other side of the river?" It was a moment before I realized I had asked my question out loud.

"Oh," Reverend English's voice was still trying to be Sunday-sweet. "I asked him to bring me some materials I needed from another neighbor."

The sound of Pa pulling the wagon around drew the reverend's face away from my own, which was good, because my look was one of sheer disbelief. I wanted to tell him that I wasn't an ignorant child and knew Pa was too busy with our own place and being deputy Sheriff to haul around materials for the Reverend who, in fact, was one of the strongest wiry men I had ever met. And this man-of God was tough too and preferred to do as much hard labor on his own as he could. I wanted to tell him he was for sure going to Hell for lying to me, but when he turned around, the look I was giving him said it all. His eyebrows rose and he almost looked afraid of whatever face I was making, but I quickly mimicked his Sunday-sweet voice, "I'll make sure the children are just fine. You and Pa take your time." I turned and left the man speechless. I smiled, proud of myself. How many young women could render their preacher speechless? But then I felt ashamed for wishing Hellfire on him, so I whispered a quick prayer up to God, hoping He had been too busy with all the war and blood to listen to my hateful thoughts.

Still, something was very wrong.

I walked between the wooden benches that were also pews on Sundays and helped the children best I could. After about an hour and growing questions from students, I began to worry. As I assured everyone that the reverend would soon return, I slowly made my way to the door to see if I could catch the men's attention. But the only attention I drew was from Jack who whinnied when he saw me, causing the wagon to lurch a few feet back. The men were nowhere to be seen.

I slowly left the cover of the door frame and walked towards Jack who leaned into me as I rubbed him behind his ears and patted his neck. "That's a good boy!" I whispered, "Where'd they disappear to?" They were not standing along the edge of the road, where the river bank's steep slope dropped off, so I walked towards the river to glance down the road. When they were not visible along the road, I looked down the river bank. Sure enough, the two men were sitting like two children on our favorite jumping off place on the side of the Davidson River. Of course they weren't wading or splashing each other, just in intense conversation, oblivious to my nearing presence.

Pa's voice was the first to reach me, ". . . do you think Antietam will make the difference?"

"Not been quite a month yet, but the Union victory is one the Confederates aren't likely to forget." Reverend English actually threw a small rock into the fast-moving water. "At least we haven't had blood shed close by yet."

Carefully finding steady footing at the bottom of the bank, I placed my hands on my hips and cleared my throat, "So talking about war or talking about materials?"

"Elizabeth Ann Neill!" Pa's immediate use of my full given name and jumping up to tower over me, quickly warned me that I may have crossed over the line to sheer disrespect. "What are you doin' sneakin' up on us and eavesdroppin'? Your Ma lets you come over here to help out with schoolin' and suddenly you're gittin' too big for your britches. I'll put a stop to that as soon as we get home." Pa was madder than a wet hen and I thought for sure he was going to find a switch and bend me over his knee right there in front of the reverend. But he didn't. He just stared at me with cheeks as red as fire.

I quickly dropped my hands and my head, "Sorry Pa. I didn't mean to make such a fuss."

Pa took a deep breath before he added, "And what nonsense are you talking' about with *materials*?"

I slowly raised my head again, not sure what to say as I looked to Reverend English whose cheeks were slowly coloring as well, but not because he was angry. Clearly embarrassed that his lies had caught up with him, he explained, "George, that's my fault. I told her you were helping me with materials." The two men exchanged looks that I couldn't quite figure out and the reverend finally shrugged like he was telling Pa *what else was I supposed to say?* The man-of-God came up to me and put his preacher hand on my shoulder. "I also shouldn't have left you so long with the children. It wasn't right. I'm sorry."

I believed him, for the first time that day. "Thank you, Reverend. I really do like helpin' you out." I looked at Pa and felt my eyes begin to blur and my throat ache, "I'm sorry I may not be able to help you anymore."

Pa shook his head like he was shaking off a bad thought, "We'll talk about it later. Right now, go get Jimmy and Sarah. We need to head on home."

"Okay, Pa." I didn't move right away because I was trying to stop the flow of tears before I faced the children; I didn't want them to worry about me.

As I wiped my face frantically, clearing any sign of crying, I felt Pa wrap his arms around me, "Pull yourself together. I reckon you frightened me pretty good. I'm not goin' to say anything to your Ma about school. Let's move on!"

"Okay, Pa." I turned and climbed up the bank toward the church, where a few faces, peering out the door, quickly vanished back inside. As I glanced back at the two men, I was surprised to see Pa turned away from me and wave his arms wildly at Reverend English. His voice was low, but his body was yelling. I knew that body language well. He wasn't angry with me. He was furious at the reverend. I quickly turned away not wanting Pa to know I had seen another private moment.

* * *

"I want to sit up next to Pa!" Jimmy's voice was chipper, excited that Pa was giving us a ride home, a rare occurrence. I would usually fight for the right to sit on the bench with Pa, but I simply jumped in the back of the wagon with Sarah-Jane, thankful to have a little distance from the anger I could feel still seeping from him.

The canvas was pulled back as usual when Pa wasn't hauling goods. But there was something different about the wagon. I stared at the usual floorboards, wooden planks that had aged over time with scrapes and stains. Deep grooves from hob-nailed boots and pitch forks. A few sticky places where honey occasionally dripped were now smudges and random tufts of hay always added the final layer of familiarity. But the smell was off. Blood. I smelled blood. I looked at Sarah-Jane who was busy up on her knees with her head facing over the edge of the wagon to absorb the new perspective of her surroundings and the rarity of the ride home.

I slowly scooted myself towards the canvas that was in a random heap to the left side of the wagon, its normal position. But as I scooted

157

along, I noticed a stain that I had mistaken as an old smudge. Its smooth service revealed the fact that it had been freshly scrubbed and buffed to look like all the other smudges. But I could not tell if it had been blood or not. I scooted myself back to where I was sitting and told myself that I was imagining things because of Pa and the reverend's strange behavior. As we pulled up to the house, Jimmy and Sarah-Jane jumped down from their spots like we always did. I stood up slowly and watched the two of them run off into the house slamming the door on their way in.

"Are you comin'?" Pa was already down and was facing me as I slowly walked to the back of the wagon to use the canvas to hold onto as I swung my legs over the edge. "Here let me help you." He walked to me and reached his hand up to grab my hand. I grabbed the folded canvas with both hands for support before I let go.

"Pa?" My voice was barely a whisper, but I could feel a cry begin to form. I looked down at both of my hands, they were covered in blood.

"Oh, my Lord! What happened?" Pa grabbed my hands, looking frantically for an open gash. "What did you cut yourself on?"

I was shaking and holding my hands out as far from my body as possible. "I didn't!" I screamed. "It's not my blood!"

Suddenly, Pa let go of my hands and scrambled over to the canvas. He lifted the edge I had climbed over and found what was left of the blood. Now only smears from my fingers. "Some blood must have dripped into the canvas and I missed it!" Pa turned to look at me as I still held out my hands like I was holding poison. He sighed and pulled me over to the water barrel that stood at the edge of the barn, catching fresh rain water. We'd scoop out buckets of water for Jack and Nellie's troughs or to use for washing clothes. He plunged the bucket in and pulled it out, leaves and all, pouring it over my hands, ridding me of the last of the blood. Then he grabbed his kerchief out of his jacket and began to dry both hands carefully, making sure that it was all gone.

"Where'd it come from?" I finally whimpered. Pa shoved his kerchief back in his jacket and picked up and tossed the bucket next to the barrel, watching it spin until it stopped. "Pa?" I whispered, and grabbed his arm, finally willing to use my hands again. "Is it somethin' bad?"

Pa finally looked at me, and a gentle smile assured me that I shouldn't worry. "Well, Elizabeth, it's not anything bad in my eyes. I was just helpin' a friend who was hurt get to safety. He had a big-old wound on his leg that I thought I had wrapped pretty well, but I was mistaken."

"Who, Pa?" I was curious now. I looped my arm through the crook of his arm as we began to make our way to the front porch.

He took a moment before he answered, "I can't tell you." I started to protest, but he tightened his arm, drawing me in. "And please don't ask me again. I need you to trust me on this one. There are some things I'm not ready for you to know yet."

"Okay, Pa," I reluctantly answered, but I had to make sure of one thing. "Do you swear you will tell me one day?"

He took a deep breath, relieved that I wasn't pushing him anymore, "I swear it!"

First, Viney with the stupid corn-husk dolls, and now suddenly Pa swearing to tell me secrets one day. I would hold them to it! That was for sure.

Chapter 12

Robert Hamilton, October 21, 1862

    The sudden shift of the wagon wheels from soft to hard ground and the clomping sound of Mae's hooves against the wooden bridge across the French Broad River, causes Robert to bring his mare to a halt. This stretch of the shaky Dunns Rock bridge traverses water that is much deeper and wider than the Davidson River; its power to pour out of its banks and cause extensive flooding is a feat of nature that the people living within this valley endure and cautiously work around. But on this calm, and chilly, autumn morning the river is peaceful and gracefully ferrying drenched autumn leaves and broken branches; their quick disappearance under the bridge a reminder of the swift current.

    Robert doesn't linger for more than a moment before moving on. Within minutes, he eases his wagon under the giant overshoot to the water wheel that powers Babe Cooper's Distillery. The planks, with random splashes of water spilling over, are precariously suspended over the turnpike. Robert will soon pass by the Hume Hotel before he heads up to the Cedar Mountain community to check on the folk. His wagon is carrying a dozen of the sacks of grain and a few bushels of apples. The beautiful Dunns Rock Hotel, which is the rock building's official name, was built by the Hume family from Charleston. In contrast to the years before the war, the Hume family is now staying year-round in the mountains, along with over twenty slaves. Life is very different than down in Charleston as Robert Hume attempts to farm his almost two thousand acres while his wife manages the hotel. Active in the local community, they had helped build the little Episcopal Church, St. Paul's in the Valley, which had been meeting in Montclove, the carriage house of the Johnstones across the river. The Masons also found their first home here under the shadow of the protruding rock cliff of Dunns Rock.

Before he begins to ascend the mountain road, he decides to pull his wagon around to the front of the hotel. Dunns Rock towers above the hotel like a friendly giant keeping watch. There are at least two wagons parked off to the side, closer to the river. One of them is clearly a carriage, indicating that the hotel is hosting at least one guest from South Carolina.

"Hello, Sheriff Hamilton." A gentle voice draws his attention to the front porch where Jane Hume is standing on the front steps with her hands pressing down her apron. "What brings you to this end of the county?"

Robert quickly removes his hat and slicks down his thinning hair, "Hello, Mrs. Hume. Good to see you this fine mornin'. I'm headin' up Mill Hill to check on the Cedar Mountain Community." He especially wants to check on Harriet McGaha, his friend Craf's wife. He still remembers watching his old friend sign up to fight with Johnstone on that hot July day and was so shocked he couldn't speak to his friend again after he had confronted him in line. He hopes one day Craf will be able to shed light on his decision to join the Confederates. In the meantime, Robert has received word of the loss of a child in the McGaha family and wants to pay his respects.

Mrs. Hume apologizes, "My husband and the farm slaves are out puttin' in some cover crops for the winter. He had even read recently that George Washington had done that over the winter. But he thought with all the rain we get here the crops might help ward off so much washin' of soil away with the winter snow and rain. Do come and sit a spell and let me offer you some warm cider before you head on up the mountain." Mrs. Hume is not *asking,* and Robert knows that it will be rude for him to hurry along without taking time to share the latest news. He climbs the rock steps and enters the hotel, suddenly finding himself in a large room with a fire crackling. A few chairs are already occupied by an older couple wearing their Sunday-best. Robert realizes that these people probably wear their Sunday best every day and have more than one set.

"These are the Whitfield's from Greenville. Their daughter is upstairs resting." Mrs. Hume gestured from the couple to Robert, "This is Sheriff Hamilton." The woman nods while the gentleman stands up and marches towards Robert to shake his hand. This distinguished man has a carefully groomed mustache sweeping down his cheeks and then bristling out in a flare. Robert has never seen anything like it and is trying not to stare.

"Pleased to meet you Sheriff." The handshake is firm and respectful.

"The honor is mine." Robert answers, not really sure who this man is, but sure that there is something important about him. "Where are you fine folk headed?"

The complex mustache twitches for only a moment while Mr. Whitfield decides how to answer. "We are planning on visiting Mr. Lankford and I thought I would bring my lovely wife and daughter for a few days into the fresh mountain air before we complete our journey."

Robert smiles, "I hope you enjoy the mountain air and your stay." He feels Mrs. Hume's gentle touch encouraging him to follow her into the kitchen. The two men finish their formalities and Robert soon finds himself in a large kitchen he believes Rhoda would make a fuss over. Two slaves quickly work their magic chopping and breading all varieties of vegetables.

"Betsy!" Mrs. Hume gestures to the older woman who quickly fills a large mug with hot cider and hands it to Robert.

"Thank you." Robert whispers. Betsy smiles as the sheriff takes the mug and enjoys his first sip, wishing he could pull out his pipe and enjoy a quick smoke, but Rhoda has fussed at him enough times about smoking around her cooking that he doesn't even dare ask.

"Hope its fitin' to have you in the kitchen, Sheriff. But my girls here and I are dyin' for the latest news."

"True!" Betsy adds. "And we got all day." Robert's wide eyes make the women laugh. He realizes he better hustle with his sharing if he's going to have any time to make his way up the mountain. He quickly divulges any news he has of war, who has already died and what families are most in need. Before Robert heads on up the mountain, Mrs. Hume insists he take a basket of apples to add to his load.

"Thank you, Mrs. Hume, for your hospitality." Robert says as he climbs on to the wagon and slowly pulls out his pipe. "You take care of yourself, and be sure to tell your husband I said hello."

"Thank you, Sheriff." Mrs. Hume nods as she pulls a wool shawl over her shoulders. "I think we can take care of ourselves. As long as my husband is around, he seems to manage the farm and Betsy manages my household. So that makes me quite free to keep an eye out on anything out of the ordinary." The sheriff wishes that *keeping an eye out* was all that it takes to keep everyone safe. It is all they really have as a community and he hopes it will be enough, even with Robert Hume as the local patrol guard.

* * *

The wagon lurches around the final bend up the mountain before it passes the powerful Connestee Falls, a double cascade of water. A few more curves later, he reaches a level and straighter stretch following yet another river. Compared to the French Broad, the Little River seems harmless and insignificant, easily crossed with a single leap, but is still destructive once heavy rains set in, flooding the small mountain community. Robert is thankful he is following the river because it means he is almost at Craf McGaha's home. He brings Mae to a halt as he pulls up to the familiar rock wall rising only a few feet, carefully crafted to invite drovers, farmers and circuit preachers to stop and sit a spell. And, if they desire to leave their stock to graze in the field or drink from the many troughs watered by nearby springs, then travelers can ascend the rock steps to the next level of earth where they are invited to step onto a friendly porch. The former notoriously busy drover and cattle-stop is ominously quiet. It is past noon and the mid-day sun offers some warmth, but there are no children running about and no signs of life at the homestead. He sighs as he climbs down from the wagon and grabs a sack from the back and climbs several steps to reach the porch. As he brings the second load of goods, including the basket of apples from Mrs. Hume, a small crack in the door is visible. It slowly opens.

"Bob?" A tired voice asks.

"Harriet?" Robert responds. "I'm sorry for disturbin', but I didn't hear anyone and I was bringin' some staples for you and your young'uns."

The door opens gently and Harriet slowly moves into the light. She is pale and very thin. Two little girls flank either side of her with equally pale faces. "Thank you, Bob. Bring them on in if you will."

"Of course!" Robert grabs the apples first and tussles the hair of the youngest girl. He can't remember their names, but she doesn't seem to mind. He walks into the log home and notices the two rocking chairs by the fireplace, one with a quilt recently occupied; the other ominously vacant. "Any news from Craf?" Robert asks as he places the apples on a long table.

After Harriet ushers her two girls to the table, she disappears into their kitchen and returns with a knife to slice an apple to into pieces. As the girls enjoy the juicy treat, Harriet takes Robert's arm and encourages him to sit in the empty chair. As she wraps the abandoned quilt around her shoulders she stares at the fire, "He writes me, you know?" Robert nods but does not interrupt her thoughts. "It's all about where they are moving around and who they meet. Although he does always wonder if he will ever see me and the children again." Her hand reaches for her mouth to stifle a small cry. She breathes deeply, "But he won't see but two of his babies." She glances back at the two girls quietly eating. "I lost Little Mitch, and my four-year old Wiley." She finally looks at Robert as she barely whispers, "And the beautiful baby girl I named Hattie only lived a few days. She never even met her Pa." Robert reaches his hand across to grasp Harriet's cold fingers. She returns the firm grip, but any threat of tears is thwarted by a hollow look.

"I'm sorry," is all Robert can manage. "I can make sure more supplies are distributed this end of the county." The sheriff shakes his head at his seemingly insensitive response. He only knows feeding people. He only knows moving on to avoid the next death.

To Robert's surprise, Harriet squeezes his hand and smiles softly. "Come with me, Sheriff." The grieving woman stands and wraps the quilt around her shoulders as she walks past her girls. Robert stands to follow Harriet, who has never called him sheriff before. He follows her into her kitchen and then out the back door. He soon finds himself looking at her version of a root cellar, and it is also filled with goods. "I'm very blessed with family and neighbors. We all take care of each other and I feed many a hungry traveler passing through." She pulls her quilt tightly around her shoulders, "I look like this, Bob 'cause I've lost so many children and I worry. But my family and friends have been making sure I eat and I reckon I need to keep feedin' myself so I can keep feedin' others."

"I meant no disrespect, Harriet." Robert's cheeks flush slightly.

"No need to get tore up, Bob," Harriet smiles. "Good to know the other end of the county is watchin' out for us up here, but we are takin' care of each other best we can. Even when our men are out fightin' each other." Her smile falters at the truth in her statement.

"Sheriff?" Another female voice emerges from around the back of the house, having clearly been in hiding. Her long dark hair and darker skin are the only indications that she is part Cherokee. When Robert stares a moment too long, she touches her chest gently and clarifies, "I'm Nancy Guice McGaha."

"Hello Nancy." Robert smiles. "It's been quite a while since I've seen   you."

Harriet moves to stand next to her sister-in-law, putting her arm around her. "Craf told us you'd watch out for Nancy while he was gone."

Robert, suddenly remembering his pledge to Craf in front of the whole campground, realizes that it must have been received by Craf as a reminder that he would protect his Cherokee sister-law. "That's right I did promise."

Nancy nods, but is still cautious. "Craf joined the Confederates hopin' not to divide our community more than it already is. But it ain't that easy. They's lots of folk don't talk to each other hardly, 'cept over farmin' and birthin'."

"I reckon that's a good thing." Robert encourages the two women. "If folks can talk over those things that matter to keep us fed and alive, then that is somethin' this war can't take from us."

Nancy nods. "Seems right simple when you put it that way."

165

Robert clears his throat. He has an idea. "Well since you are all watchin' out for each other up here, will you let me unload the rest of the staples with you? I'd sure like to return home before dark. Mrs. Hume kept me longer than I had planned."

"Anything to help you out, Sheriff." Harriet's smile returns and Nancy nods, clearly curious in what staples still need to be unloaded. Robert is relieved to see both women pull back their shoulders revealing sheer determination, a quality always associated with the McGaha family.

Elizabeth Neill, November 4, 1862

The Lankford's home was bursting with excitement, clearly visible, even as I simply stood in front of the small picket fence that must have recently been erected. I wasn't used to opening a fancy gate, but the already familiar two-story home with narrow shutters framing the open six-pane sash windows made me feel at ease, since they reminded me that I was not a stranger. I hesitated for a moment, though, because I wasn't used to the covered back porch being filled with several men laughing and smoking. I could recognize a few of them, like Mr. Gash and Reverend Duckworth. Even Mr. Poor was present and already in deep conversation with Mr. Lankford, probably comparing best selections of war-time merchandise. I figured Mr. Patton, Mr. Orr and Mr. Siniard were milling about somewhere inside. Pa always said that where business was getting ready to happen you could find all of those men in the midst. A large Confederate flag hanging from the upper right window rippled with the cold wind, reminding me that winter was making its way to the mountains. I wasn't surprised by the flag, since it matched the one Lankford had raised at the store, but I wasn't sure why Mrs. Amanda Lankford had invited our whole family to this celebration.

I had asked Pa if I should stay behind and mind the farm, but he insisted we all go. "Move!" Jimmy shoved me to the side while he pushed open the gate, "We can't wait all day for ya to open a dang gate!"

"James Gaston Neill, you watch how you are actin'!" Ma's body pushed past mine and grabbed Jimmy with one hand by the collar bringing him to a halt, while she balanced a basket with biscuits in the other. I thought she would skin Jimmy's hide right there and then, but she held him in place until he looked up at her with his best sheepish eyes. I looked back at my sister and we both smiled at each other, thankful it wasn't us that was being fussed at this time. But Ma caught us in the act and decided it best to include us all in her warning, "You girls wipe that smile of your faces! I don't want any of you three embarrassin' me or your Pa!"

"Now, Sarah," Pa had finally caught up with us after hitching Jack and the wagon a ways down the dirt road, alongside the other wagons, and a few carriages. I could see Tony watering the horses and managing two other men, I assumed, were someone else's slaves. I hadn't seen them before, but Tony was definitely keeping them busy. I didn't see Pink anywhere and when Tony saw me staring at him, he quickly nodded his head at me in acknowledgement. Pa's voice reclaimed my attention, "I'm sure our young'uns aren't that poor mannered." He walked through the gate, followed by Sarah-Jane. I quickly followed and closed the gate behind me.

"I know, George," Ma stopped a moment and looked towards the porch, hoping no one had seen her reprimand her children. "But we've never been asked to gather with folk that aren't from around here. And . . . ," Ma paused and tried to whisper to Pa, but we all heard her, "they are mostly Confederates." At this point Jimmy, Sarah-Jane and I moved in closer to Pa. Ma's nervousness even put a squelch in Jimmy's comments.

Pa sighed heavily and looked at his sour-faced family, "We do know some folk here today. I think I spotted Bob on that crowded porch. And, we have known B.C. and Amanda a long time. We are friends first and foremost and their family will be considered our family, even if they are wearin' gray. Besides," Pa waved his hand towards the

167

porch, "We know Amanda's brother too. James has already befriended us and it looks like he's home for a visit." Pa's wave was greeted with an eager return wave from the porch. One of the men was leaning heavily on the railing looking straight at us. The red strand of hair was slicked back I was sure with enough grease to keep him looking respectable throughout the day, although he still quickly wiped his hand along his lighter red strand to make sure it was still holding in place. I could feel my cheeks flush and I had to tell myself to breathe. I was staring at him. He wasn't wearing a gray uniform.

"Are you comin'?" Sarah-Jane's voice interrupted me. "I'm not standin' out in the cold any longer than I have to."

I looked away from James and tried to still my heart as I looked at my sister, who was not paying much attention to me anymore. "You go ahead. Catch up with Ma and Pa. I'll be there shortly."

Sarah-Jane sighed and shook her head. "You stay and catch your death then. Your cheeks are already like red apples!" Then she turned and ran after Ma and Pa who had already reached the back porch. While Pa was chatting with the men on the porch, Jimmy took off to a tree nearby to join two hardy-looking boys who were daring him to climb it, while Ma and my sister slipped around to the front of the house to head inside to where I was sure the women folk were preparing the meal.

James' wave had long stopped, but, with my obvious inability to keep moving forward, he suddenly began to shift his body awkwardly, like he was making up his mind if he should come out to greet me or wait for me. He looked at the men on the porch who were busy with their own chatter so he began to make his way to the steps, which he then jumped off like a boy. I smiled at him as he approached, causing me to finally find my will to move. "Miss Neill, I'm pleased you and your family could accept my sister's invitation." His return to formal names reminded me of the time that had passed. Over a year without seeing each other and dwindling letters brought a distance I hadn't realized would be so startling. But, when he reached me, we both stared at each other for longer than was deemed fitting for anyone

168

who may have been watching. His face was still the same, but his beard was trimmed closer to his face and the notoriously loose stand of his red hair was neatly held behind his left ear.

I had forgotten how blue his eyes were and found myself quickly averting my eyes. "I was wonderin' why we were invited. Especially since I know my cousins were not, only Uncle Bob and Aunt Rhoda." I looked back up at him and smirked, "She could have told me you were comin' home. I almost didn't come, but Pa thought it would be best if we all came."

James dropped his eyes to the tip of his boots and kicked a little tuft of dead grass. "Well, I'm sure thankful you didn't stay home." He swallowed and looked at me again. "You sure look pretty, Miss Neill."

My cheeks felt like flaming apples again, as I flattened out the front of my blue-striped dress. I had filled out quite a bit since he'd seen me last, but not grown much in height. Still, I almost looked him straight in the eye. "Oh, Ma made me get all gussied up. We had to wear our Sunday-best."

"Well, blue is. . ." James faltered for a moment then added, "Well... you're a sight for sore eyes!" He grinned, proud to have come up with his best way to tell me I looked pretty.

"Well, so are you, Mr. Morris." He frowned slightly at my formal use of his name. I nodded at his brown jacket and smiled, "I see you aren't wearin' gray."

"Not yet," he quickly answered. "I will, though, as soon as it looks like I'm needed."

I frowned, realizing my desire for James to avoid war was not realistic, but I couldn't help myself. "I still hope you can avoid the war."

"Elizabeth." He stepped closer to me and a longing in his eyes reached the soul of me. "I wish I could . . ."

"What are you doin'?" A loud booming voice startled James and he turned towards a young man, not much taller than himself walking towards us with full speed. "Keepin' all the pretty girls outside?" The stranger, clearly a few years younger than James, quickly slapped James on the back and then leaned on his shoulder, but fixing his eyes on me. Any tenderness in James' eyes had transformed into controlled irritation.

"Of course, where are my manners?" James shoved the man's arm off his shoulder, "Miss Neill, this is my brother, William Lewis Morris."

I was surprised to be introduced to another Morris so abruptly. I couldn't help but smile at the slight resemblance between the brothers. "Pleased to meet you, Mr. Morris." I did a slight awkward curtsy, not sure what else to do.

"You can call me William, since there are too many Mr. Morris' here." He placed himself between James and me and then had me follow his explanation with the pointing of his arm. "See that old man on the porch sitting in the rocking chair?" I nodded, although I could only see as much as a stretched-out leg and boot behind the other men blocking my view. "Well that's the only real Mr. Morris here. He's our Pa. Mrs. Morris is inside near the warm fire. She likes to leave the talk of war and business to the men."

James sighed and shook his head, "Not really, she puts her opinion on Pa and then she lets him do the talkin'."

"Anyways!" William glared at James and turned me to face the right side of the house and pointed at a man, in Confederate-gray, and a pregnant woman who were making their way to the front of the house with a bundle in their arms, "That's our youngest brother, Beverly Thomas Morris, but you better just call him B.T. He and his wife Sarah-Jane are expecting their second baby. Looks like they have their little baby girl, Rholly, all bundled up heading for the front door. Best to avoid the men folk and their talk of war when you're a Captain of North Carolina's 64th Regiment." I noticed William stand a little taller, showing off his own gray uniform, "I'm serving with him you know?"

"Well, that's good." I wasn't sure what to say. But I realized at that moment that both of James' younger brothers were already in the 64th and it was only a matter of time. "I thank you for your service." I glanced around William to look at James, begging him to jump in.

"Okay, William," James placed his hand on his brother's shoulder and squeezed, "That's enough family information for today."

"But I haven't even talked about our sisters." William protested.

"She knows Amanda well and that's enough for now." James' voice was firm. I never thought of myself as knowing Mrs. Lankford well, especially since she was closer to Ma's age than my own, but I simply nodded along, hoping that William would move along.

"Did he tell you I was his *younger* brother?" William was teasing James now and James wasn't happy.

"Confound it, Will! Move on." James shoved his brother a little.

William started laughing, "Well, James, she done set your heart a quiverin'." James' ears were suddenly as red as his hair, but his brother started moving away from us before James could give him a head slap. "Don't worry, big brother, I'll keep your little secret safe." William then turned and pretended to yell to B.T., who had long disappeared behind the house. "Hey, B.T., wait for me, I got some news!" Unfortunately, the word *news* brought all eyes from the porch to focus on this small scene unfolding. At this point even William sobered up and was embarrassed to be caught acting like a child. The three of us suddenly stood still staring at the collection of dignified men who were silent and looking to each other for answers. I noticed Uncle Bob had joined the men and was also looking at us with concern. He spoke with Pa right before Pa stepped off the porch and came very quickly in our direction. He stroked his beard nervously as he approached.

"Elizabeth, what is goin' on?" He nodded awkwardly at William and James. James' eyes were huge and I knew, if he could, he would have given his brother a likken he'd never forget.

William straightened his uniform and was first to speak, "Sir, I apologize for the commotion. My brother and I were having a fine conversation with Miss Neill, here, when she told me about ways to take care of new babies and, since my brother's wife is expectin', I was hollerin' for him to stop so I could share the news. But my timin' and choice of volume was not appropriate and brought undue stress to Miss Neill, and you, Sir." Pa, James and I stood in shock and some awe

171

of William's story. Pa looked at me and when he saw I was doing everything to keep from smiling he sighed with relief and played along.

"Well then, Mr. Morris, I accept your apology and, well. . ." Pa really didn't know what else to say so he leaned in and added, ". . . think before you start joshin' around in front of the County's Sheriff and Deputy Sheriff." Pa pointed at Uncle Bob who was watching us from afar with his arms tightly wrapped across his chest and then Pa gently opened his vest and briefly flashed his own badge.

"Yes sir!" William swallowed and he quickly excused himself, disappearing behind the house while the volume of the chatter on the porch increased.

Pa sighed and looked at me and then at James, who was visibly shaken. "Elizabeth, please head inside to help Ma." I began to object, but James looked at me and nodded for me to obey my father. I swallowed hard, suppressing my raw desire to cry and left Pa with the man I hadn't seen in over a year. The man I wanted to be with more than anything. I headed towards the front of the house, but right before I turned the corner, I glanced back to see Pa and James walking together slowly. And talking. My stomach dropped and I wished I hadn't come at all.

*　*　*

James and Pa spoke privately long enough for the food to be set and for Mr. Lankford to call everyone to attention. Ma told me I needed to head into the sitting room to invite the guests from South Carolina to join us in the dining room. I wasn't so sure it would make a difference since they would probably have to stand anyways. The beautiful home was very crowded and I guessed most guests would fill a plate and then disappear back onto the back porch or most of the children would perch themselves on the wooden staircase. I still listened to Ma and headed to the only room I guessed was the sitting room, and walked past the front door and its small foyer into another large room that had its own fireplace. It was clearly lined up with the backside of the fireplace in the dining room. I stopped suddenly and stared. A distinguished looking man with a strange mustache and his well-to-do wife were sitting on the two upholstered couches near the fire place. Ma had told me they owned one of the carriages and had come up from South Carolina. Mr. Lankford had several business acquaintances, so I didn't think much about it. But I was frozen because I saw a young woman that must have been their daughter since she had the same citified look and sat gently next to the woman. I found myself staring because she was the most beautiful woman I had ever seen. Her dress was not only the color of the most beautiful red rose, but, like the layers of a rose, it fanned out into a full skirt supported by several petticoats underneath that visibly boasted lace hems. The bodice of her dress buttoned up right-smart with brass hooks that were in the shape of leaves and her long sleeves reached down to her wrists with tufts of lace adding a finishing touch before her gentle hands folded neatly in her lap. Her jet-black air was plated perfectly into elaborate braids, like a crown, but still allowed two symmetrical curls to gently touch her cheeks.

"May I help you?" The woman's voice broke my rude staring.

I gently brushed my hands along the folds of my blue-stripped Sunday-best and suddenly didn't feel so gussied up anymore. "I'm sorry. I didn't mean to stare. But you're so beautiful." I dropped my eyes, embarrassed to have shared my thoughts out loud.

A gentle giggle set me at ease, "Why, thank you, sweetheart. That's mighty kind of you."

"It's time for gathering for Mr. Lankford to speak before the meal." I announced. "But," I added," I'm not sure where you'll sit."

The giggle returned. "Not to worry, Mother and I will wait here while Pa joins the rest of the folk." She sighed and adds. "We will wait for dinner to be served." As if on cue the man jumped up and moved towards the growing commotion.

"Oh, I'm sure dinner is already served. But I'll make sure someone will bring you and your Ma a plate." I smiled, "If that will be alright with you?"

The young woman looked at her mother and, when she nodded, the young lady responded with a single nod, "Thank you. That will be just fine."

I excused myself and moved back through the foyer, squeezing between bodies until I could see Mr. Lankford clearly.

"We are blessed to have so many family and friends with us this day! I Cain't say I've ever had this many folk here, but we will all manage to act civil once we say grace. There's enough food for all!" Courteous laughter filled the room. "Before we break bread together, I want to introduce some distinguished guests." He pointed to the citified man with the fancy mustache. "We are honored to have Mr. Whitfield and his wife and daughter visiting today. He is a business associate and my steady connection to the news comin' up from the south." Applause welcomed him and a few pats on his back may have surprised him some, but he recovered from each one with a smile and nod to the guilty party.

Mr. Lankford drew our attention to him again, "Today I want to introduce you to our guest of honor, my brother Wales Lankford." A man I thought looked almost identical to Mr. Lankford stood next to him, his gray uniform different than the Morris boys' uniforms. It seemed newer and was a better fit. "He has recently been made Sergeant Major in the First South Carolina Regiment under Capt. Peronneau." Applause and hoots filled the room so suddenly that I was immediately drawn in and I found myself clapping and smiling. Mr. Lankford raised his hands to calm us down before he continued, "Our home is honored today with the presence of our Confederate brothers." I looked around the room, and William and B.T. Morris stood proudly alongside Sergeant Major Wales Lankford, along with several other men I had never met. "We want to thank them for protecting our counties and our honor." Applause rose again and I, too, felt proud. He wrapped up his speech with greetings from others not present and finally ended with, "Lieutenant James Deavor returned in September to the service and was sorry he couldn't be here, but he has sent word of congratulations."

174

I looked to find Ma and Pa, and I couldn't see them anywhere, but Uncle Bob was close to the front door. He was clapping, but there was a familiar strain on his face. The same one I had seen when Johnstone announced that the war had begun and then again when Fourth of July came along and Andrew signed up to fight under Captain Johnstone. He saw me look at him and he forced a smile and a nod, assuring me he was all right. I knew then that Uncle Bob was a good liar, and definitely a better liar than William Morris.

After several speeches we all finally were allowed to eat. The distinguished guests were allowed to serve themselves first. I told Ma I would take Sarah-Jane with me and fill up two plates for the fancy ladies still waiting in the sitting room. Ma thought that was a generous and kind gesture. I happily filled the plates and my mouth started to water when I saw Mrs. Lankford had made her famous gingerbread and hot apple cider. I fussed at my sister to hurry so we could quickly return and grab our own fixings. As Sarah-Jane and I walked into the sitting room, I stopped, but this time my stomach dropped. James was speaking to the woman that looked like a human rose. They were lost in conversation, and I watched as James shoved his hair back twice. Sarah-Jane was busy helping the older lady and then left as quickly as possible to get her own food. I slowly walked over to the whispering couple and as quietly as possible placed the plate on a small table nearby. "Oh, hello, Sweetheart," the rose spoke. When I looked up, I saw James looking at me and his ears were turning red again. I didn't look at him for more than a second; I was furious. "James, dear, this is the sweet girl I told you about who said she'd bring me food." She reached out and squeezed my hand, but was still talking to James. "Now isn't that just the sweetest?"

James cleared his throat. "Yes, Ma'm it sure is." James began to walk towards me, but a lace-tipped sleeve reached his arm and stopped him. Surprised at the lady's forward behavior James asked politely, "Miss Whitfield, is there something else you need?"

"Oh, James, I'm sure this girl can bring me some water, while you keep me company a spell longer." She patted the seat next to her and then looked at me, "Right, dear?" My heart was racing and I was not sure what to do. What had Pa said to James? That I was a child? That he better find him a citified woman and leave his country girl to find a sheep-farmer? Needless to say, all of my thoughts were not hidden very well and my face must have begun scrunching up. "Are you okay, Miss?" The young woman had a worried look on her face.

Before I could answer, James stepped towards me and lifted my chin with his hand. "Elizabeth!" James' voice and touch shocked me. "Stop frettin'!" James smiled and winked at me before he turned to the most beautiful woman and announced, "This here is Miss Elizabeth Neill and only a few moments ago her Pa gave me permission to officially court her." He turned to face me and gently took my hands in his. "That is, if she will calm down and let me."

CHAPTER 13

Robert Hamilton, December 2, 1862

"Are you all tore up about the weather, Pa?" Camilla's words identify Robert's fears. She is busy preparing some string beans and sets them on the stove to simmer, carefully working around her father's presence.

"Yes, Millie, I sure am." From the warmth of the kitchen he looks out the window toward the mountain path the children usually ascend to head to school. The cold sleet won't let up, and Robert fears it will cause a problem getting two men over the mountain to Fletcher's home today. Robert hasn't allowed anyone to stay in the root cellar in quite a while and prefers their taking cover in the small building that his boys helped him construct to look like an additional barn. It is a little way up the holler with the creek nearby for fresh water. The natural overhang created from the gnarled Rhododendron roots and a sharp cut in the bank allow it to be hidden well and only noticeable if you come up on it. There is enough room inside to house sheep, a transformation Robert hopes to make once the war is over. In the meantime, there is plenty of room for at least a dozen grown men to sleep, even if it is only on fresh hay. Robert prays he never has to shelter that many fugitives. He is thankful, though, that the barn is dry in spite of the fact that it is not warm, since a fire would not be wise in any case. The two strangers tucked away in the new barn, who simply call themselves Silas and Leon, are deserters, Robert is sure. He promised them no more than a few nights to rest and gather supplies before they have to move on.

Robert was in a fix less than two months ago when he had a deserter bleeding from a gunshot wound to the leg. He and Fletcher had convinced George to use his wagon to transport the wounded man directly to Fletcher's barn. George did it, but Robert and Fletcher had never seen him that angry before, believing they had unnecessarily endangered his family. Robert and Fletcher still can't figure out why George doesn't tell at least Elizabeth what is happening. It would ease the already complicated efforts some.

Robert can hear scuffling above him and a few whiny notes of protest from Emily and Rachel who, at age four and six, are undergoing early training on how to keep a home clean and respectable. The older children are helping Rhoda with the discipline, but Robert doesn't hesitate to walk over to the stairs and interrupt. He yells, "Viney? John-Riley?" Within minutes, the two run downstairs without a fuss.

"Yes, Pa?" both children simultaneously respond. Viney is fifteen and Jon-Riley has turned fourteen, but any child-like excitement is gone as they stand before their father as adults. Robert sighs, aware that he has asked them to grow up quickly, but he will have it no other way.

"Head down to the cellar and grab some dry blankets and a ration of dried pork along with a half dozen apples. Then the two of you head up the holler." The two teens nod and both turn to reach for their heavy winter jackets and scarves. As they lace up their boots, Robert adds, "Be sure to hurry on back and report to me the condition of our guests. Make sure they aren't freezin' to death."

Without a word and only a nod, Viney and John-Riley slip out the door. Robert doesn't miss his son reaching for Viney's hand as they head down the steps and is equally aware of her willingness to latch on to him. Although, at times, he understands why George protects his children from the details, there are moments like these that assure Robert that maybe he isn't making a mistake.

* * *

It is not long before Blue and Grady scurry along behind Viney and John-Riley as they carry the supplies and disappear around the bend of the path heading up to the hiding-place. Robert settles into his favorite rocker for a few minutes when he is suddenly surprised by a sturdy knock on his door. He is momentarily frustrated that the dogs didn't warn him before he remembers the hounds followed his children up the path. He walks towards the door as a second volley of knocks is followed by Strawbridge Young's familiar voice, "Bob, it's me, Strawbridge."

Robert hesitates in front of the door, not sure what needs to transpire next, when suddenly Rhoda scurries down the steps from the upper level and looks at Robert with wide eyes and whispers, "You hustle to the door." She then looks at Millie who is also wide-eyed and standing in the kitchen door with one hand clutching some beans. "Millie and I'll watch for the young'uns from the kitchen." Millie nods and disappears with her mother quickly on her heels.

Robert is angry with himself for not standing watch while his children headed up the holler, but he thought this weather would keep any visitors away. Grabbing his coat from the deer horn hook next to the door, Robert steps out on the porch to welcome his friend, "Sorry took so long getting' to the door."

"I was beginning to wonder if you were home. The dogs didn't make the usual fuss over me when I rode up. I thought maybe you'd taken them hunting in this crazy weather." Robert shifts awkwardly as he watches his friend look around for the dogs and then frowns, "Where are the dogs?" Before Robert can make up a plausible lie, Strawbridge answers his own question. "I reckon they're off burrowing after a rabbit or possum."

Robert nods, relieved, "I reckon so!" Quickly changing the focus, Robert continues, "Why don't you come in and sit a spell out of this cold." His old friend quickly accepts the invitation and once the two are inside and nearing the warm fireplace, Robert asks, "What brings you out in this weather?"

Strawbridge is thankful to be out of the cold and holds his hand out to the crackling fire before sitting in the rocker nearest to the heat. Robert has already settled into his rocker and looks anxiously at his friend. "Well, Brother Bob, I reckon I needed some time to share news that only we can share without a quarrel or fear of one. We don't see eye to eye on everything, but I'll be damned if we can't still be brothers in the Lord!"

"Amen!" Robert genuinely smiles at his friend and knows he speaks a truth that even Robert keeps fearing is wishful thinking. He is frightfully aware of Silas and Leon, who don't even trust him with their real names, and, yet, Robert is risking his home, family and friends for them: strangers.

Rhoda comes and briefly greets Strawbridge and hands both men a warm cup of coffee, carefully avoiding making eye-contact with her husband, lest she give away her fears. When Strawbridge asks her to join them, she insists, "I'll let the two of you catch up. I have too much to fuss over in the kitchen to even think about sittin' a spell." And just as quickly as she arrived, she disappears back into the kitchen.

Strawbridge frowns for a minute, "That sure isn't like Rhoda, to not sit a spell." He pauses long enough to cause Robert to contemplate how he can assure his friend that her behavior is not out of the ordinary when Strawbridge adds, "I reckon she would be more likely to visit if Martha-Ann had joined me."

"Yes," Robert agrees a little too quickly, "I'm sure that's it!"

Satisfied with his own conclusion Strawbridge begins to share, "Latest news is that we hear our boy, Joshua, was transferred to Company E, 7th Battalion of the 65th Regiment." Strawbridge rests his coffee cup on his knee. "We are thankful because he has relatives in that group. So we are more likely to hear word. Although I worry something fearsome."

Robert nods and takes a sip of his coffee, making himself focus on the conversation. "He, like Andrew, had to follow what they believed was the right cause."

"Any word from Andrew?"

Robert nods, "Well, some hopeful news right now before Christmas. It seems the two sides are considerin' a prisoner exchange sometime soon. Seems both sides have some important men captured and need them back. Andrew's gift with horses has helped get a teamster role with his group, so they want him back. We are hopin'."

Strawbridge surprises Robert with an emphatic snort, "Maybe that will be safer and less of a target with horses than those with rifles, like our boy." Strawbridge shakes his head at his own outburst. "Well, that slipped out." He looks at Robert. "Brother Bob, I did not mean to compare our sons. We just worry about his life on the front lines and his thinking that he can come home a hero."

Robert shakes off the comment. "No offense, my friend. Neither of us wanted this war or the breakin' away from the Union. Our boys have been listenin' so much to the old veterans from the Mexican War and the heroic deeds they claim. It ended only fourteen years ago, but you would think it was yesterday. Thank God the Revolutionary War vets are all gone."

Strawbridge looks straight at Robert, "Have you not listened to our sons, Bob? They are comparing this war with the rebellion from England! Lincoln is being compared to the English king! They are even thinkin' they are the modern 'overmountain men' who will throw off the enemy like down at King's Mountain."

"Honestly, Straub, I've not heard our boys talkin' about this, but I did hear a speech or two recruitin' for the Confederate army makin' this argument. Also read an article or two in the Greenville paper along that line."

Strawbridge asks, "What are you hearing from the many Revolutionary War descendants we have here?"

"Well, none will argue or debate the point, but most I know are highly offended since their folks- dads or granddads- gave so much not just to fight and defeat the English at those battles in King's Mountain, Guilford Courthouse and elsewhere, but mostly to build our own country into a solid one, not ruled from overseas. The Millers, Kings and so many families in these parts struggle with the comparison."

"What about our own pioneer hero here, Lambert Clayton? His family members are all over these parts." Strawbridge raises his voice and yells, "Rhoda, you were a Clayton, right?"

Rhoda scurries into the room, but still does not sit. "Yes. I was." She scratches her head a minute and then adds. "From what I could hear from the kitchen, it seems my poor Grandpa Lambert must be turnin' over in his grave with such a comparison. But all my kin just stay quiet. They don't want to upset this younger generation with their comparison and would-be-hero status." She quickly nods and excuses herself, aware of Strawbridge's attempt to include her.

Strawbridge wonders briefly about Rhoda's strange behavior, but Robert quickly draws him back into conversation. The two men speak for some time before a sudden dropping of a pan in the kitchen startles the conversation. "Oh, I'm sorry, Ma!" Millie speaks a little louder than would be expected, especially from one as soft-spoken as she is. "I'm sure I can fetch Viney to help me clean up the mess!"

"Or your brother, John-Riley!" Rhoda adds before silence follows.

Robert feels his face flush slightly as Strawbridge looks at him confused, but when Robert doesn't react to the strange kitchen interchange the visitor quickly finishes his coffee and stands, "I'd best be getting back. Martha-Ann's Gash family seems dedicated to this fight and she is so torn apart. Her bother Leander Gash, who is such a Confederate supporter, has a son that joined the Confederacy. As a mother, she is terrified for the lives of her three sons and her nephew." Robert frowns, realizing Leander must not have told his sister about his Union-sympathizing intentions, even if they are masked by the action of his son and the presence of his slaves. Robert has greater worries and decides it is not a battle he will take on when his own challenge is very real and right in front of him.

Robert quickly stands with Strawbridge, blocking his view into the kitchen and the window directly beyond. "We understand very much. God help us all."

Robert walks his friend to the door, feeling a sense of relief, but suddenly Strawbridge reaches into his coat pocket, "I almost forgot, being almost Christmas, I have this small kerchief Martha-Ann stitched for Rhoda." With a soft white cloth in his hand he quickly turns to head into the kitchen. Robert runs after him but it is too late. Rhoda and Millie stand wide-eyed as Strawbridge is taking in the scene beyond the window. Blue and Grady eagerly wag their tails as they follow Viney and John-Riley who are helping a man in a Confederate uniform limp towards the house. A rough blanket is thrown over his shoulders, but he is clearly freezing. Strawbridge turns to Rhoda and Millie whose faces turn away, and they pretend they are busy with cooking. The visitor turns completely around to face Robert who is standing with both arms leaning against the door frame staring at Strawbridge quizzically, clearly assessing how his friend will respond. "What is going on, Bob?"

"What do you think, Brother Straub?"

Strawbridge glances at the scene taking place in the steady falling sleet and runs his empty hand through his curls. "Well, it looks like the dogs weren't off chasing a rabbit." He pauses and then glares at Robert. "And it looks like the Sheriff and his family may be harboring deserters." A gentle gasp from Millie causes Rhoda to stop moving and embrace her daughter.

"Well, are you sure that is what it looks like?" Robert walks to the window and looks out at his two children and Leon. "To me it looks like two children helpin' a man who is freezin' to death. But I reckon this man and his freezin' friend will soon have to make their way across the mountain to another friendly neighbor's house."

Strawbridge's face goes white. "I don't want to know more." He turns quickly drops the white handkerchief on the kitchen floor and begins to stomp back past the fireplace. But before he can reach the door Robert grabs his shoulder.

"Straub?" Questions hang heavy between them.

Roberts' long-time friend is shaking. "I understand that you couldn't tell me. And I am more than grateful for not having to carry the burden of that knowledge too. But it breaks my heart to know my Naomi and Fletcher are endangering their family with helping you and the deserters. It was one thing helping escaped slaves several years ago, but now that they have young'uns: don't they know that if the law catches them harboring deserters, they'll have hell to pay?"

Robert squeezes his friend's shoulder, "Straub! Listen to me!" Robert waits until Strawbridge finally makes eye-contact. The Sheriff finally whispers, "I am the law!"

Elizabeth Neill, January 30, 1863

"You are a sight for sore eyes, Elizabeth," Mammaw sighed as she brought me a cup of coffee and sat down with me at her oak table. "It's been a while since I've seen you."

"It's only been two weeks, Mammaw!" I protested as I took the cup from her. The coffee smelled so good. Coffee beans were beginning to be hard to come by and some folks were grinding acorns or chicory roots to use for coffee instead. Ma told us that we better keep our eyes out for the beautiful purple flowers when we begin to see them come spring and dig up their roots to bring home. She figured we would soon run out of coffee too and wanted to be ready.

Mammaw took a sip of her coffee and smiled at me, "Well, two weeks is a long time when I'm used to you comin' up the hill to see me nigh on every other day."

"You're right." I dropped my shoulders and looked at my coffee cup. "It's been busy with Pa bein' deputy and all, and the stress of war all around us." I looked up from the table, "but that's even more reason to check on you. Maybe you should come and live with us." I gave her a hopeful look.

"Oh, gracious no! I have too much to do here to be playin' house down the hill with you." She smiled and winked at me, "But I'll consider the offer if the need arises."

I smiled and took my first sip of coffee. I nearly choked and looked at Mammaw who was enjoying her coffee, "Your coffee is too strong!"

Mammaw laughed at my reaction. "Well, your Pappaw Neill used to always say to me, 'If you are going to make coffee make it strong, Sarah. If you are going to make water, make water.' So, I make it strong, just like Jimmie liked it!" Mammaw sighed and smiled at the memory and proceeded to savor one more sip.

I, on the other hand, put the coffee down, feeling badly, since she was sharing what she thought was a treat. Mammaw returned her focus to me, taking in all of me. "Look at you, Elizabeth! You growed up all of a sudden." My cheeks reddened slightly. Mammaw set down her cup of memories and grinned, "Oh my, is there a young sweetheart winnin' you over?"

I laughed out loud at her comment, almost surprising her. "Not young."

Mammaw was quiet for a minute and had a frown on her face. "Is it that James Morris that you told me all about last June?"

I nodded, but she waited for me to explain. I clearly wasn't going anywhere until I shed light on my statement, and red cheeks. So, I told her all about James from that awful day at the grist-mill until only two months ago at the Lankford's home where I thought I could never be happier. I had let him lead me by the hand to meet his parents and most of the rest of the day was a blur. Pa had put heavy restrictions on how courting would look, but I didn't care. There were no more guesses on James' intentions. "But," I stopped and looked directly at Mammaw, "now he's gone again to Polk County, and I don't know when I'll see him again. He said he'll write, and I have been writin' him. But it's not the same."

Mammaw grunted and stood up to clear the cups. "It's better that way! You're still too young and got more growin' up to do!"

I was shocked with Mammaw's harshness, "But you just said I was all growed up! And there's women a plenty who marry at my age, or even younger!" I was a little more indignant than was allowed. If Pa had been there, he would have hauled me outside to find myself a switch that would have left my rear stinging for a few days. But I thanked the Lord that Pa was not there, and I took a deep breath so I would not push my luck and say anything else considered disrespectful.

Mammaw calmly poured my coffee back into her coffee can, clearly not letting the dark liquid go to waste. When she was finished, she turned and looked at me with one hand on her wide hips. "No need to get your dander up. I know you are a young woman and clearly your Pa is supportin' your courting this man, but don't get in a hurry to get yourself hitched."

I took a deep breath and sighed, "Well the war is keepin' that from happening anyways."

"That may be," Mammaw came over and patted my hand, "but the war may help the two of you learn a heap about each other."

I frowned, "But he's away. How can that be true?"

"You'll know, Sweet-heart." She stood up and walked towards a cabinet. "Trust me! You'll know." She pulled open the cabinet door, grabbed a jar and handed me the apple-butter. "Now you better get on with your trip on down the road. Please hand this to sweet Mrs. Jane Patton. She likes my apple-butter and I'm sure she'd enjoy some on these cold winter days over some warm biscuits."

I took the apple-butter in my hands and was surprised that our conversation was over, but she was right. I had a sheep to deliver to the Pattons, and I still had to make my way along the foot of the hill near Mammaw's house that wound around to the Davidson River. This path, however, did not take me to the Cagle Grist Mill. Instead, it came out down the river, smack in the middle of a wide-open valley. "Thanks, Mammaw. For the coffee. . ." I cleared my throat, "Or more for the talk. I'll be back sooner next time."

Mammaw hugged me and held me a moment longer than she normally would, "It'll all work out fine. The Lord knows." I let go and hoped she was right. I wasn't so sure what crazy game the Lord was playing with my heart, but I did pray every night He would keep James safe and bring him back to me. I hoped the Lord knew.

I was actually excited to head to the Patton House since I hadn't been there in a while. The home stood pretty near the Davidson River and their land stretched for many acres. Standing in the open valley, the mountains seemed a little bit further away. I was happy that the Pattons were in need of a new ewe, and it gave me a good reason to break away from the daily routine on the farm. I hadn't returned to help with school since the incident with the blood in the wagon. Pa had been right that I was lucky to spend time at school instead of helping on the farm. I saw relief in Ma when I told her I was not going back because helping her and Pa was most important. I did miss it, though, but I helped Sarah-Jane and Jimmy all the time with their reading and figures.

The ewe followed me obediently as was in her nature, and I was thankful my wool coat, scarf, and mittens were warm enough, making the winter chill bearable. As I headed down the final stretch and saw the house begin to rise not too far in the distance, I was excited to see Pink bustling about in the front, carrying some cut wood strips from what looked like a barn out towards a large field. He did that twice before he saw me and met me with a large grin and wave. Pink had told me he knew most of the slaves the Pattons owned and there were quite a few. Pink's long legs and twelve-year old energy ran towards me, and then walked in step with me as if he'd walked the whole way alongside me. "Hi, Miss Neill. That's a mighty fine ewe. Missus Patton will be mighty happy with her."

"How come you know so much about what Mrs. Patton likes or doesn't like." I teased. "She doesn't own you!" I smiled at my statement, but saw Pink was surprised by my comment since I had never referred to him personally as *being owned*. But then I added, leaning into Pink as if we had a secret, "Since no one *owns* any slaves any more, right?"

"I ain't shore what you mean, Miss Neill." Pink was clearly confused.

I smiled even bigger now, excited to share the news with Pink, who obviously hadn't heard. "President Lincoln declared somethin' called an official Emancipation Proclamation. I think it was a few weeks ago. At least that's what I heard Pa and Uncle Bob talkin' about." When Pink looked at me, still confused, I added, "That means he out-lawed slavery!"

Pink started to shake his head and laugh a little, "Miss Neill, we live in the Confederate States of America. Did you forget?"

My cheeks turned red for a second time that day, but not for the same reason. I felt so stupid. "No, I . . . didn't forget."

Pink grinned. "Ain't no worry. We're gonna keep doin' what we do until we're told somethin' else." He grabbed the ewe's rope out of my hand. "Right now, we gonna git this ewe to Missus Patton." He looked at me and added, "And no she ain't my *owner*, but she and her husband let us gather and worship on their land. So, we shore respect 'em."

"What do you mean?" I followed Pink and the ewe, quite a sight to see I was sure. There were only a few black faces looking our way and some of them were shaking their head in disbelief. I realized Pink was well known for doing things his way and getting away with it.

"Well, Miss Neill." He pointed in the direction he had been walking earlier with the cut wood. "Along the bank, a-ways down, we got our own brush arbor that many of the slaves from the area, includin' my family, come there together to worship. It broke down in the last snow storm so we was fixin' it up good before our next gatherin'."

I nodded not sure what to say. Pa had said slaves weren't allowed to gather anywhere, but I guess that wasn't the case on Mr. Patton's land. As we reached the homestead, Pink walked us up to a young black boy about Pink's age, who wouldn't look me in the eye. "This here is, Riley. He's Jesse's grandson." Pink looked from the boy to me and then explained, "He ain't talked to any white women outside of Missus Patton." He handed Riley the ewe. "Here, take this to Jesse." Riley didn't say anything, but grabbed the ewe and took off towards the barn, with the sheep obediently following.

"I got some apple-butter for Miss Patton too." I nodded my head in the direction of the house. "I think I'll knock on her door." The two chimneys that rose up from each far end of the home shot out continuous smoke, making me hope that maybe there was a warm seat in front of one of the fires for me.

"Miss Neill?" Pink had a mischievous look in his eye.

"Yes, Pink?" I looked at him with curious anticipation.

"Remember that story about Robert F. Hamilton? Not your sheriff uncle, but the one that come home from the Confederate army all bleedin' from the mouth?" I nodded. He continued, "Well, I told you I'd find out." He looked around as if sharing a secret before he whispered, "He done stuck a stick in his mouth to make his-self bleed and then made them think he was bleedin' from the stomach. I told you he had pulled the wool over them Confederates' eyes."

I muffled a giggle. "Well, that's pretty clever."

"And you know, I heard tell that he and his woman are expectin' a young'un sometime end of summer."

"She's having a baby?" I was surprised.

"Ain't bad for a dyin' man!" Pink laughed out loud.

I shook my head as we reached the front steps. "You sure hear a lot Pink!"

He stood up straight and smiled, "Well, all folk are ready to talk! Don't matter who."

I walked up the steps, and he didn't follow me. "See ya around, Pink."

"See ya around, Miss Neill!" He turned and ran off towards the barn while I carefully held Mammaw's apple butter and knocked on Mrs. Patton's door.

Robert Hamilton, March 4, 1863

The winter months in Transylvania County remain cold and dreary, both in weather and moods. Rhoda and Robert have been stewing with no recent word from Andrew. The rest of the children have begun tapering off with asking about him, not because it is not on their minds, but because they want to avoid the fearful look on their mother's face, the only answer she is capable of offering. In the midst of the cold, Robert is grateful that Strawbridge is keeping their questionable-support of deserters a secret, but knows it's to protect Fletcher and Naomi. Strawbridge fears their two babies, his grandchildren, will be innocent victims in the war between neighbors and split ideologies. Robert is aware their friendship is strained, but they both work to keep their focus on their families and local needs, no different than before.

By March the tension of the unknown is broken when Robert, who is leading Mae from the barn, ready to head out for the day, hears Grady and Blue barking up a storm, and Joel yells from down the road that he sees Andrew walking towards them. Without a moment's hesitation, Matilda, Emily and Rachel come tumbling out onto the porch with John Riley following, snatching up little Rachel on his way. Emily's club foot stops her at the bottom of the steps, but she is surprised when Viney, slamming the door behind her, scoops her up and straddles her across her back. Millie and Rhoda follow shortly and wait on the porch with Rhoda's hands up to her mouth as if lifting a silent prayer of thanks.

Robert keeps walking towards the house, and Mae whinnies in reaction to the jubilant noise, a rare sound these days up Lambs Creek. Rhoda and Millie laugh out loud when they see the herd of siblings tackle their brother and the two hounds desperately trying to participate. Andrew's grin matches their enthusiasm. Robert quickly wipes away a tear of joy and wonders when the last time was that he had felt pure joy. He savors the moment.

Finally, Andrew reaches the house with questions, laughter and touches following him like a whirling dust cloud. When the bustling settles, the children respectfully give Andrew some space when they see Rhoda walk towards her boy and embrace him. Millie, right on her Ma's heels, throws her arms around the two of them. Then, with both arms holding her boy so she can take a good look at him and his ragged and dirty uniform, she says, "Well my boy, let's get you out of those rags and into some clean civilian clothes."

Andrew reaches to pull Emily off Viney's back into his arms, kissing her head and breathing in the memories of his little sister before he smiles at his mother and suggests calmly, "Ma, you only need to wash and patch them as best you can. I need them."

"No!" Rhoda, suddenly aghast, exclaims. "You must not go back. You have done your part!" The sudden seriousness silences the jubilance, and Robert can only watch as Rhoda tries to plea with their son. He doesn't answer his mother, but squats down with his sister still on one hip, to scratch Blue and Grady behind their ears.

Robert is finally close enough to Andrew and waits for Andrew to make the first move. Leaving the dogs, Andrew walks up to Mae and scratches her nose. He makes eye contact with Robert and then reaches out his hand to his father. Robert exhales, unaware that he's been holding his breath, and, returning the handshake, accepts his son's moment of truce.

Andrew takes a few deep breaths and finally speaks, and although he looks at his siblings a moment, he only addresses his parents. "Ma, and Pa, please understand that I was only exchanged for some Union soldier and am still in the Confederate army. I am permitted to rest a couple of weeks but gotta report back to duty by early April."

Rhoda sits defeated on the middle porch step while the children fill in the rest of the steps. Andrew joins them still holding Emily. Robert carefully seeks information so it does not appear he is being critical, "But I heard that, when the Union and the Confederate armies let soldiers go, they must sign a paper promisin' not to fight against them again."

"That's parole, Pa and it worked for some time, but it seems like it is startin' to fall apart. It's obviously not workin' and men on both sides are goin' right back to fightin'. It is not the same as exchangin' soldiers."

"Oh. I see." Robert nods his head more in sorrow than agreement and then begins to scratch his beard. If parole is no longer going to work then what will happen to the soldiers that are captured? Will each side begin to hold prisoners of war? A deep fear causes Robert to briefly shudder. The war does not seem to be coming to a close. Not soon.

Andrew tries to elevate their spirits by announcing that what he had written about has, in fact, come true: he is to be assigned as brigade teamster. Andrew smiles and stands to slap his Pa on the back, shaking Robert out of his dark thoughts. "Thanks, Pa, for teaching me about handlin' horses and wagons. I passed all their requirements and should be handlin' the horses, harnesses and wagons. I might not even have to carry a rifle and definitely will not be near our canons as they terrify the horses."

Rhoda sighs with relief while Robert says gently, "Well, son, that is certainly good news. We all do still worry for your safety. Please take care of yourself."

"Well, I ain't leavin yet!" Andrew tickles Emily and her giggle makes everyone smile.

The sudden intense barking from the dogs and galloping of hooves causes the whole family to turn to see George thundering up Lambs Creek and Andrew's face transforms into one that is battle ready, quickly handing Emily back to Viney and jumping up to follow Robert to meet George, hopefully out of earshot of the other siblings. When George stops, he briefly acknowledges Andrew, but quickly states, "You need to get over to the Young's. Joshua has been brought home, but the family is all tore up." He nods at Andrew and adds, "He didn't come back lookin' like your boy here." Robert can't help remember Strawbridge's comparison and feels guilty – thankful the table isn't turned.

"Let's go!" Robert jumps up on Mae and then pauses a minute to look down at Andrew who is wide eyed and unsure. Robert reaches down his arm and says, "Are you comin'?" Without a moment's hesitation Andrew grabs his Pa's arm and swings up on Mae and straddles his father from behind, holding him tightly. Robert notices the light weight and frame of his son, but does not draw attention to it now. Rhoda will fatten him up before he has to leave again.

Leaving the rest of the Hamilton family on the steps, disappointed, the three men make their way over the mountain, careful not to draw attention to the small path leading to the hidden shelter. Robert lifts a prayer of thanks that there is no one currently taking shelter. He will not allow anyone to stay while Andrew is home. This he is sure of.

Once they reach the Young's home, it is only moments before they see Rachel-Emma come out to wave at them to follow her inside. George, having been present earlier, decides to take Mae and Jack to the trough for some water. As Andrew and Robert enter the home, the fireplace is surrounded by Strawbridge, John and Martin who are talking intensely, trying not to raise their voices; but anger drives their movements with fists on hips and other hands waving through the air.

"Brother Straub?" Robert interrupts their silent fury, with Andrew on his heels. As soon as John and Martin see Andrew their faces brighten, and they embrace him with full force. Strawbridge looks at Andrew and then nods at Robert. "Looks like God has favored your son," he whispers. But before Robert can say anything, Strawbridge adds, "A blessing, Brother Bob. A blessing! Hear nothing else." His eyes are fierce and Robert nods. Then Strawbridge leads Robert and Andrew into a back room with Joshua propped up on a bed and Martha-Ann wailing beside him. Robert is relieved to find his sister-in-law, Maria, trying to console her neighbor and friend. He longs to ask her for any news of her own boys, John and Harrison, still at war, but it is not the time or place. Robert knows it won't be long before Rhoda will sit with Martha-Ann as well, relieving Maria, and will, undoubtedly, gather any news at that time.

Joshua clearly has a head wound with clean bandages wrapped around his forehead, covering most of his hair. A few dark tufts escape close to his ears. His left hand and arm are bandaged and wrapped tightly against his chest. But the wounds are not the frightening part. It is his eyes. They are wide open, but he sees nothing. He sees nobody. Strawbridge barely whispers, "He was brought to us like this, and he doesn't even know who we are. It is like his mind is gone."

Robert doesn't know what to do, so he places a hand on Strawbridge's shoulder and squeezes. He then does the same for Martha-Ann who has begun sobbing silently now. Rachel-Emma, brushing past the men, kneels beside her mother and rocks her gently, as Maria stands to apply fresh bandages.

Robert realizes that Andrew is no longer next to him and is not sure when he disappeared. But, as Robert and Strawbridge emerge from the room, the space in front of the fireplace is now occupied by Martin, John and Andrew quietly, but vigorously discussing. Their movements, however, are controlled and decisive. They are clearly planning retaliation. Andrew suddenly turns his head and looks straight at his father. His anger is so vivid that it causes Robert to physically step back. He tries to hold his son's glare, waiting for it to soften. But as Andrew's lips begin to tighten, Robert realizes his son has no intention to seek peace between them, despite the morning's promise. Robert drops his eyes and quickly removes himself from his son's presence. He won't be home long.

Elizabeth Neill, March 19, 1863

Jimmy and Sarah-Jane were off to school, the breakfast dishes were finished, and I had already hung out the wash on the line to gently dry in the warming spring breeze. Ma had decided to head to the Valley Store on her own, and I was thankful for a few moments to myself. I walked out to the wall that I had not climbed for some time and could hear the bustling Lambs Creek calling my name. I touched the pocket of my apron and felt the letter I had already read five times...it had a deeper pull for my attention. Sitting down on the wall and letting the warming rocks settle me, I pulled out James' letter and opened it once more.

Dearest Elizabeth,

The days do linger, and I long to see you. I think fondly on our time at the Lankford home where I was able to introduce you to my parents. They ask of any word from you often, and I am thankful I have your letters to share. Spring means I am busy with preparing for planting and I am eager to help with lambing and calving.

I hear from my brothers, and word is not hopeful. Many of our men have perished and many fight only to then rise up and run. My brother calls these men cowards and traitors. To leave your brother and family and flee, or even worse, to join the other side. We have terrible times ahead.

But I am strengthened by your letters and your words of encouragement. Please send my greetings to your family who God will bless for their loyalty to our country and our cause.

Yours,

James

I folded the letter again and placed it back in my apron pocket. I smiled. But a small aching crept in from deep inside. I pushed it away and did not want it to ruin my quiet moment of peace. Yet, I couldn't keep from worrying about what James meant when he said that God would bless my family for their loyalty to our country and our cause. What it meant to be loyal? What was our cause? What was my cause?

I stood up suddenly and surveyed the land before me. I could see up the hill and knew Mammaw' house was a stone's throw beyond the bend and beyond that the Davidson River flowed with the Deavor's and Patton's land along the banks with their slaves. But then the Cagle-Grist-mill stood proudly at the entry to the forest with clear Union-sympathizers manning its mill. I looked to the left and watched Lambs Creek road disappear up the holler to my cousins that I hardly spent time with anymore, who were acting so secretive that, clearly, something was amiss. I didn't dare ask because I was loyal to Viney's need for me to honor her secret, or Pa's need for me to honor his secrets. So, I slung my head to my right and watched the Boylston Turnpike disappear around the bend that lead to the Lankford's Valley Store and then beyond that to where a few distinguished homes were beginning to define Brevard, though the war had slowed down any real progress. The Lankford home and their proud Confederate display burned fondly into my mind. Finally, there was the campground which still offered the community a preferred gathering place, where all could come.

Loyalty? Cause? God blessing my family? I felt an unease, but I pushed it away once more and focused on the eggs I needed to gather and the hay I needed to pitch. No more thought of the war. Not that day.

CHAPTER 14

Robert Hamilton, April 9, 1863

Robert rolls the latest newspaper tightly in one hand as he shifts to his left slightly to move out of the shade cast by the preacher's tent and let the morning sun warm him. He notices several of the gathered men and women also step into the light, but, in spite of the promise of spring's warmth, a cold fear permeates Wilson Campground. Rumors of the Shelton Laurel Massacre are so strong that a special court session is called. They meet at the campground to accommodate the growing number of Transylvania folk, rather than at its previously scheduled location in Probart Poor's trading post. The absence of both the continuous sound of children's laughter and the enticing smell of slow-roasted pork, only punctuates the gathering as one void of celebration or even friendly fellowship.

As the crowd grows, Fletcher, in his role as Reverend English, strolls over to stand near Robert, trying to keep an air of peace about him. But a glance at the papers in his hands that he keeps rolling and unrolling tells Robert otherwise. He has no words for his friend. He knows that the Reverend is the only one who should share the news. Words of encouragement would only diminish the gravity of the report.

Acting chairman, Leander Gash, presides over the special court of the Transylvania County Court of Pleas and Quarter Sessions, and is busy arranging one chair and a small table under the arbor that stands in front of the Preacher's tent. Meanwhile, on two benches and four other chairs, eight more justices sit and deal with county business.

Justices Patton, Clayton, Low, Aiken, Osborn, Thomas, Paxton, and Erwin discuss paying William Deavor for the corn to be delivered to the families of soldiers. Robert watches George, as his deputy, speaks with Gash, making final plans to insure order. Once the deputy knows his orders, he leans casually against a corner of the arbor, a dry branch poking his neck. At this point Robert, as sheriff, leaves Fletcher and steps to the back of the crowd to make sure he has a clearer view of all who are attending. When it seems all who would arrive have assembled, Chairman Gash calls the session to order and proceeds to sit, positioning his tall frame as best he can behind the small table. He overlooks the crowd but is also within view of the rest of the justices only a few feet behind him. As his voice booms loud enough for all present to hear, he keeps the court process moving in an orderly fashion, aware that most gathered are not present for the mundane agenda of running the county. Not influenced by the urgency of the crowd's majority to get-on-with-it, Gash takes care of county business at hand. After he appoints a special commission to receive and distribute the county's appropriation of state funds to help families of indigent soldiers, arranging for corn to be bought and shared for such families with the help of William Deavor, and frees some of the Allison, Johnstone, and Clayton slaves from taxation, he suddenly stops. Chairman Gash decides to ask his colleagues for a few minutes. He does not want the clerk to transcribe the somewhat-private session. The onlookers, who have grown restless, finally become focused.

Deputy George Neill asks if he should clear the campground. Robert is startled by his deputy's question and jumps to attention as the folk in front of him start yelling. He sees George smirk ever so slightly, and Robert shakes his head, thinking maybe his deputy chose a poor time to joke. Yet, he has been worried about George's heavy burden, so George seeking some levity in the midst of tragedy, gives Robert some hope that his deputy and friend may be coping.

"No," Gash says, seemingly unconcerned with the fuss from the crowd; he waits a moment for them to compose themselves before he continues. "We have asked Sheriff Hamilton to invite Reverend English to give us information about recent events over in Madison County and help us evaluate if it means danger for our county. This is off the record, but not private. There are too many rumors flyin' around."

Robert moves to the front of the crowd as George jumps off the platform to move to the back of the crowd. George is still smiling to himself as a few folk in the audience fuss at him, or pretend to knock him up-side the head. Reverend English also finds his way to the front as the Sheriff steps onto the platform and begins to introduce his friend and pastor. "As most of you know, Brother English came to us from Yancey County as an itinerant minister for the Methodists but stayed with us, thanks to marryin' Strawbridge Young's daughter, Naomi. He has friends and family back there in Yancey and Madison, and has gotten a lot of mail about the recent events there. I asked him to give us a summary as best he could." The sheriff moves to the same spot his deputy occupied earlier, and also leans against the arbor.

Fletcher is aware this is not his own congregation and, due to the nature of his message, he is somewhat intimidated by the crowd of justices and visitors. It doesn't help that he is apprehensive of the glares from those who are familiar with his Union-sympathizing political leanings and actions. Yet, he steps forward with a deep sigh onto the platform to face the crowd, still holding a few pages of notes, and walks to stand next to Gash's small table to make sure everyone can see him. He looks down at the papers he is now carefully unrolling and looks out at his audience with a cautious smile, "The notes are to keep me brief and on track. Do not worry, I am not going to preach."

A few folks laugh, more from anxiety than humor, but some glares soften.

Thankful for the laughter, Fletcher begins, "As I understand from the letters I have received, the troubles in Madison started over salt, along with other provisions promised by the state. I hope you can understand how crucial that is for curing meat, tanning hides and about everything we do." A few nods in the crowd encourage the reverend to continue with his approach to building some understanding for the horrible acts they have only heard rumors about, and do not comprehend. "Here we are close enough to South Carolina to get regular shipments over the mountains, and the Charleston folk really keep it coming. But higher up in those mountains- Madison, Yancey, Mitchell counties- salt is hard to come by."

Chairman Gash, ironically the one eager to get to the point, asks, "The murders were over salt?" Some gasps rise up from the crowd.

The reverend pauses a moment to refocus and, once the crowd has settled again, eager to know more, he continues, "It seemed to start when some men from up Shelton Laurel Valley and elsewhere went down to Marshall to take stockpiled salt and other items from folks living there. It was a ragtag bunch, some Confederate deserters and some Union supporters and some simple men wanting to provide for their families after a very hard winter." Fletcher looks at his paper aware most locals in front of him do not see deserters and Union supporters the same way.

"We ain't got no sympathy for them, Preacher! We heard here they wuz bushwhackers a killin and a rapin. Keep your preachin' to your church!" A man from the back yells, but Fletcher and Robert don't even look to see who it is. It doesn't matter.

Fletcher quickly answers, raising his voice above the growing din, but holding his temper, "Not true. There was no killing and raping from these men." He shakes his head and tries to clarify, "But they did break the law and take goods, food, and salt. They roughed up some families. They did destroy some property, like some bushwhackers have done close by and in Henderson County."

"Seems, then, they wuz bushwhackers, Preacher! Ain't no doubt!" Some nods agree with the statement, but others are shaking their heads in confusion.

Trying to hold onto his preacher voice, Fletcher responds as gently as possible to the obvious anxiety in the crowd. "It's real complicated over there as most families are split in loyalty. No, I best say strong loyalty to the Union or Confederacy. I can only believe that whether these men were lawless bushwhackers or not depends on where you stand." The silence in the crowd returns. Small nods, and people suddenly not looking around at each other, brings that uneasy feeling back to Robert as he, too, shifts his gaze to look only at Fletcher. He cannot give anyone reason to question where he stands. The sudden silence speaks volumes that he is not the only one fearful of discovery or betrayal. Fletcher swallows at the change in atmosphere, but continues, waving a letter. "Maybe this will help. Some have written me to say the Confederates were withholding salt from the Union sympathizers up Laurel Valley. I cannot prove or disprove that."

"Go on." Gash clearly wants the reverend to get on with it.

Fletcher nods, "What I can say is that the Confederate 64th officers are based in Marshall. Col. Allen and Lt. Col. Keith had some big, old struggles with the families up that creek where so many Sheltons lived. They asked General Davis for permission to put down the insurrection up there."

"So did the general give it?" An anxious man in the back asks.

"Yes." Fletcher nods.

"Then what they did was legal?" Another voice rises up out of the silence.

The reverend shakes his head, "What is 'legal' in *war* or *revenge*? What they did was bad in any book. The Confederate troops went up to find most men gone, except for some old men and kids." The normally calm pastor stumbles in speech, desperately trying not to weep. There is silence as he finally composes himself; he feels Robert begin to move towards him. Fletcher does not want the Sheriff to come to his rescue, when he has yet to finish. He holds out his palm to stop Robert and offers up one short nod that assures his friend that he can continue with the news. "My old school teacher, Mrs. Riddle, now 85, they hanged and whipped. Likewise, Miz. Sallie Moore they whipped with hickory rods 'til blood came in streams. They hung two Shelton women by the neck a long time, almost killing them. On and on it went, trying to find out where the Shelton men were hiding. Finally, they took about fifteen old men and young boys as prisoners. Two escaped and they executed thirteen, including a pleading fifteen-year old boy, in a firing squad. They then stuck them in a shallow grave or ditch."

The silence is broken with a few gasps. Robert looks out at his people. Divided or not, tears are shed by men and women. One woman asks, as she wipes her face with the back of her sleeve, "What happened to the bodies?"

The reverend, at this point numb to the horrors of the story, pulls from deep within to show compassion, "The families found them near the river and re-buried them in one grave near where they were murdered."

As Fletcher pauses to let the tears and growing murmur usher the crowd into consolation for one another, Chairman Gash stands and draws attention back to the platform. Reverend English sighs and looks up at the arbor's structure, beginning to bud, before he composes himself and looks back at the chairman. Chairman Gash simply thanks Reverend English. Fletcher is relieved and quickly steps off the platform. As he does, Gash turns to Robert and asks the main question hanging in the air, "Sheriff, what does this mean for us in Transylvania? Are we also in danger?"

Robert quickly steps forward, having been warned by Gash that he would ask this question. So, with confidence, he speaks out to his Transylvania folk. "Not in the same way, as I see it. Many of our families are in tension over this war and debate who is right. But my concern is that after these guerilla actions by Allen and Keith, others will rise on both sides to continue with this horrific approach. Right now, another group on the Union side led by Colonel George Kirk is using similar tactics. 'Kirk's Raiders' they are called and they seem to run loose with little or no orders. He has many men from our area and is sometimes guided into these mountains by our own Reverend Allison here." Murmurs of confusion rattle the campground.

"Union troops?" Gash asks for clarification.

"Yes." The Sheriff nods. "I understand they can be brutal and use mainly guerilla tactics." He starts, but has to raise his voice as he hears cries of concern surge up from the already unstable crowd. Robert finally raises his hand, asking for calm. He reassures his people best he can, "It is my hope that our own Reverend Allison will help protect us!" He knows the confusing looks on some faces indicate they are not sure how Reverend Allison can protect them if he is with Kirk's Raiders, but others nod understanding that he may be able to convince them to leave us alone – that Transylvania has nothing to offer.

Robert continues, while holding up and flattening out the rolled-up newspaper, "This is big news and in all the papers we get. You all know A.S. Merrimon, Solicitor for the State and local boy, born right up in Cathey's Creek area. His mother was a Paxton. This article about the

Shelton Laurel massacre says he wrote Governor Vance, declaring these men as all 'guilty of murder and such savage and barbarous cruelty is without parallel.' The paper goes on to say that Vance said the 'affair was shocking and outrageous in the extreme.'" Robert drops the paper on the small desk next to Gash and adds. "Even Confederates condemn this massacre."

"Thanks Sheriff," Gash begins to close the session. But Robert is not finished.

Robert takes a step forward to the edge of the platform and stands facing his people, both Union Sympathizers and Confederate supporters. He sees Lankford, remembering the joyful celebration of his brother and in-laws who are Confederate soldiers, honorable men. Friends. He wonders who knows. *Who knows which of us secretly supports the Union cause and which of us does not?* He pushes away his moment of distrust and wariness, and he speaks with a certainty, true to his core belief, "Friends, as Reverend English has said, we seem to have sufficient salt and all of us are working hard to give support to all families in need, even in this special court session today. We pull together as Transylvanians, no matter which side our men are fighting on. I think that is the Christian thing here. We all want peace here!" He pauses and sees many nods so he dares to add, "We will still be neighbors and kin when it's all over. Remember that!"

Elizabeth Neill, April 18, 1863

"Here, Elizabeth." Jimmy's voice pulled me out of my thoughts as he shoved a fist full of wild strawberry blooms into my face. The fine white flowers made of a cluster of five or six pedals made me smile and reminded me of the dogwood flower that James gave me so long ago, still safely preserved in a box under my bed. "I thought ya might like some flowers." I took them from my brother and let him snuggle up next to me on the top porch step.

"Thanks, Jimmy." I ruffled his already messy hair. "What has gotten into you?"

"I miss all your teasin' and fussin' so I thought maybe you'd be mean again if I was nice to ya?" He shoved my shoulder and laughed. But he didn't move away. He was already nine, but he still wanted to play like a six-year-old, and I had been the leader of all three of us, helping my siblings build forts and pretend to our-hearts-content. I suddenly realized that it was the first spring where I hadn't hauled them out of bed on a Saturday to hit the first rays of sun warming the rock wall. I hadn't forced them to begin our chores early enough to play outside as soon as the sun let us shed our jackets and sometimes, when Ma wasn't looking, our shoes.

But not this spring, and I was pretty sure not any spring to come. I didn't wish for it anymore, and, although I longed for that inner desire, which had somehow disappeared, I also was content with being in a different place. Where that was, I wasn't quite sure, but building a fort was no longer my passion. Although, I argued for a moment with myself, I would probably never give up climbing the wall, it was still the fastest way up to the house. Giving that up would simply be impractical.

I sighed and hugged Jimmy. We sat for a moment listening to Lambs Creek's familiar babbling. Suddenly, the sound of hooves pounding the dirt made us stand to have a better look up Boylston Turnpike, wondering who would be in such a hurry. Quickly jumping off the porch and moving to the top of the rock wall, we were both surprised to find the rider's skirts flapping frantically and then abruptly turn right, heading towards us.

"Rachel-Emma Young? What in tarnation are you doin'?" I asked as my friend came to a full-stop right below us. Her hair was a mess, and her face was tear streaked. I quickly scrambled down the wall, while Jimmy stayed at the top, clearly frightened. "Are you okay?" I asked, grabbing the reins and calming down her horse.

"No, Ma's fallin' to pieces because Martin enlisted. My stupid brother thinks he is helping my family and avengin' Joshua by goin' and fightin' when Ma really needs him home to help with Joshua, who still can't put on his own clothes right." Rachel-Emma took a breath and then looked right at me. "I got to get a tincture to help calm down Ma and I'm headed to the Valley Store, but no one is better in these situations than Millie. Can you run up Lambs Creek and fetch her to come help with Ma and Joshua?" Her face became contorted and a cry rose from somewhere deep. "I can't do it anymore. I can't help Ma. She's starting to look through me. Just like Joshua!" She swallowed. "Can you help me, Elizabeth? Please?"

I didn't even think twice. "Of course! You head to see Mr. Lankford. I'm sure he's got some tincture that will help her with her nerves." I let go of the horse. "Be sure to ask him for one of those special local tinctures that may work better than somethin' from some city. I heard Ma say there's some mighty fine mountain brew that might help. Even heard some special Cherokee medicine." I paused aware that I had spoken the unspeakable about any Cherokee still being in these parts, so I quickly added, "taught to local mountain folk years ago, of course. Worth askin' about that too. I'll head up the road to get Millie."

"I can't thank you enough!" With a quick kick in the horse's side, Rachel- Emma was off, heading toward the store.

I looked at my brother, who was sitting at the top of the steps and was white as a sheet and I realized that I was responsible for my brother and sister while Ma and Aunt Rhoda were visiting Mammaw, and Pa was out and about as deputy. I yelled as loud as I could, "SARAH-JANE!"

Suddenly, my sister appeared from the back of the house with her favorite hen under her arm, "What is all the fuss? Miss Lilly here is needin' some quiet to lay her eggs!"

I sighed and climbed back up the wall. I took Jimmy by the hand and walked him over to Sarah-Jane, "Do you think you can watch your brother for an hour while I head up the road to fetch Millie? The Young family needs her bad, and I got to do this!"

Sarah-Jane dropped Miss Lilly and grabbed her brother's hand with vigor. She stood up tall and said, "Of course I can! I'm twelve you know. You don't worry. Jimmy and I will be fine." She pulled Jimmy's hand. "Won't we?" Jimmy just nodded and followed his sister into the house.

I quickly turned and scrambled back down the wall and began to run up Lambs Creek.

* * *

The familiar curve to the left in the road and a glimpse of the roof to the Hamilton's house gave me the extra push I needed to keep running. I had my skirts hiked as far up as I could over my knees without being too indecent should I run into John-Riley or Joel, even though I didn't much care, but Ma would, if word got back to her. I took a deep breath and dropped my skirts back over my knees while still walking briskly. Blue and Grady came running toward me and only barked twice before settling in beside me, keeping pace as I continued up the final incline. When I reached the porch, my initial intent to knock on the front door was interrupted when the two hounds disappeared around the corner to the sound of laughter coming from around back. Without hesitation, I abandoned the front door and scurried around back, making sure I reached Millie as quickly as possible.

The stream along the Hamilton's house was always a favorite place for Viney and me to wade and tease her brothers, so it wasn't a surprise to find most of the children enjoying their Saturday home from school with spring's fickle warm breeze chasing them to the creek. Millie was laughing too as Blue and Grady jumped into the stream, so I hustled over to them, aware they didn't know I was there. As I approached, I became excited too, since a gray uniformed man sat at the edge of the creek surrounded by the children. I thought Andrew had already left, at least Pa had said that, but maybe he was back.

As I was almost upon the small gathering, little Rachel spotted me and squealed with delight, "Elizabeth!" She jumped into my arms and I hugged her, but there was a sudden silence. I looked at all the rest of my cousins; their faces were white, and they began to move closer into each other to block the man sitting by the creek.

205

I frowned and asked, "What's wrong?" But when no-one answered, I laughed, "Come-on! I saw Andrew sittin' there! Why are you hidin' him?"

Viney was the one to step forward and put her hand through my free arm with Rachel still clasped around my neck. She strategically turned my back to the creek and asked, "Why are you here, Elizabeth?"

Aware that she was not answering my question, my heart began to race. Something was not right. I let her pull me only a few feet before I flung her off of my arm and turned back around to face the creek. A man I had never seen before was trying to scurry up the holler, but he slowed as soon as we made eye-contact. His gray-uniform was wet at his ankles with bare-feet already muddy from path, and he was carrying what looked like crusty boots. I wouldn't have thought much of it, or even thought it was one of Andrew's friends passing through, if it weren't for his eyes. They stared straight into me. And then there was his voice. He uttered only one sentence that sent a shudder through me. "Will this be a problem, Miss?"

All my cousins stood still and didn't say a thing. They actually looked at me to see what my answer would be. That was when I felt as if a blind-fold had been ripped from my eyes. I heard the baby's cry on Christmas. I saw the terror in Viney's eyes holding the corn-husk doll. I understood the blood on Pa's wagon. Not allowed to visit up the holler because we are all too busy. Lies. Secrets. All of them.

I stared back at the man and swallowed. "No, Sir." I let my eyes move to Viney's who was already wiping away her tears, not in fear for the man's safety, but in fear of losing me. I looked away and heard her gasp as I walked towards Millie and handed Rachel to her. "Millie, Rachel-Emma needs you to help her with her Ma. Now! She's in a bad place." Millie nodded and putting Rachel on the ground, ran into the house to gather her basket. By the time I glanced back in the direction of the holler, the man was gone.

I looked back at Viney who was pulling her apron up to her face to wipe away her despair. "Elizabeth, I'm sorry." She said more, but I

206

didn't hear her as I ran home with my skirts held as high as I could get them, not caring if my drawers were showing or not.

Robert Hamilton, April 18, 1863

It is already dusk when Robert knocks on the Neill's front door. It had only taken a minute from the time he arrived home until his children informed him of Elizabeth's unfortunate visit. One look from Rhoda had told him he best wait for dinner until he speaks with the Neill family and salvage what he can.

As the door slowly opens, Sarah-Elizabeth is not surprised to see Robert standing in front of her. She sighs, "Hello, Bob, I thought it might be you." She waves her hand gently towards their fireplace, where he can only see the back of Elizabeth's head and shoulders sitting in a straight back chair. The scuffle of feet above indicate that the other two children are clearly upstairs. George is leaning against the fireplace, but no fire is burning. Homemade candles light the room. He quickly turns his head as he hears Robert and waves him to come and sit down in the rocker only a few feet from the splotchy-tear-stained face, which was now as cold as the room. She does not lift her youthful blue eyes, or toss her auburn hair over her shoulder to make sure she is absorbing every detail, so as not to miss one moment of life.

Sarah-Elizabeth moves in close to her daughter and tries to touch her gently, only to be brushed-off with a sudden jerking movement. The quick repulsion from Elizabeth causes her mother to retreat to the side of her husband, who places his arm around her.

"Well," Robert takes off his hat and slaps it on his knee as if swatting an invisible fly, "I reckon you're either in or out!"

"Bob!" Sarah-Elizabeth is appalled at her cousin's flippant approach. "She's just a child."

Robert does not look at the two parents, because the question is not for them. He is staring at Elizabeth who has yet to look at him. "Is she?" After a long pause he continues, "The way I see it, with your blessin', Elizabeth is courtin' a good-old southerner whose family is in the Confederacy. Last I checked, that makes her a young woman. Isn't that right, Elizabeth?"

Elizabeth turns her head to meet Robert's eyes. She slowly answers, "Now that you've determined I'm no longer a child, what is it that you want from me . . . Sheriff?"

Robert is briefly startled by Elizabeth's use of his title since she has only ever called him Uncle Bob, but he quickly realizes that she is negotiating. "To pick a side."

Elizabeth holds him with her intensity and Robert does not dare look away. "No."

All three adults shifted awkwardly, but Elizabeth's eyes change from a hardened look to one of curiosity, waiting for her uncle's rebuttal. He searches her thoughts and finally responds, "Well, that won't do."

A very loud and sudden laugh escapes from Elizabeth's core, "Ha! What are you goin' do? Shoot me?"

"Elizabeth!" Sarah-Elizabeth regrets her reprimand of her daughter immediately when the now fierce blue eyes turn on her.

"What? Mother! You want to lock me up in the barn?" She flung her head back and again the haunted laugh escapes, "Ha! No! You are the ones who have to pick a side. Not me!"

Silence follows as the adults are baffled. Finally, Robert shifts and clears his throat. "What are you sayin', Elizabeth?"

Elizabeth looks from her uncle to her mother and then to her father. "I have always been on your side. Am I not family? Am I not the one who pretended it was a lamb when that baby cried in your damn root cellar, Uncle? Am I not the one who swore to keep secrets about strange happenings with only the simple promise that I would be told, I would be included, I would be trusted, when it was time." Elizabeth stood and faced the three of them. "Who the hell do you think you are to think this war is only suffered by you?" She walks over to the mantle next to her parents and lifts her hand to place it flat on the family Bible, "I do swear I never will endanger my family even if it means I have to hold off on my child-conceived notion of love. I do swear I will protect Lambs Creek and what my family deems right and good in God's eyes.

I do swear I will one day forgive my family when they can prove to me that I am indeed worthy of being a part of it. But not today!"

"Elizabeth," Robert stands and grabs her arm as she attempts to walk past him. "I'm sorry."

Elizabeth gently removes her arm from her uncle's grip. She lifts her eyes that have a depth to them that Robert is shocked to see. He finds himself overwhelmed by her solemn intensity as she whispers, "Not today, Uncle." Suddenly Elizabeth turns and heads out the door into the dark. No one goes after her. No one dares.

Elizabeth Neill, April 19, 1863

The familiar wooden building eased my anger some as we rounded the corner; fond memories of school and worship services lifted my spirits for a moment. Ma had told me I didn't have to go to church, but then quickly glanced away when she saw the look of horror on my face. I was furious that she would even consider that I may want to keep away from my friends, especially Viney. I needed to see her. I didn't want one more day to pass with this distance between us, one created by the adults in our lives.

We arrived early enough for me to separate myself from my family and stand along the path where the Hamilton family usually emerged from traipsing over the mountain pass. I knew they would walk today because the sun was warm and the sky was blue, the fresh sounds and sights of spring were too beautiful to miss. Sure enough, it wasn't five minutes before Rachel Emma and Joel came running first. When they saw me, Rachel Emma gave me a bear hug and then scurried on, but Joel awkwardly looked away, as did most of the others as they emerged. Viney was last, walking with Aunt Rhoda and Uncle Bob. Uncle Bob instantly understood what I was doing and nodded respectfully before taking Aunt Rhoda's hand, "My dear, let's leave Viney and Elizabeth to talk." She hesitated a moment, but, after she assessed my demeanor and was satisfied to see I was not full of anger, she nodded and patted Viney's hand before dropping it.

I waited a minute and hoped Viney would look at me, but she kept her eyes down with her hair falling into her face. I sighed, "Viney, I am not mad at you." She slowly lifted her eyes, clearly swollen form hours of crying, which made us almost look like twins.

"You're not?" She whispered.

I reached out my hand and touched her arm. "It wasn't your fault. Not one bit. You had to obey your Pa and Ma."

She nodded with her mouth half open. "I did. I hated I couldn't tell you."

I pulled her into my arms and we stood there holding each other tight both of us shaking. "No more secrets?" The question was more of a promise.

"No more secrets." Viney pulled back to look me in the eyes and then a gentle smile worked its way through her puffy cheeks. "I swear it!"

I grinned and turned her so I could loop my arm through hers. "I swear too!" Then we started walking towards the church where members were already heading inside. "Will you sit with me?"

"You couldn't keep me away if you tried." She then inspected my face. "So what will people say when they see our puffy eyes and blotchy cheeks?"

I laughed, "We'll just tell them we been cryin' over boys." She laughed and we both headed into church to sit as far back as we could so that no one could actually see our faces or ask questions.

Although sitting next to my favorite cousin was a blessing, and gave me some sense of protection, yesterday's events continued to flood my senses. As Reverend English droned on about God's will, I did not hear much beyond the occasional "Amen". My thoughts were filled with images of Ma and Pa trying to explain why they didn't want me to know about Uncle Bob harboring deserters. They hoped keeping me from being involved would spare me unnecessary pain. At one point I saw Reverend English pause in his sermon and stare at me. I don't know what he said before, but he cleared his throat and added "But and if ye suffer for righteousness' sake, happy are ye: and be not afraid of their terror, neither be troubled". I frowned and deliberately rolled my eyes. I could tell my preacher wasn't all too happy, but I knew, after Pa's lengthy confession, that my good-old teacher and preacher was also a deceiving and plotting man who would one day have to stand before God and explain himself like the rest of us.

Even before Uncle Bob knocked on the door last night, I knew I really didn't have much of a choice. I hadn't much thought of my political views, or even believed I had to choose a side, since I assumed, as a Southerner, I supported the Confederacy, by default. Yet, my last encounter with Pink, where I declared that he was free because of Lincoln's Emancipation Proclamation, did make me wonder how much I really understood. The reality was I didn't understand anything beyond what was happening up Lambs Creek and within Transylvania County. I had to think about people I cared about, and even if I didn't like some of them much, people who I knew. I could accept Pa and Uncle Bob's premise that keeping our local families and neighbors safe was their focus. Which, they explained, was why they did not make public their sympathizing with the Union like the Cagles, or fly the Confederate flag like the Lankfords. They had the notion that they would keep the peace as best they could and hoped the war would end before their secret would cause unintended irreparable division within the county. I could accept this. It seemed possible that the war would be over soon and everyone could move on with life. After all, James had not joined the Confederate Army and, I was therefore, not betraying him by not telling him.

My stomach suddenly lurched. I hoped for the first time that the war would end before I saw James again. As long as I didn't have to face him, then I did not have to keep a secret from him. The anger and sense of betrayal I felt towards my family was strong. How much greater would his be? I squeezed Viney's hand and she leaned her head on my shoulder. I took a deep breath and made the promise to myself that I would do nothing to hurt my family and, if James couldn't forgive me for this in the future, then he would need to look for another woman. I sought comfort in my reasoning, but it still settled like a heavy stone in the pit of my stomach.

CHAPTER 15

Robert Hamilton, June 25, 1863

To Rachel-Emma's delight, over the past two months Millie has spent a lot of time helping Martha-Ann with Joshua's care, so Robert isn't surprised to hear that the wounded Confederate soldier is showing some improvement and is even beginning to talk somewhat coherently. Robert decides it is time to visit the family and see for himself how they are faring. He is pleased to find Strawbridge and Martha-Ann, along with Rachel-Emma, John-Stewart and Millie, gathered outside on such a beautiful day. When Millie sees her Pa arrive, she waves him over to come sit next to Joshua who is already talking while waving his hands around as if painting a picture in the air. Robert can only smile at the renewed energy in the young man, but the lap quilt carefully tucked around the young man's legs and the drooping of one side of his face reminds the sheriff that Joshua is far from whole.

Joshua's voice stumbles at first until he is sure what he's going to say, but once he settles on his narrative he begins. His speech is slow. "It was awful. We had no chance in that gap with steep mountains on all sides. Never knew what was Tennessee, or Kentucky, or Virginia. Not that it mattered." His eyes stare off in an odd direction not really focusing on anything until he hears his father's voice bring him back.

"Were you outnumbered?" Strawbridge asks carefully.

For a few minutes everyone sits in silence waiting, watching Joshua's hands untuck and re-tuck his quilt before looking up and answering, "Don't really know. The worst was that we were outgunned.

They had those new Spencer rifles," he waves one hand frantically in a circle over and over, "You know, those repeatin' guns. Our men were just shot at many times while tryin' to pour powder and shot in the barrels of the Gillespie or Kentucky rifles. For one of our shots, they'd get ten or twenty off."

"Damn them." John Stewart's voice startles Joshua at first, but he draws his brother near with a single wave. John Stewart obediently moves towards his brother without hesitation and settles at his brother's feet. Joshua then lean towards his brother as if the conversation is only between them.

Robert and everyone else move in a bit themselves in order to hear Joshua continue, "And it was rainin'. Getting our powder wet. Awful. What really got us was that they captured our spring so we had no water for us or the horses for days. When the general surrendered, several slipped away but more than two thousand of us got held by the enemy. It could have been a lot worse."

John Stewart abruptly stands up and paces, running his fingers through is wild hair, a habit he has apparently inherited from his father. "It just ain't right! They're just ain't no fightin' fair."

Strawbridge stands too, and walks over to his distraught son. "It's war, what do you reckon happens in war? It's no game with rules that people abide by. Hell, right now the one rule of exchanging captured soldiers is no longer working. Of course, it never worked in the first place, so now they're building God-forsaken prison camps." This time Strawbridge runs his hands through his hair.

Martha-Ann places her hand gently in her lap and whispers loud enough for her husband to hear, "Go on tell them what we heard. Now's as good a time as any."

John Stewart raises his voice, "Tell us what?" Pa?"

Joshua is moving his head back and forth between parents and his brother, but the movement is awkward and jerky. Millie notices and quickly places a gentle hand on his shoulder hoping to calm his nerves.

More silence, then Strawbridge speaks, "Son, your brother, Martin, was taken prisoner last month at Jackson's Mill near Kinston. We hear they took him and some others somewhere up north to a prisoner of war camp."

214

It's Joshua's voice that responds first. "My little brother is a prisoner?"

"Afraid so. Hard to get any more information than the basics. We keep trying," Strawbridge says, as Martha-Ann sobs. The grieving father adds more bad news he knows Martha-Ann cannot give, "Your cousin, Martin Gash, was also taken prisoner at the same time as your brother in Kinston. Sent somewhere up north too."

John-Stewart can't take it anymore and runs into the house, slamming the door, leaving the small gathering sitting silently, while Joshua mumbles to himself.

"That's not all." Strawbridge breaks the heavy stillness and nods to Martha-Ann to share her news. She hesitates, clearly not sure if Millie and Joshua should hear, but Strawbridge pushes her, "Go on. They can handle hearing what a fine line we all walk."

Millie looks at Robert confused, and for a moment, Robert realizes she is worried that they are going to talk about their own secret undertakings across the mountain. He shakes his head assuring her there is nothing to worry about and her gaze softens and focuses on Martha-Ann as she clasps and unclasps her hands three times before she begins, "Well, my brother, you know Leander Gash?" She looks at Millie to make sure she makes the connection and, after Mille nods, Martha-Ann continues. "He told me that in the beginnin' of June, only a few weeks ago, he wrote Governor Zeb Vance. They've known each other for some time and my brother is quite the politician. He told me that he argued his case for leniency for the Confederate deserters." Robert's eye-brows lift in surprise and he has to work hard to suppress a smile. Martha-Ann does not notice and sighs. "It appears he is makin' a strong case for the Confederacy to understand the heavy burden they are placing on our people, especially calling up a local militia to hunt down deserters who are more than likely better trained and equipped than the local farmers turned into militia. He even says he'd harbor his own son if he were to desert. It seems Leander is pushin' the Confederacy to consider a settlement of sorts in hopes that doin' this sooner than later will allow for better terms than if the war drags on any longer."

Robert looks at his friends to assess how they feel about this confrontational letter. "It seems, maybe, this is something to celebrate. Don't you think?" Millie looks at Joshua who seems to have fallen deeper into his own world and is shaking his head, processing in his own way.

Strawbridge nods, but a frown occupies his forehead. "It can be considered that, but what Martha-Ann did not disclose is that, at the beginning of the letter, he tells Vance that he intends to criticize his conduct since it appears Vance only surrounds himself with people he presumes are friends. He even says the Confederate Army is as equally annoying as the Yankee's army." Robert can't help but chuckle at Leander's audacity. Strawbridge takes in Robert's physical response and sighs as he adds, "I know this calls for some sense of levity, but we worry that this will only mark him as a Union sympathizer, and publically so. We pray this does not bring unwanted aggravated attention to his. . ." Strawbridge pauses, ". . . our family."

Robert stands and walks over to his friend and takes off his hat to flatten his thinning hair, "I'm sorry, but it looks like the war keeps creating new challenges. Let's hope that Martin is being well taken care of and at least he is not in the line of fire. I know this is still no real assurance, but it's somethin' to hope on." Robert is talking from his own experience from when Andrew was taken as prisoner but then also exchanged, yet he won't remind them because, as Strawbridge stated earlier, there are no rules and nothing in war is fair. "And when it comes to Leander, I think he will be alright. He seems to be well respected and hurtin' him and his family would only make Vance look weak. Leander would not have spoken so boldly if he did not consider the risks, but more importantly this letter shows that he is lookin' out for those in the mountains' interest." Robert smiles and adds, "He is, after all, a politician. And more than that, one that is on our side."

Elizabeth Neill, June 26, 1863

Even though drops of sweat were converging into a steady stream down the back of my dress, I didn't mind. I was excited about heading to the Valley Store and look across the way at the Oak Grove Church with all the trees beginning to cast their summer shade. It had been so long since I had been the one to deliver honey and eggs, and was thankful Ma was too busy putting together a basket for Pa to quietly deliver up one of the hollers to help feed a family. Ever since Pa and Uncle Bob had included me in *the* secret, Ma didn't hesitate to let me know every little detail she and Aunt Rhoda were doing for families in the community. I even knew which homestead was suffering because there was a husband, brother or son who had deserted from the Confederate Army and had joined up with the Union. Every detail was no longer left a mystery to me and, to my surprise, Sarah-Jane and Jimmy still seemed oblivious to any of it, a clear relief to both Ma and Pa. I figured they had decided to change their approach. I guessed Jimmy and Sarah-Jane would ask if they had questions and answers would be provided. Clearly my parents wouldn't make the same mistake twice.

I hurried up the steps to Mr. Lankford's store. "Good mornin'." I greeted Tony and clearly startled him as he was at the far-end of the porch sweeping the remains of branches and leaves blown in from last night's thunderstorm.

"Mornin' Miss Neill." He took off his wide-brimmed hat, "You sho snuck up on me."

I placed the basket on the porch and walked over to him, "I'm so sorry, Tony. I didn't mean to scare you." Then I grinned as wide as I could and looked out from the porch toward the Oak Grove Church, as I had longed to do for some time. "I'm just so excited to be here and feel like some things haven't changed."

Tony's eyes darkened some and he put his hat back on his head so he could resume sweeping, "Miss Neill you better head on inside. Missus Lankford is a helpin' today and she'd shore be pleased to visit." He didn't share anymore, and he clearly wasn't wanting me to continue talking with him because he began to whistle. I didn't allow this to be my dismissal because I was curious why his bearing changed so quickly; something was clearly wrong. I frowned and followed Tony until his whistling stopped. He continued to work even as he asked, "Miss, is there somethin' wrong?"

I put my hands on my hips, "Confound it, Tony! That's what I want to know. You up and start whistlin' on me when we were talkin'. Somethin's not right." My eyes grew really big, "Is Pink okay?"

Tony stopped sweeping and looked at me for a moment with surprise before dropping his eyes and almost laughing, "Pink? Ain't nothin' wrong with Pink, 'cept needin' to be put in his place once in a while." He shook his head still chuckling, "No, Pink sho can take care of hisself." Tony looked at me, and this time did not drop his eyes. I had never really seen his dark eyes and suddenly Tony seemed older than I thought he was. His soft wrinkles gently rose in a smile, "Its mighty fine of you to care for that boy. Mighty fine!" He then looked away and began to whistle again. This time I accepted his dismissal and went to grab my basket.

The familiar stuffy smell of the store made me cough and smile at the same time. "Hello there, sweet Betty." Mrs. Lankford was clearly happy to see me, but a sadness continued to pour from her that I was hoping would someday disappear. I never could bring myself to tell her that I didn't go by Betty, but figured it really didn't matter at this point, and surely not something worth making her even more melancholy.

"Happy to see you this fine mornin' Mrs. Lankford." I smiled, setting Ma's basket on the counter. "I hear you are expectin' again. I'm so happy for you!" I started to help her pull out the jars and eggs, rather than make my usual investigation of new products in the store. Like Tony hinted, it seemed Mrs. Lankford could use a friendly visit. "So, when do you think this youngin' will be arrivin'?"

Mrs. Lankford seemed surprised by my congratulations and looked around the store making sure no one was around, "I guess Millie told you?" I nodded, not sure what else to say; it had only been yesterday that Millie had talked to Ma about Mrs. Lankford having the morning sickness real bad, so I figured it was public knowledge. "It's alright, I guess. It ain't arriving til late winter sometime. I ain't told no-one else yet. Want to make sure it grows first." She sighed.

"I won't tell. I promise." I put the last jar on the counter, regretting my choice of topic.

She reached out and gently patted my hand, but then began to hold it and squeeze it gently, "But I got some news for you, sweet Betty."

I didn't take my hand away. Her sorrowful eyes, which I had associated with all the sadness she had endured, were filled with a new sorrow, one that involved me. This was the same look of darkness that had crossed Tony's eyes. My heart started to pound. "James?" I asked.

She nodded, "He done enlisted this month with the 64th Regiment, joinin' his brothers." It seemed she might cry, but any crying had been long exhausted.

"He said he would enlist with them, didn't he?" I didn't know what else to say or feel except state the obvious, even with my greatest fear becoming a reality.

Mrs. Lankford squeezed my hand one last time, let go, and, with a small smile replied, "He shore did, didn't he?" She shook her head. "Well, he comes by it honest, don't he? Let's hope my brothers are as good at gettin' out of this war as they are gettin' into it." I nodded and began to help Mrs. Lankford gather the few supplies Ma needed me to bring back in my basket, but it was all a blur. I felt foolish because my worry wasn't about him joining the war, or even fighting; I knew this could happen and would happen. I had been praying for his protection ever since the war broke out. Horror suddenly filled me when I realized that my first thought wasn't fear over him dying. The truth was that I was selfish at that moment because I knew that right then I was officially supporting opposition to my James. I worried more about what he would think of me than about his dying.

As soon as I left the store, I scurried up the small hill with Oak Grove Church quietly standing vigil. I found the shade of the dogwood tree that James and I sat under only a year ago and allowed myself to cry. I asked God to forgive me for my selfishness and prayed hard for

James' life. But as hard as I prayed and as hard as I cried, I couldn't let go of my first fear. I finally argued enough with myself and God to settle on the reality that I had, in fact, not really lied to James, since we had not spoken. I told myself that this would be okay in God's eyes, as well as James'. It had to be.

CHAPTER 16

Robert Hamilton, July 14, 1863

Robert tries to focus on the garden and is thankful for the sun, but recent news of great losses at the battles of Vicksburg and Gettysburg only causes Robert to be on edge since the reality of the aftermath has yet to unfold. He is startled out of his deep thought. "Daddy, Daddy. A rider is a-comin'." Matilda screams as she runs up Lambs Creek road, her skirts flailing in the kicked-up dust.

Robert stops hoeing the vegetable garden, as do two of his children, Joel and Emily. At nine and seven they are pleased to be helping their father rather than playing, like their little sister Rachel, who is conveniently under Millie's watch inside the house. Even Emily, with her club-foot, shows her Pa that she can pull weeds and tie up string beans as good as any of her siblings. Uncertain as to what the news might be and whether it is friend or foe, Robert puts down the hoe and reaches for his Gillespie rifle, conveniently resting against the nearby fence. As he signals with one swoop of his hand for Joel and Emily to run up the gentle slope to the house, he carefully leans on his rifle. He doesn't want to take any chances. The children don't question their father and as Matilda reaches the fence, she climbs over it quickly and follows her siblings. She hurries them along as they try to look back at their father, a solitary soldier, but one they knew should still be feared.

As soon as the rider becomes visible the sound of a familiar voice breaks the tension, "Bob!" A long, lanky arm waves wildly. "It's me, Fletcher!"

As Robert smiles and places his rifle back against the fence, he hears the scampering of feet behind him. He turns to see his three children had not made it to the house yet and were already running, not toward the garden, but toward the road. Robert shakes his head as he follows his children to meet his old friend. But he is not the first to greet Pastor English. "What's up, Preacher?" Joel tries to ask calmly, but is clearly out of breath and excited to have beat his older sister to their guest.

The unexpected visitor smiles at the children, but Robert notices how quickly the smile fades. Robert is keenly aware that Fletcher rarely comes up Lambs Creek to visit, since over the mountain is a shorter ride. Cause for greater concern is that Fletcher rarely remains in his saddle. Reverend English looks from the children to Robert, and Robert can tell that Fletcher is not sure if he should share what he has to say in front of the children. But Robert does not shoo them away, a sign to the reverend that they have nothing to hide. Robert comes up to the horse and reaches up to shake his friend's hand, "Can you come sit a spell and tell us what is new?"

The reverend leans down and grabs the sheriff's hand, but he does not let go, pulling Robert in closer to hear his news. "Just thought you needed to know; the militia has set up camp on our campground."

Robert raises his eyebrows and clarifies, "The Wilson Campground?"

As the reverend releases his grip, Robert asks, "Who?" The children are all wide-eyed, the playfulness is gone.

Fletcher has an urgency to his answer. "Troops. Not from around here, maybe Buncombe County or down the mountain."

"Are they flying a flag?" Robert asks and tries to sound calmer than he feels.

"Yep. Stars and Bars." Reverend English takes a deep breath, still seeing the image of the Confederate battle flag waving from the top of the preacher's tent, sacred ground during the camp-meetings.

Robert is still grappling with why they would be occupying the campground. "You are sure they are not those rascals with Kirk and his supposed Union boys?"

The reverend exclaims, "Oh, yes, I'm positive. The few that have uniforms are wearing gray."

"Matilda," Robert turns his head and addresses his daughter, "Take Joel and Emily up to the house and tell your mother I have some business to attend to, then saddle and bring me Mae." Matilda doesn't ask questions, but pulls her siblings toward the house.

"I can walk myself!" Joel fusses at his sister as he pulls away his hand.

"Then walk!" Matilda yells. They both look back at the two men who are not amused. The two quickly look away and break into a run with Emily on their heels. Before the door slams Robert hears Matilda yell, "Viney! Millie! Ma! The war's done come to Transylvania!"

Robert turns his head away from his family shaking his head at Matilda's outburst, but aware that it is of his own doing. Yet, his daughter's outburst, although overly dramatic, still speaks to the real fear they all have, but don't voice. When Fletcher doesn't say anything, Robert stares down the dirt road with a look of growing concern, letting his show of strength waver some, now that his children are gone. "I have heard from some Allison friends that their own Rev. Allison was sometimes guiding Kirk and there was talk about comin' this way to check us out. They have undoubtedly heard about what we are doin' here with so much movement across the mountain. I really do not need to be seen talkin' to Union folks or I'm a dead man."

Reverend English shifts in his saddle and looks around cautiously, "Bob, you know our secret is safe. You are the bravest man I know, doing what you feel God is leading you to do. And I *know* without a doubt they are Confederate militia, no chance of you running into a Union troop. I reckoned you ought to know because there may be problems. Our wonderful campground has been such a spiritual place for all these years. The meetings and spiritual gatherings have really brought us together during these tense times. It's simply a sin having those troops there." He slaps his own knee really hard and grunts, "You got to do something!"

Surprised by his friend's urgency for Robert to stand toe to toe against a Confederate militia, Robert raises one hand. "Well, hold your horses, have they been causin' any problems?" Robert watches Fletcher hesitate for a minute and then reluctantly shake his head. "Well then we might be fussin' over nothin'. However, as Sheriff, I know I need to check out their intentions." Robert turns to see Matilda leading Mae by the reins with one hand while holding his holster and Colt in the other. He is surprised at first how quickly the mare was saddled, but then he sees Rhoda stepping onto the front porch. His wife must have already known he would need to leave. She catches his gaze and simply nods before she heads into the house. Robert looks back at his friend and continues, "Not that I can do or say anything. I am sure the local folks are expectin' me to call on them and let the community know."

Robert quickly returns to the fence post to grab his rifle and, after securing it to his saddle, he takes Mae's reins from Matilda and kisses the top of his daughter's head, while carefully relieving her of his Colt. He sees Joel and Emily have settled themselves on the porch steps just as Millie and Viney step halfway out the front door with Rachel hiding behind their skirts. He knows all of his children want to see real soldiers, but it is a solo job. Reverend English rides with him only to the end of Lambs Creek road before they part ways, agreeing that Fletcher's reputation may not benefit Robert any at this moment.

The preacher heads north while Robert turns south, soon reaching the Valley Store where he is not surprised to find a small crowd beginning to gather. Robert recognizes several faces including his brother-in-law, Henry Mackey. It is Pink, however, who spots Robert first and eagerly draws everyone's attention to their law-enforcement sauntering up to them. "Hi, Sheriff!" Pink doesn't wait for Robert to respond, but jumps into his own narration of the militia occupying their campground. There are two young white boys about Pink's age listening intently to Pink and excitement seems to fuel their giddy movements.

"I know, Pink!" the sheriff interrupts the boy and addresses everyone who is waiting for him to discuss the issue. Pink doesn't move, but stares up to the sheriff still straddling his horse. "I have no more news than the rest of you, but I'm fixin' to head over there and assess what their intentions are."

"Well, I'm comin' too!" Henry steps forward wanting to support his brother-in law. His statement causes others to chime in and half of the group start to move towards their sheriff.

"That is mighty kind of all of you, but I need you waitin' here while I go alone." Robert quickly stops the protest with a raised hand, "What message will it send the militia if a flock of farmers marches with their sheriff down a hill towards them? It might look like we are tryin' to start some ruckus of our own." Robert sighs, since he really does wish to have his own little army with him, but he continues with confidence. "I will come back shortly and report what I find out." He looks directly at Henry to be the voice of reason in the small crowd. Henry nods at Robert and begins to face the others, putting in his own two-cents worth of logic to which the small crowd begins to slowly agree.

Thankful for Henry's presence, Robert turns to leave the Valley Store behind him and rides across the hill with Oak Grove Church to his right. He hesitates for a moment at the top of the hill, taking in the scene below him with sounds of hammering metal and outbursts of harsh laughter mingled with the smells of burning fires and roasting pork. But missing are the laughing children and lifted hymns. He pulls out his pipe and lights it, takes a deep draw and lets the tobacco ease his nerves. With one hand on the reins and one hand holding his pipe the sheriff descends down to the campground.

It's only a few minutes before a young, nervous guard stops him. "Halt. Who goes there?" Robert can only see the back of the tents, all tightly placed next to each other. From years of meeting inside this campground where the tents create a perfect rectangle, it is clear why the soldiers have chosen this spot, a make-shift fortress, but with walls of canvas. "The Sheriff of this county." Robert speaks with as much authority as he can muster. "I want to speak to your captain or whoever is in charge." Tactically the sheriff chooses to stay mounted, a weak defense, but all he has, short of drawing one of his guns.

"Not possible!" The guard is dressed in a dirty gray jacket with two buttons missing, the only piece of uniform to indicate any particular allegiance. Robert notes that this soldier's blue, not gray, trousers are a few sizes too big and, from the dark red mark clearly visible along the right thigh, probably one he pulled off a dead Union soldier. For the first time, Robert is forbidden from entering the inner yard of Wilson Campground and feels anger surfacing. He takes another draw from his pipe. He questions the wisdom of coming, but remembers that he is not at war with these men. He simply doesn't trust them.

"Sir?" Robert calmly blows out his smoke and says firmly with as much of a cunning smile as he can muster, "It stands to reason your commandin' officer may be unhappy if he finds the local sheriff came by without bein' informed." The soldier frowns, but allows Robert to finish. "But likewise, he may commend the man who makes sure the sheriff does not go away without bein' questioned."

After one moment the young man's eyebrows lift and he smiles ever so slightly. "Wait here!" He yells and turns and runs between two tents to disappear into the inner courtyard. Robert stares straight ahead, hoping he made the right choice to persuade the soldier to grant him audience with a higher-ranking officer.

It isn't long before a young man with lieutenant's bars saunters out and sneeringly asks, "Yeah, who are you and what do you want?" He finishes buttoning up his jacket and looks like he is annoyed his nap was interrupted. The young guard quietly slides up next to his commanding officer, not sure if he has made the right decision to announce the sheriff.

Mae, startled by the loud angry voice, requires calming before the Sheriff can answer the angry greeting. "I am Robert Hamilton, High Sheriff of this County, checking on you and what your plans are here."

The lieutenant walks right up to Mae and grabs her bridle, as close to the bit as he can get and jerks her head to the side. "It ain't none of your business what we are doin' or nothin' else. It is war and we are now the authority. Do you understand that?" Mae stomps her hooves and Robert is trying best to calm her and not show his fury at this man's disregard for his horse.

Robert speaks firmly without losing his feigned appearance of respect, "Of course, Lieutenant. But whenever you leave, my job is to help keep order and I'd appreciate any help you can give or leave me with all your army expertise."

"Well, Sheriff whatever your name is, I got no time for this. Be on your way." The youthful commanding officer lets go of Mae and waves the sheriff away dismissively. However, almost as if he is recollecting his orders, he looks Robert straight in the eye and continues without hostility, "We'll be on our way when we check on the training group up in Cherryfield." He turns his back and marches briskly and with some seeming authority down the eight-foot-wide passage way between two tents. Robert lingers a moment to watch the officer head straight to the central booth, originally set up for the campground evangelist. He does not like the thought of a training area being set up in Cherryfield, still in the County, but several miles further south. He tries to be thankful it is only for training. As the young soldier moves quickly to resume his orders to guard the tent fortress, Robert slowly turns Mae away from the scene as he shakes his head, his only outward display of the great sadness he feels for the desecration of this holy ground.

"Sheriff, that man shore didn't seem to care none!" Pink's voice startles Robert as he is hardly a few feet from the tents. He must have quietly followed the sheriff, and, as he glances up the hill, two other seasoned oaks have pale faces peering from behind them. The situation is clearly a game to the boys. Pink, however, is at Robert's stirrup and glancing up at him with innocence and curiosity.

The sheriff whispers loud enough for Pink to hear. "What in the hell are you doin' Pink? Get yourself clear on up and outa here! Now!"

"Who's that talkin'?" The young guard grabs his rifle and scurries around Mae and is quickly pointing his weapon at Pink, whose audacity is suddenly wiped from his whole being.

"He's only a silly boy. Nothin' to bother over." Robert puts out his pipe and stores it in his coat pocket, aware both hands may be needed. He hopes his calm movements will assure the guard to let this situation dissipate on its own. "I'll make sure he doesn't bother you none." He begins to reach down to grab Pink, whose small dark hand is already reaching for the sheriff.

With the butt of his rifle, the guard knocks Pink to the ground, startling Mae who whinnies and moves sideways. Robert jumps off of Mae and calms her while moving in close to Pink who is whimpering on the ground, blood glistening from his hands that are gripping his head. The guard spits on Pink. "Ain't no slave gonna insult the lieutenant!" He looks at Pink's simple cotton shirt and trousers and a smirk spreads across his face. "Where are your papers, boy?" Pink's eyes, still closed, absorbing the pain, quickly open in terror and glance for a moment into the accusing eyes of the solitary soldier. Suddenly a boot strikes Pink in the stomach. "Don't look me in the eye, you filthy scumb. Ain's you learned your place?"

Robert quickly moves to stand between the guard and Pink. "Sir, I'll make sure he's punished to the fullest. Let me take him."

"Oh, I see you protectin' that slave boy! You ain't gonna punish him none! I think he should get a thrashin' right here."

"What's goin' on?" B.C.'s loud commanding voice emerges from inside the campground tucking a gold coin into his breast pocket. Tony is next to him, carrying two empty baskets, clearly a successful exchange of goods has transpired. Tony's eyes glance at Pink and he stiffens, keeping his face downcast and his shoulders low. Yet, Tony's eyes hold a firm grip on Pink who has stopped whimpering, finding unspoken direction through Tony's unwavering focus. B.C. and Robert exchange glances and no words are needed to assess the gravity of the situation.

"This here slave-boy needs to be shown his place. I'm fixin to holler for the lieutenant to come lash the skin off his sorry ass." The guard loses a little of his appetite for vengeance when he realizes three grown men are moving in closer. "What's all this?" He begins to lift his rifle.

"No need for shootin' or lashin' anybody, friend." B.C.'s voice is calm and he gently pushes the barrel of the gun to face the stirred-up dirt ground. He calmly reaches his finger into his breast pocket to retrieve the freshly earned gold coin. "Looks to me like you could use some new pants, maybe somethin' in gray and not blue." The guard's face reddens and he stares at the gold coin now extended to him in B.C.'s very calm hand. Robert is impressed with his friend's ability to command authority. His clean-cut white beard and impeccable tailoring of his own clothes only remind the guard of how much he could benefit from the coin. "In fact," B.C. adds in a jovial tone, "I am sure I have some fine pants that may fit you. If you head on over to my store later on, I'll be sure to make you look like a distinguished soldier."

The guard swallows and quickly grabs the coin, tucking it into his boot. He then heads right back to his post and turns his head the other way as Tony, without waiting for permission, quickly lifts Pink up off the ground and hands him to Robert, who, back on his horse, settles him best he can across his lap. Pink awkwardly stretches one bloody hand around Robert's neck while still holding his head where the bleeding has slowed some. The Sheriff then urges Mae to gallop up the hill to the Valley store tucked away on the other side.

Only once he reaches the porch does he stop and notice that several local folks are still gathered, including two of the Justices from the County Court, Patton and Paxton. They are in dialogue with Henry, who is clearly filling in all that previously transpired. Suddenly they all turn to watch the scene from a distance. Robert carefully hands Pink to two men who stretch him out on the porch. Amanda Lankford hustles inside the store to gather some bandages. Immediately Robert is barraged with questions.

"What happened to Pink?"

"What do they want?"

"Who are they? Not any of our local troops."

"How long will they be here?"

"Are they looking for deserters or scalawags?"

As the sheriff stands up on the porch next to more than one woman now fussing over Pink, he replies, "Pink didn't follow my directions and was in the wrong place at the wrong time. As to the militia, I cannot answer your questions as they do not wish to talk with us."

"But you are the Sheriff!" a young man yells and the crowd's anger begins to grow. B.C. and Tony arrive, and Tony quickly disappears behind the store with the empty baskets. B.C. walks up to stand next to Robert.

B.C.'s voice booms, "Listen!" For the second time in less than a half hour B.C. has come to Robert's aid. The two justices are clearly pleased to see B.C. standing next to the sheriff, so the two men walk to the porch steps to show their support as well. Robert feels Henry move in to stand next to his brother-in-law.

Henry leans in and whispers, "Are you okay, Bob? Not hurt, are you?"

Robert smiles gently at Henry and answers, "I'm fine. But I reckon I'd much prefer feeding my sheep right now."

"I reckon so." Henry looks out over the small crowd who have finally calmed down. "But, the way I see it, you got to deal with this cantankerous flock right now."

Robert nods and takes a deep breath. He doesn't want to spread more fear than necessary, so he tries to stay calm as he answers, "For the army at war, bein' sheriff is not relevant. I suggest we be nice to them," Robert pauses and glances at Pink who is allowing himself to be bandaged, "Even after what they did to Pink, let them be and go in peace. We don't want to bring more trouble on ourselves than we already have with so many bushwhackers doing their evil deeds and with so many families hungry with fathers and sons away or dead."

"Now go on home, unless you have some business to take care of. In that case come on in and I'll be happy to help you find the supplies you need." B.C. tries to lighten the mood. The two justices laugh, and some others in the crowd chuckle.

Henry says a few final words to Robert and then jumps off the porch to head towards his mare tied up at the hitching post. As the small gathering follow his lead and begin to disperse, they are suddenly stopped when one very nervous man from the upper county Quebec area calls out loudly, "Sheriff, how do we know they will not come back to camp later and take our stock and food like they are doin' down in South Carolina?" The dwindling crowd stops and turns to listen to the farmer. He comes in closer and is speaking to all, not just his sheriff. "I hate to say what my cousins in Greenville County are telling about our own troops comin' through, sayin' they got to feed their troops and animals. Some of my own kin are comin' up here a-beggin' for food for their families 'cause they were cleaned out." The men, women and few young boys have all gathered back together and are once again facing their keeper of the peace. Robert sees Henry has remained with his horse, but has not mounted yet, clearly waiting to hear how Robert will respond.

Robert looks at each one of the fearful faces; some he has known his whole life; others are new to the county, making a fresh start. He glances at B.C. who shakes his head slowly; he has no words. The store-owner is clearly doing business with this militia and they are not desperate enough to plunder. Not yet. So, Robert explains, "I do not know all the rules of war, but have heard that when militia are not supplied from somewhere, they have the right to take what they need to keep goin'." His gaze shifts to the campground not far behind them. He weakly underscores a haunting truth, "At least the lieutenant is not takin' more from us than our sacred campground." He pauses and sees small nods of acknowledgement followed by silence, as individuals finally disperse and go on their way; even Henry decides it is time to ride on home.

Only moments after everyone has left, Robert hears a small voice, "Sheriff?" He turns to see Pink sitting up with his legs dangling over the side of the porch. His head is bandaged and his eyes are filled with tears, "I'm so sorry." He chokes on his sob and Robert lets the boy gather himself together. "I didn't know it could be so bad."

Robert squats down and settles himself on the edge of the porch next to Pink. B.C. stands alone, but doesn't move as he watches the sheriff face the boy. Robert shakes his head. "You were lucky, Pink. You've been lucky your whole life." Robert suddenly has memories of his own brother John-Wesley, who never for a moment trusted whites outside of his family. He had told Robert several times that Robert would never understand what it is like to be black and that only if you were on his side of color could he truly know. Robert misses his brother and hopes that he finds real freedom wherever he is now. Robert sighs and gently pats Pink's leg. Pink is black and white to the folks who know him and yet, to the guard, and to anyone not from around here, he is only black, only a slave. Robert nods his head in B.C.'s direction, "You better thank Mr. Lankford. He bought your hide."

Pink stands up quickly and faces B.C. "Sir, thank you. I'm shore Pa will pay you back."

B.C. nods at the young slave now beholden to him. He laughs suddenly, awkwardly, and gently slaps Pink on his back, "Or your grandpa Frank Allison will take care of it. I'd never hear the end of it, if I'd let someone hurt an Allison!" Then B.C. points in the direction of Little River, "If I were you, I'd hustle outa here before that guard decides to come buy himself some gray pants." Quickly, Pink jumps off the porch and takes off.

B.C.'s smile fades as he turns one last time to acknowledge Robert. A seriousness settles heavily on both of them. Had the loyal Confederate family just helped a slave? Even with his Allison justification, they both know that nothing is easy. Boundaries are blurred for everyone.

Elizabeth Neill, July 30, 1863

"Get up!" Ma's hushed voice pulled me out of my deep sleep and, from the flickering reflection of the candle light on her face, I could tell something was wrong. "Throw these on and pull your hair back." Ma flung a pair of trousers that she and I used interchangeably when either one of us needed to work the garden or field without the nooks and crannies of skirt-layers inviting small critters into their crevices. We never wore the trousers anywhere in public, but I wasn't questioning Ma in the middle of the night, since I at least figured I wasn't going to pull any corn. I did wonder if I was being asked, for the first time, to help hide a deserter or maybe keep watch, so I was quick to obey without question. "And hurry! Pa and Bob are already grabbing empty buckets and will leave without you if you aren't ready. But they really need as many hands as they can get."

I reached under the bed to blindly find one of Pa's old shirts and pulled it out before I threw off my night shift. I was buttoning up the shirt when Ma ran her one free hand through her graying hair, "But I'm goin' to wait here with your brother and sister." She started to pace, like she was not sure if she should haul them out of bed too... they were already sitting up in bed and yawning. Ma waved at me to follow her into the hallway and I obeyed, awkwardly hopping on one foot while pulling up my trousers. Once we were in the hallway, Ma finished her thought, "I'm still not ready for them to be involved. I'm simply not!" Then I realized Ma was asking me for permission to leave them out of whatever crisis I was getting ready to face.

I wrapped the grass rope belt until my trousers were securely in place. We were moving down the stairs when I realized Pa and Uncle Bob were making an awful lot of noise outside yelling at each other, something about buckets; too loud to be implementing a secret mission. At the bottom of the steps I found my boots ready for me and, as I frantically laced them up, I tried to look at Ma, a hard task with the single flicker of a candle. "Ma, I am not sure what is goin' on, but you know better than I do what Jimmy and Sarah-Jane should see or not see." Ma seemed relieved and I realized, for the first time, that I had not yet let her or Pa know that I had moved on from their deceitful approach. In retrospect, I allowed her to suffer, intentionally at first, but then it became second nature, something I was suddenly ashamed of. As I headed to the door, I quickly turned around and slung my arms around Ma's neck, causing her to awkwardly hold her arm out so the candle flame wouldn't set my hair ablaze. Her empty arm, though, hungrily received my embrace and I could feel her body relax as I whispered, "Ma. You are doin' everything right."

I released her. But she held on a moment longer. As she reluctantly let me go, she whispered, "Be careful."

"I will," I confidently replied, carefully shutting the door behind me; then I frowned as I stood on the porch in the dark of night wondering what I was even blindly agreeing to do. The moon was about as full as it was going to get, and it actually seemed brighter outside than inside the house. I guessed it must have been pretty early in the morning since the moon was already creeping towards the tops of the trees heading up Lambs Creek. But there was no sign of dawn. Not yet. Especially since the nocturnal Whip-poor-wills were still busy calling out to each other as they searched for unsuspecting moths, ignoring our unusual night-time commotion.

I could hear Jack whinny in protest as Pa suddenly appeared with the wagon and Uncle Bob on his own horse following close behind. "Let's go!" Pa yelled, and I jumped as quickly as I could onto the back of the wagon, surprised by the joy I experienced from the daring leap my trousers encouraged. Before I was even settled, the wagon lurched forward and I knocked into several pails, all empty.

I tried to lift myself up on my knees enough to get Pa's attention, "What's goin' on?"

Uncle Bob was the one to pull up next to me on his horse while Pa was hustling Jack to move at a quicker pace than his usual gait. My uncle yelled. "The campground is on fire!"

"What?" I frowned.

"Someone is tryin' to burn down Wilson Campground." The wagon lurched, so Uncle Bob pulled away to take the lead. I lowered myself onto the wide boards and held on as best I could. At one point a wooden pail knocked into me, depositing the remains of loose corn-pone. I brushed it off my leg and continued to stare into the night wondering what I was getting ready to face. I knew there had been Confederate soldiers occupying the tents, but they had moved on a few days earlier. As Pa guided the wagon past the church and over the hill, he pulled to a stop next to Uncle Bob who was already shaking his head. I quickly scrambled to my knees again and my heart started to race. It looked like a large crown of fire, like each tent had been deliberately set ablaze. The crackling and popping of the wooden platforms were only outmatched by the sudden collapse of an upper beam, causing any remains of canvas to cave in. The flames only calmed for a minute before the fire suddenly reignited.

"It's too late!" I cried out loud.

Pa ignored me and drew his wagon down the hill, following Uncle Bob. He made a wide birth around the blazing inferno. We found ourselves quickly on the other side of the campground closest to the creek. Hauntingly, the moon and the flickering flames lit up the grimy and horror-stricken faces of several folk who were already creating a feeble water brigade, with too much running and not enough pails. Other wagons were pulling up as we arrived, and I didn't have to be told what to do. I started to throw the pails in the back of the wagon towards any free hands meeting us. I then grasped the last pail with my own hands and jumped off the wagon, and headed straight for the creek. I filled it and handed it to the first pair of reaching hands that would take it, and then I ran to where the empty buckets were being returned and repeated filling buckets. I don't know how much time passed but it was long enough for my initial energy to succumb to a steady deliberate motion. I felt my hands begin to ache, but I pushed through, not daring to complain.

I didn't know who else was around me, not at first. But, as first signs of dawn began to soften the harsh contrast between the dark night and the fire, familiar faces appeared. "You done good, Miss Neill." Tony's voice was the first to draw me out of my intense focus. His hand rested on the bucket I was holding, with water barely reaching half-way, at that point all I could muster to lift. "It's over now. You can stop." I dropped the bucket, letting the water recklessly spill back down the creek bank. I looked up and saw a smoldering fortress.

"What's that?" I pointed into the middle of what remained of the old campground.

"Well, I'll be!" Tony rubbed his aching neck and a smile reached across his face.

Pa suddenly leaned in from the other side of Tony. I hadn't realized he'd been hauling water only a few feet from me. "Well, look at that! The whole campground was burned, except the preacher's booth in the middle."

Tony shook his head in disbelief and walked down to the creek to begin cleaning off some of the grime. Since my trousers, boots and my feet were already drenched, I sat on the muddy bank and sighed as Uncle Bob appeared with an empty bucket that he proceeded to toss next to mine.

With both hands free, Uncle Bob reached for his pipe, "Well, I'll be dogged. Reckon it was bushwhackers?"

Pa shook his head, "Hard to say, but nobody knows or saw it, except for the fire. Could be bushwhackers or angry locals. I'd say at least some of them were either religious or superstitious!"

"How come?" My voice caught them a little off guard as I looked up at the two men, who didn't realize Tony and I were still listening to them.

Pa looked at me and then pointed back at the one standing structure, "They left the preacher's booth. I simply wonder if they thought God might get them if they messed up that little pulpit."

"Well the devil sho has 'em already!" Tony stated to which Pa and Uncle Bob nodded their agreement.

As the pink streaks across the sky gave way to blue, Uncle Bob and Pa took in the scene before them with exhausted neighbors shaking their heads and recalling the night. Others gathered up buckets, and some folk were already picking their way through the smoldering mess to find any salvageable items. Uncle Bob gave Pa a quick firm pat on his back, "Well shucks. I had hoped we could use that special camp ground once again after this awful war to bring our people back together again. Worship and music can do that." I pushed away the heavy knot in my throat, caused by the memory of those celebrations and revivals.

"You are right, Bob," Pa said as he began to reach his hand out to me, eager to head on home, "but I fear our many little churches must do that job. Those community gatherings may be in the past. I understand that the property is supposed to revert to the Wilson family when this mess is over, assumin' it is not likely to be used as a religious campground anymore."

Tony helped us gather up our pails and then headed on up to the Valley Store, which would undoubtedly draw many folks later that day to do business and discuss the night's events. Uncle Bob made his rounds to those still milling around and continued to see if any more evidence had been gathered. After acknowledging that he still had no answers, he walked with Pa and me back to the wagon, "You head on back and get some rest. In the meantime, I need to get word to the county leaders and court justices that their alternate meeting place has been burned." Before he mounted up, he came over to me and awkwardly patted my hand. He never was one to show me much

236

affection, but I could tell he, like Ma and Pa, was trying to make things right. "You sure did your part on the water brigade."

I smiled and gently squeezed his hand, "Sheriff, you didn't do too bad yourself!"

"Your Pa and I are tryin'." He quickly mounted and took off.

I sat up on the bench next to Pa on the ride home and, for the first time, understood that Pa and Uncle Bob were trying to be the law, even when they were breaking it. Pa caught me smiling, "What are you smilin' about."

"Nothin'." I moved in closer to him as he let Jack take his time pulling our wagon home. At one point I rested my muddy face on his shoulder. "Thanks for takin' me with you." He didn't say anything. He didn't need to.

CHAPTER 17

Robert Hamilton, August 1, 1863

Robert is thankful for morning worship at the little Methodist church on Davidson Creek, especially after the events of the past week. After service, Reverend English notices Rhoda heading down the path with all the children, leaving Robert behind to hang around in the shade of the trees, pretending to read the Good Book. He knows his friend needs to talk and, after the last of the other parishioners leave, he walks over to Robert who doesn't hesitate to shoot straight. "Can you be my preacher right now, even outside the walls of that little church behind you?"

Fletcher laughs out loud, but quickly realizes Robert is being serious, "Well, am I not always your preacher?" When the reverend watches his friend's eyes drop to the dirt and the sound of the bustling Davidson River and the lingering hoots of children fills the silence, he realizes his answer is, maybe, not accurate. He waves Robert to come sit on the church stoop with him. Both men lean their backs against the already locked doors; Robert carefully places his Bible next to him. "Okay, so there are times that, maybe, I don't quite seem the 'Man-of-God' that you want me to be, someone without fault or a dark side. But you already know that. So, what is it Bob? Spit it out!"

Robert rests the back of his head against the white-washed oak door. "Fletcher, we both know that what we are a-doin' up Lambs Creek is against these new Confederate States and what most local folks feel. Besides that, it puts my family and your family at great risk."

Fletcher continues to look out towards the river. "Bob, I knew it had to be bothering you. Can I ask a couple of questions?"

Robert sits up and faces Fletcher with curiosity, "Course."

"First, when you were made Sheriff of Transylvania, did they require you to swear an oath of loyalty to the Confederacy?"

"No. Word was just then comin' in from Asheville and Greenville that North Carolina had seceded. Nothing was said."

"So, you did not break a sworn oath."

"Well, no."

Robert slowly pulls out his pipe and lights it as his friend, now his preacher, continues, "Secondly, are you and George Neill doing the best you can to keep peace, collect taxes and help folks in this new county with all the limits you have."

Robert, with the pipe in his mouth answers, almost mumbling, "Well yes. I reckon we work hard tryin' to do that during this awful time. We are simply two men tryin' to cover all this mountain land with only a little help from local rangers and home guard. Mostly old folks with all the able-bodied men gone to war."

"And, Sheriff," Fletcher stands and Robert smiles at the use of his formal title and his friend's court-like tone of voice, "if I may say, you and George have been checking on so many of the families left devastated by the loss or absence of husbands and fathers, folks see you as some kind of savior."

Robert quickly stands, pulling the pipe out of his mouth. "Preacher, that's too far. We are not that, just a-tryin' to do what is right in these trying times."

Fletcher's voice softens again and he settles again on the stoop. He slaps the dirt off the cuffs of his pants and looks right at Robert. "Well, Bob, is what you are doing up Lambs Creek also what is right? You are saving lives!"

Robert settles again next to Fletcher. "In my heart- and for the family and the Neill family- we know it is right. You just preached on love and how great the love is when one 'lays down his life for his friends'. So, we see the risk as based on love."

Fletcher takes a minute and leans over almost as if he is praying. Suddenly, he sits up straight again and quietly asks, "So, does this come down to keeping a secret from the community? Is that what is bothering you?"

Robert blows out a very long plume of smoke. "I reckon so. Big secret it is. I just wonder if it is all right to hide it, even if I know it is the right thing to do."

"Well, Bob, I have an idea. See that Bible on the stoop that you carried here? Tonight, sit down with Rhoda and read the Gospel of Mark."

Robert reaches for his Bible and wipes off the dirt from the step. "How come? Does it tell me such a secret is right or wrong?"

"Just read it and see how many times Jesus tells his followers not to tell something- about who he is and so on. Jesus himself had to tell folks to keep secrets! There's a time to tell and a time not to."

"So, I'm in good company, Preacher?" Robert smiles weakly, still heavily burdened, but he taps Fletcher's arm with his Bible. "I guess you *can* be my preacher when you want to!"

Fletcher returns the smile and stands to head on home to his family. "I reckon so. And I guess you can be my sheriff when you want to! Now go figure out who those damn bushwhackers are that burned our sacred campground!" And with that one statement the old Fletcher returns.

Elizabeth Neill, August 25, 1863

"Make sure you are careful with that plate." Mammaw reminded me, as she did every time I came to stay the night, about how Pappaw had made a trade of two of his fine Jimmie-Neill hats for some uppity dishes. I wondered why she didn't keep them tucked away in her cupboard, but I figured it was the reminiscing that drew her to use them. I loved staring at the blue designs swirling around the edges moving from intricate flower scenes to boats at sea and the center an elaborate garden in front of a fancy home. The boat-at-sea always drew my attention, something I couldn't quite understand. To think about such a large body of water that expanded so far you couldn't see the other side, made my head hurt. We'd learned about it in school, but to see the picture on Mammaw's plates always made me wonder what it was really like. I finished drying the plate and carefully stacked it onto the other three that were already occupying their space on the shelf. I then followed her outside to enjoy the coolness the summer evening offered. "I told you how my Jimmie gave those to me one day." Mammaw sat in her rocking chair as I leaned against the porch railing.

"Yes, Ma'm, many times!" I smiled at her, knowing it didn't make a lick of a difference if I'd heard it before, she was sure to tell me again. I stopped short of telling the story for her as she began. "He'd been goin' on about how we would have to sell a few of our sheep to make up for some hats that he hadn't got paid for." Mammaw's eyes had that familiar twinkle, "But he was one awful liar. I could tell he was up to somethin'." She began rocking softly and I breathed in the gentle breeze and listened to the crickets greet the night. An occasional fire-fly would alight, bringing back memories of my own catching of the docile fire-flies and releasing them back into the night. Mammaw's gentle laughter drew me back to the familiar story, "I knew he was up to no good, but he was still sly as a fox and managed to surprise me one morning when I walked into the kitchen and, sure 'nough, the table was all set with those four beautiful plates."

I couldn't help but smile as Mammaw began to hum her favorite camp meeting song, *I am Bound for the Promised Land,* and I found myself humming with her.

As the moon and the fireflies became brighter and the darkness signaled time to head to bed, a sudden pounding of hooves startled us both. It was coming from the direction of town, and a man was yelling something. Mammaw hustled us into the house, and fumbled behind some brooms, surprising me when she suddenly grasped a rifle. I stayed close to her as she blew out the three candles that offered any light. As the pounding came closer, the man's voice was repeating over and over, "We're under attack… Protect yourselves!" Just as suddenly as he had appeared, the man's yelling faded as the hooves pounded on heading north, in the direction of the Cagle Mill.

Mammaw and I found ourselves sitting on the floorboards leaning against the front door with her rifle straddled across her lap. "What in tarnation was that all about?"

"I don't know, but maybe we should go back outside and look," I feebly suggested. I could feel my heart race, remembering the night at the campground.

I couldn't see her face, but her *humph* told me she wasn't smiling, "Now that ain't protectin' ourselves, now is it?"

I sighed and I settled with placing my head on her shoulder and her patting my knee. We must have sat in the same spot for over a half hour waiting for more hooves and more yelling, but nothing happened. I could feel Mammaw's body begin to relax, and I wondered if she was nodding off, but the sound of a wagon approaching from the north made me jostle her enough so she was paying attention too; after all she had the rifle. The sudden stomping of boots on the porch and the frantic knock on the door, vibrated through our backs, forcing us to stand up as quickly as our stiff legs would allow. "Mrs. Neill? Sarah? Sarah Clayton Neill?"

I could feel Mammaw breathe easier and quickly light a candle, "I'm comin', William." She nodded for me to open the door while she lit a second candle. I opened the door to find Captain William Deavor standing with his suspenders clearly holding up his trousers over a worn night-shirt. His scruffy beard covered most of his face, and one hand anxiously kept combing over his beard and mouth.

He glanced at me and then at Mammaw who was now carrying a candle to the door. "Are you two alright?"

"William, what in the Lord's name is goin' on?" She waved her empty hand around frantically, "Some crazy man come stampedin' through here like the whole Yankee army is a followin' him. But we ain't heard nothin' except you."

Captain Deavor looked away from us and toward town. "I heard too and that's why I came this way to find out more. But I thought I'd make sure you are doin' alright since my Margaret told me I better not return without word from you." Mammaw had been friends with Margaret Deavor since she was a Patton, and I knew that was way long ago.

"You tell Margaret I'm doin' fine, but I sure want to know what is makin' everyone so fretful." Mammaw and I followed Captain Deavor out to his wagon.

"I wish I could have sent my son, James, who sent word that he will soon be assigned to Hendersonville, closer to home. It seems they could use some more hands dealin' with bushwhackers and deserters in the area as well as help with feedin' the troops." He ran his hand over his beard again, "I know, if he were here, he'd already know what is goin' on."

"May we come?" My voice surprised both adults. "Maybe you could drop us both off at my home and take Pa with you."

"That's up to your grandmother." The elderly Captain Deavor said and then looked at Mammaw to see if she agreed with him.

Mammaw looked at me and then looked at him for a minute, clearly contemplating my proposal. "I think that would be a grand idea." She promptly blew out her candle and had Captain Deavor help her up into his wagon. I quickly followed by jumping up into the back of the unfamiliar wagon, but was thankful to find only a few sheaves of freshly cut hay occupying the space. I sat on one of the hay bundles that was close enough to the edge for me to hold on to as the wagon lurched forward. I couldn't believe this was happening again, and I couldn't wait to get home where I always felt safe.

It was only a few minutes before the wagon pulled up and, as Mammaw and I were climbing off the wagon, Pa came running out the door with his own rifle. "What is happenin'?" I led Mammaw up to the porch while Pa and Captain Deavor discussed if they should head up to get Uncle Bob first. Suddenly, I heard Pa yell, "Elizabeth, come here." Mammaw patted my arm and headed inside while I returned to the wagon,

"Yes, Pa?"

"Saddle up Jack and head up to Uncle Bob. Tell him somethin' is happenin' heading south and we don't know what yet." He jumped up on the wagon and then looked at me. "Then ride with Uncle Bob until you find us. That way William can take his wagon home and you and I can ride Jack." He didn't wait for me to repeat any of the instructions, but glanced for a minute at Ma who was now standing on the porch, alone. She nodded and then went inside closing the door behind her as I ran to the barn.

* * *

Uncle Bob and I rode steadily and swiftly side by side, past the Valley Store and Oak Grove Church, both of which were completely dark. I could feel the absence of the campground to my right as we began to encourage our horses to gallop. As we headed towards what was designated as Brevard's center, we followed the dirt road to the left as it wound up the small hill that would one day hold our courthouse. Pa had told me the plans were in place, but funding the project was not possible since the war was eating up any money that might have, under other circumstances, been available. A George Clayton and Ephraim England had already made plans on building a temporary courthouse, and were eager to get started. As we rode past Lankford's beautiful home, lit up from inside, we saw that several wagons and people ahead of us were gathered at what can only be considered the top of the hill. Torches burning made the scene so frightening, but I kept myself from cowering and running in to see if Mrs. Lankford would let me wait with her. I was slightly comforted when I saw Pa in the distance, standing on Deavor's wagon, attempting to calm the crowd.

Once Uncle Bob and I reached them, we finally heard someone, who was frantically pointing, say *Dunns Rock* and *Hume Hotel*, so both Uncle Bob and I turned our heads to look at a faint light high in the night sky coming from far in the distance. Another fire. A massive fire if it was in the Dunns Rock community.

244

Pa's voice boomed, "We don't know who set the Hume Hotel afire."

Uncle Bob jumped off of his horse and asked, "How do we know it's the Hume hotel?" Pa simply pointed to a young black boy who was shaking and holding onto a gelding that had no saddle. Uncle Bob frowned, clearly not sure who this boy was and approached him, "Son, can you tell me what happened?"

The boy, maybe no older than ten, nodded and first asked, "Are you de sheriff?"

Uncle Bob nodded, "I am."

"Good. Ma told me I couldn't come home till I talked to de Sheriff."

"Your Ma?" Uncle Bob was clearly confused.

"Betty. Missus Hume's Betty." The boy was hoping that the sheriff knew what he was saying, because his eyes were moving between the flickering torches and all the white faces.

"Yes, I know your Ma." Uncle Bob smiled, setting the boy at ease. "Go on. Tell me what happened."

"Not too shore. But some fellas come and set the hotel afire." The boy pulled and fiddled with the reins causing his gelding to whinny. "Ma told me I should come and tell that no one was kilt." He swallowed, "And since Mr. Hume is gone on business, Miss Hume is safe tonight with Ma and Pa."

"In the slave house around the corner from the hotel?" Uncle Bob asked.

"Yes sir." The boy held his head up in spite of some of the shocked responses. He added, "But they'll move her tomorrow . . . somewhere... probably the Hanckle house, on Chestnut Hill. They's her friends." Murmurs of agreement rippled through the small crowd.

"How'd you get here without getting' hurt by the men who burned the hotel?"

"Pa told me to head on in as fast as I could to tell and that I'd be all right since de men wusn't headed towards Brevard." The boy shuffled again awkwardly, feeling quite overwhelmed by the whole evening.

"Was Babe Cooper's distillery also set ablaze?" Uncle Bob asked.

The distillery was around the bend from the hotel, so we all suspected that it would have been an easy target to burn along with the hotel. But the boy shook his head. "No sir. Seems dey pick whiskey over people's lives."

"Looks like you may be right." Uncle Bob patted the boy's shoulder, "You done good. Tell your folks I'll be out to talk with Mrs. Hume in the mornin'."

"Yes sir." The boy jumped back up on his horse and took off clearly thankful to head on, even into the dark of night.

Uncle Bob jumped up to stand on the wagon with Pa and addressed the crowd, "We will deal with this in the mornin' when we have daylight. The men who did this appear to be gone and Mrs. Hume is clearly safe. There's nothin' else we can do except let me know if you hear of any suspicious talk." There was more nodding and agreement, and soon everyone was heading home, including Captain William Deavor and his wagon.

Before long, the moon was the only light left to give up any sense of where we were standing. I looked around at the small town we were trying to build and wondered how many more places would burn before the war was over? I knew everyone was afraid for their own homes, their own crops, their own lives. As if reading my thoughts, Pa said to Uncle Bob who was mounting his horse. "At least no lives were lost."

Uncle Bob waited for Pa to mount up behind me and, as we began to trot back down the dirt road heading out of Brevard's center, he finally responded, "Not yet."

Robert Hamilton, August 26, 1863

The fresh biscuits and ham offer some comfort after Robert's very restless night. He worries that maybe neighbors around the county will build more distrust among each other because he has asked them, both at the campground and last night, to listen and report any suspicious talk or behaviors. He gulps down the last of his coffee. The woody chicory flavor reminds him of the simple pleasures he takes for granted that are impacted by the war and states to Rhoda, "I need to leave now and go out to Dunns Rock."

"Can you tell me why?" Robert's wife frowns slightly as she begins to clear the empty bowls. Robert quickly stands, and it only takes one look from their father for the procrastinating children to jump up and clear the rest of the table. Millie steps up to her mother and grabs the bowls in her hands, "I got this, Momma." Rhoda gently smiles and then nods at her husband to step onto the porch with her.

Robert follows his wife down the porch steps to stroll along the road. The cool morning breeze will soon give way to the summer heat, so Rhoda takes a deep breath to calm her nerves as she waits for him to speak. He grabs her hand and lets their leathery fingers intertwine. His voice is deep and gentle, but cautious, "I need to try to figure out more about the burnin' at the campground and the Hume Hotel. Do you remember what I told you last night?"

Rhoda takes a deep breath, "Yes, the bushwhackers burned down the Dunns Rock Hotel. It's awful! I bet there's nothin' left but the stone." Robert squeezes his wife's fingers. She won't cry. She won't show fear. But he knows she worries. But her support remains unwavering.

Robert stops at the edge of the barn and looks at his wife. "One of Hume's slaves told me last night that Reverend Hanckle, from the nearby St. Paul's in the Valley Episcopal Church, has put Mrs. Hume up at his house right now."

"And you want to go speak to her?" Rhoda asks a little relieved.

"Yes," Robert is a little confused. "What did you think I was going to do? Hunt down some bushwhackers single handedly?"

Rhoda rolled her eyes, "Well . . . maybe!"

A loud guffaw echoes all the way into the house, making the children feel relief, although they don't know from what. After Robert pulls himself together, he manages to kiss his wife's smiling face. "I may be stubborn, but I'm not stupid!"

Rhoda leans into her husband. "I'll be the judge of that!"

* * *

As the heat begins to claim the day, Robert is relieved as Mae trots under a lush canopy of chestnut trees, still unperturbed by the sweltering heat, and then ascends a small hill to the beautiful Hanckle house, fittingly know as Chestnut Hill, overlooking the river. He lifts his hand and waves, followed by a "whoop", as he approaches the large two-story home. He does not want to startle any folk fearful of strangers, especially after last night's terror. As he approaches, he is thankful he is recognized as sheriff by the waiting party on the porch whose guns are tactfully laid down. "Hello, Sheriff, we've been expectin' you."

Robert dismounts and ties Mae to a nearby post. He steps up onto the porch and heartily shakes the hands of Rev. J.S. Hanckle and two other men, a seemingly large group to be actively guarding this home. Robert asks, "Is Mrs. Hume available? I need to speak with her. I need her help."

The men nod at their sheriff and, as the reverend turns to head into the house, he quickly steps back as the usually exuberant Mrs. Hume, looking stately, steps from behind the door and asks, "Hello, Sheriff, how may I be of help?" She does not move beyond the door frame. Her eyes cautiously scan the road and the trees.

For a moment Robert glances over his shoulder to see if someone else is coming. Realizing her recovery from the burning of her hotel will take time, he quickly returns to his task at hand. Taking off his hat, he offers his condolences and listens to her recollection of details. Once Mrs. Hume is clearly finished, Robert asks her about a particularly curious detail, "Ma'am, word is out that before those awful men burned your hotel out, one of them warned you just before and thus saved your life."

Mrs. Hume nods slowly. "That's about the essence, Sheriff."

Not wanting to upset her, he tries to change the urgency in his voice to an air of casual conversation, "Did he perchance say more, anything else about fires, destruction or folks hunting them?" He leans against the side of the building as he waits for her to answer.

She shifts her weight and relaxes against the door frame, "Not that I remember. Wait. There was some odd comment about 'God not

protecting them campers anymore.' Does that make any sense to you?"
She seems genuinely curious, some of her fearful state giving way.

Robert chuckles slightly, "Yes. And I am much obliged."

Rev. Hanckle sits back down on to one of the roughly hewn benches
that had been tactically placed for watching the road. He clears his
throat and asks, "Would you share with us what this strange statement
might mean?"

"Of course." Robert stands up straight again so he can address his
entire audience. "It seems that the same rascals that burned the Hume
Hotel also burned the Wilson Methodist Campground where your
Episcopal Church folks also held services from time to time. It now
looks as if the evil purpose was to keep the troops from camping there
again and maybe capturing or stopping the bushwhackers' outlaw
activities. Army troops are far more threatening to bushwhackers than
me and my deputy George. Seems like the hotel was another place that
could be used to benefit a large gathering and they weren't goin' to wait
and see."

Those listening are not sure they all agree, thinking Robert gives
bushwhackers too much credit for actually having a plan, but they are
willing to listen to Robert's arguments. As the conversation turns to
crops and weather, Hamilton feels relief. If his suspicions are correct
that the bushwhackers had committed both crimes, then some county
residents were most likely not the perpetrators, unless of course they
were secret members of those bushwhackers. He quickly pushes that
thought away and enjoys some needed casual talk. As he leaves, he
says, "And Reverend Hanckle, not sure if I ever said to you how much
I appreciated your preaching at the Oak Grove Methodist Church
formal opening back some years ago. Good that you folks could use it
so much during the summer as well. We all have to work together." He
rides off feeling a little uncomfortable that maybe he overly played the
"together" bit since most local slave-holders were in his congregation.

CHAPTER 18

Elizabeth Neill, September 1, 1863

I climbed up and settled myself on the roots that twisted and curved into a saddle, still my favorite spot along Lambs Creek, but I didn't come to play. I opened a small envelope where James had roughly scribbled my name on the front, a hurried feel that his handwriting continued to display through the whole letter. His usual calm and intentional lettering with few errors and carefully planned out words had given way to raw emotion and a haunting fear.

Dearest Elizabeth,

I am at a loss why I have not heard from you. Your letters are my hold to what is good and right in this world. I fear any letters you have sent have assuredly been lost in delivery as we no longer remain very long in one place. I long for news from home. How are Amanda and my sweet nieces? Those young girls' laughter could be a precious remedy to lighten the melancholy that abounds. I long to see your auburn hair and blue eyes. I know it is futile to have such home-sickness. Please keep writing, even if they do not all reach me. At least I know you are thinking of me. Tomorrow we continue our march toward Cumberland Gap in Tennessee. It is worrisome. Hug Amanda and the girls from me. With God's protection I will soon be home.

With greatest fondness, Your James

I sighed and felt such a deep connection to James that I had feared was lost in the midst of our separation. I knew then why he longed for my letters since they gave him the same closeness that his shared with me. Guilt welled up inside of me because all the letters that he dared to believe had been lost had never been written. I had felt any letter leaving out *the secret* would be a letter full of lies, but I knew at that moment that I was wrong, very wrong. I dismounted my root-saddle and scurried home to write James about everything that he would want to know: about the occupation of the camp-ground, about the fires, about his family and, most importantly, about how I missed him too. They were all truth and I didn't want him to miss out any longer on the day-to day life of our community, a community and people that he drew strength from.

Robert Hamilton, September 2, 1863

The rain has been relentless since dawn and finally causes Robert to seek some shelter, at least until the downpour gives way to a steady drizzle. He is thankful to have an excuse to head into Lankford's Valley Store to catch up on news from around the county. As expected, the store has several men already gathering under the porch cover, sharing news, rumors, and war stories as well as discussing where creeks are rising and what fields are already flooding. Others disappear through the door to reappear with a fresh can of tobacco, reminding Robert his own tobacco is running low.

One face surprises Robert. "Well, hello Captain Duckworth," Robert reaches out and shakes Duckworth's hand, "How goes it with our new home guard?" Robert had wondered how long it would be before the army hired Duckworth to seek out deserters, without needing the local law's permission, and was not surprised when word came.

Duckworth straightens his military cap and Robert can see the young man is proud. "Sheriff, I'm not used to the title. I've only been doin' this a month and only found a couple of deserters and no bushwhackers.

251

Not easy in these mountains with so many hidin' places. I even heard some deserters were hidin' on that ledge in the middle of Dunns Rock, but I can't get to them or catch their women droppin' food in baskets from the top."

"Captain?" A voice yells from the side of the porch closest to the front door causing both men to turn and look. Robert recognizes James Clayton, the county's first coroner.

"Yes, Lieutenant?" Duckworth responds officially. Robert raises his eyebrows surprised to hear the county's coroner being referred to as a lieutenant.

Clayton points at the front door and yells, "I'm headin' insides for some supplies."

"Make sure to see if Lankford's got anymore coffee and grab a box of cartridges." Duckworth nods his head towards Robert. "I'll sit a spell with the sheriff here."

Clayton acknowledges Robert with a single nod. "Sheriff."

"James." Robert responds, realizing maybe he should have said lieutenant, but was clearly confused. Clayton does not seem bothered and quickly disappears inside.

Seeing the confusion of Robert's face, Duckworth explains, "James Clayton is also part of the home-guard and my lieutenant."

"I see." Robert contemplates the news a moment before he adds, "Seems a mighty fine addition to the home-guard having the local coroner on hand." Robert wonders for a moment if he has offended Duckworth, who takes his responsibilities very seriously. To his relief the captain chuckles.

"So true!" Duckworth smiles and motions to Robert to sit a spell with him.

Robert and the new captain settle on two empty chairs and Robert lights his pipe. He contemplates the previous information concerning Dunns Rock. "Well, I'll be dogged, Captain, about that news. You know, the trouble with people hidin' under the ledge. I reckon there may have been some bushwhackers up there too and could be some connection to burnin' Hume Hotel."

Duckworth, pleased to have contributed the information, smiles. "I reckon there is."

The thunderous burst of rain causes Robert to raise his voice. "Deserters are one thing, but for my work as sheriff, the bushwhackers are far worse with all the evil deeds, the murders, rape, theft, and all. The difference is that the deserters are tryin' to take care of their families and crops. The bushwhackers are thieves and outlaws taking advantage of this war opportunity to do their evil deeds."

Duckworth is suddenly taken aback. "Are you defendin' the deserters, Sheriff?"

Robert, realizing he may have overestimated the level of friendly discussion, tries to ease the sudden challenge in the captain's voice. The sheriff shakes his head and answers, "Just noting big differences. That's all."

After a grunt, audible even over the relentless deluge of water hitting the porch roof, Duckworth leans back in his seat and crosses his arms. "Well, Sheriff Hamilton, since we are on the topic, can you figure out or guess when somebody is about to desert or supports the other side?"

Stealing time to respond, Robert takes another slow draw from his pipe, wondering where this is going and whether Duckworth has suspicions that could impact Lambs Creek. He finally asks, "What do you mean?"

Keeping his arms tightly crossed, his eyes are clearly scrutinizing the sheriff. "It has to do with one of your relatives, Robert Franklin Hamilton. Did you not wonder about him and his getting out of our army with blood coming out of his mouth?"

"Can't say that I did. Wonder what?" Robert does his best to look Duckworth in the eye, realizing he blatantly lied, but did not feel beholden to the home-guard. Family business is family business.

Duckworth slings one arm out pointing nowhere in particular. "I saw him when he first got back and saw him spit blood. I thought it was from his mouth, not his stomach or lungs like he said."

Robert nods and frowns as if concerned. "Captain, I did not see that, but I have the feelin' you are wonderin' about more."

Duckworth leans in and Robert can see an intensity building. "As you may know, he has been home about a year now and last week his wife delivered a baby boy."

Robert, surprised by the seriousness of the statement, laughs and says, "That does happen when couples get together!"

Duckworth suddenly stands up and paces, shaking his head. "You have no idea!" He finally turns and faces Robert who is holding his pipe, but remains seated, not sure where this is going. Duckworth smirks, "Did you know, Sheriff, that they named that boy Thomas Lincoln Hamilton?"

Robert's surprise is genuine. He feels his mouth drop and suddenly he realizes he is sweating. With his Uncle Joe fighting on the Union side and other family members being questioned, he decides to respond very carefully. "No, I had not heard that the baby had arrived, or named such."

Duckworth suddenly smiles at the genuine shock on Robert's face and then comes over to settle back in his seat. "Maybe you didn't know that Thomas is the name of Abraham Lincoln's youngest son." Robert is aware that Duckworth is unable to name him as 'President Lincoln," but chooses not to say anything as Duckworth adds, "You think there is any clearer sign of loyalty to the Union?"

"I reckon not." Robert lifts his pipe, but then stops with sudden concern and quickly asks, "Where is my cousin now?"

The captain shakes his head and waves his hand dismissively, "With his baby Lincoln, I guess. I can't arrest a man for what he names his baby, now can I?"

Relieved, Robert lifts his pipe again, "I reckon not."

Duckworth smiles and adds, "But I've got my eye on him."

"I'm sure you do," Robert weakly smiles back, but carefully steers the conversation to how family is faring and what other news is brewing. Robert listens half-heartedly, and is relieved when a steady drizzle sets in.

Elizabeth Neill, September 16, 1863

September came quickly with more sad news from so many families about their men and the increasing poverty at home. The need for help was almost stifling. Ma and Aunt Rhoda helped Pa and

Uncle Bob as best they could to distribute what neighbors were willing, but more accurately, able, to provide. The mud had finally hardened enough for me to hitch up Jack to the wagon and make rounds to some community folk who had indicated they could provide some needed supplies, especially with the growing chill of the fall nights taking longer to be chased away by the morning sun. Blankets and clothing were in need in addition to the basic food staples. I was happy though, most of all, because Viney was making the rounds with me. I pushed away the reality that Ma insisted I didn't travel alone anywhere anymore, not until the war was over. At first, I was upset with the restriction, but I muffled my objections once I realized it meant that Viney and I could spend more time together.

We giggled most of the way to the Patton house and caught up on any gossip. She filled me in that James-Henry Cagle was still sweet on Emma-Rachel and he had yet to enlist in the Union Army, something all neighbors had suspected he would have done long ago. Emma-Rachel was happy since it meant she didn't have to worry about him going off and getting killed. I listened to Viney talk and talk, but the more she talked the more our giggles gave way to serious concerns and some naïve strategizing of our own. At one point she suggested that, when James came back, I should hide him up the holler until the war was over, but she and I knew it was silly wishful thinking. Our voices soon gave way to silence as we turned the last corner and faced the beautiful home in front of us. Mrs. Patton's slave, Jesse, and his grandson, Riley met us and Jesse took Jack by the reins as I jumped into the back of the wagon to hand Reily some empty baskets and burlap sacks.

"I'll take that, Miss Neill." A familiar voice drew my attention and, at first, I didn't recognize Pink. It wasn't because he was taller than me now, it was his unfamiliar distance.

I handed him the last two sacks and smiled, "Hi there, Pink. I haven't seen you in some time. You need to come around again, Sarah-Jane and Jimmy have been askin' about you."

Pink's eyes glanced to Jesse who, I could tell, was shaking his head ever so slightly at Pink. Pink dropped his eyes and answered, "Thank you Miss, but I ain't comin' round no more." Something snapped and I couldn't help myself. Before Pink knew what was happening, I grabbed him by the front of his shirt and tugged him over to the side of the wagon where Jesse wasn't standing. We must have been a sight, especially since he was looking down at me, but I was still older and he knew it. "Since when do you not go where you want to go?"

Pink swallowed and gently lifted his hands to carefully pry my hand off his shirt. "Miss Neill." He then lifted his eyes and looked right at me. The Pink I knew spoke. "Ever since I was almost killed by that soldier." He gently touched his head. "You didn't see none of it, Miss Neill, but it was somethin' awful." This time I dropped my eyes, because Uncle Bob had told me what had happened. I never figured anything could change Pink.

"Miss?" Jesse's voice interrupted my private moment with Pink. He kept his eyes down cast, "I think it better if Pink help carry the sacks now."

"No!" I said defiantly. This made Jesse stand still since he wasn't sure what else to say and didn't dare.

"Elizabeth!" Viney's voice pulled me back from my rage, just long enough to realize I had just treated Jesse like a slave. Something I had never done before. "What has gotten into you?"

I looked at Pink who was standing wide-eyed on one side of me and then glanced at Jesse whose eyes were downcast and he was slowly retreating. I felt tears well up, yet Jesse deserved an explanation. "Mr. Jesse, I only spoke harshly to you because I don't want you treatin' Pink like a slave. I've never seen Pink as a slave and you're not goin' to turn him into one right in front of my eyes!"

"Confound it, Elizabeth! That's enough!" Viney was looking around frantically, "I'm afraid Mrs. Patton's not much goin' to like you makin' a fuss like this. She's bound to step out on that porch right soon."

"Miss Neill," Pinks' voice was familiar again, "Thank you, but you ain't gonna change who I am." Pink straightened his shirt and smiled, "Even if you are as strong as an ox."

I couldn't help smile, "Now that's more like it!" I turned to face Jesse. "Mr. Jesse?"

He lifted his eyes, "Miss, I'm only protectin' not hurtin'." I could see I had offended him, but then his serious intensity softened and he added, "But I see you doin' the same." I nodded and he suddenly brought us back to the task at hand, "Pink, Riley, let's fill up these baskets and sacks so Mrs. Patton can visit with the ladies." Riley and Pink quickly scrambled to follow Jesse's lead.

I turned my head and Mrs. Patton was rocking in her rocking chair on the porch waving at Viney and me to join her. My face grew red and I looked at Viney who whispered, "I swear I didn't see her." Neither one of us knew how long she'd been sitting there.

As we walked towards her and stepped onto the porch, we timidly settled together on the one long bench. "So good of you girls to gather the supplies for those in need. The need is only going to grow." She unfolded a newspaper that was sitting in her lap. "It seems the South has been dealt another crippling blow."

"Ma'am?" I tried to read the black letters from where I was sitting but could only make out the date, September 9th. "What are you saying?" I tried to sound as proper as I could. Mrs. Patton was a fine lady with a heart for everyone, and she was well read and educated. "We haven't heard the recent news."

"Well," She lifted the newspaper to check her facts before returning it to its folded state. "It seems the Confederate army surrendered at Cumberland Gap. In fact, North Carolina's 64th Infantry regiment was totally disbanded, and prisoners were taken captive if they weren't killed." As I felt the blood rush to my head, I barely heard her add, "I know many of our local boys were in the 64th. May God bless their souls."

I don't remember much more of that moment except Viney, once again, yelling at me to pull myself together because, as she informed me later, I obsessively repeated, *James, James, James* over and over again until Viney explained to Mrs. Patton that James was a part of the 64th. She apologized profusely and, once Jesse and the boys had loaded grains, apples and cured meats along with some blankets onto the wagon, Viney quickly thanked her and said goodbye. She then took the reins and, as we turned the corner, leaving the Patton house in the distance, I began to sob uncontrollably.

Robert Hamilton, October 18, 1863

The hues of orange, red and yellow leaves are still brilliant as fall demands attention in the midst of the war-stricken nation. Rhoda and Robert, along with their children, have joined several church members and others living along the Davidson River and up Avery Creek to gather at the Young's home for a pot-luck after church. Even the Tinsley and Osteen families have traveled from way up the river where they live in close proximity to the large rock mountain known as Looking Glass and the powerful waterfall nearby, bearing the same name. It is a rare moment of festivity, and Robert enjoys watching what feels, in part, like a Young family gathering. Fletcher and Naomi greet Emma-Rachel and James-Henry, who is now openly courting the Young girl. Rhoda leaves Robert to gather Naomi's toddler into her arms while Martha-Ann takes her youngest granddaughter out of Fletcher's arms and cuddles her with delight. Ladies of the church eagerly set up two wooden tables and place the food they can offer to the collective table to share. It is not the lush spread of fixings that the small community is accustomed to, but it is still enough to share. Some families clearly come empty-handed, but are eager to help prepare the tables and are outwardly thankful for inclusion in the fellowship, a clear message Reverend English emphasized only moments ago in the small church. All are to feel welcome. Robert smiles at the thought that no one would dare miss coming, and clearly want to avoid the likelihood that Fletcher would reprimand them for not feeling welcome.

Rhoda suddenly leaves Robert's side as she spots Maria and Henry Mackey appearing from the other side of the Young's home, followed by their five children that are still at home and not off to war. Their son, also named Strawbridge, is fifteen and is carrying his brother Alex, who is four, on his shoulders. The three girls, Martha-Jane, Sarah and Harriet, all suddenly slow to a stroll together with Harriet rolling her eyes at her older sisters who are trying to fix their hair-ribbons. Rhoda embraces Maria, since it has been a while since the sisters have had time to catch-up. Henry, realizing his wife is otherwise occupied, quickly moves towards the tables, eager to deliver the fixings in the two baskets he is carrying.

As Sunday dinner is still in preparation, Robert heads over to the random collection of indoor chairs and rockers added to the out-door weather-beaten benches and chairs to make a larger setting for visiting. Joshua, who did not come to church that morning, is already sitting in one of the stiff-backed chairs, eyeing every parishioner that comes to greet him and then, after an awkward moment, quickly moves on to speak with someone else. Joshua clearly continues to suffer at home, not only from his emotional trauma of the war, but also from constant grave news of Confederate losses. Martha-Ann told Rhoda that her wounded son tries to help around the house and garden but cannot do much. Like many other church members from the little chapel on Davidson River, now sometimes also called Young's Chapel, Rhoda and Robert try to offer as much support as possible; but they find that often it is simply best to listen to him relive his trauma, a burden they are willing to share.

Robert sits next to Joshua; both take in the bustling of friends and family and seem content to settle into respectful silence. The peaceful moments are short-lived as Fletcher and Strawbridge make their way to join them. "Reverend." Joshua acknowledges Fletcher with a brief nod.

"You seem to be faring better each time I see you." Fletcher pats Joshua on the shoulder before sitting on the other side of him.

"He is doin' as best he can." Strawbridge answers for his son, whose gaze has already drifted to the sudden burst of laughter from two boys armed with long sticks pointed at each other, screaming *pow, pow*. The

259

youngest boy yells at the older one that he shot first and that the other one should die. Fletcher jumps to his feet and encourages the boys to play along the creek, a little way beyond where all the people are trying to visit. The boys obediently move on with the sounds of *pow, pow* fading. Strawbridge nods his thanks and then continues, "Never know what will take Joshua's mind away. It can even be the sudden flash of lightning and thunder that has always been a regular sign of mountain life, a time to get out of the rain and set a spell."

He then runs his hand through his curly hair, "Then there's been no word from my other boys, not since the battle of Chickamauga. Word has it that the Union Army used the Spencer repeating rifles and thousands died, no final count yet."

Robert had heard the battle of Chickamauga had been a victory for the Confederate army, but with great losses. He tries to encourage his friend, "Let's hope your boys have simply not found time to send word yet." Robert knows his words are weak, but he sees Strawbridge nod his head, thankful for at least a positive word.

Joshua suddenly stands up, eyes focused again. "Ain't likely! I know they're dead!" His eyes turn to Robert, but they hauntingly stare through him. "I feel it! The damn Yankees kilt them!"

"Joshua!" Strawbridge stands too, "Don't talk that way. We don't know."

Joshua's eyes move from Robert to his father and then he tucks his head awkwardly and begins to slowly shuffle towards the creek where the two boys are still playing. The men left behind barely hear him answer, "I know."

"He's been prophesying for days, and Martha-Ann and I don't know how to keep his mind and spirit well." Strawbridge feels he needs to explain his son's behavior.

It's Fletcher who responds quickly, "We all are on the edge of being haunted. My own dreams wake me full of images that I can't even begin to share without frightening Naomi." Fletcher is still following the shuffling image as the wounded soldier finally settles on a bench along the creek. "God's got his own way of speaking to each of us."

Strawbridge looks at his son-in-law and gently smiles, "I think you'll make a fine preacher after all." Then Strawbridge's smile falters, "Even when you continue to endanger my daughter and her children."

"I think it's almost time for prayin' over Sunday dinner," Robert interrupts, as he looks around anxiously. He hopes no-one heard Strawbridge's last comment, although it is likely only the three of them know what he is referring to.

To Robert's relief, Fletcher does not challenge his father-in-law but nods accepting the truthful statement. Strawbridge takes a deep breath and pulls himself together before he stands, "Yes, let's pray."

Once the three men join the bustling congregation all clustered around the tables, Strawbridge, being the host, offers up a lengthy prayer, clearly reminding those gathered of his own earlier preacher status.

To Robert's relief, he is able to enjoy a plateful of cornbread, fried okra and a sliver of ham accompanied by simple talk. He welcomes advice on the best fishing holes as children's playful banter fills the background.

As the afternoon begins to wind down and a few families have begun to say their goodbyes, those left are surprised to hear a rider approaching. Robert quickly moves away from the circle of chairs and checks his Colt, but still leaves it holstered. He moves around the corner of the house and is surprised to find Captain Duckworth briskly drawing near. As Duckworth approaches, he yells, "Got a letter for the Strawbridge family, Sheriff." He pulls a letter out of his coat pocket and waves it.

Robert takes his hand off of his holster and walks towards the horse. "Well, this is a surprise. Thanks for bringing it. Must be pretty important for Lankford to send it up with you on a Sunday. Never thought you were one to deliver mail."

Captain Duckworth smiles, "I told him I was headed this way since it is quite the holler known for suspicious activity. Never know when I might run into a deserter."

Robert swallows and waves for Duckworth to follow him around the house, "We are havin' a church gatherin', at least some of us are left.

261

You're welcome to deliver the letter and I'm sure we can find you some food."

Captain Duckworth seems pleasantly surprised with the possibility of eating and immediately dismounts, a successful deterrent for continuing the conversation of scrutinizing the holler. As they join the rest of the congregation and neighbors with greetings, some more guarded than others, Henry suddenly steps forward and shakes hands with Duckworth and Robert moves in not caring if the behavior may seem rude. Duckworth, though, doesn't hesitate to respond to Robert's presence by addressing him directly. "Well, Sheriff, this here James Mackey is my newest member of the home-guard." Robert fails to cover his surprise and looks right at his brother-in-law, hoping he will tell the captain to stop joshing.

Robert's stomach begins to feel queasy as Henry nods, removing any doubt. "I figure since my two oldest are fightin' for the South I better do my part as best I can. Captain Duckworth has assured me that he will only call for me when he needs men."

Robert forces himself to speak and finds some relief in the fact that Henry won't be on the hunt every day. "I reckon that will be good to have the home-guard right here on the Davidson River." Robert has to remind himself that Henry lives close to the Cagle Mill, where he is probably keeping his eye on James-Henry. His eyes betray his thoughts as he glances over at Emma-Rachel and James-Henry who are sitting together and laughing.

Duckworth and Henry both absorb Robert's thoughts, causing Duckworth to snicker, "Yes, it will help keep an eye on suspicious activities." Robert, embarrassed that he is so transparent, notices that Henry is not laughing. It is a burden he is bearing, but he is doing it to honor his boys, not to play a game of spy-master.

Interrupting the private conversation, Martha-Ann brings Duckworth a small plate of food, enough to make anyone grateful. "Thank you, Mrs. Young." He gently takes the food and then quickly remembers, "Oh yes, I came to give you this letter." He hands Martha-Ann the small envelope and then makes himself comfortable on one of the open benches.

Martha-Ann takes a minute as she stares at the envelope and then looks at Strawbridge who quickly comes to her. She barely whispers, "It's from my brother. Leander wrote us." Her hands begin to shake and she hands the letter to her husband.

As Robert and Rhoda quickly come to stand next to their friends, the whole family begins to gather. The remaining guests and parishioners remain seated along with Duckworth who is enjoying the last corn on the cob. Strawbridge suddenly hands the letter to Robert, "Please read it for us."

Robert does not hesitate; his voice is loud enough for any dwindling conversations to dissolve.

> *Claytonville NC*
> *Oct 8th 1863*
> *S Young & Family*
>   *Dear Relations.*
>   *It is my painful duty to inform you that I greatly fear that your son John was killed at Ringold. Mr. Gullick's son wrote to his father that John Young of Capt Gashes company was killed with three others of the Battalion on Friday evening at the commencement of the fight. He named no others. We therefore conclude the three other men were from some other neighborhood. We have not a word from the other boys and fear more of them may have been killed since then. The Lord only knows why so many of the innocent are taken whilst so many of the guilty escapes. It may be that they are taken from greater troubles yet in reserve for us. We must submit as best we can. That is our duty to ourselves and few remaining friends yet alive but really there seems to be but little left worth living for. I hope we will get the particulars soon. I have feared there was bad news is why we are so long getting the news. We are all well as usual.*
>   *Your affectionate Brother,*
>   *LS Gash*
>   *S & M A Young*

The sudden wail released from Martha-Ann's soul is only matched by her daughters' sudden sobbing. Strawbridge can barely hold up his wife, causing him to quickly join her as she crumbles to the ground. Fletcher and James-Henry each console Naomi and Emma-Rachel as Robert and Rhoda ease themselves to the ground with their friends. No words, only desperate cries of anger and sorrow fill the small clearing where the vibrant colors continue to boast beauty that can't find time to mourn. It is only the soft shuffle of Joshua that causes Robert to lift his head. The wounded Confederate soldier looks straight at Robert this time and, without-emotion, states, "I told you." Then he turns and heads back to his spot at the creek.

As the initial shock and agony gives way to the reality that the afternoon is waning and people must soon return to their homes, Martha-Ann and Strawbridge disappear into their home without a word as the remaining folk clear the area of any left-over signs of the festivity. Chairs are returned and goodbyes quietly whispered. Even Duckworth helps Joshua into the house, speaking in whispers about Confederate woes.

As Captain Duckworth un-hitches his horse, he asks Robert to join him for a bit. Robert obliges and walks alongside the young man as he leads his horse to the other side of the house. On the other side, the two men observe the Mackey family ahead of them disappear into the forest as they head on home. Once they are alone, the captain's voice is low, "Sad news today. Another loss of one of our own."

Robert nods, "Yes, it grieves us all."

The young man stops as if preparing to mount his horse, but then pauses and faces Robert, "Did you know that your cousin Robert Franklin Hamilton took off to join the Union forces?" Duckworth draws out the Hamilton name slowly, if not facetiously.

Surprised by the sudden change in not only subject, but tone of voice, Robert answers honestly, "Hadn't heard."

Duckworth looks back in the direction they had come from and then leans in and says a little more quietly, although clearly getting worked up, "More than that, Caleb Orr, James-Henry Cagle's brother-in law, left his grist mill just down the Davidson River and signed up with them too." He looks again over his shoulder aware he is in Cagle and Orr territory. "I'll bet money that James-Henry is sure to follow soon."

Robert, still grieving from John's death, can hardly believe he is having to discuss this now. "I'm not sure about your timin'! We have received horrible news and you are talkin' about this?" Robert is relieved a bit when he notices that Duckworth is a little embarrassed.

"I'm sorry about John's death." The captain pauses a moment, "But even with poor timin', the issue is still one that is time sensitive, as Sheriff, you know?"

"No, I don't know." Robert is baffled.

Duckworth drives on, "So will you arrest him or shoot him?"

Robert waves one hand in the air, "Who?"

Captain Duckworth frowns, confused by Robert's baffled response. "Your cousin, of course. He must have obviously faked that bleedin' to get out of Confederate service and now has gone over to the enemy. I knew he was one of them after namin' that baby!"

Robert feels heat creep up his neck, and he takes a deep breath before he moves as close as possible to the young leader of the home-guard, "Now hear me well, Captain." Duckworth does not budge; he is attentive, but clearly surprised by the sheriff's intensity. "Robert Franklin Hamilton had legal discharge papers from the Confederate army based on a medical doctor's evaluation. I know not where you got your medical degree and when you examined him to determine otherwise. Like many in our county, he has chosen to fight on another side. I am tryin' to keep the law here and not in a combat role. So, he is your worry, not mine."

Duckworth, who is clearly taken back by the very firm words from this lawman, quickly mounts his horse. But Robert is not finished. He grabs the horse's reins and adds, "Further, it is not my job, or yours, to judge what names are given to new babies. Look around our community at the names of Grant, Washington, and many famous leaders. How many Lambert Claytons are there in our County that are named after our own Revolutionary war hero?"

After a moment of silence Robert releases the reins and takes a deep breath. Duckworth nods and firmly responds, "You do your job Sheriff, but if I can catch that deserter or anybody trying to recruit in these parts, I'll shoot him for sure. That *is* my business."

Elizabeth Neill, October 30, 1863

The knock on the door caused Jimmy to rush to answer it before Sarah-Jane could beat him to it. I didn't pay them any attention since I was eager to finish cleaning up dinner. I wanted to head outside for a few moments before the setting sun completely chased away my chances of getting some fresh air before the dark and the cold set in.

It was Pa who settled down my sibling's fussing, and I didn't even try to listen to him talk to yet another person asking for help. There had been a steady flow of strangers and neighbors asking for support. Ever since my trip to the Patton House I reckoned word had spread that we were helping with the distribution of supplies. We never figured people would knock directly on our door instead of waiting for us to visit them. Ma told me I needed to realize that these were desperate times and people didn't care anymore about who knew they were in need.

"Elizabeth?" Pa's voice pulled me out of my focus and I quickly hurried to place the last chair in its spot around the table before Pa could ask me to fetch another basket of supplies or some blankets. I didn't want to have to come back to an unfinished chore.

"Just a second, Pa," I yelled. "I'm almost finished!"

"Elizabeth," His voice was closer and softer, "You have a visitor." I turned around and, next to Pa, stood James. His gray double-breasted jacket was neatly buttoned all the way to his collar, which boasted a deeper gray that wrapped around his neck. His red hair was greased back, but his light red stripe was still fighting to fall into his face. Beneath his full lips was a red beard that had grown until it substantially protruded from his chin. Although his presentable appearance was impressive, I could see he was still healing from scratches or wounds of some sort on the left side of his face, but nothing disfiguring.

The green of his eyes dominated and, as I continued to take inventory of the soldier standing before me, his eyebrows shifted from what seemed almost like an anxious grimace to a playful smirk. "Well are you goin' to stand there and stare at me all evenin'?"

My cheeks flushed, and I awkwardly stumbled towards him, stopping within reach. I hesitated and we both looked at Pa who was still taking in the whole scene. He wasn't smiling, but he wasn't frowning either. He took a deep breath and nodded his permission. We finally embraced and I could feel all my tension melt and all I could whisper was his name. Pa awkwardly cleared his throat, "Why don't you come outside and sit a spell." James released me first, pulling us out of our lengthy embrace.

"Yes, Sir. I would very much like that." James followed Pa out onto the porch while glancing back at me, soaking up my huge grin.

Ma's voice startled me, "Well at least take off your apron." She and my sister giggled as I untied my apron and flung it at them. I couldn't remember the last time I heard my mother giggle, but it only added to the giddiness I was feeling.

"So, ya have a boyfriend?" Sarah-Jane was grinning.

I was thankful Pa and James had already settled onto the front porch. "Yes, I do!" I smiled and then smoothed down my hair and ran upstairs to grab my Sunday-shawl. It was a soft blue which Ma always said made my eyes almost Cagle-blue. I scurried back down the stairs and then calmed myself with a deep breath before opening the door to join Pa and James who were already in deep conversation. I noticed Pa took the only two-seater bench forcing James and me to sit in rockers, but I didn't mind because I sat in the one closest to him. James looked away from Pa and smiled, "I'm happy you could join us, Elizabeth."

"Me too, James." I smiled and didn't care that I had interrupted their conversation. "What did I miss?"

James hesitated for a moment, so Pa jumped in, "He was beginnin' to share with me his account of his regiment's battle at Cumberland Gap."

James hesitated again and then finally stated to Pa, "Sir, I ain't so sure it is proper to talk about it in front of Elizabeth."

267

I could feel my giddiness vanish and give way to defiance, but Pa saw it too and quickly answered, "James, I reckon the Elizabeth you used to know couldn't have handled the news you are about to share, but she is a young woman now." Pa looked at me and, seeing my gratitude added, "And, if you are going to court her, it is best she knows all you have been through."

James nodded and then looked at me quizzically. I held his gaze and didn't drop my eyes or shy away. He nodded softly and then slowly dropped his eyes to the floorboards as if looking for something he had lost, "It's hard to tell a story I'd rather forget, but I will tell you what I recollect." Pa and I were quiet as James began to tell us of how he, under the command of his brother Captain B.T. Morris, along with his brother William and a cousin also named William, tried to take control of the key passageway along the Cumberland Mountain range. It strategically allowed for movement of supplies and men between Tennessee and Kentucky. "We were outnumbered and they had the advantage. We finally surrendered and those of us who could, fled." James continued to stare at the floorboards, and I could see him reliving the horror as his eyes widened. "The cannon fire from above was somethin' awful. Like the sky was fightin' against us too. Those Union troops had their thick fortifications way up on the ridges around that narrow passageway through those mountains. There were bodies everywhere. Once I knew we were done for, I tried to climb over a bloody heap of men to get myself to a thicket of trees and bushes, the only place I knew I could hide. I tried not to take notice of all the death around me. B.T. had taught me to harden myself to death. Harden myself to dead bodies and killin'. He said it would be the only way to live. So, I listened to my brother. But the eyes. . ." James stopped and swallowed slowly, "the eyes told their stories. When I saw the empty eyes starin' at me, it was like I felt their souls steal a part of mine." He shook off the images and slowly caressed his beard with his right hand. "So, I got myself hid in the thicket and kept movin', never been so thankful for Rhododendron before. Once I found myself at the bottom of the gap where the valley spread out a little, I waited 'til dark before I tracked a swiftly movin' creek that was wide enough and loud enough to muffle my movement, and I followed it until I could climb on the bank once I was sure no one was around. I was thankful it was a mild night, but I was very hungry and thirsty so I drank some of the creek water, but it tasted like blood. I couldn't see anything except what the moon lit, so I drank what I had to drink. As soon as the sun turned the gray shadows into color, I saw the creek had bodies that had been dead for longer than the heap of men who had protected my body from the last volley of cannon fire. I wretched up any bloody water that was still settled in my gut." James suddenly looked at Pa, "You know what I thought about when I stopped to drink our clear mountain water this mornin'?"

Surprised at the sudden change of direction, Pa shook his head, "I can't even begin to guess."

James smirked, "I drank blood. I drank blood from men who died, and I'm still alive." He shook his head. "You reckon Jesus is proud of those men? Givin' their blood?"

Pa and I couldn't respond at first. I was thankful Reverend English was not there to hear James' confounded statement. Pa sighed and shook his head, "I'm sure that only Jesus knows who he is proud of or not. And I'm as sure as the sun rises that it's not for me to judge."

James nodded and continued, "I found my way back along the valley we had marched through and was fortunate enough to meet up with B.T. at a location where we had made camp on our march to battle. We still don't know where my brother, William, is or my cousin." James paused for a minute and I remembered his brother William teasing me at the Lankford's beautiful home. I was suddenly afraid for him, even if I barely knew him. James continued, "B.T. was torn to pieces over the losses, but we made our way home. He is pulling together what is left of our regiment. We think we are goin' to be stationed at Farmer's hotel in Hendersonville for some time."

"So that means you aren't headed off again into battle?" I quickly squashed my desire to jump up with joy, but he could see it on my face.

He grinned at my response. "Yes, for now at least it looks like we will be helpin' provide supplies needed to our troops and seekin' out deserters and bushwhackers who are a growin' nuisance."

I saw Pa shift awkwardly for a moment, but he quickly covered it with a large stretch. He stood up and walked over to James, "I thank you for your willingness to lay down your life, and I pray your brother and cousin are safe, but I'm hopin' you don't have to face any more battles." Pa glanced at me, and I could see now that his inability to smile out of happiness or frown out of disapproval earlier was because he felt neither, he clearly was consumed with worry. He didn't know what the future would bring, but there was a deeper chasm to cross now that James had been in battle and not only felt but tasted death.

* * *

"Is your Pa still on the porch?" James' voice was almost a whisper. Pa had agreed to let the two of us walk to the stone wall and settle ourselves on the edge, with our legs dangling.

"Yes, he will be there 'til you leave, now won't he?" I smiled and leaned into James. The red hues from a brilliantly painted setting-sky only deepened the red of James' hair and beard. I reached up my hand and tugged playfully on his beard. "You let it grow." I grinned. "I like it." He took my hand from his beard and didn't let go, but folded it into his hands. The warmth of his palms was soothing as the night chill was moving in. My Sunday-shawl was beginning to feel too thin, but I didn't want to risk James leaving by running inside to get a real coat.

"Thanks for writing me." His voice was deeper than usual, "The letters that I did receive let me escape from the horrors. I didn't have to protect myself from death at those moments. I wish I had received all of them."

My stomach flipped and I didn't know what to say. I couldn't tell him that I hadn't written him for a time period, but I wasn't going to lie. "I loved your letters too!" I answered truthfully. "But now our letters only have to travel between Hendersonville and Brevard. Right?"

James's smile returned, "Yes, you are right, and when I have leave I can come and see you." He squeezed my hand. "We can really begin courtin'." He turned his head to look at Pa who had not taken his eyes off of us. "I think your Pa is still in agreement, though he seems more tore up about it."

I leaned in again. "Don't worry about Pa. If he weren't still supportin' you courtin' me he would never have invited you to stay and especially not let you sit here and hold my hand."

James leaned in to me this time, only a breath away. I heard Pa get out of his rocking chair and clear his throat. James smiled, "It's not like we're gettin' hitched. At least not yet." My eyes grew big. Had James just proposed?

"Well, you better ask Pa first? I think he's on his way down here." I could hear Pa move on the steps.

James suddenly stood up and helped me to my feet. Right before Pa reached us, he whispered, "I will." And then he took my chin in his hand. We were standing almost eye to eye, "But let's finish this damn war first." He reached his lips up to gently kiss my forehead before Pa caught up with us and promptly expressed that dark had set in and there were chickens to feed in the morning.

CHAPTER 19

Robert Hamilton, December 25, 1863

The crunching sound of the fresh snow feels like a small offering of peace this Christmas Day. The flakes fall softly as the cousins run about holding out their tongues to snatch as many as possible before they reach the frozen ground. Robert notices that Elizabeth is not joining in the game and has settled on the bench against the wall closest to the front door. She is clearly warm enough, bundled in her winter-wool, but she still has her hands tightly tucked between her knees as if trying to keep them warm. Blue and Grady are resting snuggled against each other at Elizabeth's feet content to keep their paws warm, at least for now.

"Looks like you're missin' out on some Christmas joy." Robert sits down next to Elizabeth. For the first time he realizes how small she is compared to his own children and, now that she is sixteen, he believes she has likely reached her full height. However, he is quite aware that her strength and tenacity make her seem a giant at times.

"It's fun watchin'," Elizabeth answers politely. She is clearly not wanting to engage, and Robert settles for several minutes of silence. He can hear George and Sarah inside talking with Rhoda and their muffled sounds and laughter only add to the tranquility that he hasn't allowed himself to seek out or enjoy for many months. He quickly pushes away the thought of those who are hungry and cold, and focuses on the moment, even if only for a few hours. He is drawn out of his lull when Elizabeth shifts and looks at him. "How do you do it, Uncle Bob?"

Robert knows exactly what she means. He doesn't hesitate more than a moment because he sees a depth in the young woman's intense stare, her blue eyes almost translucent. "Because it's right."

Elizabeth's brows narrow, "How do you know that?"

Robert sighs and pulls out his pipe. "I just do." He begins to prepare the tobacco. She does not say anything since she is waiting for him to explain himself. She watches him carefully light the pipe and take his first draw, before he finally continues. "It's like a deep knowin'. I've been taught since I was a boy how to treat others and how we have to take care of each other. That's what's most important to me, my pa and his father before him. So I do what's fittin' to what my family stands for."

"So, the whole notion that blood is thicker than water?" Elizabeth looks at her hands, tucking them in her pockets. "You do what your family believes no matter what?"

"It's like this, Elizabeth." Robert points his pipe toward the laughter and the snow falling. "I believe no one is better than me and no one is less than me. God put me here to take care of those I'm responsible for, and if that means it's a friend or stranger knockin' on my door, then I take care of them. *Their* story is between them and their family *and* God."

"What about Andrew?" Elizabeth's question was innocent, but it still takes Robert by surprise. It is the one fault in his plan. It's the one aspect of his philosophy that is not working out as he would like it to and, as the war continues to rage, it is the one ember that simmers deep within that he cannot seem to extinguish.

Robert looks at Elizabeth, and since he has promised her to keep no secrets, he drops his fatherly pretense and whispers, "I may lose him. In fact, think I already have, but it's the price I will have to pay."

"I don't want to lose anyone, Uncle Bob." Elizabeth looks out at her cousins. "I don't think I'm willin' to pay any price and choose any side, not if it means that the ones I love will hate me forever." She holds up her hand before he can react, "I know, I know I have chosen my own blood and support the possibly treasonous actions we engage in. But I'm going to do what I can to not lose those I love in the process of me still doin' what I think is right. Yes, I have been taught to follow our ways just like those on the other side are followin' what they've been taught. There's got to be a way for us not to end up hatin' each other. There's got to be away for us to have it all . . . I mean all that matters. Don't you think?"

Robert knows Elizabeth worries about James and his family who she has grown close to over the last few years. He, too, wonders about how his friends like the Lankfords will respond when the war is over, but he does not dwell on what he cannot control. "If you figure out how to do that then let me know." Robert smiles at Elizabeth.

She looks at him and tilts her head slightly, allowing a small smile to appear. "I will, Uncle Bob. I'll figure it out and when I do, you'll be one of the first to know."

Elizabeth Neill, February 22, 1864

I could hardly believe I was sitting on the fancy couch in Lankford's living room, next to James. The place was as elegant as I remembered, except I was happy the beautiful young woman that looked like a human rose was not visiting. James had asked Pa for permission to pick me up and take me to Sunday dinner at the Lankford home. Pa agreed with the understanding I would be home before dark. This, of course, was more time than I could ever have imagined, especially since it meant I was able to sit next to James in the front seat of his wagon, alone. The biting wind only made it better, since he tucked an extra wool blanket around me and pulled me closer to him. I couldn't believe that I actually would have traded sitting next to him, now on a soft couch in front of a warm fire, for more time on the wagon.

"It's mighty fine you both could join us for Sunday dinner today." Mrs. Lankford gently patted her bulging belly and slowly, with the help of her husband, settled herself into an upholstered chair. Mr. Lankford tucked a soft blanket around her shoulders. "Ain't much longer and this baby will be here. Right, B.C.?" I could see worry cross her eyes as she quickly looked up at the strong man who was still making sure she was comfortable.

"It'll, be alright, Amanda." He touched her shoulders one last time before taking the one rocking chair, clearly his favorite. "It'll be different this time. You'll see."

"That's right." She smiled and added, "Maybe even a boy!"

James took in the interaction between his sister and her husband, and I could tell he was obviously pleased. "You are in good hands, Amanda, and you have our sister, Betty, headed up here to stay with you soon." James' had written me that his other sister, Elizabeth, shortened to Betty, had promised she'd come and stay for the last few months of the pregnancy and through the birth. The reminder seemed to relieve Mrs. Lankford, since her eyes began to close.

When she didn't open them again, I frowned and looked at James and he then looked at Mr. Lankford, who promptly explained, "She nods off quite a bit these days. Sometimes she sleeps all day." Mr. Lankford's beard was groomed as usual, but his sudden scratching of his beard left it in disarray. "I guess it's normal." There was some doubt in his statement, but I figured she was probably pretty exhausted with her little baby, Hattie, almost two. Even with the three older girls helping out, it must have still been exhausting, especially since visitors were all too common. After all, Mr. Lankford was a key business man in the community.

As James and Mr. Lankford began to discuss business I tried to listen, but my attention was often distracted by one of the girls running in to grab little Hattie who would wobble her way to her mother, still sleeping, only to be swept away mostly by Susan, who was, I guessed, around eleven or twelve. The girls continued this pattern and enjoyed the attention they received from me as I smiled at them and their new-found game. I thought about James' sister, Betty, and realized suddenly why Mrs. Lankford must have thought it okay to call me Betty for so long. I was thankful, though, that James had taught her to call me Elizabeth, a habit that was hard for her to break.

275

It was Mr. Lankford who drew me suddenly to attention, "Did you hear James Henry Cagle has signed up as a Union recruiter?"

"Well, heck fire!" James stood up suddenly and began to pace. His sister stirred for a moment, but didn't manage to open her eyes. "I reckon it was only a matter of time."

"He's always been open about supportin' the Union, but I hoped he'd keep it all talk and no action." Mr. Lankford was clearly grieving. He'd been doing business with the Cagle Mill for years. I had heard from Emma-Rachel that the Confederates were beginning to take control of several mills and had moved the Linsey-woolsey mill's production out of the county. I wondered if that pushed him over the edge.

"That bastard!" James' sudden cursing did startle Mrs. Lankford to open her eyes.

"James! Not in front of the girls!" As James apologized to his sister, the very pregnant woman worked herself out of the chair and intercepted little Hattie this time on her own, taking the toddler by the hand and waving her children out of ear-shot. She did not return. I found it curious that she wasn't concerned why her brother was so upset, but she clearly had no desire to add to her own burdens.

Once the three of us were alone, James continued, "How could he go against us? He's been ornery for sure, but it ain't like him to be completely ignorant." James resumed pacing. I was thankful he was not looking at me because I could feel heat begin to rise up my neck, and I was sure my cheeks were beginning to betray my emotions. I swallowed and told myself to listen and not say anything stupid.

Mr. Lankford shifted in his rocker to face the fireplace, "James you know that we are a split community. It ain't a secret that half of our families are fightin' on either side. It's a cryin' shame, but it's the truth of it!"

"But I know James-Henry!" James slowly drew one hand through his hair to slick his red strand of hair back into place. "I don't know any others." He then stuck his finger out and pointed it at his brother-in law, "And I swear to God, I will have my regiment keep a watch out

276

for him. He'll be one lucky son-of-a-bitch if he's not dead before the war is over."

Mr. Lankford looked at me for one moment, making me sit a little straighter. I wasn't sure if it was that he was suddenly aware that I was still there or if he had his suspicions. His glance was only fleeting, and I chose to chalk it up to coincidence. He began to rock, "I wouldn't get too caught up feelin' betrayed. Right now, we have to take care of protectin' ourselves and our families. If that means your regiment keeps an eye out for the new Union recruiter then that seems fair enough." The thought of James seeking out James-Henry to kill him was too much, and I began to feel my eyes become blurry. I held as still as I could and didn't dare lift a hand to wipe away the tears that were beginning to escape. Mr. Lankford cleared his throat and nodded towards me.

It was as if James suddenly remembered I was there and looked at me, quickly returning to sit next to me, gently taking my hands in his. "I'm sorry Elizabeth that you have to listen to all this. I can see you're all tore up." I sighed, thankful that my red cheeks were mistaken for having a frail disposition.

I let myself wipe away the tears, pushed away my need to run away and scream, and managed to assure him, "It's only that Emma-Rachel is my friend, and I know this must be hard on her too." It was the truth. James quickly rooted through his coat's pockets and, within seconds, triumphantly presented me with a clean kerchief, at least he said it was clean. I was thankful, regardless. I made a note to myself to never leave home again without my own kerchief, clearly a vital accessory. After wiping my eyes and nose, I gently smiled at James. "Thank you." I then reached out and grabbed his hand, "Could you take me home?" I couldn't get out of there fast enough and realized too late that I was suddenly running away after all, but it was too late to retract my request.

James was a little surprised, but nodded with understanding, at least the understanding that I hoped he still believed. "Of course, Elizabeth." He stood and helped me stand up. I looked at Mr.

Lankford who was examining the scene that was unfolding. I dropped my eyes, ashamed that I had ruined their Sunday afternoon, one that would have naturally unwound into napping, some laughter and a delightful cup of *real* coffee, with some apple pie I had made a fuss over earlier as I helped set the table for the meal. I couldn't wait to enjoy it, and now, suddenly, I was eager to leave.

"I'm sorry, Miss Neill, that our conversation upset you so much." Mr. Lankford stood and walked over to where we were gathering together the warm outer coats and my extra wool blanket. "I assumed you hear a lot of upsettin' news at home with your Pa bein' deputy sheriff."

As I buttoned up my jacket, I managed to look at Mr. Lankford again, "I do hear some things, but Ma and Pa have always been particular in what they tell me."

Mr. Lankford put a hand on my shoulder. "I have only ever seen and heard of a strong Elizabeth Neill. The one my boy, Tony, tells me fought a fire, holdin' her own until she almost dropped." The weight of his hand, I realized, was to assure me. "I think you are stronger than cryin' about your friend."

"B.C." James' voice was suddenly protective. "What are you doin'? She's upset. Cain't you see that?"

Mr. Lankford took his hand from my shoulder and straightened out his tufts in his snow-white beard. He didn't look at James, but continued to look at me. "Yes, she is upset." I felt the red begin to reclaim its presence in my cheeks. It was strange him talking about me to James, but looking at me at the same time. "Don't be fooled, James." His grin was suddenly genuine and so wide I could see most of his teeth. "She's one tough woman."

James shook his head at his brother in law, clearly confused. "I know she's no weak puppy, but I'm respectin' that this was too much and will take her home. Is that so wrong?"

Mr. Lankford finally looked at James and his grin dwindled to a soft smile, "Yes, James, you are doin' the right thing takin' her home. All I'm sayin' is she's a good one to keep your eye on." He winked at me and then turned his back to us to head towards one of the back rooms, "I'll tell Amanda and the girls there's more pie for us."

James shook off Mr. Lankford's behavior, and I couldn't quite figure out what to make of it myself, but I did know he was more curious than suspicious. He had seen me grow up, and I guessed he knew me better than I thought he did.

"I don't know what got into B.C.! I'm sorry, Elizabeth." James was already guiding his mule to move the wagon out of the Lankford's cleared meadow that had been mostly reduced to frozen mud.

I pulled the blanket up over my head to cover my ears from the cold. "I think it's because he's watched me grow up. He's part teasin' and part serious."

"I reckon you're right." James glanced at me. "What do you mean by serious?"

I let the blanket drop to my shoulders and I looked straight into James' eyes. He suddenly frowned at my distinct change in intensity. "Will you really kill James-Henry?"

James pulled his mule to a stop. We were half-way down the small hill that lead away from the ridge that was now slowly being developed into downtown Brevard. The mule wasn't too happy, jerking the wagon twice before stopping completely. "If I have to. Yes." James was frowning and our eyes were locked. "I don't think you understand that he is now our enemy."

My eyebrows raised up. "No, maybe your enemy. But he's still my neighbor." I couldn't help feeling my chin lift.

"Elizabeth! You can't be serious." This time I saw James' cheeks begin to redden, and it wasn't from the wind that had resumed its intensity. "You are not to consider him your neighbor anymore! Nor should you speak with Rachel-Emma since it causes you to forget yourself."

"Excuse me?" I was turning my whole body towards him without completely falling off my seat. "Since when can you forbid me to speak to a friend? Since when do you determine who my neighbor is and who is not?"

James's face came in really close and the space between us was filled with a heat that was not one I had ever thought could rage, not with one I cared for so deeply. I could feel him spit his words. "Since you agreed to be my girl."

We held the intensity. I had never seen into the depths of him. The gray of his eyes dominated, and I could see he wasn't full of hate. He was full of fear. I softened my stare and suddenly closed the gap between us, my lips gently brushed his. He moved back in shock as I stated emphatically, "Yes, you are right. I did agree."

He took his one empty hand and wrapped it around the cradle of my neck and pulled me into him. The kiss was not long, but when it was over James held my gaze one moment longer and asked, "You reckon B.C. was warning me about you?"

I smiled and answered from the heart of me, "I do believe he was."

Robert Hamilton, March 29, 1864

"I can't believe this is happenin' again!" B.C. speaks quietly to Robert as the two men brave the cool evening, pacing on the porch as a screaming storm rages inside the fine walls of his home.

"At least she's screamin'," Robert dares to share some weak offering of hope. "I heard that as long as the woman is screamin' then she's still pushin' that baby out." The two men had occupied the back porch on and off since yesterday and Robert is thankful for the warm spell. The dogwood trees are being fooled to think spring is here and already reveal some early budding.

As the two men face the yard with the promise of grass peeking through the softening ground, another wild outcry brings B.C. to grasp the railing and cringe. "But it's been goin' on since yesterday." B.C. looks at Robert with wide eyes. "She ain't that strong. She could barely hold herself together for a full hour without fallin' asleep. How's she going to make it through this?"

Robert has no words to offer his friend, so he stands by his side as the turmoil inside continues. Millie is once again helping with the birthing process along with Amanda's sister, Betty, and two other women. Viney is also inside with the young girls and has brought them outside often to get fresh air and play as best they can, but their mood is considerably downcast.

"I have somethin' to show you." B.C. suddenly straightens his shoulders. "Wait here." Robert is confused with his friend's directive, but he nods and waits as B.C. disappears through the back door and reappears within seconds. Robert raises his eyebrows as B.C. waves a newspaper in the air. "Confound it! We've got to talk of somethin' else or I might go plumb crazy."

Robert reaches for the newspaper, also relieved for the respite. Staring at the front page he asks, "Why have you kept a copy of *The North Carolina Standard* from February 10th?" Robert is always grateful for B.C.'s ability to keep up with the latest news with newspapers, but why he would keep this particular one and bring it home seems somewhat odd.

B.C. leans on the railing and sighs. "You won't believe it. Look at the public meeting announcements."

Robert skims the headlines until he reaches a collection of documents published. Robert's heart begins to beat faster so he settles himself in one of the rockers and begins to read, "*At a public meeting held in the town of Brevard, on the 30th January, 1861, Major Samuel Wilson was called to the Chair, and Rev. J.H. Duckworth requested to act as Secretary. On motion, the Chair appointed the following gentlemen as a committee to prepare a preamble and resolutions for the action of the meeting, viz: O.L.Erwin, L.S.Gash, James Hamblin, Robert Hamilton, and Squire Morgan, who retired a short time and reported the following preamble and resolutions, which were unanimously adopted by the whole meeting.*" Robert raises his eyes towards B.C. who has his back to him and is still leaning on the railing. "They go on to print all of our resolutions on why we should not secede. They actually printed our feeble attempt to avoid this cantankerous war."

B.C. turns around and shakes his head. "They sure did. And they include several official requests from other communities as well."

281

Robert scratches his beard and stares back and forth between B.C. and the newspaper. "I don't understand. Why now? We are in the middle of the war. It's been three years!" Robert feels the heat rise, despite the cool breeze that ruffles the pages of *The North Carolina Standard*. "What in heaven's name is goin' on?"

B.C. shrugs and reaches for the newspaper. "I reckon that the editor..." he scans the page until he finds the name, "William Holden has somethin' to gain from this. Seems a might risky to be printin' this now. Seems he may be sendin' a message to the North, in case we lose."

Robert remembers William Holden, who openly tried to keep North Carolina from seceding. "Maybe he's aiming for public office, once this war is over." Robert is trying to skim through the other headlines and adds, "Maybe there is somethin' here we're missin' about the war bein' over soon? Maybe he knows somethin' we don't."

B.C.'s humph is loud and surprises Robert enough to glance up at the large man, whose unkempt white beard and hair only enhance the wild look in his eyes, "He's a traitor for sure. And he's put all of us who signed our names that day, back before the war, in danger. All the news I receive from my family do *not* show that we are surrenderin' to the Northern aggressors."

Robert swallows hard and folds the newspaper slowly. He is not going to remind B.C. of the losses at Gettysburg or the defeat at Chickamauga, or any of the numerous battles where many of our own southern men perished. In essence, he was right. Until absolute surrender is imminent, we are still at war. He stands and walks toward his friend, extending the newspaper to him. "Thanks for not sharing this with everyone, no need to spread deeper worry than is necessary. Bein' a small mountain community, let's hope this seems insignificant in the scheme of the whole war."

There is suddenly a wailing sound that abruptly shifts the atmosphere. A high pitch scream that can only come from a baby causes B.C. to suddenly stand tall and proud. He doesn't hesitate to rush past Robert, leaving the back door wide open. Still holding the paper, Robert waits as the baby seems to settle and the house recovers from the endless onslaught of the last twenty-four hours. It is Millie that comes to find her father on the porch, but Robert is struck by her weariness. She looks at her father and shakes her head, "It don't look good, Pa."

Flinging the newspaper onto the empty rocker, he pulls his daughter into his arms. "Are they goin' to lose this baby too?"

Millie tries to muffle her sobs in her father's coat, not wanting to upset the girls that Viney is watching on the second floor. She's been told to keep them occupied until they can clean up the birthing mess in the living room that had been transformed into a bedroom three weeks earlier since climbing the stairs had become too difficult. Robert waits patiently until Millie finally lifts her head, "I don't know if the baby will make it or not. He don't look too good." Robert is immediately filled with joy from her indication that B.C. finally has a boy, but he quickly checks his unbridled emotion as he hears his daughter's account. "He's so small and his color is sickly. But he is breathing and cryin' so that is somewhat hopeful."

"I should think so." Robert reassures his daughter.

But she is not finished. "Pa, its Amanda. She lost so much blood that it's like a bloody battlefield in that room and all the way down the cellar steps into the kitchen where we kept changin' and boilin' sheets. I think this birth sucked all the blood and life out of her, Pa." Robert can tell she wants to give in to sobbing again, but she takes a deep breath instead and, nodding to her father, she returns to where she is needed.

Robert slowly enters the house and follows the trail of blood. He finds B.C. next to his wife with a small bundle wrapped in his arms. The tiniest hand Robert has ever seen reaches out of the fold of the soft blanket and B.C. gently touches it. He looks down at Amanda and whispers, "You did it!"

Amanda's voice is weak, but a small smile crosses her pale lips. "I promised you a son, didn't I?"

"You sure did." B.C. kisses his wife's head.

"Tommy." Amanda whispers. "We're callin' him Tommy, right?"

B.C. tries to place the baby in Amanda's arms. But she can't lift them up, so he takes her arm and lifts it to wrap around her child as tears begin to flow. He glances at Robert, who sees that B.C. is vividly aware that he is losing his wife. He kisses her forehead again. "Yes. Tommy is a good name."

"You take care of him now." Amanda seems eerily at peace. "Betty said she'll help you." Robert hears Amanda's sister suddenly sob behind him and then scramble to the bottom of the stairs to yell to Viney to bring down the girls. B.C. does not protest as his four girls enter the room, although little Hattie remains in Viney's arms and is not sure what is happening. The older three move to their mother's side. Amanda can only barely move her head, enough to see her girls, "Now don't you fret none. I'm goin' to be with your sister Amanda-Thomas, she's waitin' for me." The girls wrap their arms around their Ma best they can, kissing her and crying. Millie and Viney, still holding Hattie, join their father as they leave the room allowing the family to say their final goodbyes.

As Robert and the girls step onto the back porch, he sees the newspaper, having been blown off the rocker, flutter haphazardly, almost toppling off the porch. He manages to grab the unfurling pages and quickly scrolling it as tightly as possible he shoves it into his jacket pocket. Observing her father's curious behavior with the paper, Millie asks, "What was that, Pa?"

Robert smiles gently and shakes his head brushing aside his odd behavior, "Trust me, it is insignificant in the total scheme of life."

Elizabeth Neill, April 5, 1864

Pa pulled the wagon up in front of the Oak Grove Church, and I managed to jump to the ground still holding a wicker basket. He motioned for me to wait outside while he quickly slipped inside the small church to check on the Lankford family. I followed the sound of metal hitting dirt until I found the familiar scene. I couldn't believe that Tony was already digging a second grave, a smaller one, next to Mrs. Lankford's grave. Little Tommy was too weak to live past a few days, but Pa told me that Mr. Lankford was thankful that the baby didn't die first, so Mrs. Lankford had passed on, content that she'd birthed a baby boy.

Tony and the shovel seemed to be fighting the hard ground. Bitter cold had returned with a vengeance only a few days ago, killing the poor dogwood buds. Pa said these dogwood winters were mean tricks nature played on the beautiful trees. My favorite trees. I still kept the carefully pressed dogwood bloom safely preserved under my bed. I couldn't believe it had been almost three years since James had given it to me. I walked up to the same tree we sat under and reached up to touch the dying bud.

"Miss Neill, are you okay?" Tony's voice drew me back to the task at hand. I was helping with making sure I gave Betty a basket of Ma's honey, biscuits and some salt-pork, when they left after the burial. Pa and I had arrived too early, but we wanted to make sure we didn't miss them and we didn't want to disturb their privacy. They weren't having another big funeral like they did for Mrs. Lankford where her whole family had come up from Polk County and James and his brothers had managed to take time away from their regiment. Although I had been thankful to see James again, the circumstances did not allow for us to pick up where we had left off only a month ago, especially not with his brothers around. He had squeezed my hand before he left and told me he would write soon. James and his brothers had stood at their sister's funeral with such hard-faces like they had lost all ability to cry. I guessed to them it felt like another loved-one lost in battle. I cried, though. Viney told me every detail on how it had been like a battle for Mrs. Lankford during childbirth only to end up dying once her son was born, so I cried and cried. But it felt different standing at the graveyard with Tony and a slowly emerging small grave. I didn't have any more tears.

"I'm fine Tony." I pinched off the dead bud and turned to face Tony who was leaning on the top of the shovel, taking a quick breather. "It sure is funny how nature will trick even other elements of nature. You'd think they'd be workin' together."

Tony scratched his head, "Ain't never thought of that. Lord works in His own way."

I held the crumbled bud up in my palm and looked at Tony. "Don't understand why the Lord would let somethin' so beautiful begin to bud, just to let the frost set in and destroy it."

Tony shook his head and grasped the shovel again digging with renewed energy. I was pretty sure it was fueled by anger, but I knew he'd never say it. I walked over to the grave, and Tony stopped for a moment wondering at what I was doing. I took my open palm and turned it, letting the dead bud, now almost powder, slowly fall into the grave.

CHAPTER 20

Robert Hamilton, May 1, 1864

"I swear to God they're bushwhackers!" James Deavor is fuming and his horse struggles to keep close to Robert who is trying to listen. The morning chill rapidly dissipates as the lingering fog lifts. Rays of sun filter through the wisps of white as they finally yield and reveal the brilliant blue sky.

"What makes you so sure, Captain Deavor?" Robert tries to regulate the speed at which the two men head along the road towards Dunns Rock. He needs to find out more about why James Deavor is furious, so he hopes, by using his newly appointed title, he can calm him into a more tactical and less emotional state. James Deavor's relocation to the area to hunt down Bushwhackers and deserters has been met with much joy from his family, relieved to have him closer by and not off in battle, but it has also caused Robert to have to accommodate this young captain's hunches and suspicions.

Captain Deavor does respond favorably to his new title and seems to pull himself together, sitting up straighter and calming his horse enough for the two men to more effectively ride in tandem. "We all know the Kuykendall boys signed up to fight with the Union."

"True." Robert nods.

"Well, some neighbors reportedly saw the boys workin' the fields. They told the neighbors they were home foragin'."

Robert has received numerous reports over the last two springs from neighbors and friends throughout the county about soldiers from both sides coming home after telling their regiment leaders they had to *go foraging*. Planting for harvest season seemed a plausible enough reason to stop fighting and leave for a spell before heading back into war. When Robert first heard this, he didn't believe it was possible, but when several families suddenly had fields planted and reports of sightings of sons and fathers began to emerge, Robert no longer questioned its accuracy. In fact, he is proud of the men who were able to convince their leaders that this was a valid reason for taking leave. "This still wouldn't make them bushwhackers, Captain." Robert realizes they are almost within sight of the Kuykendall log home and the two fields that are clearly freshly plowed.

"I know that, but they could be *and* more importantly they are *or* were Union soldiers fightin' aginst us, so we have to catch them in the act." He abruptly stops and dismounts. "Quickly, get down." Robert dismounts and follows the captain behind a cluster of fairly thick bushes. "Let's watch. You'll see!"

"I really don't think it's a crime to feed your family. You know as well as I do that both sides have. . ."

"Shhhhhh." The captain's finger is up to his lips and his eyes show clear disappointment in his sheriff's unwillingness to engage in what Robert feels is a game of spy-master.

Robert sighs and squats down beside Deavor and is close enough to see several beads of sweat begin to expose a level of fear Robert has not noticed before. Captain Deavor has, after all, been actively engaged as a soldier so fighting bushwhackers and capturing deserters is a daily ordeal. Robert sighs and counts his blessings. In spite of witnessing the pain and suffering from hunger, grieving over the loss of loved ones and dealing with the agonies of basic survival, he has truly not encountered the horrors of war first hand.

"See, look at the boys. They are headin' around back." Captain Deavor's voice is quiet and he is pointing at two figures that are plainly carrying some supplies to the back of their home. "Let's go!" Captain Deavor's boldness returns and he mounts his horse quickly and takes the lead by urging his horse into a full gallop towards the log home.

Robert, shocked at the sudden action scrambles to get Mae to calm down and let him mount her. "Wait, James." He tries to yell over his shoulder. "You don't want to risk bein' shot!" Robert is aware that every family is on edge and the intensity of the gallop will only be seen as a threat.

By the time Robert guides Mae out from the bushes he sees Mr. Kuykendall on the porch with a pistol. At first, he can only hear hollering, but by the time the sheriff is within ear-shot, James Deavor is already off his horse and heading towards the man who is now screaming for the approaching figure to leave. As soon as the captain begins to reach for his own pistol a gunshot rings out causing every bird in the surrounding brush and trees to abruptly take flight.

Robert pulls Mae's reins hard, not moving any closer to the angry Kuykendall father still pointing his pistol at the captain who is stumbling backwards holding his right side. "Put your gun down!" Robert yells.

Mr. Kuykendall, clearly in shock, looks at Robert with wide eyes. "He was goin' shoot me, Sheriff!"

"I reckon that's what it felt like." Robert begins to dismount, but doesn't step closer. "Put down your gun so I can check on the Captain."

"Are you goin' to arrest me?" The man places the gun on the porch's top step.

"Not today, I reckon." Robert begins to walk faster and finally reaches James Deavor who is still buckled over. But he is clearly breathing.

"I've been shot!" Deavor's eyes search Robert's face for some understanding.

"Of course you have! I would have shot you too if you'd headed to my house like that. Drawin' your gun and all. Yellin' and screaming'." Robert doesn't coddle the young captain. "You should know better than that!"

"But you got to arrest them. They're bushwhackers!" Captain Deavor's stubbornness doesn't seem to wane any, even with a bullet lodged in his side.

Robert shifts the wounded man so he is sitting up-right. "If they were bushwhackers, they'd have no need to plant. They'd be livin' off their spoils."

"Oh, I hadn't thought of that!" Deavor grunts as Robert lifts up the jacket and finds blood oozing.

"Well, it looks like we need to stop the bleedin' pretty quickly." Robert notices movement behind him and turns to find Mr. Kuykendall heading towards him, unbuttoning the shirt he is wearing, and quickly removing it by the time he is upon them. He doesn't say anything as he hands the sheriff the shirt, but quickly retreats at least ten paces, his pale-naked belly and chest looking sickly in the spring sun. "Uh, thank you." Robert nods and wads up the shirt, careful to avoid the sweaty material and only presses the dry cloth against Deavor's wound.

"You can keep that." Mr. Kuykendall's voice is awkward. "Won't be needin' it no more."

"I reckon not." Robert acknowledges his unintentional host, but quickly frees the man from any sense of obligation, "If you help me get him on his horse, then we'll be on our way."

The half-naked man quickly closes in to help hoist the wounded man onto his horse. The captain only grunts and curses, but Robert and Mr. Kuykendall ignore his complaints, fussing at him to stop protesting and keep pressure on the wound. As the farmer leaves the scene and Robert makes sure James Deavor is strapped down well enough, a bloody hand suddenly grabs Robert's arm. "I'm gonna die! Aren't I?"

Robert unfurls the tight grip. "I don't think so. Especially not with that grip. But if we don't get you cleaned up and looked at then only the Lord knows what will happen."

"Take me to Fletcher. He'll know what to do!" Captain Deavor's grave look is worrisome, but it is not what surprises Robert.

"Fletcher?" Robert scratches his beard. "Confound it! What're you talkin' about? He's no doctor and you both think of each other as sorry-good-for-nothin's. Why would you want me to take you to him?"

James Deavor sighs and holds uncomfortably onto the flap of his saddle to steady himself. His voice is urgent. "Take me."

Robert shakes his head, quickly mounts Mae and grabs the other horse's reins so he can guide the wounded captain to see Fletcher, his "sorry-good-for-nothing" neighbor.

* * *

Fletcher is easy to locate since he told Robert that he spends consistently more days trying to assist George Clayton and Ephraim England with downtown Brevard's building plans. Robert slowly leads Captain Deavor to what looks like the beginnings of a wooden building which will one day be the temporary courthouse. Although it has been a welcome warmth during the early morning hours, the mid-day sun's intensity is beginning to chase people into the shade. From the shadows of a large Oak, Reverend Fletcher English emerges to meet Robert and Captain Deavor, who remains hunched over. The two men pull the injured man off his horse and, as Deavor grunts, they pull him into the shade, leaning him up against the Oak.

"What happened?" Fletcher quickly moves to Deavor's side.

Robert looks at his friend and shakes his head in continued disbelief. "It seems Captain Deavor has been shot and only wants to speak to you in what he feels are his dyin' moments." Fletcher raises his eyebrows, clearly confused, so Robert fills him in on the happenings of the last two hours as Robert opens the jacket again to find Mr. Kuykendall's shirt, now mostly stained dark red, has hindered anymore loss of blood.

"Fletcher?" Captain Deavor reaches a shaky hand up, which is met by a sturdy grasp from the reverend.

"Yes, James, I'm here." Fletcher is frowning and continues to hold his neighbor's hand. "What do you need from me?" Reverend English's sincerity is not lost on Robert.

Robert resumes scratching his beard dumbfounded by the odd pairing. As he notices other curious faces approach, he asks one to fetch the granny-woman down the hill to tend to the wounds. Once James Deavor has his words with Fletcher, Robert will insist he have his wound tended to, but Robert is pleased the bleeding has stopped. He feels the situation is not as dire as the captain feels, but he is not the one who has been shot, so he tries to respect the man's wishes.

Deavor lets go of Fletcher's hand and digs into the inside pocket of his jacket and retrieves a small Bible and a pocket watch. He hands the Bible and watch to Fletcher. "Please give these to my family, and I want you to take my last will and testament." Fletcher obediently takes the two heirlooms and tucks them into his own jacket. He runs to his own saddlebags and returns with a steel pen, ink and some paper.

Robert chuckles at his friend's preparedness to pen a sermon where-ever he may be. As long as this Sunday he doesn't mistakenly preach from Deavor's will and testament. At this point Robert figures it is fitting to find a seat in the shade and retrieve his pipe and tobacco and settle in for a good smoke.

Finally, the "last will and testament" is completely dictated and signed. After Fletcher has returned the writing instrument to his saddlebags, Robert rises and comes over to Captain Deavor and Fletcher and can simply no longer remain quiet. "I thought Hell would freeze over before I saw you two talking like you'd been pickin' flowers together your whole lives. Can you *please* explain to me why you wanted to see Fletcher?"

James Deavor looks at Robert like it should be obvious and seems almost insulted that Robert should even ask. "Hatin' a man 'cause of his thinkin' and his ways is one thing. I may not agree with his political leanin's, but I trust Fletcher with my life and family." Deavor cocks his head to the side questioning Robert's grasp of this seemingly simple concept. "Ain't that the same for you, Sheriff?"

Pleasantly surprised, Robert suddenly laughs. "Yes, Captain Deavor. It sure is!" Robert looks at Fletcher who is also smiling. There is a profound moment of relief that both men willingly embrace. Robert doesn't hesitate to reach for Deavor's hand and squeeze it. "Captain, I do believe you are going to live." The sheriff then nods to the granny-woman with her herbs and bandages, along with some helpers, indicating they can now take the captain as their patient and care for his wound.

Elizabeth Neill, May 4, 1864

"I know the best place for fishin'!" John-Riley's excitement made me feel like it was 1860 again, when heading out to fish along the Davidson River meant an afternoon of splashing each other and bringing home three or four trout to fry up with a fresh pan of corn bread. But the two wicker baskets Viney and I were carrying kept the situation real. Their side slits had enough space to let water seep through them, but keep fish from escaping, and acted like very large nets. The two straps woven into the sides allowed the baskets to then transition onto our backs to carry home more than just food for dinner that night for each of our families. John-Riley was carrying rope, a pouch full of corn-nibbles, and a hunting knife was strapped to his britches. Ma and Aunt Rhoda were ready to clean and salt what we could bring home, ready to preserve as much food as possible for the growing hunger in the county. Neighbors all over these mountains were hunting and fishing trying to feed each other as best we could. Uncle Bob's son, William, was busy trapping and hunting beaver, deer, mink, muskrat and possums. He was still able to sell, on rare occasions, some of the valuable furs through Lankford's store when there was a desire to buy some down South, but it was the meat that was crucial and in demand. There were times I heard Pa talk about how William had climbed clear up to the mountain's ridge tracking a buck big enough to feed a few families.

The morning sun had already begun to hit the tops of the trees when we wound around the school house about twenty minutes earlier. My heart ached when we passed it because I realized that I considered the building my church but no longer my school, even though I hoped that, when the war was over, I could maybe help Reverend English again teach the younger children. But I didn't dare wish anything out loud, not when I was busy catching fish to feed people; no one quite cared at that time about reading and arithmetic.

As we moved through the forest, I made a mental note on where the Chestnut trees were standing. Come fall I would be sure to return and gather chestnuts, since I knew Mr. Poor liked to sell them at his trading post. It seemed every tree, plant and animal were carefully considered as potential food.

"See! Over there." John-Riley pointed at a spot along the river where it looked like the water rippled over stones that had at one point been placed into a V formation. The bank was low and flat enough for us to easily reach the water without having to climb over roots or scoot down a steep dirt ledge, so John-Riley was the first to have his shoes off and pants rolled up. As his bare feet plunged into the water he yelled, "Dag nab it! It's cold!"

"What did you expect?" Viney fussed at her brother as the two of us placed the baskets down on the soft soil. "It's always cold even in the blazin' hot summer." I tried not to laugh when John-Riley made an I-know-what-I'm-doing face at his sister, but it was too funny as he gave up pretending he could handle the cold and finally came scrambling back up onto the bank, plopping himself next to us and rubbing some warmth back into his feet.

"You'd better start usin' that gourd of yours." Viney teased.

"And you better stop all that yackin'. You probably already scared away all the fish from here clear-to Pink-beds up the mountain!" He rubbed his feet a few more seconds.

I hated being the one to remind us of our task at hand, but I wasn't going to spend my day listening to the two of them nag each other. "I think we better get goin' if we are goin' to fill these baskets and get home before dark."

John-Riley and Viney both nodded with sudden seriousness, clearly used to shifting from family life to somber intensity. I was instantly ashamed to have taken their light sibling bantering away. They had, after-all, been playing with treasonous fire longer than I had. John-Riley, thankfully, broke me away from my darkening thoughts. "The deeper end is over on the other side of the river, but maybe if we head up the river bank a bit longer, we can find other deeper places along this side." John-Riley began to put on his socks and shoes as Viney and I slung the baskets back over our shoulders.

I let John-Riley and Viney take the lead since I hadn't been this far up the river before. We found one spot where the river had formed a natural pool and the darkness of the water was a clear sign that it was deeper than the generally shallow nature of the Davidson River. The bank was steep though, so John-Riley scrambled down with my basket and straddled two wide roots, shoving the basket into the water. He pushed it down deep enough with a forked branch he had cut off of a

294

nearby tree. With one hand holding the stick to keep the basket submerged and the other hand tightly wound around the rope he had tied to the handles, he waited patiently. Viney dropped corn-nibbles from above his head and they slowly sank into the depth of the basket-trap. As soon as he saw some movement, quick as lightning he drew the basket up, capturing at least three fish. He then handed that basket to us for us to pour the fish into Viney's basket. I stood patiently waiting for each catch. Sometimes he only caught one, other times he managed five. Anytime there was one that was too small he'd throw it back into the river promising to come get it when it was grown. But once the time between catches drew out unbearably long, and only one fish had dared to seek out any corn-nibbles, John-Riley hauled himself and the trap back up the bank. "Time to move on."

Viney's basket was filled with at least twenty fish, beautiful trout, mainly motionless; but a few would still squirm and gasp for air. "My baskets goin' to be too heavy for me." Viney didn't say anything as John-Riley grabbed her basket and effortlessly slung it onto his back. She raised her eyebrows to me, clearly impressed, but she would never tell him, so instead she fussed, "I was just sayin' maybe we could put some in Elizabeth's basket."

John-Riley glanced at his sister and me, with the empty wet basket strapped to my back soaking my dress. "We still need to use hers to catch some more, then she can use it to carry the fish." Viney and I didn't protest. I was especially thankful that the water seeping through my dress and into my britches was at-least river water and not the oozing liquids of dying fish.

We came around a wide bend and found that the bank was beginning to feel farther away from the river. We were clearly heading uphill and the river was not. The steepness was due to what looked like a rock formation that gradually rose along the bank. We reached the top and could look straight down into the water that was pushing at the base of the rock wall. "Look at that dark pool of water!" John-Riley was pointing straight down.

"But there is no way to get there!" I carefully stepped back from the edge, holding onto the branches from a tight cluster of rhododendrons.

John-Riley surveyed our surroundings more clearly. "If we go back down the way we came, it looks like there's a wide stretch with shallow water. We could hustle across it, if you ain't scared of some cold water, and then come up the bank on the other side."

Viney and I were tired of looking for any more perfect spots, so his plan sounded reasonable to both of us. Once we descended back to the level of the river, we all took off our shoes and socks and scurried across the wide shallow stretch of the river. I held my skirts above my knees, managing to avoid any more water absorption than was already on my back. Adding any more water weight would make the walk home unbearable. The water, though, did remind me that I needed to relieve myself pretty soon.

We worked our way up the other side of the river to find the best way to reach the dirt bank we had spotted from the small cliff. As soon as I saw that we were close, I suggested, "How about you two head on and I head into these bushes for a minute."

"That's fine." Viney reached out her hand, "Let me have the basket so we can figure out the best place to set the trap." I eagerly handed her the basket and watched the two of them disappear around the final bend. I tucked my head and shoved some bushes out of the way to look for a spot where the brush wasn't so thick. I didn't like getting poked. I finally squatted down and felt relief.

From the lower angle I could see some lighter green ahead of me, which meant there was probably a natural clearing. I was curious, so once I was finished and pulled up my britches, I quickly broke through the last bush. I froze. It was a clearing. Not very large, but large enough for a roughly assembled fire pit, clearly made from the river's rocks and what looked like five make-shift tents. Someone had taken some fancy carpets and tied them to some small trees. A large frying pan was carelessly tossed next to the cold fire pit and there were a lot of bottles laying around, some half broken in the fireplace. I had to tell myself to breathe and was finally able to when I realized that I was alone. The camp-site was empty. I couldn't tell if anyone was planning on coming back, but I wasn't going to find out. I scrambled through the bushes, not caring if my face was scratched and found Viney and John-Riley, who hadn't had enough time to set the trap up yet. They could see I was clearly upset, and it made me so mad that they didn't think it was anything serious at first, probably some families out hunting. They even suggested that it could belong to the Tinsley family since they still lived a way on up the river. I hated to return, but I made them put down the baskets and follow me through the thick brush to the campsite where someone had turned carpets into tents.

"Oh my God!" Viney's hand covered her mouth.

"Carpets?" John-Riley was confused. "No mountain family would make a tent out of carpets!" He scratched his head and then added. "Who in tarnation would even own fancy carpets like that?"

"The Hume Hotel," I whispered.

"They didn't say they had carpets stolen." Viney corrected me.

I whispered, "They wouldn't know. Remember the building was burned."

"Bushwhackers!" John-Riley gasped.

I shoved Viney and John-Riley's shoulders. "We better get the hell out of here. Now!"

John-Riley and Viney quickly followed me back to the river and grabbed the two baskets. We crossed back over the cold river, but sat hidden in the deep brush on the other side before we put our shoes back on. John-Riley carried the full basket while I carried the empty one, but I said nothing as John-Riley guided us safely back home. We had to find Uncle Bob and Pa as soon as possible.

Robert Hamilton, May 4, 1864

Once Robert alerts George, the sheriff does not hesitate to search out Captain Duckworth who quickly gathers Lieutenant James Clayton and Henry Mackey, calling them to duty as part of the home-guard. It is midafternoon by the time Robert and his posse head to the suspicious camp-sight. Robert never thought he would be happy that Henry is part of Duckworth's men, but having family alongside him allows him to trust, a virtue he has never shared with Duckworth. As Robert's legs grip the horse, John-Riley's arms are tightly wrapped around his father's waist as he whispers directions into his father's ear to guide him and the other four men, also on horses, to the camp. The five horses slowly approach the bend close to the campground and, after they guide their horses through the shallow water, all six men quietly dismount. Earlier, Robert suppressed the notion that John-Riley should not be with them since he needed his son to guide them. He still does not like it but is thankful the three youth were not captured or injured during their discovery. The sweat-soaked boy, who smells like fish, looks at his Pa and nods as he pushes aside the brush they had moved through that morning.

As they move in closer Robert feels a hand touch his arm, "We will take the lead." Duckworth's voice is barely a whisper. Robert nods, relieved as he watches the Captain signal to Lieutenant Clayton and Henry to move in from different angles. George joins Henry as they disappear to the left.

Robert and John-Riley follow the captain who crouches behind the last branches before they reach the clearing. He waits and observes. Only when there is a sudden cry from a woodpecker followed by a wren's call does Duckworth relax and answer with his own bird chirping, closest in resemblance to a finch. He waves his hand at Robert and John-Riley as his body straightens, "All clear from all sides. Let's move in."

Robert raises his eyebrows as they enter the campground at the same time as George and the other two men, who instantly split up to start investigating. John-Riley steps in only far enough to hunker down at the foot of the bush they came through. Robert, however, quickly moves to stand next to the captain and looks at the young man. "That was quite some whistlin'. I'm impressed." Duckworth smiles at the sheriff and nods his appreciation.

"Look at this!" George draws their attention to behind the carpet-tents. The men quickly find themselves facing a trunk poorly hidden in the thick rhododendron bushes. It is full of random items including silverware, china-dishes, women and men's clothing, candles and candle holders, and at least nine jugs, which, after opening one, George confirms is some form of alcohol. "This camp-site is definitely not abandoned."

Lieutenant Clayton walks briskly to the river-stone fire pit and bends down for a few moments. He shakes his head. "But the fire's been cold for quite some time. They haven't been here for at least a couple of weeks."

Robert walks over to the fire-pit and turns to take in the whole scene. The rain-soaked carpets are hanging low, burdening the branches; the edge of one tent has already snapped free, occasionally flapping haphazardly. Aside from the abandoned frying pan at his feet there are no other signs of recent use. He takes a deep breath and strokes his beard. "They may not be here now, but they're aimin' to return. They're like a pack of wolves coverin' a wide area. No doubt they'll be circlin' back around." He faces Henry and begins to open his mouth, but Henry quickly shakes his head and then nods towards the captain. Robert raises his eyebrows and quickly remembers to specifically address Duckworth. "Captain, if you and Henry and James are agreed, we should leave the camp-site as it is. The trunk and all. We want them to think no one has come upon them. It's my intention that we catch them when they make their return."

Captain Duckworth looks at Henry and Lieutenant Clayton for unspoken acknowledgment before he turns back to Robert and smiles. "We're agreed, Sheriff."

CHAPTER 21

Elizabeth Neill, June 4, 1864

The discovery of the bushwhacker campsite caused me to be fearful about moving freely about the forest, which I resented. So, to set my mind straight, I found myself spending more time at Mammaw's helping her with her garden and managing her grazing sheep. Since she lived right on the Boylston Turnpike, we were frequently visited by weary Confederate soldiers on their way home on leave or, when they hobbled by with a limb missing, they clearly had been discharged. Mammaw always offered them cold well-water and an apple or two from her root-cellar. A large watering trough, that my Pappaw had hewed out of a big log, still sat under my favorite willow tree, its branches always seemed to be waving at me to come and sit underneath them. I had heard that in the past, our men who had gone all the way to fight in the Mexican War, had stopped under these trees on their way home. They had watered their horses and had chosen to sit a spell. It seemed these current Confederate war-weary soldiers found comfort in following in some of their families' past footsteps. It seemed the shade of the Willow trees would always lull them into telling their stories of war. No two stories were ever the same.

That day there was one man in particular, John Byrd Allison, that sat down in the shade and told us a story I could hardly believe. He stretched out against the base of the willow tree and placed his hands behind his head as he began to share, "I walked through piles of bodies on my way home. My shoes were so badly worn through that I thought I'd not make it home. But doggone it if I didn't come across a young colored boy with new boots on. I told the boy I needed the boots worse than he did." Mr. Allison chuckled. "The boy didn't hesitate none, seeing the sorry condition I was in, he took them off and said I could have them." I watched Mr. Allison wiggle his feet in his boots, although I would not have called them new. I figured *new* meant *not ruined*. Mr. Allison smiled. "I told him I was much obliged to his willingness to surrender the boots. He told me it was nothin' since he had plenty more. I figure he was right smart collectin' boots off bodies." I quickly excused myself, thinking that I might not keep down breakfast. When I finally pulled myself together, I quickly thanked God that James wasn't clawing his way through dead bodies anymore and that he didn't have to scavenge for boots.

Once Mr. Allison left, Mammaw said she wanted to head down the road to the Valley Store for some staples. I was happy to head in with her and avoid working the garden in the rising heat and humidity. I looked forward to seeing how the Lankford girls were doing. I knew Susan was helping her Pa a lot in the store while Betty, Amanda's sister, was still helping watch the younger girls at home.

I had every intention of heading into the store with Mammaw, but I saw Pink sitting on the edge of the porch with his legs dangling over the side. He didn't jump up and greet me, like he had a few years ago, but he did smile and wave, then returned to rummaging through a large basket he was awkwardly balancing on his lap. "I'll wait out here, Mammaw, if that's okay?"

She was already halfway through the door when she acknowledged my request, with an indifferent nod. She began to eagerly call to a friend, "Well, I declare! Sally, is that you? I ain't seen you since..." As her voice was muffled by an equally enthusiastic cheer, I turned and headed towards Pink.

"What're you doin?" I slid down to the edge of the porch next to him and looked into his basket. There were several pairs of shoes.

"I've got to make shore I match up pairs before I hand off the shoes to Mister Lankford. His customers ain't gonna be happy if their shoes git mixed up." He pulled out two shoes that looked like a pair and handed them to me. "What do you think?"

"That looks right to me?" I smiled.

"Well, you're wrong." His teeth flashed a brilliant smile as he snatched the shoes out of my hand and then pulled open the shoes for me to look inside. "See there's numbers inside that you got to match up." He then pulled another shoe out and showed me how it was, in fact, a better match. "It's a good thing you don't work for Pa. He'd tan your hide for miss-matchin' shoes." It was good to hear him laugh.

"I thought your Pa was a blacksmith?" I was surprised to see the pile of shoes. "I expected a basket of horse-shoes."

"Pa is mostly the Allison's blacksmith, but he's their cobbler too. He makes shore everyone's got shoes that ain't got holes. He does git awful angry at anyone that wears their soles down so it's almost impossible to patch. That goes for my black *and* white cousins." Pink continued to pair shoes together by tying laces together and then checking his matches at least twice.

"I haven't seen you since that day at the Patton's house. I'm sorry about that, you know?" It felt good to finally apologize for my irrational behavior in front of Jesse.

He stopped for a minute and smiled at me. "Oh, don't you worry none about that, Miss Neill. It helped me remember that I have friends." I smiled back. "Pa also told me I needed to git back to helpin' him, which means I cain't be afraid of leavin' home since I need to be the one to deliver his shoes and pick up scrap metal where-ever I can git it." He returned his attention to his basket to finish his final shoe-matching task.

"I haven't ever seen your Pa." I stated as a matter-of fact. Leaning back on my hands, I looked at Pink with a little more scrutiny than usual. His hair was not real curly like Tony's. Instead, it lay flat against his head slicked down, just like James' hair. His long narrow nose also set him apart as different. "Is your Pa whiter than you?"

Pink stopped looking into his basket and placed it down next to himself on the porch. He looked at me with a slight frown on his face, like he was confused or maybe even surprised. He looked around the porch, and I could tell he was making sure Tony was not anywhere around. "Well, Miss Neill, if it were anyone else askin' I'd high-tail it outa here."

I shifted awkwardly and could feel myself turn red. "I'm sorry, Pink. You don't have to answer." I sat up straight and awkwardly straightened out the folds of my skirt.

Pink watched me for a minute, contemplating how he should answer. He finally sighed. "Pa don't ever leave the farm because he *is* whiter. He don't trust nobody else but the Allisons and those who live around us." I stopped straightening my skirt and looked at Pink who suddenly appeared older than a fourteen-year-old boy. I knew he had aged after the campground incident, but I was beginning to learn that there was a great deal more to his story. So, I didn't say anything and listened. "He always says that my grandpa, Frank Allison, is a good white man and raised him with Pa's older white brothers, Uncle Elisha and Uncle Elijah, but no matter how much I want to believe it's all good, I cain't." He paused a minute wondering if he should tell me anymore. He checked his surroundings again and his voice became a whisper. "I ain't ignorant. My Granny Lucinda. . ." Pink looked at me, his gray-green eyes narrowed as he clarified, ". . . she's a black slave, in case you wondered." I nodded thankful for his explanation, since I'd never talked about this before with anyone. I was most definitely overwhelmed with the direction of the conversation. When Pink saw that I understood, by what must have been a shocked look on my face, he continued, "So, this means, she ain't *Grandpa* Frank's wife, yet she had his baby. But no one talks about it. They all just say '*that's the way it is.*'" Pink shook his head.

I swallowed hard. "I don't know what to say." I stood up quickly hoping to give Pink permission to stop talking about something that I had never really thought of, something that seemed so strange and unsettling.

Pink jumped up too, the basket of shoes waiting patiently at his feet. "I'm sorry I upset you, Miss Neill." His eyes were full of worry.

"Oh, Pink. I'm the one who should apologize for asking such a question." I dropped my eyes. "There is so much I don't understand."

"Well that makes two of us." Pink tried to lift my spirits like he always did.

It was my turn to look around and make sure we were still alone. "I reckon if the South loses the war you will all leave?" I could feel my nose burn as I tried to suppress tears. It was not my right to cry. Still my vision began to blur.

The quiet chuckling coming from Pink surprised me. I quickly wiped away my tears and frowned at the smile coming from the boy in front of me. He picked up his basket and shook it so I could hear the shoes clunking together. "Oh, Miss Neill. Where would we go? Here Pa has work and I'm for shore a good hunter and trapper and can practically catch a fish with my own hands... well almost."

I put my hands on my hips. "After everything you just said, why would you stay?"

"Why would we go somewhere where we know no-one? Especially Pa and me. We are, at least, considered family by some of my white relatives, even if others pretend we don't exist. We know what to expect here and we already got plans for makin' it on the other side of the war." I raised my eyebrows, so he continued. "Jesse's already teachin' me how to read and write, just like Missus Patton taught him."

My face lit up. "Oh, Pink, that's great! Maybe I could help?" All the times I had helped the younger children at school came flooding back and my longing to focus on schooling again clouded any clear-thinking.

Pink's smile faded and he shook his head. "I'm much obliged, Miss Neill, but that shore ain't a good idea. I don't reckon it's legal and it shore wouldn't be looked upon too kindly by others." He sighed and then smiled again, "Maybe one day it will be considered fittin'."

I nodded, knowing Pink was right. But I held my chin high, determined not to cry again. "Yes, maybe one day."

Robert Hamilton, June 30, 1864

"Well I'll be damned! Look at this, Bob! Looks like we may have a leg up after all." Robert has stopped by the Valley Store to check in on the latest war-news. He is not surprised to be greeted with B.C. grasping several newspapers he has procured from merchants coming up from Greenville, South Carolina.

Robert leans against the counter trying to look at the newspaper, but B.C. is excitedly tapping it with his hand, so Robert asks, "What's got you all happy like a flea on a dog's back?"

B.C. speaks not only to Robert, but a father and son who have been gathering their supplies and have emerged with their arms full, are also clearly listening. As they place their items on the counter B.C. summarizes his readings. "The Yankees tried to mess with General Early up in the Shenandoah Valley, right on up our Blue-Ridge Mountain range. Looks like the Yankee's General Hunter underestimated all our boys raidin' their supplies and ammunition so they were plum out of luck when they faced General Early. Looks like our men are headed to Washington now." The father and son nod and smile politely, but Robert notices they are eager to leave. Since their items contain a variety of remedies, it is not hard to conclude there is clearly sickness at home.

B.C., also aware of their need to head on, lets them pay and head out the door before he looks at Robert and then turns the page of the newspaper. "Then look at this." He points his finger to a section, but Robert doesn't try to read it, he waits for B.C. to share the news. "We managed to hold off that damn Sherman and his army last week at Kennesaw Mountain in Georgia. He thinks he can move on through the South? He'll never make it past our boys."

Robert nods and listens to his friend, although he feels very different. Now that the war is being fought with growing frequency to the south of Transylvania County, it means they are *caught in the middle* more than ever. He will face new challenges that will place his loved ones and himself in greater danger.

Elizabeth Neill, July 30, 1864

I had promised Ma I would help her with gathering and shucking fresh corn and was eager to harvest the new ears before the sun began to hit the field. It wasn't hard getting out of bed that morning since I had heard Pa make quite a commotion tumbling out the door way before dawn. He had the wagon hitched to Jack in no time and was gone before I felt the first light peak through the shutters. I hadn't been able to go back to sleep, so when Ma's gentle footsteps were finally making their way along the creaking hallway floorboards, I hopped up and followed her down stairs into the kitchen. When I asked Ma where Pa was, she gave me that "you know" look that informed me it was simply Pa and Uncle Bob undermining the law again. I was thankful Ma didn't lie, but she looked more worried than usual. I hoped she would tell me more over breakfast, but first I had corn to pick. I yelled up to Jimmy and Sarah-Jane that they better get up and come out soon to haul the full baskets up to the house. However, I didn't wait for their whining responses since I knew Ma would send them soon.

I was thankful for a little time without their fussing at each other. So, I entered the corn field, heavy with morning dew, wearing my corn-picking britches and a wide brimmed hat that would keep the wooly-worms and gnats from bothering me too badly. As I picked corn, my mind began its routine assessment of daily news and events that were, unfortunately, becoming commonplace. Pa had told me that Captain Duckworth and his men had checked on the hidden campground consistently, but hadn't found any sign of movement. I secretly hoped the bushwhackers were dead and were never returning. Then I asked God to forgive me for wishing anyone was dead. I moved so quickly between fear, hate, guilt and then a strange sense that everything wasn't real, and I was a plum fool to trust any of these unbelievable stories. Ma had told me the best thing to do was keep on with chores, take good care of Mammaw and help our neighbors. Ma said, "We can only do what we can do." But when I spent time with Viney she would fill me in on all the news she had heard of war and battles. I was quite upset when she told me that a General Sherman was attacking Atlanta and that there were so many Confederate casualties that there was real worry that Atlanta would fall soon. Didn't help any when James told me we should be watching for the Union Army to turn and head up through North Carolina and wreak havoc on us. I hoped they were overreacting.

That early morning, I kept trying to push my thoughts back to the corn. Did the silk look brown enough? Which ears needed a few more days? I had been harvesting corn for a while, wondering when Jimmy and Sarah-Jane would begin hauling the full baskets to the porch, when I heard Pa and the wagon pulling up to the field. I expected to hear the wagon continue on up Lambs Creek to Uncle Bob's, but instead I heard Jack whinny as it came to a sudden stop and Pa hollered, "Elizabeth? Come here!"

He didn't have to ask me twice. I had heard this tone many times before, and I knew immediately that I needed to drop my basket and head towards him as quickly as I could. I ran down the corn row, shoving stalks out of my way, and emerged quickly, almost tripping over the baskets already full of ears. Pa was sitting on the wagon gripping the reins tightly. The wagon had the tarp drawn over the "supplies" he was hauling. As soon as Pa saw me, he waved me to him. I obeyed. As soon as I reached him, he jumped down and whispered, "You take the wagon up to Uncle Bob. Right now!"

"Pa?" I could feel fear rise. He never had me take his wagon, especially if he was hauling a load of deserters to safety.

Pa hesitated a minute trying to decide if he should yell at me to *do as he says* or to explain. He kept to his promise to not treat me like a child. "I ran into Captain Duckworth and his men up the road and they said they were headed this way. Had to water their horses first at the creek near the old campground." Pa's voice grew desperate. "You take the wagon now, and I will see if I can keep him from headin' up to see Bob. At least long enough to unload." I knew what he meant by *unload* and I felt sweat begin to bead on my forehead.

I began to scramble up the wagon and grasped the reigns, but the sudden trampling of hooves behind me made me stop and turn my head to see who was coming.

Pa waved to the arriving guests with a forced smile on his face as he whispered to the tarp "Don't move! Don't breathe! Sure as hell, don't cough!" I knew he wasn't talking to me. But then he looked at me and said, "Don't leave yet. Won't look right. I'll tell you when." I nodded and tried to wave and smile at our early morning guest.

Captain Duckworth and one of his home-guards came right up to the wagon. "Hi, George. What a surprise to see you headed through the valley so early in the mornin'." I could see Pa move in closer to the Captain and lean calmly against the side of the wagon. Captain Duckworth gently lifted his cap for a minute to greet me, "Mornin' Miss Neill." He replaced his cap while I returned his greeting with a nod.

"So much need in the county as you well know. Got to get to families and sometimes I have to follow leads at the crack of dawn, even if they are only random deer trails, leadin' me nowhere."

Captain Duckworth nodded and looked both ways up Lambs Creek as if making sure no one was listening to their conversation, "So you heard too?"

"About what?" Pa came up to the horse and looked up at the Captain in all seriousness.

Captain Duckworth glanced at me, "Ma'm I don't mean to frighten you."

308

I looked right into his eyes and didn't lie, "Trust me Captain Duckworth, you can't frighten me any more than I already am."

"Yes, it is a shame the fear we all live under." He looked at Pa and added, "Seems there's been a sightin' of Union soldiers, they look like a rag-tag bunch of escaped prisoners-of-war comin' up from South Carolina headin' through our county."

"Union Soldiers?" I spoke before I realized my own surprise caused Pa to look at me with a moment of fear.

He pulled himself together quickly and shook his head, "I heard that too, but didn't find a thing."

"We are headed up to talk with the Sheriff, to see if he has word." Captain Duckworth turned his horse and his home-guard followed his lead.

"How about I go get him for you?" My voice was a little louder than I meant it to be. The men turned their horses and looked at me, as did Pa with his eye-brows lifted. "I'm headed up there right now and I know Ma is fixin' breakfast. I'm sure there is plenty of biscuits and Pa's famous honey to share."

When Pa saw the men considering my offer, he jumped right in. "I know my Sarah-Elizabeth would be delighted to have some visitors."

At that moment Jimmy and Sarah-Jane came tumbling down the wall and heading towards us. Jimmy yelled, "We're getting the baskets of corn now. I promise! Don't tell Pa we were late!" My sister and brother each grabbed a bushel and turned and fled back to the wall, one climbing it while the other one passed the bushels up. The scene caused everyone to laugh and Pa added. "Got some fresh corn too if you care to shuck a little and have a fresh cob along with your biscuits?"

"I bet Uncle Bob will be down here to join you before the corn is cooked." I added.

Captain Duckworth smiled and sighed with relief, "I sure am famished. A good breakfast would be welcome. We can shuck corn and talk. Doesn't hurt to enjoy life a little." He and his home-guard dismounted and started following Pa towards the house. Pa looked at me one time and nodded. My signal to move on out.

* * *

With Grady and Blue greeting me with confused barking that settled into recognition once I called their names, I pulled the wagon behind the Hamilton house, away from the view of the dirt road, in case Captain Duckworth changed his mind and headed on up. But I was pretty sure that our plan was solid. Uncle Bob came to meet me with his colt already strapped to his waist. I realized he had been expecting the wagon load. He, however, like the hounds, was surprised to find me manning the reigns. "What happened?" His face was clearly stricken.

"Pa's fine if that's what you're askin'." I saw his shoulders drop with relief, but as I told him what lead to me arriving alone with his precious cargo, he quickly stood at attention again. He yelled for John-Riley, who quickly emerged from behind the barn with an empty feed-basket. I could hear the sheep softly bleating, eager to devour their pile of corn husks.

"You need to take care of our guests while I head down to George's. Captain Duckworth is needin' to talk to me." John-Riley nodded and watched his father hustle to the barn and within minutes he had Mae saddled and they were headed down Lambs Creek.

A strange silence grew as John Riley looked at the tarp, and I slowly climbed down from my seat. I stood next to him and waited until he shifted awkwardly. "You know what's under this tarp?"

I put my hands on my hips and tilted my head. "I have my guesses and reckon it's not your usual load."

John-Riley stepped up and grabbed the tarp and slung it up with such force that the three mud-streaked faces beneath immediately shielded their eyes from the sun, still casting its morning rays through the trees. Their bodies flat and stretched out, suddenly coiled ready to jump and flee. But, when they saw we were unarmed and only staring at them, they settled into a crouch and looked around at the farm, safeguarded by hills and trees. Their blue uniforms, even dirty and worn, clearly marked them as the enemy, and I could feel my stomach lurch. If I had already eaten breakfast, I would have not been able to keep it down. Thankful for my empty stomach, I managed to swallow hard. Even if I couldn't muster a smile, I nodded to the men to let them know they could get off my wagon.

"Welcome to Transylvania County." John-Riley said with some gusto, not sure what he was supposed to say to Union soldiers. But they interpreted my nodding and his awkward greeting as a sign it was safe to move about.

"We were informed there was a Sheriff that would house us." One of the soldiers spoke with an accent I had never heard. "We did not believe such words could be true, but after listening to the discussions from underneath the canvas, we stand quite corrected." The man ran his dirty fingers though his greasy hair. "Seems there are several of you we must thank with utmost gratefulness."

"Let's get you on up the holler, before you keep thankin' me, mister." John-Riley waved for the men to follow him, since they clearly did not know what a holler was. The men nodded at me and awkwardly followed John-Riley through the path on up the mountain. Soon the thick Rhododendron bushes hid the blue of their uniforms. I shook my head and thought to myself that no one would ever believe that this little mountain valley suddenly had Yankees hidden up one of their hollers.

Robert Hamilton, August 2, 1864

"Are the soldiers gone yet?" George asks as he climbs the steps to the porch. He hasn't even sat down yet in the rocker before he burdens Robert with the question that is still weighing on the whole Neill family. Elizabeth especially keeps asking and, although he has assured her that her Uncle Bob has it under control, the little doubt that has grown within himself can no longer be managed.

It's a warm evening, even the breeze doesn't offer its usual relief, but Robert is already enjoying his pipe, with the dogs resting at his feet. "Sit down, George." He waits for his deputy and friend to settle down. Rhoda comes out to hug her cousin and offer him some coffee. He quickly says he will forgo her offer, but when she fusses at him to find some time to accept hospitality, he sighs and agrees to coffee *and* a piece of apple pie. Once she disappears inside, George stares at Robert, clearly irritated with his delay in offering details. Robert waves his pipe at George, "Oh stop that frettin'. Yes, the soldiers are gone. I sent them up and on over the mountain to Pink Beds and gave them directions on how to find their way into Tennessee. They were in good form, so I fed them one night and sent them on their way the next mornin'." George lets out a deep breath and finally sits back in his rocker. Robert continues, "I was only willin' to keep them on for one night. And I will stick to a one-night stay, if I can, makin' space for any others that may come a-knockin'."

George stops rocking. "You have a desire to go through this again?"

Robert's face grows serious. "No, I don't *desire* it! But I don't see how we can get around it. I'm afraid Atlanta will fall soon and the war in the South is only goin' to get worse."

"You may be willing, but I am NOT puttin' my family through that again."

Robert takes a long draw from his pipe and blows out the smoke with slow intention. "I agree. So, I have already ridden up to Cedar Mountain, in case more come, like these last soldiers who came up through Jones Gap to get into our mountains. I made some arrangements with folks who will bring any union soldiers directly to me, and through the woods, not by way of Lambs Creek. I've made a plan, but I need you to keep alert."

George shakes his head. "If anyone needs to see *the sheriff*, I can't keep them from goin' up the road to find you."

"That is absolutely right. So, you should be High Sheriff and I should be your deputy." Robert lowers his pipe as Rhoda joins them on the porch with coffee and pie. George is so distracted that he almost spills his coffee.

312

"What's got you all riled up?" Rhoda teases, and then settles next to Robert in her own rocker.

As George finally manages to place his coffee on the railing next to him so he can hold his pie and fork, he answers. "Your husband is makin' no sense."

Rhoda laughs, "Wouldn't be the first time. But I reckon most times he is fixin' to explain. Right, Bob?"

Robert shakes his head. "If you two would stop talkin' I could explain."

George lifts his fork and takes a bite of pie, but Rhoda takes her empty fork and waves it in front of her husband, "Well, go on!"

Robert chuckles at his wife, but then transfers his focus to George. The sheriff's shift to an earnest demeanor, is a welcome relief for his deputy. George needs to understand what Robert is planning and feels he no longer has time for pleasantries. They simply cannot take any of their circumstances lightly. Robert finally explains, "I have a real burden as I go all over this county tryin' to collect taxes from folks who cannot feed their families, cannot harvest their crops, if they have been fortunate to even make a crop or garden. This war is hell on families. So many men have died, been wounded or are still out there gettin' shot up."

"Bob, I agree, and we have chewed on this, many times. So, what's different now? What's that have to do with the soldiers? What are you thinkin'?" George grabs his coffee from the railing and takes a sip, pleased to taste a hint of real coffee mixed in with the chicory root, a real treat.

Robert blurts out, "I think you ought to run for Sheriff." Shocked, George tries to keep from spewing his sip of coffee all over the porch. He notices that Rhoda is calmly sipping her coffee like it is a fine summer evening; clearly, she is already aware of this approach.

George quickly swallows and looks right at Robert. "What on earth are you talkin' about? You are the Sheriff, and I could never run against you! You know how everything is done and I only help. What would you do if you're not sheriff?"

Robert nods reassuringly. "First of all, I would not leave you a-hanging. I could be your deputy and guide you when needed." Robert

313

removes his pipe from his mouth and waves it, pointing down Lambs Creek. "I got word that the State has begun issuing cards to assist wives and widows of soldiers who have died in combat. They are basically ration cards that will provide staples like beans, cornmeal, dried fruits, and the likes to these families. They are calling for 'Card Agents' to carry this out. And I think that, as a card agent, I could best help with the work we are already doin', especially since we never know when our own supplies will no longer be enough."

George takes a moment to process this approach and is shocked to find that this is being offered, but he quickly realizes that no one in Transylvania knows better about the many suffering families than this sheriff. "So, it's not only about keepin' people from headin' up Lambs Creek?"

Robert shakes his head, "Rhoda and I talked about this before our latest blue-uniformed guests arrived." Rhoda nods and reaches to squeeze his hand. As he returns her affection, he adds, "We realize that it is time to make some changes, even if they are only slight. This way, as Deputy and Card-Agent, I am still in the county and can keep an eye on families."

George sighs and takes another sip of coffee. "Well, Bob, I reckon you are the best one to sort out the wheat from the chaff."

Robert frowns. "What on earth are you talking about?"

George laughs as he responds, "How many times have you, when collectin' taxes, been able to figure out that somebody is tryin' to con you into thinkin' they have nothin' to give or cannot work off their taxes due on the road projects. I reckon those same folks will try to get some cards for themselves and take from those who really need such support. Hard to believe we have moochers in such hard times."

"I guess you are right, George." Robert's face grows somber again. "All I know is that many of our folks are hungry and need help. It's so bad that, hopefully when this war is over, we can build a county home for those who have nothin'. It's called a *poor house*."

George looks past the porch railing a little way to the large vegetable garden still yielding abundance. "What a terrible name, but I guess there is no doubt that those with the worst need would be thankful to live there."

314

Robert shakes his head, "With what I have seen these past few years, we will have many knockin' down the doors."

Elizabeth Neill, August 9, 1864

I was eager to write James, so I lit a candle and gathered my steel pen, ink and paper from under my bed and carried them quietly into the kitchen. I was so tired, but I needed to let him know what was happening. My heart ached to tell him of the Yankee holler, but of course that could not happen. Yet, I realized that, by writing, I at least felt closer to him, even if I didn't tell him everything. I shoved my nightgown sleeve up above my elbow, avoiding ink stains that would also avoid fussing from Ma in the morning. I paused before starting, making sure the paper was sitting just right. It felt good to hold the pen again.

Dearest James,

We have been weary, working from dawn to dusk harvesting corn and every vegetable Ma thinks can survive the root cellar. We have slaughtered a few sheep and a hog we bought from the Orrs. Preparing salt meats for the winter isn't only for our own family, since many families are in great need without their husbands and boys to help. I do think we will be in good form since Mammaw's field is yielding good crops as well. This, of course, keeps me working her fields and ours, but it is nothing to complain about since Jimmy and Sarah-Jane are helping with great vigor. It appears Pa will no longer tolerate tom-foolery from them.

Your sister, Betty, appears satisfied caring for Amanda's girls and at times I have witnessed laughter arise, a welcome sound in the midst of such darkness. I do not see the Lankford family often, since we have been preoccupied with harvest season. I do look forward to visits with you when you return.

Pa came home today and told us that this morning in the August 9, 1864 term of Transylvania Court of Pleas and Quarters, they elected him to be Transylvania County Sheriff. It appears that Sheriff Hamilton, my uncle, made a strong recommendation with assurance that he would accept a deputy nomination if so offered to him in the September court session. It appears that my uncle is interested in being made Card Agent, a new position that will help meet the needs of the poor. Although official proceedings will not declare him a deputy or the card Agent until September, Pa said it is only a formality at this time. It feels curious knowing Pa will now be Sheriff and Robert Hamilton his deputy, but we will all adjust to the changes.

I am happy to work so hard since it keeps my mind away from this treacherous war and am anxious for the day when you will no longer be a soldier. I know you are proud to be a solider and I am proud of you too for your bravery, but my heart cannot bear the thought of you in danger. May God keep you and your brothers safe from the cruelty of this war.

Yours,

Elizabeth

I blew on the paper, hoping the ink would dry quickly since I was fighting to keep my eyes open. As I waited, the relief in writing James gave way to the gnawing doubt in the validity of my actions. I knew that Pa becoming Sheriff meant I didn't have to hurry up to fetch Uncle Bob, because it would be our door that people would knock on to summon the Sheriff. I had not realized until that day that, for me, I felt we were somewhat justified with Pa being a Union sympathizer as the deputy, following his sheriff's orders. But with Pa actually being the sheriff, I was afraid we would never be able to defend our actions, if we ever had to.

CHAPTER 22

Robert Hamilton, August 11, 1864

Naomi English is sitting conspicuously in the front pew with her mother and father next to her, helping keep Fletcher's two little girls in line while he attempts to deliver a sermon. The protruding belly signals that it will not be long before Reverend English and his wife have their third child. Martha-Ann and Strawbridge are clearly proud grandparents and Robert smiles at the rare moment of joy within the war-stricken family. After the death of John Young, the already struggling Joshua seemed to withdraw even more into himself and Martha-Ann told Rhoda that he swore he would not return to church. They have occasional word from Martin who is still being held as prisoner in Elmira, New York. They hold on to the hope that at least he is not on the battle lines and will come home when the war is over.

A sniffle from the back of the church catches Rhoda and Robert's attention as they turn to see Rachel-Emma trying to muffle her sound with a kerchief to her mouth and act as if she is gracefully blowing her nose. But the red eyes and blotchy cheeks reveal that she has been crying for a while and that the sniffle is her attempt to keep from falling back into her despair. Rhoda taps Robert's arm and whispers, "Don't stare!"

He raises his eyes at his wife and whispers back, "I only looked 'cause you looked first."

"Well, poor girl is probably bereft over her brothers, so we need not stare." Rhoda holds her head forward with intensity and nods at Fletcher's latest statement, clearly not having heard a word.

Robert tries not to laugh at his wife and has to lift his hand to cover his mouth and finds himself feigning attention as he scratches his beard with thoughtful strokes. He has to force himself to concentrate even harder when Rhoda nudges him with her knee. Suddenly, his five-year old daughter, Rachel, speaks aloud with concern, "Ma? Why are you hittin' Pa?"

As the parishioners take a moment to chuckle and turn their heads, Reverend English pauses to shake his head at the scene.

Elizabeth Neill, August 11, 1864

I scrambled to stop Rachel-Emma outside the church before she started to cross over the little bridge to their house. She was clearly not waiting for her family, who were all standing around and asking Naomi questions about how she was feeling and if she had had any signs of labor pains yet. I wished I had sat with my friend, since I didn't notice her distraught condition until we all turned around to look at my cousin embarrassing Aunt Rhoda and Uncle Bob. The horrified look on Rachel-Emma's face at the sudden attention drawn to the back row was enough to make me wish I could have run to her at that moment, but she would have been more mortified than she already was.

"Will you stop already?" I finally said out of breath almost catching up with her on the other side of the Davidson River. "I never have seen someone able to move so quickly in their Sunday skirts."

Emma-Rachel finally slowed and waited for me behind the first bushes hiding her from the church across the river. "Hi, Elizabeth." She wiped away fresh tears, but tried to smile. "I'm sorry you had to run."

"What's wrong?" I came up next to her and looped my arm through hers, encouraging a slower stroll.

318

She welcomed my arm with a gentle pat, clearly appreciating that we could talk without me staring any more than necessary at her poor composure. "It's James-Henry."

I had flash-backs to the day Rachel-Emma and I were pulled into the fight at the Cagle-Mill between James-Henry and her brother John, along with my cousin, Andrew. I suddenly couldn't quite catch my breath for fear of the worst, "Is he dead?" Everyone knew James-Henry Cagle was a Union sympathizer, and I was surprised he had survived this long without incident.

"Oh Lord, no!" Rachel-Emma clasped her chest. "Don't even say that!"

I breathed a sigh of relief, "I'm sorry, I thought by the way you are cryin' that surely something awful has happened."

"He's joined the Union!" Rachel-Emma barely uttered the words before another sniffle caused her to retrieve her kerchief from the fold in her skirt.

"I'm sorry, but you knew he would." I said the words without hesitation.

"Elizabeth!" She stopped in her tracks and dropped my arm to face me clearly shocked. "How can you be so harsh?" She crossed her arms, but her bottom lip began to quiver.

"Oh Rachel-Emma, I meant no harshness. I swear." I came up to her and placed my hands on her crossed arms. For the first time I felt older than her. I had always looked up to her, being six years older than me, and so beautiful, but I figured despair could even make the strongest woman react like a child. "I was only saying that it is not a surprise. But it doesn't make it any easier."

Rachel-Emma nodded slowly, dropping her crossed arms and letting me loop myself back into the crook of her elbow. As we slowly continued our stroll, she tucked away her kerchief. "I know you are right, Elizabeth. But I thought that, as long as he was all talk, then I had a chance that he wouldn't go into battle. I'd have a chance that maybe he won't come home like Joshua with his mind not-right, or be

319

held prisoner like Martin, or worse get a letter about how he's dead, like John."

"I think you have a right to feel the way you do." I had felt much the same way about James when he joined in, but I had not lost a loved one to death. I wondered if I should say anymore or simply walk in silence. Still, I decided maybe I could help her understand one thing that I had seen in my James. "If James-Henry only ever speaks the words, will he feel proud in the end?" Rachel-Emma looks at me and is clearly confused. So, I continue, "He has some strong convictions and wants to stand for what he believes in. To him it has to be more than words only."

"Did he tell you this?" Rachel-Emma grasped both my hands. "He said those words to me too."

I shook my head. "No, he didn't tell me."

Her grasp relaxed some, "Then how do you know this?"

I smiled reassuringly, "Everyday I'm learnin' that there are many reasons for the choices we all make. I do know that deep convictions stand pretty high on the list of important reasons."

"But what about love?" Rachel-Emma's question was honest.

I thought for a minute before carefully answering, "How can a man love if he has no deep feelings about fightin' for what is right, to protect his loved ones?" Rachel-Emma nodded and we both continued in silence, winding around another bend along the dirt path. I wondered if the statement was true for myself, in some way. But, regardless of my notion, I recognized that many of our men believed it. I took Rachel-Emma's hand and swung it playfully, "Maybe there's something in the air or in the water that makes them believe it; maybe war stories from the glory days handed down instills this notion. Or maybe it isn't for us to understand."

Rachel-Emma smiled weakly, "Maybe so."

Had I just embraced the notion that we, as women, didn't or maybe even couldn't understand our men? Reality was that I understood more than I wanted to admit. I was doing the same thing. Taking a stand. And clearly, although secretly, taking a side. I was fighting for

320

those I loved. I never intended to feign ignorance to Emma-Rachel, but it was simply easier.

Robert Hamilton, November 5, 1864

The sun has long set and inside the home the long wooden table is blessed with enough food to feed the Hamilton family. Robert and Rhoda sit with their children and laugh as Joel retells how Reverend English almost raised a gun to the church rafters yesterday at school to shoot what he thought was another snake, but ended up scaring the heck-fire out of a possum. Robert can't believe Joel is already ten and privately laments that his children are growing up so quickly.

"Reverend English must be losin' sleep with his new baby boy cryin' at night." Millie smiles as she takes another bite of potatoes. Robert is happy for the birth of Fletcher's son, Charles, who was delivered last month with no complications. He is aware that Millie is weary from helping with births that produce dying babies and dying mothers, so she deeply treasures a healthy birth.

As the family laughs freely, outside Blue and Grady begin bellowing up a storm. The family suddenly quiets down and looks at each other, trying to figure out what the dogs are fussing over. The high intensity of the barking, intertwined with growling does not sound like their typical curiosity in a passing raccoon or eager greeting of a friend. John-Riley is the first to stand, but Robert holds out his hand to stop him and steps to the door alone. He grabs the Colt and its holster, out of habit now, and quickly straps it to his waist.

He opens the front door and does not see anyone approaching. "Blue! Grady! Hush!" But the dogs stand a few feet from the bottom of the porch and are vigorously barking at the forest not too far beyond the vegetable garden. Robert yells, "Who's there?"

A quick reply emerges from the dark, "A friend! Can you please call off the dogs so I can come closer?"

Robert whistles and the dogs immediately run towards him and settle at his feet. Slowly, two black men emerge from the field followed by five white men, mostly in uniform. Robert waits for them to come close enough to see if he recognizes anyone. The two black men quickly explain that they have been sent as guides from up Cedar Mountain to bring the five Union soldiers to him. He does not ask for their names. Robert thanks the guides, clearly a father and son undertaking, and lets them quickly disappear back into the thicket.

Robert quickly invites the men in without any formal introductions or any clarification on the reason for their late visit. The awkward silence is nothing new to the Hamilton family as the strangers enter the warmth of their home. It is only moments before the five very hungry escaped Union soldiers sit around the table and await the blessing. Robert's children take their own plates to settle around the fire, leaving the benches for their guests. Rhoda, dividing out what is left of their dinner onto five plates, encourages Robert to say another dinner blessing since the men obviously are expecting it. The children, with mouths half-full obediently bow their heads and let their father doubly-bless their meal.

"Amen," rings loud and clear across the room.

Robert is not the only one in his family observing the unique collection of men vigorously eating their food. They all have beards, but one is so long it reaches the broad-shouldered man's chest, while another has a short-cropped beard that accentuates his slender frame. The other three men's beards fall somewhere in-between the other two extremes. Only two men have a Union soldier's cap. Three men have some form of blue jacket or vest, which cause Robert to suspect they could be officers. One escapee is dressed in no uniform at all while the last man is clearly wearing a Confederate uniform with a Confederate cap.

It is Joel who speaks first to the man in gray, "So, Mister, are you a Confederate soldier?"

"Joel!" Rhoda's voice is anxious, "Let's leave the men to eat."

Joel drops his head and scrapes his fork against an already empty plate. He would have licked it, and he thinks he may still do that when no one is looking.

"No problem, son." The man smiles. "I am a Union officer. Name's Lieutenant Hastings. I thought it would come in handy to be dressed like a Confederate when I needed to find out the loyalty of those who we needed help from." He grins. "Worked too! Got us this far."

"Sheriff Hamilton?" The one man that looked like a full Union soldier with cap and jacket addresses Robert directly.

Robert hesitates a moment and wonders if he should correct the title and inform the men that he is actually the deputy sheriff, but the detail really is insignificant at the moment so he responds, "Yes?"

"We are much obliged for your hospitality. I am Captain Langworthy." The captain finally shares his identity and then proceeds to introduce the men. "You have spoken with Lieutenant Hastings, but this is Lieutenant Terwilliger." The man with the long beard nods in acknowledgement before Captain Langworthy moves on and taps the shoulder of the man to his right wearing no uniform, "Captain Starr." He ends with a final nod at a soldier who has almost cleared his plate. "That is Captain Aldrich."

"Pleased to meet you all. Do tell us a bit about your journey. I find it somewhat odd that you are all officers?" Robert encourages the men to speak freely.

The officers immediately look to Captain Langworthy who does not hesitate to begin, "We were captured in Plymouth, North Carolina, on April 20th and then loaded into cattle cars and transferred south, until we were unloaded in Andersonville, Georgia." The men place their forks on their empty plates and, although they could clearly eat more food, they are thankful for what they have received. "It was a strange ordeal. A Captain Wirtz met the officers who were delivering us and informed them that he could only take the enlisted men; not the officers. He demanded that all the officers step forward; there were around seventy five of us, and then proceeded to imprison over seven hundred of the soldiers that had made the south-ward journey with us. The captain of the guard tried to insist Captain Wirtz imprison us too, but he said he had no room for officers. Something about his European background and respect for fellow officers. The guards had to decide what they would do with us, and so we boarded the train again and were then deposited in Macon where they quickly built a stockade around us using a team of slaves. We were there a short time, and I procured turpentine in case we should be fortunate enough to escape. But before we were able to do so, we were transferred to Charleston. You see, our Union troops were on nearby Morris Island and firing on Charleston. Moving captured Union soldiers, like us, in their line of fire was a hearty attempt by the Confederates to encourage our Union troops to cease firing on the city." Captain Langworthy pauses and looks nervously at the children sitting near the fire place, all listening intently, except Rachel and Emily, who play quietly in the corner, only concerned with who will spin the top next. "Are you sure I should proceed with your children listening?"

Robert nods. "We have no secrets. They are as much a part of this war as you and I."

Captain Langworthy frowns at the truth of the statement, but he proceeds. "While we were within such close proximity to Andersonville, I was able to ask some Catholic Sisters if they had word from the prison camp where my men were taken. She spoke of such horrors. I was sick to hear of men she tended, where she wiped maggots from their skin because of deplorable condition. I think nightly of the horrors of my men who still remain prisoners. It is not likely many will survive." The Union soldiers look at each other, acknowledging the weight of the statement. "From Charleston, we were transported north to Columbia in hopes that we and the other officers would not all succumb to the fever running rampant further south. Once in Columbia, they marched us to the Saluda River and placed us in a large field with guards. It was clear to us all that we should escape before a stockade could be built around us, like we had seen happen in Macon. The five of us managed to escape with the help of my turpentine that we rubbed on our shoes to keep the dogs at bay. We could hear them whining when they found our scent, but they were confused and upset and could not continue. We had many encounters along the way and what a surprise as we made our way up the mountains to find the Sheriff a loyal Union man."

John-Riley quickly interrupts, "Pa, ain't no Union man." Rhoda and Millie quickly rise and head into the kitchen busying themselves with dishes. Viney follows them and returns with mugs for some chicory-coffee.

Captain Langworthy is startled by the young man's statement and the sudden bustling of the women, clearly uncomfortable with the discussion. Robert quickly offers a soft chuckle, "Please excuse my son and my family. We're all very weary from talk of loyalty and tire of the ragin' battle between North and South, but also between neighbors. I do sympathize with your cause, but I would ask you to be cautious with how you label my family. Please consider us friendly mountain folk who saw it fittin' to welcome you in on your journey home."

"I did not mean to offend." Captain Langworthy apologizes, but is not entirely sure he understands. He accepts the mug from Viney and watches her pour coffee for each of the men still sitting around the table. He takes a sip and tries to explain, "I was a physician in New York City before the war and I never encountered anyone who was sick and cured at the same time."

"Well, I wish it were that simple, Doc." Robert sips his coffee. "You see, I have neighbors and friends on both sides of the war and they don't mind shootin' each other if they think that it's the right thing to do to defend their side. It's quite a place to be in the middle. You see my boy over there?" Robert points at Joel. "He and each of my children." Robert falters a minute as he thinks of Andrew and corrects himself. "At least all of my children who are here, I have raised to be honest- God-fearin' Christians. But each one of them will lie quick as lightnin' if anyone asks if you were here tonight." At this point Rachel and Emily are crawling into Joel and John-Riley's arms yawning. "A fearsome way to raise my children." Robert nods for the two boys to haul their little sisters upstairs. Robert observes pity reflected in his guest's eyes. "Oh now don't you worry none about us. We don't need your pity. I am proud that we follow what we feel is right in God's eyes."

Captain Langworthy raises his mug and holds it as the other officers raise their mugs as well, causing Robert to be perplexed. As the mugs are held stock-still half-way raised, Captain Langworthy speaks, "We honor you and your family!"

Robert awkwardly raises his mug to match the men's actions, "Well, I thank you."

325

The men then unanimously chant, "Hear, hear!" and take a drink of coffee, so Robert sips his as well. Captain Langworthy smiles and explains, "It's usually more impressive with glasses of strong spirits, like cognac."

"I guess you have some strange ways of honorin' people up north!" Robert smiles, "Around here we honor each other by sittin' on the porch and listenin' to each other." Then Robert lifts his mug. "But there is always a strong cup of coffee!"

The laughter is welcome and settles everyone into an evening of stories and fellowship. Robert and John-Riley eventually show the men to the shelter up the holler and settle the men in with hopes they can leave the next morning.

Elizabeth Neill, November 6, 1864

The down-pour made it difficult to do anything but stay put. I was thankful for an excuse to stay inside for a bit and enjoy the fireplace and spend more time cooking, a chore Sarah-Jane was claiming as her own while Jimmy and I helped Pa outside. It felt good to spend some time laughing with Ma and my sister in the kitchen while we finished canning the final sweet potatoes not stored in the root cellar. That afternoon, after the kitchen was clean and before it was time to prepare supper, I settled onto my bed upstairs, listening to the rain beat the roof with a steady rhythm, making it hard to keep my eyes open. But I wanted a few minutes alone to read the letter from James again. Although I had received the letter the day before, I had read it twice and thought it wouldn't hurt to read it again, since it reminded me that he was still very much alive.

Dearest Elizabeth,

It seems I will have to wait with taking leave to see you since the numbers of deserters, bushwhackers and escaped Union prisoners coming up from the south has increased with such vigor that it keeps my regiment on highest alert. We patrol Hendersonville and the surrounding area with such vigilance that I am confident few of the likes of them will slip by our patrols.

Please keep us in your prayers as we continue to protect our families and country.

We have received word that my brother, William, and my cousin are prisoners of war at Johnson Island. It is my hope that they remain in good form while being held and do not succumb to sicknesses that are reported to kill so many of our soldiers. But I do not wish to burden you with more of my worries, my love.

I hear word from my sister Betty that she and B.C. are becoming steadfast friends. It is my hope that she will remain with him and his girls. Time will only tell.

I am very pleased to hear that you are persistent and continue to persevere in the hardships of life. But I know you are strong. In more ways than one.

I hope to take leave as soon as I am able.

With fondest greetings,

Your James

I traced my finger over his words *But I know you are strong. In more ways than one.* These words felt very real and sincere. It was a truth about myself I was beginning to embrace. I hoped that, because he already believed that about me, that he would one day still see those words to be true.

Robert Hamilton, November 7, 1864

Hopes of a one-night-stay is literally dampened when heavy rain sets in. After two days, Robert finds himself bringing the men in to his home for what he hopes is the last meal before they leave the next day. The downpour of rain is so strong that only Viney hears a knock at the door. Blue and Grady are inside and only start barking when Viney reaches for the door handle. She looks at Robert first and he holds up

327

his hand for her to wait a minute. He waves the five officers to quickly follow him into the small back room behind the kitchen, where the men awkwardly cram into the small space, including Robert.

Viney opens the front door slowly and another Union solider stands in front of her completely drenched. "Hello there, I am what they call a Yankee soldier. I am heading North." the man yells slowly. Only half-way listening to the man's patronizing description, Viney drops her shoulders in disbelief, and doesn't say anything. Instead, she closes the door on him and turns to her Ma. "It's another one, and I'm pretty sure he thinks we're ignorant. Do you think we could maybe not let this one in?"

"Viney!" Rhoda quickly walks past her daughter who proceeds to sit in the rocker in front of the roaring fireplace so she can have a good view of what will happen next. "Of course, we will let him in!" Rhoda opens the door and the man quickly explains, in the same patronizing manner, who he is and that he is looking for the Sheriff. His crisp, precise, but simple language perturbs Rhoda as much as it did Viney, so she stands and looks at the soaking man for a moment and does not offer her usual smiling gesture of hospitality. Instead, she nods for him to follow her as she leads him to stand in front of the fireplace; she then proceeds to open the door to the backroom. Viney is not disappointed in her expectation of being entertained as Captain Aldrich emerges from the backroom to embrace the wet man, who is leaving quite the puddle on the hard-wood floor. He is quickly greeted by the remaining officers, all oblivious to Viney. She settles into a rocking chair, carefully positioned to observe every detail.

Captain Aldrich quickly introduces his friend to Robert, "This is Lieutenant Conley who was captured with us at Plymouth in April." He then addresses the wet man. "I can't believe you have come all this way alone!"

The new guest waves his hand at the door, "Well, there are six more waiting in the brush. One of them a Confederate deserter."

A loud laugh escapes from Viney, and she exclaims. "Great day in the mornin'! You got to be joshin'!" The men, though, don't hear her, but Rhoda glares at Viney and pulls her out of her rocker to help her in the kitchen while Robert encourages the newcomer to invite in the rest of the escapees.

Elizabeth Neill, November 8, 1864

"You won't believe this!" Viney had her arm snaked through mine as she led me around the final bend to their home. "It's a whole flock of soldiers campin' up the holler."

"You mean Yankee Holler?" I teased, as I tried to avoid stepping in a large puddle. The rain had let up a bit, and the sun was peeking through the dark clouds, offering a little respite, and warming the day enough to walk along Lambs Creek. It was only a matter of time before the heavens poured again.

Viney laughed, "Well ain't that the perfect name!"

"Are you sure you should be bringin' me up here?" I stopped her before we were in view of the front porch. "Won't your Pa be upset?"

Viney shook her head and nudged me to continue walking beside her, so I complied as Blue and Grady scampered down the muddy road to join us. She explained, "I told Pa that I was goin' to fetch you to help us some with pullin' together the sacks of provisions that we are makin' for each soldier. A collection of salt-meats, some bread and some apples. Not sure what else, but Millie is in charge."

I stopped her again. "Now, Viney! Don't you know I have plenty to do at home and at Mammaw's?" I teased, but she could feel I was serious at the same time.

"Oh, come on, Elizabeth. You would never believe this if you didn't see it for yourself. I promise if you just take a look and help us for a bit, then you can head on," Viney begged. "Some of them really irk me. A few think we are some ignorant folk and talk to us like we are as slow as molasses." She giggled for a second and pulled in really close and whispered, "So I mess with them. Turn it right back around. You got to come and see!"

I sighed and reluctantly nodded. "Oh, all right!" I was curious, but I worried too since it seemed that maybe so many people hiding in one place was really not *hiding* at all. It would be so easy for James and his regiment to run into a large gathering of Union soldiers and deserters. I was trying to absorb some of Viney's lightness in the midst of the absurd and push away the words from James' recent letter.

"Besides, I think Millie is sweet on one of the men, a Lieutenant Hastings. She's been offerin' him more coffee than others and talkin' to him about our community and all. I saw Pa fuss at her a few times to stop talkin' to him, but she cain't help it." Viney sighed. "This rain has kept the men here too long and if they stay much longer, we may have to begin marrying some of them." She laughed at the horrified look on my face. "I'm only joshin'!"

We came around the corner of the house; our boots making squishy noises as we attempted to follow the normal path, but then decided it was best to climb to the grassy area that offered less of a chance of falling flat on our faces. The normally tranquil stream that ran through the middle of the holler and offered summer relief from the heat was a rippling force of mud and water well above its normal flooding level. It wasn't the stream that fascinated me the most, though; it was the collection of benches and chairs that were brought outside of the kitchen door to allow a crowd of men to enjoy the few moments in the sun. At first, the men hardly noticed us because they were busy with shoe repair or shuffling through backpacks. Others simply sat partially reclined closing their eyes for a moment to let the warmth lull them. However, one man quickly stood and anxiously walked towards us as the other men suddenly gave him their attention.

"Miss?" The man addressed Viney as his eyes bounced back and forth between her and me nervously. "Have you brought a visitor or is this a sister that has been tucked away?"

Viney rolled her eyes. "Yes, Mr. Conley. I have so many sisters that we take turns comin' out of the house." Her sarcasm shocked me.

"Lieutenant." The man corrected, "I'm Lieutenant Conley."

330

"Oh, that's right!" Viney's voice was too sweet. "I forgot for a minute." I quickly realized this was one of the men that she is fed up with and hoped that Uncle Bob wasn't listening. I was sure he'd have a fit if he heard her be so disrespectful.

The Lieutenant was clearly not pleased with Viney's feigned ignorance. His face went red trying to decide if he should reprimand her, but then, glancing at me, he decided to focus on the task at hand. Since she was not giving him the answers, he addressed me directly. "Miss, I hope you come as a friend and not a foe?"

I smiled and truthfully answered, "Sir, I am a cousin from down the road and my father is the sheriff and a union sympathizer. We are all in this together and I have come to help with packin' provisions for you and your men."

Lieutenant Conley was quickly joined by another man in uniform who was wearing a Union cap. "Did you say your father is sheriff?" When I was surprised to be addressed by someone else, he quickly took off his cap and bowed his head with a quick nod, "Excuse my poor manners. I am Captain Langworthy. My men and I arrived here first."

I did my best awkward curtsey, "Pleased to meet you sir. I'm Elizabeth." I decided my last name was not needed. "And yes, my pa is sheriff."

The captain and lieutenant frowned at each other and then both looked at Viney. Captain Langworthy spoke with hesitancy, clearly trying not to offend, yet there was an obvious air of suspicion. "I thought *your* father was the sheriff. What is the meaning of this?"

Vineys eyes grew wide and she clearly respected this Captain Langworthy, especially concerning a serious matter of mistrust. "Oh, Captain. It's a simple matter. Nothin' to worry over."

Captain Langworthy replaced his cap, but did not ease his intensity. "Do tell."

"Well Pa was what we call High Sheriff until a few months ago and Uncle George was deputy Sheriff. Then they basically switched. Well, there was an official election and all, but basically mostly people call them both sheriff, dependin' on who is talkin'. But now Uncle George

331

is the High Sheriff. But people just say sheriff..." Viney was turning red, "Well dag nab it, it sure is a strange thing." Viney looked all forlorn at Captain Langworthy and shrugged. "I guess that may seem suspicious, but around here it's normal. You'll have to just trust us, I guess." She looked at Lieutenant Conley and with as much respect as she could muster she added, "Considerin' the hospitality and Pa's relentless search to collect supplies for you from folk that don't even have a pot to piss in, I think you should believe we are more than poor ignorant mountain folk."

"Miss! We do not think that!" Captain Langworthy quickly rebutted, deeply offended.

Viney's voice softened and she regarded the captain with respect, "No, sir. I know *you* don't. But some of your men do." She turned her head to Lieutenant Conley. "Ain't that right, Lieutenant?"

Lieutenant Conley's face reddened as Captain Langworthy turned to face him. He cleared his throat and stood up straight, clearly pulling himself together, trying to find a way to save face. "Miss. I stand corrected. It is my sincere hope that you accept my deepest regrets. I have much to learn about ... about... your people." Captain Langworthy's eyes grew wide and he looked at Viney and me to see how we would respond to this equally offensive statement.

Viney's jaw dropped and I covered my mouth, but then I couldn't help but begin laughing. The poor man was serious, and he really was apologizing. Viney also began to chuckle. "Oh, my dear Lieutenant Conley. It sure is clear who needs some educatin'."

Robert Hamilton, November 9, 1864

Robert is weary after having spent two more days gathering enough supplies for the company of twelve men to travel on through the mountains. He finally gathers them together for the last time. The fireplace offers the last warmth the escapees will feel for days, but Robert is not concerned with them. After hearing their escape stories and their ability to make it this far, he believes the men will fare just fine. But he does have one concern. "Who will be the lead officer while you travel from here?"

The men look at each other and then Captain Langworthy answers, "We are all officers. No one is in command?"

Robert frowns, "Are you sayin' that in the Union Army you have no one that is in command? Are you sayin' that everyone simply does what they like and don't follow orders? Because if that is what you are sayin', then the north won't have a chance in hell winnin' this war. And I have put my family in danger for nothin'."

The collection, of escapees, awkwardly scratch their heads and look at each other, confused at what Robert is insinuating. Captain Langworthy quickly rebuts, "Of course we have different ranks and follow orders. It seems we have not had need of it on our escape route."

"Well, you do now. With as many of you as there are, you better decide who is in command since there will be times one of you will have to make the decision for all of you." It takes only moments for the men to agree that Captain Langworthy is indeed the highest-ranking captain and so Robert looks seriously at all the other men. "Does this mean you are all willing to follow his command?"

The men quickly answer, "Yes, Sir."

"Good! Then it is time for you to move on." Robert pulls out a roughly drawn map on a piece of paper. Millie and Viney are moving in and out of the room with packed provisions in small sack-cloths and laying them on the table.

Captain Langworthy asks, "How do we do this? What do we need to know?"

"First, we hope a guide will show early tomorrow. I'll not give his name in case you are caught and questioned." Robert flattens out a hand-sketched map on his table as the men gather around, leaving no more room for Viney and Millie to finish their task. So, they stand and lean patiently against the doorframe into the kitchen. "If he does not show, or if you lose him, I will try to give you some direction."

Captain Langworthy interrupts Robert before he moves on. "If he doesn't show is clear, but what do you mean by 'lose him'?"

Robert sighs, "Well, I hope you understand that the few helpers we have are really aware they may be shot if caught guidin' you. At the slightest sign of Confederates or home guard or bushwhackers nearby they may well disappear into the thickets without notice. We encourage that tactic to keep them comin' to help." Robert does not mention his own brother-in-law is part of the home-guard, but he knows that Henry is busy farming and, besides, inspecting his neighbors and kin up the Davidson River, according to Rhoda, has got him all tore up. He reports to Duckworth that all is well, and his Captain lets it be, and no-one is the wiser.

"You mean they would abandon us in these mountains?" The lone Confederate deserter voices his concern.

Robert nods. "Yep. You are escaped soldiers and could be re-captured and treated as prisoners of war. To help you is regarded as a far more serious crime and may mean simply being shot on the spot. In fact, two helping men were just killed over in Cruso, in the Pigeon River Gorge."

Captain Langworthy looks seriously at Robert, and almost whispers, "Gracious, Sheriff. Again, we know that what you have done here is really a big risk for you and your family. We are deeply indebted and will never forget it." All of the men chime in and nod solemnly.

Robert tries to be gracious and accept their appreciation, but he is ready for these men to leave and does not desire for this seemingly growing rag-tag battalion to expand any larger. They need to leave before more arrive. To him it is as simple as that. "Thank you." Robert manages, but then directs everyone's attention to the sketched map. "Now back to the directions. This trip will take you over the hill as you face the holler where you are hidin'." The men follow his finger as he moves it along squiggly lines. "Follow the trail to the creek we call Davidson River upstream, to your left. Under no circumstances go right, downstream, or near any voices in that direction."

"But one of your daughters was telling us that there is a friendly church there?" Lieutenant Hastings, still wearing his stolen Confederate Uniform, asks.

Robert nods, and then frowns at Millie who quickly disappears into the kitchen with reddening cheeks. Viney quickly follows trying not to giggle. For a moment, a hand reaches back into the room and places the final provisions on the floor where they had been previously standing. Robert ignores his daughters and continues, "Yes, but very close to where we once had a grist mill and linsey-woolsey mill, the Confederates are working iron. The Cagle grist mill is run by another man and the Cagle family moved to Cedar Mountain." Realizing that none of these names mean anything to his guest he returns their attention to the map. "When you get to this wagon road you may see that church on the right. Be sure you study the dirt on the road carefully to look for more than one set of fresh hoof prints heading up the mountain where you want to go. If so, turn right onto the little road heading up Avery's Creek, only a few yards from the church. It will take you past some small farms, a saw mill and up the mountain to that community, called Pink Beds. Your guide will do the same alternative if it looks like a patrol is on the way up. Otherwise, stay on the wagon road with the river, past the falls on your right, then the large mountain of rock on your left. It's called 'Looking Glass Rock' by the Cherokee in their language. The road will level out into a small settlement, Pink Beds, with houses on both sides of the road. The folks are friendly, but very scared and cautious. They will not bother you or ask who you are. But if you ask if anyone is watching the Wagon Road Gap ahead, they will nod 'yes' or 'no.'"

"What do we do if they nod 'yes'?"

"Just past the houses, a road or trail on the right, will lead you to the next ridge taking you through Yellow Gap instead. When you get there, turn left and climb the ridge itself. It will lead you over to Mount Pisgah, about the highest in the area. Stay to the left and go down the mountain edge to the river, Pigeon River."

"And what if the Wagon Road Gap is not watched?"

"That road will lead you down to the same river, only further upstream."

After an awkward pause one officer asks, "This Mount Pisgah you mention- is that perchance the one I heard belonged to the Confederate General Clingman? Is it safe to go there?"

"Well yes. It is all rough woodland and neither he nor his men are nearby. You are safe." Robert focuses the men to the map again and points to the other side of the mountain ridge. "Others will help you once you are on the other side."

The men begin to step away from the table and grab the provisions that Viney and Millie have already placed on the table or left abandoned on the floor next to the kitchen. Robert sighs and is thankful to get the men on their way. "Gentlemen, time for some rest. You have a big day-hopefully several days ahead. Go in peace and with our prayers."

Chapter 23

Elizabeth Neill, November 24, 1864

I was surprised that we were actually attempting to have an official Thanksgiving meal with the Hamilton Family. It had been a year since President Lincoln had declared the fourth Thursday in November a national holiday, a celebration Uncle Bob had educated us about through the years, but not a celebration all, yet, completely embraced.

The Hamilton family journeyed down Lambs Creek to gather in our home. Clearly Pa and Uncle Bob agreed it was the best way to avoid worrying about unexpected guests. They knew, from experience, anyone seeking shelter would wait in the bushes until they arrived home and, secondly, anyone seeking "The Law" to help them in the county would stop by our house first. It was good to hear laughter, and the smell of turkey roasting made my stomach growl for several hours. My cousin William had taken my brother Jimmy hunting for the first time and Jimmy was proud to shoot his first turkey. He beamed with such pride when we sat around the table and exclaimed how delicious it was.

Although the meal was enough for everyone, there was an unspoken understanding that we all took only as much food as we needed to fill our plates once. Ma carefully rationed out the servings for my youngest cousins since any waste was not acceptable. The slew of Union soldiers earlier that month left a substantial hole in our rations. We still had plenty, if only our families were to be fed, but it was never only us. None of us dared to complain aloud since our parents reminded us at the beginning of every meal with a lengthy prayer to God how fortunate we were to be so blessed. To argue that our blessings were diminishing, would have been blasphemous. So, I secretly counter-prayed to God to help at least some hungry people knock on other doors so I could eat two biscuits again in the morning instead of one.

As dinner came to a close and family began to spread out for a lazy late afternoon, Pa and Uncle Bob grabbed a cup of coffee, as they still liked to call the brown hot liquid, to head out onto the porch, braving the cold afternoon chill, for Uncle Bob to light up his pipe. There was a serious look on Pa's face when he nodded to Uncle Bob to head over to the far end of the porch, so I looked at Viney and whispered, "Quick follow me." Viney didn't question why as we both scurried upstairs to my siblings' and my bedroom. The one bed was beginning to feel tight since Jimmy was quickly growing. Pa promised me he'd build me one as soon as the war was over. I told him not to worry and that, if it got too awful, I would sleep at Mammaw's every night. I was about ready to make the move.

"What are you doin'?" Viney finally asked as she followed me to the one window facing Lambs Creek.

"Shhhhh." I whispered as I carefully cracked the window. We were right above the conversation below.

"Should we be listenin'?" She whispered with feigned concern.

"Hush," I held my finger to my lips and then added, "And don't you go gettin' all uppity on me! I just beat you to the idea."

She nodded and whispered, "True 'nough."

Uncle Bob's voice silenced our whispered bantering. "What's happen' in the county, *Sheriff*?"

Pa chuckled at Uncle Bob's emphasis on the title. "Come on Bob. You'll always be the sheriff in my mind, and I couldn't do this without you. Most folks will always see you as High Sheriff." Then Pa cleared his throat. "Anyway, word has come in that James-Henry got shot a couple of days ago, somewhere between Boylston Road and Little River Turnpike." I stifled the small gasp that escaped and looked at Viney who was frowning.

"Cagle?" Uncle Bob asked for clarification, but I knew exactly who Pa was talking about. Emma-Rachel's fears had become a reality. Uncle Bob continued, "I heard rumors that he returned quietly as a member of the 3rd Regiment of North Carolina Infantry to help in the cause he now believes in." Uncle Bob paused briefly before he sighed. "I had been givin' thanks that he and his friend, W.W. Hamlin, could do this recruitin' as individuals, an assignment that I thought had them in much less danger than riding about with that radical, Colonel Kirk. Seems like I was mistaken."

"Yep. He has some kind of big record for recruitin' Union soldiers in these parts. He must have been enlistin' new recruits when he was shot." Pa explained.

Uncle Bob's voice revealed deep concern. "Is he severely hurt? Did they catch him?" Pa took a minute and Viney and I wondered what was taking him so long to answer. I raised my hand to my mouth and pretended to drink, suspecting maybe he was taking a sip of coffee. Viney nodded, agreeing with my assessment. Pa finally answered, "We heard that he was hit in the chest and hip and escaped with the two recruits with him, John Wood and one of the Galloways from up in Wolf Mountain and Balsam Grove. Rumor has it that they are carin' for him somewhere up in the mountains. Wood may have been interested in fightin' for the other side." I felt some relief knowing that James-Henry wasn't dead and hoped that Emma-Rachel was receiving the same information.

Uncle Bob asked the questions weighing heavily on me. "Who did it? The home guard?" My heart raced in fear that Pa would say it was James. But then, surely, he would have told me if that was the case.

"It appears Captain Deavor called on the 64th Regiment to keep watch between here and Hendersonville for a Union recruiter. The 64th took note and moved into action not really knowin' if they would encounter bushwhackers or the recruiter. Seems James-Henry is lucky to be alive comin' up against the likes of them."

I slumped completely to the floor and looked up at the ceiling. My heart was pounding with the thought of James and his regiment being the ones to shoot James-Henry, someone James knows well. Viney slipped down next to me and grasped my hand and squeezed it as she whispered, "You don't know it was James!"

"But it was his regiment!" The words were barely audible, mostly because I was trying not to sob. I suddenly felt very cold, but it was clearly not only the chill coming in from the window. Viney reached for the quilt on our bed and pulled it down to cover us.

Pa's voice drew me back to their conversation. "Bob, what's the latest on the war?" I wanted to stand up and scream out the window that moving on with the conversation was not appropriate. The warmth from the quilt kept me from following my instincts.

Uncle Bob's voice quickly set me straight. "Awful news, George. Everywhere. The word is that General Sherman is marching across Georgia destroyin' everything in sight."

"What?" Pa's shock reached Viney and me as we looked at each other with a new fear pounding in both our chests.

Uncle Bob explained. "Somethin' called a 'scorched earth' military maneuver. Nothin' left for food or roads or civilian livelihood. Not just military destruction."

"And he is already in Georgia?" Pa's voice was softer as if he didn't want to alarm anyone inside.

"Unfortunately," Uncle Bob responded, "Atlanta is wiped out and he hopes to march to the sea. This may break the back of the Confederacy." We all wanted the war to be over, but soldiers losing their lives was one thing, families and property intentionally destroyed was something else.

Uncle Bob pauses before he grieves aloud. "You know, George, as much as we did not want this war or the country to split, I am sorry for all the sufferin' on both sides. No winners, only losers. Let us hope the end is near and some order can be restored."

340

Viney and I stayed laying on my bedroom floor for some time while I tried to pull myself together before we joined the festivities downstairs. When we finally came downstairs the grief on my face was greater than the guilt I felt for eavesdropping. So, I quickly pushed through the front door to the porch and walked right up to Pa. He saw my face and then looked up at my still-open-window. Instead of fussing at me, like he would have a couple of years ago, compassion and shared grief swept open his arms to gently embrace me and let me cry. No questions asked. No answers needed.

Robert Hamilton, December 7, 1864

A light dusting of snow still covers the ground as Robert makes his way to Lankford's store where George said he would meet him at noon. Both men hope to negotiate with B.C. on what it will take to extend store-credits for specific families in the community. As Robert enters the store, he welcomes the stuffy-warmth and is pleased that no one else is present, allowing for an attempt at confidentiality. George, taking advantage of the privacy, is already at the wooden counter and in earnest conversation with B.C who is methodically stroking his white beard with one hand. They break their intensity as Robert arrives. George smiles. "There he is! Bob I was just talkin' to B.C. about our concerns."

"Hello, Sheriff." Lankford catches himself and looks at George. "I guess you both will be called sheriff and that will be the way it is." He laughs heartily, "I cain't be bothered to keep it all straight."

Robert smiles and nods with acceptance, "I think that's a fine idea. It appears we're both already used to it." Robert comes in closer and returns the focus to business. "So, have you made any headway on what might be worked out with extendin' store credit?"

B.C. returns his hand to his beard and shakes his head, "It ain't that easy, Bob."

Robert interrupts B.C. before he can go on, "As card-agent, I've got several ration cards that can offer you payment for some of the

341

supplies." At least Robert hopes that the cards will be reimbursed, but is leery that there is money readily available.

The storeowner keeps shaking his head. "It's not about the ration cards or the credit. It's about the staples. Even Probart Poor's trading post is strugglin', and he started with quite an abundance." Robert frowns and then looks around the store for the first time noticing that the only shelves that are still stocked are the ones with the non-essential items. An assortment of fine china is collecting dust in the corner and several baskets of bunch-yarn along with several yards of a blue-striped fabric are waiting to be transformed into winter scarves and dresses. Dying materials seems to be a luxury as well since indigo and madder appear on the shelf in greater abundance than usual. Robert's stomach flips, however, when he sees that crates and barrels usually full of sacks of flour, salt and cornmeal are almost bare. B.C. shakes his head, "I'm strugglin' with keepin' basics in stock for those who *can* afford to buy them."

Suddenly the door opens and Captain Deavor enters with two privates. They quickly head to the stove to warm their hands. Robert is sincerely happy to see that Captain Deavor recovered from the gun shot, which few knew he had suffered. Reflecting back to that day, Robert thinks it is probably a good idea *not* to ask Deavor about his recovery. And, clearly, it is wise for Deavor to not say too much either, since Fletcher is a Union sympathizer. Still, Captain Deavor nods respectfully at Robert, which Robert genuinely reciprocates.

"What's the news, Captain?" B.C. asks, trying to be open and friendly and steer George and Robert away from further discussions of store-credit.

Captain Deavor turns his back to the stove to face the three men standing at the counter, but he swings his hands around his back to keep them as close to the stove as possible. "Not much since we have an impossible job gettin' supplies for our troops. The Union has blockaded most supply channels and all this destruction by Sherman has cut off anything more from the south. We have been over three or four counties here in the mountains actually beggin' for vittles for Confederate troops, even though we can pay for them. Folks do not even have food for themselves, so money ain't the issue!"

Robert looks at B.C who raises his eyebrows and nods. "That is exactly what I was explainin' to Sheriff Neill and Sheriff Hamilton a minute ago."

Captain Deavor looks at Robert and George and shakes his head as he laments, "It's a bad situation."

"Did your Pa have any staples he could spare?" George asks gently.

"Yeah, he and Ma gave two bags of flour, but I felt real bad takin' from my own folks at their age. Pa said back when he was in the militia, they never had this kind of problem, even in the worst of times."

Robert, trying to show solidarity with close neighbors, says, "Your father was a real protector of us all as a Captain in our local militia. We were lucky to have him here."

"Thanks, Sheriff. A lot of people still address him as 'Captain' like most of us still call you 'Sheriff'."

There are some chuckles that fill the room, albeit a little forced.

Young Captain Deavor turns to B.C. and asks, "Have you seen John Duckworth lately?"

The sudden change in topic is no surprise, since there appears to be less time for casual conversation. B.C. shakes his head. "No. Never know when he will drop in. He and his home guard boys are constantly lookin' for deserters which seem to be increasin' in number."

Captain Deavor leaves the stove and walks towards the counter. "Thanks, B.C. Please give him a message for me. Tell him that the higher priority these days is to stop, catch *or* kill these bushwhackers. They are doin' unspeakable deeds in Henderson and other counties, even here in Transylvania. Tell him that deserters are in with them. That will motivate him more to go after them!"

Robert and George look at each other and wonder if Duckworth is still checking the abandoned campground. If the bushwhackers are making their rounds in neighboring counties then they will be back soon, if not already. B.C. responds without hesitation. "Will do."

With little more than a nod to his two men, Captain Deavor instructs them to grab the only two sacks of flour still in the barrels and the last three sacks of salt. He pays B.C. and slips out the door to ride down the turnpike toward Hendersonville.

B.C. sighs and considers Robert and George a minute before uttering words he clearly dreads. "I am really sorry I cain't help the families more. I am worried the few shipments that arrive once a week will dwindle to none. And even those that do come often only carry what someone has managed to gather from their area. I have managed to keep apples, potatoes and several salt meats available, but I ration out what I have. We are blessed to at least have the mountains with game and fish and fresh water."

Elizabeth Neill, December 24, 1864

It didn't feel like Christmas Eve, but my parents tried their best to remind us of our blessings, once again. Christmas Day's traditional meal up Lambs Creek was going to be changed, just like Thanksgiving. The whole Hamilton Family would gather at our home and bring food to share. At least Mammaw came to spend the day with us and helped us prepare some food for the next day. Using the dwindling supply of sugar, Ma made a pumpkin pie earlier that afternoon and already had it sitting on the back porch where the winter cold would keep it fresh until the next day. It was, of course, covered with a heavy dish to keep out any small critters that may find their way under the back-porch door. It wasn't much of an opening, but those field mice could squeeze their little bodies through the smallest cracks.

As evening set in, one of Mammaw's quilts was tightly wrapped around me as I settled myself by the fireplace in my favorite rocking chair near Mammaw. The both of us watched Jimmy and Sarah-Jane eagerly settle onto some smaller stools near my parents as Pa read the Christmas story out of our family Bible. His voice was deep and in full-story-telling mode, carrying our minds, for that moment, to a little manger in Bethlehem. I surrendered my current grievances and allowed myself to smile at the peaceful moment. A knock at the door broke Pa off mid-sentence, leaving the *shepherds in the field keeping watch over their flock by night.*

No one moved, since we all knew that Pa was the only one to open the door nowadays, at least during odd hours. Pa handed the Bible to Ma, and we all watched Pa walk to the door.

Jimmy quietly complained, "Aww. That's my favorite part! The angels talk to the shepherds." As Ma whispers for him to be patient, he adds, "Why are we called farmers and not shepherds, Ma? We got sheep too!" Mammaw chuckled at Jimmy's statement, but Ma was not paying attention to either of them as she focused on the second knock on the door. Someone was eager to get our attention.

Pa glanced through the side of the window first, which caused his face to light up as he eagerly opened the door. "James. Well, I declare! Come on in!"

My heart about pounded out of my chest as I stumbled to my feet, tripping over the quilt I was struggling to untangle myself from. By the time I had managed to free myself, James was already inside and grinning at me. "Merry Christmas, Elizabeth."

"James, you're here!" I came close to him and then didn't hesitate to embrace him, burrowing my face into his gray uniform. I welcomed his smell mixed with wet wool and mud, but Pa broke up the lingering embrace.

"Come join us at the fire." Pa practically pulled him into the living room.

James frowned and stood straight, suddenly looking like a soldier and spoke directly to me. "I can't. I am actually on a mission movin' supplies along the turnpike. There's only a few of us. I thought, since we are so close, that I could stop by. I had to take a minute to see you. My brother told me he'd slow the wagon down to a crawl if I could hurry and catch up." He saw the disappointment on my face. "I thought a few minutes was better than not at all, right?"

The look in his eyes, apologizing for dropping in, made me reach out and grab his arm. "Yes. You know I would prefer to see you even for a minute than not at all!"

I suddenly felt the quilt I had recently untangled myself from covering my shoulders. Pa was wrapping its warmth around me. "I think it would be fittin' for the two of you to speak a moment in private on the porch." We both looked at him with surprise that quickly transformed to gratitude. He smirked and quickly added, "But I'll be watchin' you from the window."

I hardly heard Pa's words, or Ma handing James one of our oil lamps as I threw on my boots and followed James onto the porch. The winter cold caused me to bring the quilt up to cover my ears as well. "I'm so happy that you are still unharmed." Then I added without hesitation, "Especially after that skirmish where James-Henry was shot." I hadn't intended to jump right into what had been on my mind, but our time was too short.

James shook his head. "I wasn't there." The light from the lamp allowed me to enjoy watching his red-strand of hair fall into his face.

"But I heard it was the 64th Regiment."

"It was part of the regiment," he explained as we both sat on the one long bench together. He leaned away from me for a moment to place the lamp on another stool close by. "Just like today, we are sent often in groups to help with other missions, especially movin' supplies safely."

I reached one hand through the fold in the quilt, keeping as much warmth trapped as possible, and grabbed his hand. "I am so thankful you weren't part of it! It would have been awful."

He squeezed my hand in return and, shoving his strand of hair behind his ear, leaned in closely. "I know how you feel about Emma-Rachel and James-Henry, but I promise you it's all awful! We've caught some deserters that I knew before the war. They used to come into the store and talk about the newest calf that was born or we'd speculate on who was courtin' who." He paused a minute, "I cain't explain what it was like to arrest them as deserters and traitors and take them to their death. . ." James' didn't cry, but it was only because he had moved beyond the shock of it.

"I'm so sorry, James!" I didn't look away as he observed me. I was not a young girl anymore. I was turning eighteen soon and my features had changed quite a bit over the last four years. But more

346

than anything, in spite of my occasional childish grievances, I was very much a woman.

He outlined the curve of my chin and smiled gently. "I didn't come here to talk of war."

James reached into his pocket and pulled out a piece of fabric carefully folded with a piece of twine holding it closed. I felt untamed joy well up and my grin didn't hide any of it from James. Suddenly, he felt the need to harness my expectation, "It ain't much. Just a little somethin' I had to get you. B.C. gave me a fair price for it."

I quickly opened the material and the most elegant blue ribbon uncurled as I lifted its silky texture towards the oil lamp. "It's beautiful."

"I thought you might like some new ribbon for your hair that matches your eyes." He smiled, obviously pleased with himself.

"If I remember correctly," I teased, "I thought you said my old flour-sack ribbons were prettiest?" I leaned into his shoulder and he placed his arm around me.

"They still are, but I thought you might like to try somethin' new once in a while." His face became somber. "Somethin' that doesn't feel like war."

"I do love this ribbon." I pulled the ribbon under the quilt with me and then looked up at him, his breath on my cheek. "Thank you!"

We sat together for only a moment longer before he stood, "I have to leave before the wagon gets too far ahead." I stood up too and followed him to the porch steps. He glanced at the window to check on Pa, and satisfied with the fact that Pa had clearly resumed his seat in front of the fire, James came in for a soft kiss. When he pulled away both of us smiled, "I'll see you soon, Miss Neill."

I joined into his gentle banter, "Not before I see you first, Mr. Morris." I stood on the porch until I could no longer hear him galloping up the turnpike. As I returned to the warmth of the fireplace and finished listening to Pa's reading, I realized that maybe it was okay if Christmas wasn't always the same.

Chapter 24

Robert Hamilton, February 9, 1865

A quiet evening has chased the Hamilton Family to their beds and Rhoda and Robert are nodding off to sleep when Blue and Grady begin bellowing frantically.

"Oh, confound it! Not again!" Rhoda fusses. "I hope these Union soldiers brought their own food this time! We can't handle more mouths to feed this winter!" The dogs' familiar bellows have become constant pains of worry. Even a friendly rabbit chase gives Rhoda pause. She takes a deep breath as she grips the covers tightly.

"Rhoda, we've made it this far, and spring's comin' soon." Robert is already half dressed as Rhoda remains under the covers. When he sees she won't move he facetiously adds, "I'll take care of this one on my own then."

"Yes, dear, that would be mighty fine of you!" She grunts. She regrets that her attempt at humor falters.

"Rhoda! You know darn well I can't do this without you!" Robert is beginning to worry and finally glances at his wife who is tightly clinching the covers. Her weariness is visible, but he needs her.

Before Robert utters another word, Rhoda sighs and then sits up emphatically. "I know! But I thought I could maybe wish it away." She suddenly tilts her head confused, "What's that noise?"

A loud clanging noise from down the creek is getting closer. "That's a cow bell!" Driven by curiosity and relief that it can't possibly be fugitives; Rhoda quickly jumps out of bed and begins to follow Robert down the stairs before she is stopped by the children standing at their bedroom doors. Joel's yawn transforms into a question, "Ma, do we need to get dressed and come and help?"

Rhoda looks at her children, who are ready to jump in and do their part much more quickly than she was a moment ago. She is proud of their stamina and gently smiles at them as she waves them back up the stairs. "I will let you know. Go back to bed. I don't think it's any guest for us to take care of tonight. If so, then they are sure makin' enough ruckus to give away their hidin' place."

The children seem relieved and obediently return to their beds.

By the time Rhoda joins Robert on the porch they see the kerosene lantern coming and the familiar voice of George calls out, "I need your help. Come quickly. A shootin' nearby."

Rhoda gasps and covers her mouth, but before she can clasp her husband's arm, he reaches for his holster to strap on his Colt. Rhoda grabs her wool shawl and wraps herself tightly as she follows Robert to the barn, struggling to keep up. Robert finishes buttoning up his heavy jacket as he and Rhoda enter the barn to find George has already grabbed the saddle for Mae. "Who was shot?" Rhoda finally asks.

"Old man William Deavor. Captain James Deavor's father." George lets Robert take the saddle from him. George is breathing heavily, and he tries to temper his nerves as he adds, "We don't know more than that."

Rhoda doesn't ask any more questions as she watches the men swiftly finish preparing to leave, but as soon as Robert prepares to mount, Rhoda grabs his arm. Before she can say anything, he speaks, "Rhoda, I'll be back soon. Don't fret over this." He smiles gently and speaks the only truth he knows. "I reckon this can't be any more dangerous than what we've already been through."

Rhoda nods, but the haunting look in her eyes reveals her doubt.

*　*　*

The moon is nearly full, which allows the majestic Deavor house to be eerily lit up as Robert and George climb the small knoll to the very large front porch. Two large male slaves stand protectively between them and the front door as they approach, but upon recognizing that help has arrived, the men move to the side to expose Margaret Patton Deavor weeping over her husband's body.

Robert signals to one of the slaves, he remembers as John, to hustle up the out-door steps to the second level porch that runs parallel to the one they are currently occupying. He wants the man to keep an eye on any suspicious movement while they attend to the wounded man. He asks the other slave, Moses, to wait nearby. As Robert pulls Margaret off her husband it is immediately clear that the man is dead. His eyes, wide open, stare at nothing and the huge pool of blood, originating somewhere from his torso, has already slowed to insignificant seeping. "Oh my God!" George's voice interrupts Robert's investigation of the body. He looks at George who is already putting his arm around Margaret. "I am so sorry." She leans into George and her bloody hands reach out to squeeze his hand. George does not pull away but holds her until she stops crying, while Robert gives Moses, who is still standing nearby, instructions on where to move the body.

As Moses effortlessly lifts the corpse, Robert turns to Margaret and finally asks, "What happened?"

Still holding onto George, Margaret nods at Moses to do as Robert says. She watches her husband's limp body disappear around the corner of the porch before she slowly composes herself and responds, "We heard a call from the dark for 'Captain Deavor.' Naturally, William got up and went to the porch, thinking someone was needing help. He always helped people; you know?"

Robert, nodding his head and glancing briefly at the corner of the porch, answers, "Yes, of course. A great help to many others." Eager to avoid eulogizing William Deavor, Robert clears his throat and attempts to bring the focus back to the murder. "Please tell us what else happened. Any detail might help us find who is responsible."

Still clasping her hands, George leads the widow to the nearest wooden bench and gently helps her sit down as he sits next to her. Margaret's eyebrows scrunch up and she thinks for a moment. "I'm quite sure it was one shot. But Moses said he heard several voices in those bushes over there and a bustling of bodies leaving."

Robert frowns slightly and pulls up the closest rocker to sit directly across from Margaret. "This is important, Margaret. So, it seems there was more than one person. Did you see anybody?" Robert leans in as George squeezes the widow's hand.

"Not really. It was so dark in the bushes. But it must have been several. As they ran away, they seemed to be arguing some. Somebody was laughing. Their horses were not far away."

George lets go of her hand and gently asks, "Any idea what they were arguin' about?"

She begins weeping again and George wraps his arm around her shoulder. Sudden movement at the end of the porch draws the lawmen's attention. Moses appears, now with William Deavor's blood on his shirt, and steps forward. "If I may speak, Sir?" The man's eyes are looking at the ground as he faces the sheriff.

Robert stands up and, realizing the man is addressing him and not George, doesn't point out who is actually sheriff. Instead, he encourages the man, "Of course. What have you seen?"

The slave, with his eyes still lowered, shakes his head, "Not seen sir. I heard somethin'."

"Well, then, what did you hear?" Robert keeps his eyes on the man, expecting him to look up, but he doesn't dare. Robert realizes that he doesn't know this man or any of the slaves on Deavor's land very well at all and only knows their names from listening to the Deavors addressing them over the years. Why should this man even trust him? He is grateful this man is at least brave enough to give his account. Having been given permission to speak, Moses begins, "I was out in the kitchen tryin' tah warm some milk fer mah sick young-un. I heard somebody yell somethin' 'bout it a-bein' not the right one. Somebody yelled back, 'Don't matter.' They rode off real fast."

Robert and George exchange glances; in the flooding moonlight they can tell what the other one is thinking. George doesn't hesitate to speak first, "Sounds like the bushwhackers to me."

Margaret looks up at Robert, who is now towering over her, and then at George who still has his consoling arm wrapped around her shoulders, and shakes her head slowly. "But I don't understand? They didn't take any of my possessions. It was as if they only came here to kill my poor William. What did he ever do to them?"

Robert quickly sits again and nods, "You are right. Which leads me to believe they came for your son, not your husband. They shot the wrong Captain Deavor."

"Oh my!" Margaret gasps. "But why do they want to harm James, my son?"

Robert looks wearily at George, his mind is racing on what their next steps should be, so George quickly takes over explaining, "A large part of James' role as captain is goin' after the bushwhackers, so they must have thought they were stoppin' him from pursuin' them. Wrong Captain."

Margaret begins to cry again. "That means they'll probably come back again to kill my boy too!"

Robert raises his voice. "Not if we stop them first."

"This is all too much." She quietly thanks George and Robert and then raises her voice, "Mary!" The front door quickly opens and a young black woman, who neither Robert nor George have ever seen before, appears with eyes down cast. She quickly moves to the frail woman and, without a word, helps her leave the lawmen behind, disappearing into the warmth of the Deavor home.

George and Robert are suddenly aware that they are awkwardly standing on the front porch alone with Moses, who is still waiting to be dismissed. However, before Robert utters a word, there is a sudden scurrying down the steps from the upper porch and John quickly stands next to Moses.

With eyes still down cast, Moses' voice is low and cautious, "Sheriff, when do you reckon Master Deavor will return."

George raises his eyebrows and looks at Robert who also realizes that with both of Margaret's boys off to war, she now only has her slaves to protect her. Robert pushes away his deep desire to scream at the absurdity. Instead, Robert clears his throat and sounds as official as he possibly can. "I will send word in the mornin', and I reckon at least James will return shortly." He does not know the loyalty of the Deavor slaves, nor the relationship between them and the Deavors, so he settles on trusting the present moment. He must simply move forward.

Elizabeth Neill, February 9, 1865

The moonlight outlined the men gathering in front of our house. Pa had told me to stay inside, but I had managed to follow Ma out onto the porch and stand next to her as she pulled me under her wool shawl. Her warmth and the familiar call of the Whip-or-wills eased my nerves some.

"What's goin' on, Ma?" I whispered.

"I'm not so sure." She responded as we shuffled to the edge of the porch. The small gathering of men huddled together in secrecy was a strange sight to behold with the moonlight transforming them into a muddled dark mass of moving limbs and shaking heads as their saddled horses behind them were unusually restless. We could hear Pa and Robert frantically discussing with B.C. and Captain Duckworth with occasional cursing accompanied by hellfire and damnation reaching our ears. A fifth man galloped in and dismounted before his horse came to a full stop. I didn't recognize him until Mom whispered, "Oh, my! It's James Clayton." When I looked at her confused, she explained, "Means Duckworth is gatherin' the home-guard. Somethin' awful has happened." Pa suddenly looked up from the intense discussion and saw us, his shoulders dropped and he excused himself, causing instant silence.

"Sarah, please take Elizabeth inside." Pa's voice was pleading with Ma. "William Deavor was shot dead and we are trying to make plans on what to do next. I need you all to stay inside." When Ma didn't respond he continued, "Please make sure you have our shot gun loaded and ready while I'm gone. And sure-as-hell do NOT open any doors until I return."

Ma was desperately shaking her head, so I answered Pa instead, "Okay, Pa." I pulled Ma towards the house as she continued to suppress her desire to argue, she was not going to make a scene in front of all those men.

Pa looked at me and nodded before quickly returning to the men. Once I closed the front door and locked it, a rare necessity, it was only

353

minutes before I could hear all five men galloping along the turnpike heading towards the Davidson River. The sound outside instantly disappeared as Ma slammed Pa's shotgun on our table with one hand while pouring shells onto the table with her other. As she angrily loaded the gun she growled "God-damned war!" Ma's blasphemous words no longer gave me the childish justification to use them one day, instead they propelled me forward to calmly take the loaded gun from her hands. I had only ever shot small game, but I knew how to use it. Ma didn't protest, instead she headed to the fireplace and rekindled the already dying fire, so we both could feel some warmth as we settled into some rockers and waited.

Robert Hamilton, February 9, 1865

Dark clouds begin to block the moon's ability to lead the way along the Davidson River as four of the five men quietly reach Strawbridge Young's home. Only minutes earlier, Captain Duckworth instructed Lieutenant Clayton to fetch Henry Mackey and meet them shortly. It is no surprise that the two men have already arrived by the time Robert informs Strawbridge of their suspicions. The old preacher saddles and leads his horse to stand with the other men whose horses' reins, dangling in their hands, fan out behind them. Lieutenant Clayton and Henry have already joined the small posse and have dismounted to listen to the ongoing deliberations. As Robert contemplates his initial anticipation of the bushwhackers' return to the abandoned campsite, he never imagined it would be under the circumstances of murder. As he greets the men with a nod, he doesn't dare question Henry on recent news of his son's death. In fact, he doesn't ask any of the men, how they are faring, since news of the growing collective dead, comprised of Union and Confederate soldiers, is impacting all families. Neighbors help one another grieve, but few questions are asked and circumstances often remain vague.

Robert tries to push away the noise in his head to focus on the task at hand.

"Gentlemen, thank you for your help. It seems that the murderin' bushwhackers are hidin' in one of the old campgrounds up Davidson River, way on past Avery's Creek. For years some of the loggers set up camp there and it is well hidden." Robert addresses Duckworth directly, "We don't know if these men are criminal civilians or military combatants, so it is not clear if Sheriff Neill should command this posse of if Captain Duckworth is to take the lead." Robert scratches his beard. "But before we head up that river into whatever hornets' nest is waitin' for us we need to be clear on who is in command, no questions asked, or else we *will* fail."

B.C., shouldering his shotgun, and Strawbridge, shoving his Colt into his belt, both nod in agreement, although their movements are barely visible. Henry and Clayton remain quiet, waiting for their commanding officer's directive. Duckworth, however, turns his head to face the shadows where George has been reduced to a large dark mass. The momentary silence is a clear sign that the current sheriff is processing Robert's directive. A massive cloud momentarily breaks, allowing the moon to illuminate George's face. His concern is visible and, even in the cold of the night, beads of sweat glisten. Robert knows that George is torn about relinquishing his authority to Duckworth, a man they have actively undermined for years. But Duckworth's calm demeanor, whether from experience or cockiness, is not what sways his decision. It is Duckworth's willingness to let George make the decision, rather than claim it, an obvious surprise to both Robert and George. The sheriff nervously nods as he speaks, "Captain Duckworth, if you are willin' I think it is best you take the lead since you have more experience with the likes of these men."

"I'd be honored!" Duckworth nods and immediately takes charge. "Just past the church we will take the main trail a bit. Then we'll dismount, and after securin' the horses, go quietly on foot the rest of the way." The clouds are still permitting moonlight to seep through the darkness, enough for Duckworth to see six heads nodding, so he continues, "Robert, B.C. Henry, Lieutenant Clayton and Strawbridge, you go around the camp carefully to cover the open trail in case they try to escape. Spread yourselves out so it appears they are surrounded. Sheriff Neill and I will quietly approach the camp from this end and will aim to wait a spell. Once I know you are all in position then we will move in first."

"How will you figure we are in position?" B.C.'s voice is low, and he is breathing rapidly.

B.C.'s white hair and beard are the only visible parts of him, but Duckworth still faces him. "Can any of you whistle like a bird? My men have their bird calls, but that will not be enough." Robert remembers when they first discovered the campground, and the home-guard brilliantly communicated using the cry from a woodpecker followed by a wren's call ending with Duckworth's chirping finch.

"I've been told my wild turkey call is tolerable." Strawbridge's immediate response is a relief to the others.

"That will do." Duckworth nods, "So when I hear a woodpecker followed by a wren and a turkey unexpectantly hollerin' in the middle of the night then I will know it's time. Let's hope the bushwhackers won't find the sounds suspicious."

"Highly unlikely," Robert interrupts, "considerin' all the bottles of moonshine we found broke around that fireplace last time. They are probably celebratin' right now."

"That's right." Duckworth draws attention back to his plan. "Remember, shoot only if they fire first. We have to make sure there is no doubt these men are the ones we are lookin' for."

"Then what?" B.C. asks.

There is a long pause and the darkness does not allow for clarity. Even Duckworth is clearly gauging the weight of any suggestion he might make. The continued silence, however, is a clear sign to Duckworth that the men are holding true to letting him lead. He clears his throat. "We will try to capture them, but if they shoot, then we all need to be ready to use our weapons." He pauses and then adds, "If you are not willin' to use your gun, then I strongly suggest you stay behind." The silence that follows is only broken by the sound of the men mounting their horses and silently slipping into the thick forest.

* * *

The crackling fire and the loud laughter of the bushwhackers easily conceals the rustling of men moving through the thicket, approaching them from all sides. Lieutenant Clayton and Henry lead the way as Robert, B.C. and Strawbridge follow them, carefully spreading out to take their places, with Strawbridge aiming for the farthest end. Robert didn't like to leave George and Duckworth at first, with the clearest path to the campground, but he is fiercely aware that the odds are in their favor if they appear to establish an invisible stronghold within the shadows. Alone, Robert carefully approaches the final Rhododendron that stands between him and chaos. Suddenly, there is an overwhelming stench that causes Robert's insides to lurch. He squats down and through the bush he can barely make out steam rising from what appears to be a pile of someone's dinner and booze that they couldn't keep down.

"That Billy Boy, he cain't handle this fine moonshine!" A large man wobbles towards the bush and points towards the direction where Robert crouches motionless. "Billy!! Ya hear me? Don't come back if you cain't be a man!"

"General?" A voice closer to the fire calls out causing the large drunken man to quickly pivot, almost losing his balance. "I don't think Billy Boy is intendin' to come back."

The General pivots again to face the darkness as if contemplating his options. He settles for another sip from his bottle and yells, "Don't come back here you yellow-bellied coward." Then he nods satisfied and turns to his men, "Seems we lost our little errand boy. Didn't trust the bastard. I think he told those Hume hotel people we was comin'. Said he was stuck in bushes with some fearsome stomachache, but when he come back, he didn't look sick none. Then what-do-ya-know the hotel don't have no people when we burned it down." Robert's jaw drops at the unsolicited confession and suddenly stands up with an urgency to emerge from the safety of the forest to arrest these men. But before he takes a step, he remembers that Duckworth is in command and that he still hasn't heard the bird calls to indicate everyone is in position. The former sheriff settles for fuming anger. He focuses his attention and rage on the large so-called "General" who plops down next to two men who are already beginning to nod off. "I reckon I should have shot him. Well, I figure the wolves will git him." Suddenly a woodpecker cries out followed by a wren and only moments later a wild turkey cries out. It sounds like a cross between a donkey and a chicken screaming, and ends with a strange warble. Robert is quite impressed with Strawbridge's talent.

One of the men next to the General laughs, "Or gobbled up by wild turkeys!"

The General suddenly seems to sober some, "Hush up! That don't make no sense. Turkeys should be roostin' at this hour!"

"You are right!" Duckworth's voice booms as he and George move out of the shadows with their guns drawn and Henry, Clayton, Robert, B.C. and Strawbridge each enter from their sides, to surround what appears to be a total of six men. Two are in full Confederate uniforms, one wears a Union cap and jacket, two wear clothes with no identification and the one, who calls himself General, dons a Union uniform, clearly taken off an officer. Yet, his head is covered with a Confederate cap. The men quickly stagger to their feet and begin to reach for their guns, but they freeze as Duckworth shoots at the ground near their feet and yells, "Don't move! You are under arrest."

The surrounded men slowly raise their hands, but the General crosses his arms in defiance. "Since when do men get arrested for drinkin' in the forest?"

"It's NOT the drinkin'! It's the thievin' and murderin'." Duckworth's words cause the General to squint and glance around at the seven men with pointed weapons. The shadows cast by the crackling fire seem to eerily magnify the size of the unexpected company.

The General saunters a few steps towards Duckworth as he slurs, "And by whose authority?"

Duckworth does not hesitate, "I am Captain Duckworth and am under the authority of the Confederate States of America."

A loud guffaw erupts from the General as he slaps his thigh. He turns to his men who are slowly lowering their hands. "Boys! Looky here. This here man thinks we recognize his beloved Confederacy." Forced laughter erupts from the General's cronies, but their eyes keep darting between the seven armed men still surrounding them.

"Don't matter what you recognize or don't." Duckworth continues, "You have to pay for what you've done."

"We ain't done nothin'." The General slowly moves to the fire as if needing to warm his hands.

Robert's voice booms, "You just admitted to burnin' down the Hume hotel."

The General pauses, weighing his next words carefully, but before he can say a word, one of his men, wearing the Union cap and jacket, pipes up. "Well, you ain't got proof of that! And no evidence we shot that Captain Deavor neither."

"Shut up!" The General quickly shoves his man to the ground.

Robert is quick to point out the obvious. "The camp is full of Hume Hotel plunder and your fine soldier just admitted to the murder. None of us told you who it was and, since it happened today, only we know… except, of course, those who shot him would know too!"

The General, now fuming, kicks his man on the ground and turns to face Duckworth. "We still won't go with you since we don't recognize no Confederacy." He throws one hand in the air and scoffs. "I'm a General among my men. So, I out-rank any captain."

Duckworth begins to shake his head, clearly tiring of this absurd discussion. "If you're a real general then I declare myself as a real general right now!" His voice suddenly gets louder. "As General Duckworth of this here band of men, I command you give yourselves up peacefully or suffer the consequences."

Robert feels sweat drip into his eyes, but he doesn't dare take a moment to wipe it away. His first hope of the men surrendering without bloodshed is beginning to waver as the bushwhacker General crosses his arms again. Robert slowly glances at B.C. and Strawbridge who nod at each other to indicate which bushwhacker they are targeting. Henry and the lieutenant each mark their men as well, leaving Duckworth the extra gun for any error, with hopes George marks the man closest to him. Robert is the last to nod to his posse, indicating that his target is the confessing bushwhacker still closest to him. Suddenly, the General grunts and makes one more attempt to buy time. "Well you ain't got no authority as captain or as general."

"Enough!" George's voice is strong although he quickly glances to Duckworth who seems eager for someone else to intervene in the absurdity. "As far as I'm concerned you are in Transylvania County and that is non-disputable. As High-Sheriff of this county, I arrest you for the crimes against MY people!"

The General's arms drop and he glances at his men who, within a split of a second, reach for their weapons. As he lunges for his weapon, the General screams, "Like hell you will! Take 'em men!"

Surprising the posse, Duckworth shoots first, hitting the General square in the chest before the imposter can fire his pistol. Without hesitation, each of the five men surrounding the bushwhackers take down their own targets. Having marked the General as his man, Henry manages to shoot the General a second time as the large man, writhing on the ground, doggedly tries to aim his gun at Duckworth. At the same moment, George shoots the man closest to him, but only wounds the bushwhacker's left shoulder. However, Duckworth delivers a final shot to the wounded man, but not before the bushwhacker manages to take a shot at George. As the final man crumples to the ground, George finds himself stumbling to his side and grabbing his shoulder. The rest of the men move cautiously through residual gun smoke and kicked up dust towards the bodies to confirm no one is playing possum. As the smoke clears, the men finally let down their guard as six very still bodies lie around a slowly dying fire. When Robert finally looks at George, he feels the blood drain from his face as he swiftly moves across the campground towards his friend, who is now sitting on the ground with his gun carelessly tossed to his side and his right arm clutches his left shoulder.

"Are you shot?" Robert asks as he squats down and quickly reaches for George's shoulder.

"I reckon so." George sighs. His lightness puts Robert a little more at ease. "Think the bullet just grazed me."

Robert pulls off George's jacket and feels his spirits lift as he sees only a small amount of blood staining the shirt. "It appears the bullet did more damage to your jacket and shirt than to you." Robert shoves one finger through the jacket's ripped material.

"Yes, but the sting of it sure gave me a fright." George inspects the small wound, no worse than a briar scratch. "I am sure Sarah will have somethin' to say about this."

At this point, Duckworth and the other men are gathering around and are relieved to find George in good spirits. But his last statement causes Robert to glance back at the lifeless bodies and the reality of what has transpired. This is as close to war as he ever hopes to be. He doesn't have to look at Strawbridge or Henry to know that his friend and brother-in-law share his worry for their own sons, those who haven't yet died, who still face unmatched daily horrors.

B.C. clears his throat, breaking the silence and asks, "Do you reckon we should look for that Billy Boy they were talking about? The one that run off?"

Robert points towards the bushes where he hunkered down only moments ago. "By the look of the pile of his innards that he unloaded on his way out of camp, we can be rest assured he high-tailed it outa here." The men all nod in agreement and are clearly thankful to avoid a manhunt, so Robert stands up ready to get on with business. "Captain Duckworth, what next?"

Duckworth glances back over towards the bodies and responds, "The first thing is to look for identification. That is in case any families seek the bodies. Also, to make a record of their death. But then burial as soon as possible is crucial. And, of course, as always, away from the river and burry them deep. Don't want critters a'diggin' them up. Don't have a hankerin' for burryin' these murderin' thieves twice." Duckworth pauses to consider what he is missing. Satisfied with his explanation he adds, "Lieutenant Clayton will take care of the needed documentation."

Robert swallows and keeps his thoughts to himself as he watches James Clayton, the county's coroner, nod at Duckworth. It hadn't been too long ago that Robert had teased Duckworth about how convenient it must be to have a coroner on hand. Robert can't believe how right he had been. B.C. and Strawbridge both step out of Clayton's way as he moves toward the closest body while reaching inside his own coat pocket and extracting a small notebook and a whittled-down wooden pencil stub. He pauses a moment and scratches his beard, contemplating the task. He turns to face the rest of the men and explains in a matter-of-fact tone, "It would be right smart if I had more light to inspect these bodies and write down my findings. I'd be much obliged if you men could build up the fire."

The men seem satisfied with this directive and quickly add logs to the fire until it is once again ablaze so they have enough light not only for Clayton to do his full investigation of the bodies, but also for the rest of them to help search for identification. Reluctant to search the corpses, the men leave that task to their coroner. Instead, the men readily drag satchels and barrels towards the fire circle, settling onto worn-down logs, and spend over an hour trying to find identification.

B.C. stands to once again stoke the fire and, as he watches the latest handful of dry brush ignite, he states, "Seems these men don't exist." B.C.'s words cause the rest of the men to stop searching, except Clayton, who is still busy writing down his observations. As the rest of the men inspect the scattered objects, Robert is especially unnerved by the collection of several souvenirs from the bushwhacker's thefts, including silverware from the burnt Hume Hotel.

"They don't deserve to exist." Strawbridge's vehemence shocks Robert.

"Straub!" Robert looks at his friend and is taken aback by how Strawbridge's drawn face is harshly illuminated by the fire.

"We have to think of our kin and our people first." George draws their attention. "I say that we have put forth good effort to identify these men, and only need to bury the bodies."

"I agree with the sheriff." Duckworth stands and begins to move towards the closest body.

"What are you suggestin'?" Robert asks as he sees B.C. and Strawbridge have the same confused look on their faces.

"Lieutenant Clayton?" Duckworth looks at the coroner, who takes a moment to finish a final scribble. He stands to face the rest of the men as he closes his notebook and neatly tucks it and his pencil back into his inner pocket.

"Yes, Captain. I'll help shed some light." Clayton adjusts his hat a moment before he begins. "As coroner I have all the needed documentation to write an official report. It appears the men died of gunshot wounds."

Robert raises his eyebrows. "Is that all?"

Clayton pats his jacket pocket. "Wrote down every detail of every shot, includin' that every man was holdin' their own weapon."

"That shows they weren't shot in cold blood. Right?" Strawbridge adds as if trying to make sense of it all.

The coroner looks at Strawbridge and shakes his head. "It isn't for me to make a judgement on the details. Just report them."

"But you were a part of it!" Strawbridge's voice begins to sound desperate.

"Wait a minute!" George raises his voice before Clayton offers a rebuttal. "Strawbridge, he is going to file the official report of their deaths. A factual, legal account of his findings. What we say about the actual encounter is up to us. It seems that this is simply another report from the coroner filed away concerning bushwhackers. It will only draw unwanted attention if we choose to tell everyone we know what happened. This would not be in anyone's interest." George pauses and the silence confirms everyone's understanding. "I won't and can't keep you from sharin' this night with others. But I suggest you think long and hard who you trust and who you don't." George takes a deep breath and looks directly at the fire. "Since the war is not over yet, we have to still protect ourselves from any bushwhackers who may hear of what we did and come in to seek revenge."

At this point B.C. is nodding in agreement, and Robert knows he is thinking of his family and business. Robert feels a heavy weight, but keeps quiet. He finally understands what the home-guard as well any Confederate soldiers, like Captain James Deavor and James Morris are up against every time they patrol these parts. He wonders how many coroner reports have already been filed.

Duckworth laughs suddenly. "I'm not sure why there is so much frettin' over this. The way I see it we have two law men and myself, a captain, and two men from my home-guard, who hunted down murderers and thieves. We gave them a fair chance to surrender and they didn't oblige. We made a good faith search for identity and they left nothin'. The county coroner took a detailed report and will file it first thing in the mornin'." Captain Duckworth waves towards Strawbridge, "All that is left is for us to bury them and Reverend Young here can pray for their God-forsaken souls." Duckworth sees

Strawbridge nodding in agreement, so he adds, "Seems the rest is between them and God. As far as I'm concerned, I got no regrets."

"But you shot first." Robert states what has been on his mind. George opens his mouth, shocked that the former sheriff is pointing out a detail that George, as well as the others, have quietly overlooked.

There is silence for a minute as Duckworth contemplates the facts, but then he smiles. "Well, I guess I did. But I do believe the foolish man's war cry to *git em*, was a shot enough for me. We'd all be dead if we had waited for them to shoot first."

George, takes a deep breath, grateful for the captain's recap of the facts, and unapologetically stares at Robert as he pointedly states. "It appears we all have secrets we will have to live with after this war."

Robert raises his eyebrow at George. It is the first time he has reminded Robert, in front of others, of their own treasonous operation up Lambs Creek. Robert slowly nods at George and answers slowly, "I reckon you are right." Robert should not be pointing fingers. He suddenly stands up and throws the log he was sitting on into the fire. "Okay, *General* Duckworth, let's bury these bastards."

Elizabeth Neill, February 10, 1865

I only remember Pa coming home a few hours before dawn. I had tried to wait up with Ma, but the familiar lull of the crackling fire caused us both to drift in and out of restless sleep. I do remember Ma embracing Pa and I finally felt I could welcome sleep so I didn't even try to listen to them as I climbed the stairs to scoot under the warm covers next to Sarah-Jane. Her arm immediately slung over my shoulders, a familiarity that quickly allowed me to peacefully slumber, even if only for a few hours. It wasn't until morning before I noticed Pa was shaken more than usual, but I figured he was grieving Mr. Deavor's death. I still remembered the night Mr. Deavor rode up Boylston Turnpike when Mammaw and I were hunkered down on her kitchen floor. In the midst of our panic, he picked us up in his wagon to ride with him toward Brevard, where we discovered the Hume

Hotel was burning. Those moments didn't seem real anymore. I couldn't believe Mr. Deavor was dead.

Pa told me they were sure the murderers wouldn't return, but he wouldn't tell me how he knew that, except that they were long gone.

Something in Pa changed that night.

Robert Hamilton, March 5, 1865

Rhoda's scream echoes up the narrow valley flooded with moonlight. Terror-stricken, the children scramble from their beds and tumble down the stairs only to find their Ma weeping into their Pa's arms with their Uncle George standing in the wide-open doorway. A cold night breeze causes the children to huddle together, so George quickly closes the door behind him; but he does not remove his jacket. His wide-brim hat slowly migrates from his head to his chest where he holds it in solemn reverence.

"Pa? What's wrong with Ma?" Viney's voice carries over her mother's wailing.

"Uncle Henry Mackey was shot," Robert answers, but does not look at his children. He has no words. Only two weeks earlier Maria shared that she and Henry were expecting another child in the autumn. The transformation from uncontainable joy to horrific grief is too much to bear. Instead, he looks at George, who is standing like a frozen statue in front of the door, his face only lit from bellow by the flickering lantern at his feet.

George realizes that Robert expects him to explain what has happened, even in front of the children. He clears his throat and begins. "Seems Henry thought somethin' was getting' his cattle all riled up, and he went out to his porch to see what the commotion was. He thought maybe a panther was on the prowl. By carryin' his own lantern Henry gave bushwhackers a perfect target. They made their murderin' shot and hit their mark." The narrative is followed by continued wailing from Rhoda and a few sobs that rise from the cluster of children. George takes in how the ominous shadows cast by the flickering lantern do not help the situation any. Without asking for permission, he opens up the front door and closes it only for a minute, leaving the family inside befuddled. But moments later he opens the door with his hat back on his head and an armload of firewood he has clearly gathered off their dwindling stack along the porch. The sheriff deposits the firewood next to the fireplace, still warm from the evening's embers and manages to rekindle a small fire, slowly adding some dry bark off the logs. It is not long before he adds the larger logs, anticipating a roaring fire that will help warm the room.

Robert settles Rhoda into the rocker closest to the fire place as their children embrace the familiar draw of the warm orange glow and swiftly move into its presence. John-Riley is carrying Rachel in his arms. Even though she is seven, she is not ready to grow up like the rest of her siblings. Rachel's silent whimpering and the presence of her children causes Rhoda to contain her wailing. Silently, tears flow as she begins to vigorously rock.

Robert leaves his wife's side and stands next to George who has already moved back to the front door, clearly preparing to leave. "I was afraid this would happen."

George shakes his head. "Don't go drawin' any conclusions yet! We don't know why they shot Henry. It could be simply because he is part of the home guard. It could be the same reason William Deavor was shot. It seems that his role in the home-guard gives bushwhackers reason enough." Robert knows that George is assuring him that he does not believe it was revenge for last month's encounter along the Davidson River. But doubt still haunts both lawmen.

"What will we do now?" Robert asks.

George looks at his friend and points his finger into Robert's chest. "There is no *we*. You will stay here and let me take care of this." Robert glances at his family and knows George is right. It isn't only Henry's death that they have to grieve, but it is the fact that they know, all of them know, they are not any helpless and innocent family. They are a family that could be anyone's target if their secret is exposed. Robert nods and rephrases, "What will you do?"

George opens the door and, as the cool breeze hits Robert's face, Sheriff Neill turns to answer. Robert is not surprised to find George's grieving demeanor transform into one of dogged resolve. "I'm going to find General Duckworth and Lieutenant Clayton."

CHAPTER 25

Elizabeth Neill, March 28, 1865

"What in tarnation are you doin', Sarah-Jane?" I yelled at my sister as she walked past me while I was sweeping the front porch. I wouldn't have made such a fuss if she hadn't been trying to slip by me while holding a carefully wrapped bundle in her arms. It seemed she had not gone out the back door in order to avoid Ma, who was still in the kitchen. She was clearly up to something.

She turned her head briefly and glared at me. "None of your business!" I raised my eyebrows and before I could say a word, she slipped past me and around the corner of the house. Although my sister, now fifteen, was as tall as me, I still didn't like her thinking she could talk to her big sister that way. So, as is expected from an older sibling, I did what was only right and followed her. Without her noticing, of course. I didn't have to follow her very far. She slipped into the barn for a moment to grab a shovel, and then reappeared, quickly disappeared behind the barn and then abruptly stopped a few feet away behind a large oak. I was going to jump out from behind a bush and fuss at her, but I was suddenly very curious and decided to hold my tongue a little longer. She carefully placed the bundle at her feet and then took the shovel and began to dig a small hole. I couldn't imagine what she would be burying and found my initial curiosity transform into worry.

"What are you doin'?" I asked, as I slowly moved out from behind the small bush, surprised it hadn't given away my sneaky behavior.

She barely looked up and struck the ground one more time with the shovel. "Diggin'."

"Well, I can see that." I came up to her side and looked down at what looked like one of Pa's old shirts tightly wrapped around something. "But what are you goin' to bury?"

As I began to squat down to touch her bundle, she reached out one hand and pushed me away. "Don't touch that!" I found myself stumbling backwards and my sister's eyes grew wide, as if she hadn't expected her shove to impact me.

"Sarah-Jane!" I quickly found my footing and managed to avoid falling into some briars. "What has gotten into you?"

She dropped her head, looking suddenly twelve again, and then reluctantly answered, "The war."

"What in heaven's name do you mean?" I frowned and moved to the bundle again, but this time I waited for her to squat down next to me. She slowly unfolded the bundle to reveal our family bible, a silver hair pin she received from Mammaw, and Sarah-Jane's favorite childhood doll, a patchwork collection of materials that Ma had carefully pieced together. Still frowning, I looked up at my sister.

"I'm goin' to keep them safe by buryin' them where Sherman's army won't find them." She smiled gently as she patted the yellow yarn down around the doll's face.

I suddenly realized my sister had been listening to the conversations about war after all. Even though Ma and Pa were talking about the war in front of us, I still believed my brother and sister were not impacted the way I was. "What makes you think you should bury these?"

Sarah-Jane cocked her head to the side a moment to gather her thoughts. "Well, I heard tell that this Sherman and his army were wreckin' havoc all the way through the South, and now they are headed up towards the Carolinas. I heard tell they are plunderin' and takin' everything." She took the sleeves to Pa's shirt and folded them across the small collection of items.

"I don't think Transylvania will be a place they care to plunder, Sarah-Jane." I tried to sound calm. "The mountains aren't the most likely path. I think they'll be aimin' for other places that are more fittin' to their cause."

"But do you know that for sure?" Her eyes were dead serious, and I could see a glimmer of hope.

I shook my head slowly. "No, I can't say that for sure." I wasn't about to make promises about the war, since I had already experienced its unpredictable nature. As she began to tighten the bundle, I reached out and touched her shoulder gently. "Can you wait a minute? I'll be right back." At first, she hesitated, her eyes suspiciously narrowing, but when she saw I was waiting for her to answer, she nodded. I scurried around the barn and into the house and, within minutes, quickly reappeared at my sister's side. "Here." I handed her two well-worn hair ties. "Can you hide these too? I was wearing these when I first met James and would sure like to keep them safe." Sarah-Jane's smile couldn't have been brighter as she gathered my precious ties into her bundle.

I helped her shove the dirt over the hole. Together we then shoved the largest stone we could find on top of the stirred-up dirt. Suddenly we found ourselves giggling as we collected leaves and smaller rocks to add beneath the larger rock. "That should do." Sarah-Jane looped her arm through mine and leaned her head against my shoulder. "Thanks, Elizabeth."

I patted her arm and whispered, "That plunderin' army won't find this hidin' place." Although the words felt silly, it seemed to give my sister some peace, and that was all that really mattered.

* * *

My sister and I didn't linger long before we returned to our chores. We planned to keep our small endeavor secret, a secret we both knew would only last until evening when Pa would begin to search for the

Bible. But until then, I promised her that I would say nothing. She would then share with the rest of the family her small feat against the war. In the meantime, I grabbed a basket of freshly folded laundry and jumped from the rock wall down to the dirt road below to begin the short walk towards Mammaw's house. I would probably spend the night with her, so I'd have to hear from Sarah-Jane how Pa felt about her burying the family Bible. I still spent most nights with Mammaw and found that Pa preferred that his mother was not alone more than she needed to be, especially since Mr. Deavor and Henry Mackey had been shot.

As I reached the final climb up the small hill, I paused at the mouth of the small dirt road that wound towards the Patton House. Out of habit, I glanced down that road and was surprised to find Pink's huge grin facing me from a distance. He held a heavy canvas bag in one hand, and waved the other arm, clearly asking me to wait for him. I hadn't seen Pink since last summer, so I wasn't surprised to find that he was lankier and clearly a few inches taller. "Hi, Miss Neill!" Pink continued to smile as he came closer. He shifted the bag to the other shoulder once before he reached me.

"Hi, Pink. What you got there?" I asked, suddenly realizing maybe that was a strange way to greet him after such a long time. But it seemed the most natural.

"Gatherin' some rabbits and squirrels that were unlucky to fall for my snares." Pink proceeded to shove his arm into the bag and pull out a small rabbit by the ears. "Here you can have this one if you want."

I took the dead animal and felt the soft fur, thinking about how Mammaw would be quite thankful for some fresh meat for dinner. "Thanks, Pink!" I glanced at the weight of the canvas bag, but didn't ask to look inside. "Seems you have quite the catch today."

Pink nodded and closed the top again, tightly winding a rope around it, and ended ceremoniously with a strong yank. "For shore! Family and neighbors call me lucky and look forward to what I can leave on their porches. But ain't no luck. Pure skill is what it is!"

371

I laughed out loud. "I guess you got a right to brag." I lifted my rabbit and swung it gently. "I'm lucky I ran into you before you catch all the small game in the county."

Pink smiled. "I'm shore there's a plenty."

Suddenly the conversation was over and we both stood awkwardly. I wanted to ask him how he was doing with the war and all, but last time I had my eyes opened a little too much. So, I bit my tongue and tried to think of what to ask him. Finally, I raised my eyebrows and became excited, "So how is it goin' with learnin' to read?" As soon as the words were out, I realized I had messed up again, so I looked over my shoulder hoping no-one had heard my question. Seeing that the only things moving were squirrels busy chasing each other, I looked at Pink. "I'm sorry. I messed up again."

"Aw, Miss Neill. Don't matter none." He eyed the two squirrels briefly before he looked at me again. "I shore am learnin' fast. Can write too." He bent down and picked up a small stick and then carefully scribbled *Pink* into the dirt. As soon as he was finished, he stood up and used his boot to grind the word back into dirt.

I was genuinely excited. "That is great, Pink! When this war is over, and you have your freedom, you will already be a step ahead."

Although Pink's grin was still slightly visible, his eyes held a serious mood. "My Pa told me that in January the Congress passed what they call the 13th Amendment. It abolishes slavery." He wiped his foot once more over where his name had been scribbled. "Don't mean it's law yet. Don't mean we ain't slaves no more. Not yet." He sighed and added. "But I think it shore is comin'."

I looked at Pink and for the first time saw a man. "I believe it too, Pink. With everything I'm hearin' this war has got to end soon."

"Then things will be different won't they, Miss Neill?" He looked at me as he lifted his heavy bag of small game over his shoulder.

"I'm sure they will be, Pink." I smiled as he walked away. As I turned to walk the final stretch to Mammaws, I looked one more time at the disappearing figure slinging the satchel to his other shoulder and whispered, "I pray to God that things will be different."

372

Robert Hamilton, April 27, 1865

A loud sneeze erupts from Robert who has just arrived at the top of the small incline, reaching Probart Poor's Store, and is surprised to find several faces among the gathering crowd turn to look at him.

"That's one way to announce your arrival!" George, who is tying up Jack at the small hitching post, teases Robert.

Robert nods politely at the staring faces as he dismounts to leave Mae alongside the other horses. He looks at the budding trees flaunting their triumph over winter. "Seems my nose isn't as fond of spring as my eyes are." He quickly pulls out his pipe and, within moments, smoke rises between him and those who have gathered to hear the news. Robert recognizes most faces, but not all. It appears, among the curious onlookers, there are some soldiers wearing their Confederate gray. Most, Robert knows, have returned home with war injuries, and both he and George took time with their families to recall their war stories and find ways to rally around them as they recover. He smiles, pleased that they appear well enough to be present today. However, there is one curious man, in gray, that Robert does not recognize. He nudges George and points his pipe towards the stranger. "Seems to be quite the crowd here today. Even outsiders are drawn in. Hope he's not lookin' for trouble."

"Could be someone's kin!" George dismisses Robert's worry. "Not every stranger in gray is our enemy!"

Robert nods and draws deeply from his pipe. As he slowly exhales, he answers, "I reckon you're right."

George walks a few feet with Robert towards the gathering crowd, but they decide to stay at the back, not wanting to draw more attention to themselves than the sneeze already did. Everyone is facing the front porch, a seemingly small structure compared to the towering building. Although it is officially a two-story house with four chimneys, the attic has a substantial dormer, with a small living area. Robert remembers how much of the local legal proceedings took place here before they decided to meet down the valley a bit in B.C.'s store, and then, later, at the Wilson Campground. Although Robert still grieves the loss of the campground, it feels appropriate to resume legal proceedings at Poor's Store, especially since the town of Brevard is slowly taking shape, even if only in the form of a few roughly established dirt roads along empty lots, clearly marked by wooden stakes in the ground.

"I reckon word is out and some have heard rumors." George's smile quickly fades as he faces Robert. "You think it's only rumors?"

Robert narrows his eyes and takes another long draw on his pipe. As he exhales, he points his pipe in the direction of the front porch. "Let's hear what the officials have to say."

George turns to face the porch along with what looks like over a hundred folk. Children have already found each other and have run off across the dirt road to weave in and out of stakes that mark potential building spots. As the adults ignore the children, Probart Poor offers Leander Gash a seat in one of his rockers. Leander is acting chairman for this meeting, and Robert finds it fitting for Leander and Probart to be the two sharing the news. This only solidifies for Robert their intent to support peace. But Chairman Gash waves Probart away, eager to address the crowd. Poor's stout figure nods and stands to the side of Gash, like a formidable statue, bringing greater attention to the business at hand.

Without hesitation or unnecessary preamble, the chairman announces, "Friends, as many of you know, General Lee surrendered to General Grant at Appomattox Courthouse earlier this month. More than forty men from our area were there." A visible wave of relief sweeps over some in the crowd, but an equal number of heads drop in visible defeat. Robert and George's soft nods, only visible to each other, are all they dare to reveal their joy and relief. The chairman waits for the crowd to settle before he adds, "We have also received word from Asheville this morning that Union General Stoneman's army under the command of Union Brigadier General Alvan Gillem, marched on Asheville only days ago, but the Union army was met with a flag of truce. The Confederate Brigadier General Martin had received word of Lee's surrender as well as General Johnston's surrender to General Sherman." The crowd, listening intently, is fiercely aware that less than forty miles away several friends and relatives have come close to tasting the ruthless tactics that have destroyed much of the southern neighbors. Relieved, many nod and begin to discuss the news, but before the crowd becomes too loud Chairman Gash draws their attention once more. "We also received word that a few days after Lee's surrender, a man named John Wilkes Booth shot and killed Abraham Lincoln, the Union President."

Suddenly frowning, Robert and George glance at each other, both surprised by the latest news on Lincoln. They are not sure if they should still be rejoicing over the war coming to an end or grieve over the president's death. Clearly others are equally baffled, giving rise to rumblings and murmurs in the crowd. Some break into tears and a few simply nod their heads, unclear if they are agreeing with the assassination or that maybe the awful war is about over.

Amid the confusion, the stranger in a Confederate officer uniform marches to the porch, pushing folks aside. The young man doesn't ask to speak but steps up onto the third step with his hand on the sword at his side, underlining his authority. Leander and Probart look at each other, baffled, and before they can ask him what his intentions are, the man turns his back to them and faces the crowd. "Ladies and gentlemen, we are at war. I am a Lieutenant and assure you that what you have heard is only a temporary setback. It is clear from the latest news about Stoneman reaching Asheville, in spite of Lee's surrender, that there are still many Union forces roaming our territory. The Confederacy lives! Even as we speak, our President Jefferson Davis is in our state rallying the true Confederates. He wisely departed Richmond and is in Greensboro now calling again to re-organize."

Dumbfounded, Chairman Gash and Probart gape at the man. Before they can say anything, the man begins to walk through the crowd towards his horse, carefully tied up next to Jack and Mae. He draws his sword dramatically and calls out, "Follow me all you brave-hearted, real men!"

Sheriff Neill and Deputy Hamilton, having not moved very far from the hitching post, find themselves face to face with the drawn sword. They note that several folks in the crowd don't hold back their rage and start to move toward the young lieutenant. However, they stop when they lay eyes on the two lawmen who assert their own authority, each with one hand on their pistols.

While George moves in close to the soldier, Robert raises one hand to address the crowd, "Easy now, folks. This young fellow has no idea how many we have lost and how you suffer here." He looks at the formerly active soldiers, clearly healed from their physical wounds, who seem torn between the message and the crowd's anger. Robert continues, "All of us believe the war has ended because we have received *official* word of three surrenders." The wavering men raise their eyebrows, suddenly pulled back to reality and nod at Robert with understanding.

However, the lieutenant sees an opportunity and waves his sword again yelling, "Don't listen to this man! There have been no terms of surrender negotiated yet. And that is fact!"

"Listen to this!" George pulls out his gun and points it at the young man. "Negotiatin' surrender is still surrender, so you best have that sword sheathed lickity-spilt before you hurt someone." The suddenly befuddled man quickly places the sword back in its scabbard.

"Sheriff Neill ain't bluffin'." One of the men who is still wearing his own gray cap walks up to the hitching post and unties the soldier's horse. "Be gone. Jefferson Davis won't find many bodies left to fight, not here, not anymore. We are done with this war." He glances at his Confederate friends and as they all nod their approval; he faces the intruder one last time. "All of us."

* * *

Leaving Sheriff Neill to answer questions and catch up on local news with the dwindling crowd, Robert unhitches Mae and begins his journey home. As he takes in the quickly moving clouds casting their dancing shadows across the majestic mountain ridges, a sudden lightness causes him to smile. Something feels different. He can't remember the last time he enjoyed the beauty surrounding him. For the first time since he was appointed Sheriff four years ago, he believes there is more than only surviving.

As Robert begins to pass the Valley Store, he decides to head over to the charred campground. He wants to find the small preacher's booth, the only remaining structure, and offer up a prayer of thanksgiving. But, as he reaches the campground, he is aware that he is not the first one to seek out the spot. His smile widens as he realizes his old friend Strawbridge Young is sitting on the edge of the platform. He remembers that Strawbridge was not at the meeting, so he is excited to bring him the good news. As he draws close, he realizes Strawbridge is hunched over, shaking, with one hand covering his eyes. "Straub, are you all right?"

Startled at first, Strawbridge straightens up; recognizing Robert, he suddenly looks horror stricken at his friend and shakes his head. Robert can see that Strawbridge has been crying uncontrollably and is not surprised at the catch in his throat as he tries to speak. "No. We received word. . ." He gives up trying to explain and instead hands Robert the crumbled piece of paper in his hand, clearly from the Union POW mail system.

Robert takes the letter and unfolds it and reads to himself. *I am sorry to inform you that your son Martin Alley Young, age 38, prisoner of war here in Elmira, New York died 1 March 1865 of diarrhea.* The joy he had felt only moments earlier is instantly replaced with a sick hollowness. He folds the letter slowly and moves in to sit next to his friend. "I am so sorry." He doesn't know what to say. Looking once more at the crumpled paper, he finally adds. "Is there anything you reckon I can do to help?"

Perched on the edge of the preacher's platform, the two men sit in silence watching birds alight on the bushes and young trees that are already growing through the rubble. Robert finds himself lifting his prayer, but not of thanksgiving. He is full of anger and silently condemns God's timing. He quickly asks for strength and for healing, but as he caresses the letter he is still holding, he lifts up a prayer of protection for Andrew. He doesn't know how he could ever recover from the death of his own son.

Finally, Strawbridge, running one hand through his unkempt hair, reaches over to take the letter from Robert. He takes a deep breath and explains, "I was on my way to the meeting. But B.C.'s daughter, Susan, came running out to greet me as I was passing by. She was waving this letter." He looks at Robert and suddenly Robert realizes that no one else knows. Robert drops his shoulders in anticipation of the grief still to come. Strawbridge stares out again and observes a rabbit burrowing under one of the bushes. "I reckon I would be much obliged if you did help."

Robert looks at his friend and nods, "Whatever you need."

"Maybe you could have Rhoda come over to help Martha, also Millie or one of the other girls." He looks down again at the letter. "Don't rightly know how to break the news. But I'm sure your women will be better support than I."

Robert, wishing he could keep his family from this grief, knows that he will honor his friend's request. "Of course, my friend. The Hamilton womenfolk are great support and most understandin'."

The men delay their departure and sit in silence. Remembering the morning's news, it is Robert who speaks first. "They announced that General Lee surrendered to General Grant at Appomattox Courthouse as well as other Confederate strongholds that surrendered within the last days."

Strawbridge nods, still observing the small rabbit now daring to move in closer. Speaking with little emotion, he answers, "I heard talk of such. Good news, I reckon."

Robert decides not to add that Lincoln was shot, since he is aware his forced attempt at bringing Strawbridge up to date, is the only hope he knows to offer. "Yes, it is good news." As Strawbridge unfolds and refolds the letter, Robert realizes it is futile trying to be positive. Robert slowly stands and begins to move towards Mae, who is happily grazing on the bright green patches of wild grass along with Strawbridge's mare. As he grabs both sets of reigns, he leads the horses back to Strawbridge, and he adds, "But, over or not, seems the war is still claimin' its souls."

Strawbridge slowly stands and walks towards Robert, who is holding out the mare's reigns. As Strawbridge places the letter in his coat pocket and takes the well-worn leather straps in his hands, he hesitates to mount. Instead, he frowns, and his eyes meet Robert's worried look. The old country preacher finally asks, "How long? How long do you think it will be until it is all really over?"

Robert shakes his head. "God only knows."

Elizabeth Neill, May 14, 1865

I had Sarah-Jane weave the blue ribbon into one long braid that she skillfully wrapped around the back of my head twice, leaving me to wonder if this was too fancy for a trip to the Valley Store. I wanted to surprise James with wearing his gift and hoped we would have a little more than a few minutes to talk with each other.

A few weeks earlier, he had come by our home one evening still wearing his uniform. He looked weary but wanted to assure us that he was alive and that he was headed to Polk County for a short visit to make sure his family was faring well with the news of surrender. James, along with the rest of his regiment, had continued to wear their uniforms until they had official word to disband, although many of the men didn't wait and headed on home once they heard rumors of surrender. No one tried to stop them. James, however, was loyal to his brother, B.T. He had been with him at the end of April, camped near Asheville, when Stoneman's army, under the command of Union Brigadier General Alvan Gillem, attacked Asheville. From what James said, the Union army was met with a flag of truce. James explained that it seemed to be, at first, a simple surrender in Asheville, agreeing to the same terms as Johnstone's surrender to Sherman. But a few days later, Stoneman's army returned to ransack the city under the direction of the authorities in Washington who had rejected what they believed to be lenient terms agreed on by Sherman. Once Stoneman's raiders had left their destructive mark, they high-tailed it on out of the mountains, on to their next victims. I hadn't been aware of Stoneman's march through the Western part of North Carolina, so close to us, destroying railroads, storehouses and towns. I was thankful that James was not injured, even though I could tell he was shaken by the turn-around of events. He cursed the false promise of a peaceful surrender. I wanted to hold him and not let him go that night; I had waited so long for the moment it would all be over. But

James only nodded at my parents and me and told us he would be back soon.

As Sarah-Jane gently pulled on my hair, I felt foolish that I had assured her there would be no interest in attacking our mountains. The family bible was only buried for a day, since Pa wouldn't have God's Word covered in dirt, but Sarah-Jane had only recently uncovered her hairpin, doll and my old hair ties. At the time she hid the items, she had honest reason to be afraid, I was simply ignorant of how right she was. As she finished the final knot on my blue ribbon and turned me to face her, a huge smile lit up her face.

* * *

As Pa and I sat in the wagon, he glanced at me once and smiled. "You sure look pretty." I blushed and didn't say anything. As we began to pull up to the Valley Store, he leaned in and whispered, "James better be home or you might catch the eye of some other young whippersnapper."

"Pa!" I fussed, shoving him away. "Stop embarrassin' me." Pa could see the pleased expression on my face in spite of my words so he laughed and pulled Jack up to the hitching post, alongside other horses, indicating Mr. Lankford had several customers inside. Before he dismounted, he leaned in once more and was a little more serious. "Everything I told James, about courtin' you, still stands, especially now that I reckon he will be around more."

Eagerly climbing off the wagon, I smiled and nodded. "I know, Pa." I didn't wait for him as I began to walk towards the front porch. As soon as I reached the steps, the door opened and a man stepped out with loose denim trousers held up by suspenders over a brand-new red-checked, cotton, button-up shirt, which made his red hair stand out even more than usual. "James!" I practically screamed as I scrambled up the steps to embrace him, breathing in the new cotton smell mixed with lye soap. I figured that his sister, Betty, had convinced Mr. Lankford to let her make James some new clothes. He held me tightly and only the intentional cough from Pa caused us to finally pull apart. But only a few feet. He was smiling and gently touched my hair, appreciating my effort to display the blue ribbon.

"Elizabeth. Ain't you a sight for sore eyes?" His voice was soft. Only the two of us could hear the sweet words of affection and hope that passed between us. I longed to find a private place to talk, but the front door swung open once more with Uncle Bob and Mr. Lankford coming out to greet Pa who was now climbing the stairs. So, James and I backed up along the edge of the porch to give the men room. Even though I was looking at James, I quickly noticed a change in his manner as he focused on the three men gathering, clearly intending to avoid the customers' curiosity inside. I began to ask him a question when he stopped me. "Elizabeth, hush for a minute." Taken by surprise, I frowned and then he nodded in the direction of the men, indicating he was trying to listen. I quickly forgave him his gruff behavior and decided it was best to listen as well.

Mr. Lankford looked between Pa and Uncle Bob as he held a paper in the air. "News from Asheville that was telegraphed from Raleigh is that Governor Vance has been arrested." Mr. Lankford flattened down his loose unruly curls in his beard. "But that ain't the derndest. It appears that President Andrew Johnson has appointed William Holden as our Governor."

Uncle Bob's eyes grew wide. "You mean the old editor of *The Standard*?"

"Yep, the very same man who published our official request for peace, the one we made before the war." Mr. Lankford shook his head in disbelief.

"Wait a minute!" It was Pa who seemed confused. "I never heard about this."

Uncle Bob shifted awkwardly, and I suddenly knew another secret was unfolding before my eyes. "I didn't want to burden you, but, yes, Holden, during the midst of the war, published ours and other communities' official plea to avoid the war."

Pa was frowning and glanced at me for a minute, not caring whether we heard or not. "Seems a pretty important piece of news."

Uncle Bob nodded but didn't seem bothered too much by Pa's reaction. "Was not important enough to me to cause more worry. Wasn't anything we could do about it, so it wasn't anything anybody else needed to know."

Pa reluctantly accepted Uncle Bob's explanation, but still asked. "Why in tarnation did he do it?"

Mr. Lankford waved the paper once more as he answered, "Seems clear to me. He obviously was sendin' Washington a message of his political loyalties. And now he's got what he wanted."

"Governor of North Carolina!" Pa stated the obvious.

"Seems he took quite the risk pullin' all of us into his schemin'." Uncle Bob took out his pipe and began to prepare his tobacco.

Pa suddenly lost his frown and his eyes widened. "You think since Washington trusts Holden now, you think they will be lenient on the counties that wrote those letters?"

Mr. Lankford, stroked his beard once again. Shaking his head, he looked back at James before he turned to face Pa and Uncle Bob. "I ain't countin' on Washington for lenience. Not after what they just done to Asheville."

I suddenly felt James tug my hand. "Come on, let's go. Had enough talk of war." He quickly led me down the steps off the porch. Pa glanced at us a few times but continued to be pulled back into the intense conversation. He finally stopped checking on us once we reached the small hill heading up to Oak Grove Church. My heart began to flutter remembering back to the times we found ourselves in this very spot. I sat down on the ground as lady-like as possible as James stretched out his legs next to me.

"I sure missed this view." James' voice was soft again, and I was thankful for his desire to be alone with me, even if Pa was keeping an eye on us from a distance.

"Me too." I smiled and fiddled with a loose thread on my skirt.

"I cain't wait any longer." James turned to me and leaned in so close I could feel his breath on my lips. "Miss Neill will you be my wife?" The shock of the question and his urgency took my breath away, and I was unable to answer. He watched my eyes intently and was pleased with the surprise I was feeling. He closed the small gap between us and gave me a soft kiss. Pulling away he asked again, "Well, do you have an answer?"

I wanted to answer, but was slightly confused. "Aren't you supposed to ask Pa first?" A mischievous grin told me all I needed to know. "You already did?" He nodded. "When?"

"That night at B.C.'s house when I talked to your Pa." He smiled and came in close again, hoping for another kiss.

I pushed him back, though, to look him straight in the eyes. "That was over two years ago!"

"It sure was. But your Pa said not until after the war, until then, I could only court you." He quickly came in to finish the kiss he had started. "So, now I'm askin' you to marry me."

I couldn't believe the one thing I had been waiting for was really happening. I glanced towards Pa who was now turned towards us with his back to Uncle Bob and Mr. Lankford. Suddenly his teasing me about James on our way to the store made sense. He was suspecting that James would be asking me soon. Pa nodded at me, knowing that I needed to feel his approval. I turned towards James, with his red strip of hair falling into his eyes. Before he could tuck it behind his ear, I reached out and gently took hold of the strand and tucked it for him. This time I came in close. "Yes, Mr. Morris, I will be your wife." This time I came in to kiss him and a new urgency reached the core of me. I pulled away, quite aware that Pa was still watching and instead took James' hand in my own. He squeezed it, understanding that, for now, we would need to settle for each other's presence.

As the moments passed, they were filled with catching up on his lengthy marches to engage in small skirmishes and the times he was thankful for his regiment consisting of rough mountain men, something not all the officers appreciated or understood. I listened intently and found myself pulled into stories that seemed like tales of the distant past. As he recalled his encounters, a slow but steady nagging began to emerge from deep inside, first in the form of a tight knot in my stomach, but then grew to an uncontrollable struggle to breathe. I abruptly stood up and, turning my back to James, took a deep breath.

"Are you okay?" James hopped up and moved in close behind me. He gently squeezed my shoulders. "I didn't mean to upset you with my stories of war." When I didn't respond he added, "I figured you needed to hear what I've been through. I cain't keep this from you."

I quickly spun around to face him, and somehow managed to swallow the knot in my throat. "You are right. We need to both know what the other one has been through. Right?"

James smiled and took my hand in his again. "Oh, my dear Elizabeth. I reckon this war has been hard on you, too. Worryin' about me and all."

I breathed in a deep breath and then glanced down at the three men still in discussion on the porch. Would Pa and Uncle Bob understand? I couldn't worry about them; I could only trust that this man that I loved would also protect my whole family. I looked back at James and almost whispered. "It's more than that. But you have to promise you will keep my secret."

James frowned, but then lifted his eyebrows almost amused. I guessed he was expecting a silly girl's secret of sorts, but I didn't say anything until he responded, "Of course I will keep your secret."

"You swear?" I asked, suddenly feeling like the young girl again, when Viney and I swore ourselves to secrecy over childish pranks.

James smiled and went along with my request. "I swear."

So, I told him. Everything. From helping deserters escape discovery to concealing escaped Union prisoners of war, including the flock of Union soldiers up Lambs Creek. When I was finished, I felt a lightness that I quickly assumed was freedom bestowed on me for doing the right thing. However, the lightness quickly crumbled into darkness when I realized James was not holding my hand anymore and his eyes, once full of longing, were transformed into pools of disgust. He started to back away from me and shake his head as if he was seeing me for the first time. "James?" I tried to move towards him, but he held out his hand for me to stop.

James' voice, although low and controlled, did not hold back his raging fury. "Are you sayin' that, while I was covered in the blood, brains and limbs of my Confederate brothers, my woman was at home helpin' harbor the very men who tried to kill me?" He stepped in closer, but this time all affection was lost, and his hand rose, pointing an accusatory finger at me. "Are you sayin' you were a yellow-bellied Union sympathizer, while your Confederate neighbors and friends were layin' down their lives?" I could hardly breathe and my vision began to blur as tears spilled down my already red cheeks. His finger stopped short of touching me. "Is that what you are sayin'?" When I didn't answer, he growled, "Is it?"

I wanted to yell that it wasn't that simple, but I had no words, so I reluctantly nodded. He quickly backed away again and started to walk down the hill. I ran after him and grabbed his shoulder, causing him to stand stiff as a board. "James, please. It is much more complicated than you think."

He turned to face me, and the anger in his eyes had faded some into sheer disappointment. "Is it, Miss Neill?" He nodded formally and then stated as a matter of fact. "I will leave in the mornin' for Polk. They need another hand for plantin' season." He paused and then added, "And in the fall."

I let go of his shoulder and, falling to the ground, could not control my own despair beginning to consume me. "But . . . I thought we were gettin' married?" I sobbed, but he was already moving on towards the store and away from me.

Since we had obviously made quite a scene, both Pa and Uncle Bob came running out to me as James passed them without offering a word. They both quickly squatted down next to me. I looked up at Uncle Bob and grabbed his hand. "You were right, Uncle Bob!"

Uncle Bob, confused, looked at Pa, who shrugged, clueless as well. Looking back at me and my tear-streaked face he asked, "About what?"

I looked at him and squeezed his hand tightly. "We can't have it both ways. We have to pay a price, even if it means losin' someone we love."

CHAPTER 26

Robert Hamilton, July 20, 1865

The early morning coolness is beginning to burn off as the small crowd gathers around the porch of Probart Poor's store. Frequent official gatherings are becoming the norm as Transylvania tries to move forward with establishing themselves as a county with a real town as their county seat. Brevard has yet to be incorporated and funding to build a courthouse is still a struggle, especially in the wake of numerous war-torn families. Robert joins the rest of the small crowd, made up mostly of justices and office holders of sorts. George told him that they had all been requested to be present at today's meeting. George, as Sheriff, is on the porch alongside Court Chairman Gash, who seems to be prematurely sweating through his shirt and jacket.

As Robert stands at the back of the crowd, he finds himself scrutinizing every look and every comment. It has been over two months since Elizabeth endangered the safety of both the Neill and Hamilton families. George had assured him, although with some clear uncertainties of his own, that James has it in him to keep it to himself, despite his anger. It has taken Robert time to believe that James, in fact, has kept his word and not shared their secret with others. Or, Robert wonders, if B.C. does know, if he is keeping it to himself. In any case, Robert worries about who knows and when he will receive unexpected vengeance. As Transylvania Court of Pleas and Quarter Sessions is about to begin, with Chairman Gash hitting an old gavel on a small wooden podium, Robert is aware of someone coming to stand next to him. He smiles genuinely at John Duckworth, wearing denim and a basic blue plaid shirt; without his uniform he is clearly transformed. The two men shake hands, but, before they can speak to each other, the pounding of the gavel finally brings everyone to attention.

Leander Gash clears his throat and announces, "I am as uncertain as all of you are of how everything from Washington will impact us as we continue to build our county." He swallows and continues, "We have much work to do. But first, all of you who are a Justice of this Court raise your right hand . . ." Gash holds up his right hand to demonstrate, but quickly drops it as he sees no one is following his example.

Those gathered begin to murmur to each other, wondering if they have missed something that the chairman has said, but it is George who quickly addresses the issue. "Wait a minute. Tell us what we are doin' this for!"

Chairman Gash turns red and apologizes and, as he observes the many confused faces, he clarifies the matter. "President Andrew Johnson offers amnesty to everybody in the rebellion with the understandin' that all property is returned to former owners. All property except slaves, that is." As the faces turn from confused to surprise, the chairman lifts the document, as if he is reading from it, although Robert can see he is needing something to look at besides his friends and neighbors. "The exceptions are for Confederate leaders who must apply directly to the President for amnesty. Since we have none here, we need not to worry. So now all Justices will swear allegiance to the United States." When he dares to look up again, his eyes are clearly begging for compliance, not demanding it. "It is somethin' we must do." Robert is pleased that Leander is trying to help with the very precarious transition, moving North Carolinians back into the United States. According to Martha-Ann Young, his sister, the majority of his slaves left the farm to find their way north. However, his son's favorite slave, Ben, has chosen to stay and continue working the farm and even took the Gash's last name. Again, Robert reflects on Leander and Probart's visit at the onset of the war and realizes there was indeed truth to their desire to seek peace, even though their push for a less dramatic transition was not realized. Robert watches Leander

388

hand George the document and has him read the oath as the men repeat their swearing of allegiance. Robert is suddenly confused why Gash is sitting down and wiping his forehead with his kerchief, not swearing the oath himself.

"Chairman Gash?" Robert's voice carries over the heads of the men who have completed the task. "I mean no disrespect, but why are you not swearing allegiance?"

Gash sighs heavily and then stands up again, moving in next to George. "Well, Bob. Several of us in the county who held government jobs, as in my case bein' postmaster of Claytonville, also have to write an official petition to the president for amnesty." There are some murmurs. "I sent mine two days ago." Then seeing the somber mood, Leander Gash's small mischievous grin begins to appear, and he adds, "Who knew deliverin' mail was somethin' from which I needed to ask a pardon!" He points his finger at several individuals. "And I hold all of you who sent mail as partners in crime!" As soon as he drops his hand, he lets out the loudest guffaw shattering any somberness, and everyone begins laughing, some with relief and others from the sheer absurdity of it all.

As the court session refocuses and takes care of business, including officially electing George Neill as Sheriff under the new allegiance as well as many other county officers, Robert is aware of John Duckworth leaning into him. His voice is so low Robert can barely hear him. "I have to as well."

Robert turns to face the young man, who has clearly aged over the last four years. "Do what?"

Duckworth nods his head toward Chairman Gash who is continuing to conduct business, clearly more at ease than he was earlier. "I also have to write a letter of pardon. I'll do it soon."

Robert looks directly at Duckworth, whose brief forced smile fades as Robert leans into him. "Is it because of your position as a captain in the Confederacy's home-guard?" Although they have never spoken about it, the look in both of their eyes indicate they are both remembering the night they buried the bushwhackers.

Duckworth drops his eyes and lets out a small chuckle. "You would think, wouldn't you?" He looks back at Robert and he nods again towards Gash. "But no, it's because I was postmaster of Cathey's Creek." Robert nods, having nothing to add to the strange revelation, and begins to pull out his pipe. Duckworth watches him pack in the tobacco and, as the first signs of smoke rise, the former captain adds, "It is strange it bein' over and all. I think I may have been too eager at times." Robert looks at Duckworth as he slowly releases ringlets of smoke between them. Duckworth lets the smoke hit his face and coughs slightly. For several minutes they both reflect without saying a word, but Duckworth is suddenly compelled to share one key fact. "I'll tell you one thing, though." Robert hesitates to take another draw of tobacco and raises his eyebrows as he encounters the sincere look on Duckworth's face right before he whispers. "I'll never forget that you trusted me to lead."

Robert smiles and reaches out to pat the young man on his back. "You will always be General Duckworth to me!"

Elizabeth Neill, August 1, 1865

I had stopped resisting Ma's requests for me to head to Lankford's store for staples. My fear of running into James was beginning to move from intense stomach pains to a dull ache. Mr. Lankford and James' sister Betty were always kind to me when I came in with Ma's list and left with the staples, but there was clearly an awkwardness. I didn't dare ask them how James was doing, and they never mentioned his name. I comforted myself with the reality that I could at least see Mr. Lankford's girls who were old enough to take on several of the jobs once occupied by Tony. It was strange not seeing Tony, and when I once inquired where he might be, Mr. Lankford only commented that he was not sure. He had wondered if he was working a farm nearby, but since he hadn't seen him in a while, he guessed he was long gone. I wasn't sure why I thought I'd get a chance to say goodbye, or that it would even matter, but still, I felt an emptiness. When I said something to Ma about how upset I was that Tony left without saying goodbye she told me I was overreacting because of how James had suddenly left. I figured she was right.

I took my time that morning leading Jack towards the store, so when I saw Pink's familiar grin waving at me from down the Boylston highway, walking my direction, I came to a stop and waited for him. He was clearly headed to the store as well, carrying some sort of pole full of pelts.

"Hi, Miss Neill," Pink greeted me and continued to walk next to me as I coaxed Jack to start moving again.

"Hi, Pink!" I smiled, happy that Pink and his family had not left. Although, I wondered to myself if that was okay for me to feel that way, so I didn't say anything.

"Pink Smith!" He grinned at me.

"What?" I was confused.

"My name is Pink Smith." He was still grinning and then he started laughing at my confusion. "Oh, Miss Neill. You gonna tell me you didn't know I didn't have a last name?"

I stuttered awkwardly, "I, uh, thought it was, uh, Allison."

"Well, Pa was known to some as Doc Allison, but now he ain't no slave no more, so he took the name Smith. Now he's Doc Smith since he is a blacksmith and all."

"Well that is great!" I smiled and then asked, "Did all the freedmen take on other names?"

Pink shook his head. "Naw. There are plenty who kept their former masters' names. He thought for a minute, "I know Lish King and Bill Erwin kept their names. Then there are some that are too young yet, like Jim Aiken who is only a child. His pa was also his master, Ben Aiken. I reckon time will tell what he will do. Then there's Jesse and Riley, they took on the name Gaston." Pink continued to talk about people he knew, many that I had never heard of before. "Then there is George Orr... who was born with a white daddy and black momma, and is bein' raised by his white Grandma Orr. I reckon he'll keep his name."

We were almost at the hitching post, but I wanted to ask Pink so much more before he unloaded his pelts. "Pink, can I ask you a question?" When he nodded and stopped to face me, I saw the same confident Pink I hoped would return. I couldn't help myself, but Pink always told me more than he was probably supposed to. So, this was my only chance to ask. "Are most freedmen leavin'? Are you and your family goin' to leave?"

He shook his head again, and shifted the pole to his other shoulder. "Naw, at least *we* ain't gonna leave. I cain't say for shore for everyone. Right now, my white Allison kin are makin' shore we can have a place to worship on their land. Several families keep comin' together to worship and most work on the same fields that they worked before the war. I heard tell many have gone to nearby farmers to work their fields instead of their old masters. I know Pa is still a blacksmith and cobbler." He scratched his head a minute before he added, "Then some folk took off, but I ain't shore whereto."

"Like Tony?" I stated as I slowly wrapped the lead reign around the hitching post.

Pink's chipper voice faltered as he shifted the pelt again. "Yes, like Tony." When I didn't say anything else, he cleared his throat and tried to reclaim his earlier positive demeanor. "I do know he called himself Tony Bowman. And, Miss Neill, we gotta be happy for him. That's the truth of it."

I held his gaze a minute, and I realized that I was very selfish in wishing Tony had stayed or at least said goodbye. "You are right, Pink!" I paused a minute and then corrected myself. "I mean Mr. Smith."

Robert Hamilton, August 26, 1865

Noon has already come and gone as folks representing the townships from around the county find their way to Probart Poor's store. The heat has chased several individuals under trees to gather in clusters as they greet each other; for most it is the first time since before the war. Robert smiles at the scene as old friends reconnect, but his smile falters as he remembers why they are all present and in particular that he has been asked to chair a special board, a role that will be announced at this meeting. He finds the responsibility of what is to come somewhat overwhelming, so, not wanting to dampen any joyful reunions, he slips through a scattering of trees. Within moments he makes his way across the dirt road to stumps that are the only reminder of a forest that has been felled in hopes of building homes and business. He settles on a stump that still allows him to have a view of the gathering folk, even if it is slightly obstructed by the few trees that identify the store's property line, so carefully laid out by Leander Gash when he built the store. Robert bows his head for a moment trying to find some peace before the meeting begins. At the beginning of August, Maria Mackey gave birth to a son and named him Henry, a fitting honor in memory of his father. Everyone had rejoiced that Harrison, her oldest boy, had returned from the war in time to see his baby brother born, but the soldier's wounds were deep and he died less than two weeks later. Robert is trying to clear his head from the extreme lurching between joy and grief, all the while trying to move forward as a county. He quietly prays for strength.

Suddenly footsteps approach. "Sheriff Hamilton!" Robert lifts his head quickly, surprised to hear his old friend, Craf McGaha's voice.

"Haven't been Sheriff for a while now." Robert smiles as the two exchange a hearty handshake. Robert is thankful for the distraction.

"Never had the opportunity to use it, except that day you wore that title for the first time." Craf settles on a taller stump that requires him to look down at Robert, a unique position to be in considering Craf is quite a bit shorter than Robert. Robert, though, decides not to tease his old friend about this rare opportunity. He is simply not up for his usual friendly banter.

"It has been a long time." Robert's emerging joy quickly fades as he remembers his conversation with Craf's wife, Harriet, up in Cedar Mountain, almost three years ago. He has made several visits since then, but the day he heard how many of their children had died from sickness, is still etched in his memory. "Sorry for the loss of so many of your young'uns." The pendulum swing continues.

Craf takes a deep breath, clearly accustomed to the repeated condolences he has received. "I never thought that while I was at war, so much death would strike down my family here at home." He looks down at Robert and shakes his head as he adds, "Or that so many families would suffer from divided loyalties. Up in Cedar Mountain we have some healin' to do." He forces a small smile, "I reckon you don't have much to worry about, seems like you handled the county quite respectably while you were sheriff."

Robert hides his sudden discomfort by standing up and checking on the growing crowd. It is almost time to begin. Now he is suddenly looking down at Craf and forces a smile, "Well, Craf, I reckon it was more tolerable for us than other folk." He is satisfied that he didn't lie, but he is weary of telling half-truths. Pulling himself together to focus on the task at hand, he nods in the direction of the trading post's front porch where an empty chair awaits his presence. "Craf, I want to forewarn you we will be talkin' about somethin' that might worry you some, concernin' your fear for Nancy's safety, but I assure you I have a plan to make sure I keep my word I gave you."

Craf frowns. "What are you talkin' about?"

Probart hollers for Robert to come start the meeting so Robert looks at his friend one more time. "Trust me." He waits for a nod from Craf before he turns to cross the dirt road.

* * *

Before he settles into it, Robert bends down to wipe off some cornbread crumbs from the wooden chair, clearly pulled from Probart Poor's dining table. Once he is seated, Overton Erwin, who is the current chairman, stands at the podium and uses the committee's gavel to bring to order the Special Term of the Court. It is only moments before the clusters of visiting folks come out from their shady havens and focus their attention on the small porch. "Thank you for gathering here once again. It is our hope that George Clayton and Ephraim England will soon have our temporary court-house built for us to begin to gather for court." People nod and whisper pleased to know the long delay may soon be over. But the chairman does not allow for much chatter and continues. "Ladies and gentlemen, we now have orders from Governor Holden to set up a board to administer the oath of amnesty to all Transylvania citizens." As Robert expected, murmurs and shouts of frustration accompanied by shaking heads interrupt the chairman's opening. Robert glances at Craf, who suddenly seems pale. Robert knows, without a doubt, his friend is worried if this means official visits will be made to the Cherokee relatives safely hidden within families all over the county. He glances away from his friend as the chairman hits the gavel three times before order is restored. "I have asked Robert Hamilton to chair that board and see that it is done. As our former beloved Sheriff, he is well-known and respected, able to face many questions that will come."

Robert stands and walks to the podium while Erwin takes his place on the wooden chair. He looks out at the familiar faces to help him remember why he agreed to chair this board. He is immediately aware that they are all quiet and waiting for him to speak. He knows that these people have faith in him, and he wants to make sure that they feel they can still depend on him in the wake of this directive. He sees Craf take a deep breath, clearly hoping Robert's earlier perplexing request to trust him will soon be answered. Robert manages to produce a slight smile, as he begins, "Friends, I know this seems strange, but in order for us to all be considered loyal to the United States of America we must all swear allegiance to it." Robert pauses only briefly, but before anyone can ask him questions, he continues, "All of our families have suffered during this war and many families have lost loved ones during the war . . . on both sides." No one says a word when he pauses and observes the sea of faces. With jovial reunions seemingly forgotten, everyone is suddenly avoiding eye contact, hoping not to remind each other of their divided loyalties. Robert continues, "Even now word continues to arrive of deaths in POW camps, and many of our soldiers are still makin' their way home." Robert leaves out the fact that it is the Union soldiers that have not been discharged from their units yet, since much of the South remains under occupation. "It is up to us to move forward as a community. I believe it is fittin' that I, personally, come to each township and administer the oath of allegiance in the communities.

This will be less of a travel burden to those families. It is our hope you take word of this back to your community so they are not befuddled by this directive." Robert clears his throat before he adds, "This is for *all* families, whether your husband, father or son fought for the Union or for the Confederacy . . . there is no seperatin' the sheep from the goats." As Robert looks at the crowd again, he sees some relief sweep across the faces. Especially Craf seems relieved. He finally understands how his old friend will keep his promise. If they don't have to single out families, then secrets, whether known or not, can be kept secrets.

Without warning, a tense voice from the back breaks the healing atmosphere, "And what will you lawmen do with those traitors John Henry Cagle and your cousin Robert Franklin Hamilton?"

Robert's heart begins to beat harder as he squints his eyes, trying to make out the figure coming out of the cool shadows into waning afternoon rays of sun. "Andrew?" His voice is full of hope, wondering if his son has really come home. The figure is soon clearly visible, wearing his old patched pants and favorite green vest over the new, white shirt Rhoda had made for him in anticipation of his return. Robert discerns that his son has already been home, and as Robert begins to smile, he notices the small canvas bag Andrew has strapped over his shoulder and realizes his son is not staying.

A harsh tone, making Andrew's voice almost unrecognizable, pushes through Robert's thoughts, "Well, Mister, ain't you gonna answer my question?"

Chairman Erwin quickly stands up and moves towards Robert. "You don't have to answer this. It really has no bearing on. . ." Robert holds out his hand to the chairman, urging him to back off and that he is okay. Erwin simply nods and reclaims his seat.

The gathered folk, full of curiosity and thankful the attention is no longer on themselves, position themselves to witness this odd exchange by creating a narrow clearing. As Robert observes this unusual parting-of-waters scene he is aware that most folk know that this is his son, and those who do not are quickly informed through conspicuous whispers and nods of understanding. Although Robert wishes they didn't have an audience, he also recognizes that this may be as close as he gets to talking to his son. So, he decides to engage. "First of all, Andrew, they are not traitors as you say. Be careful, for according to the law and constitution, we in the Confederate States are the traitors about to be forgiven. When John Henry Cagle is finally discharged from the Union army, he will be welcomed back to help rebuild our county." With heads in the crowd moving back and forth between the two men, Andrew continues to stare down his father, but Robert does not break his son's gaze. "Secondly, my cousin Robert Franklin Hamilton, and *your* relative as well, has heard a call to preach the gospel and has returned to preach love and *forgiveness.*" He pauses only a moment before he adds, "As you well know, these are greatly needed as we seek to come together and heal as a community."

The crowd, nodding in response to Robert's statement, are unaware of their sudden participation. Andrew, however, clearly finding his approach is back-firing, shakes his head as his crimson cheeks proclaim his level of anger. "Ain't no backward preachin' gonna save what some people have done. Secrets that some people are holdin' and will take to their grave can never be forgiven."

The crowd, suddenly feeling convicted themselves, begin to shift awkwardly. Robert realizes some people wonder what and who Andrew is talking about, once again confirming the reality that the extent of the secrets and divided loyalties reach far beyond Lambs Creek. He speaks as softly and reassuringly as he can. "It is time that all of us move on and find forgiveness. Each of us had to do what we really believed was best for our families and our communities." As worry is replaced by nods, Robert continues, "And I want to remind *everyone,* that even in the midst of the war, regardless of your loyalties, we took care of each other." He looks intensely at the people. "Remember when you helped harvest each other's corn fields even if you fought your neighbor, or your brother on the battle fields?" Nodding becomes more vigorous. "Remember when you made sure a widow had firewood, even if her husband lost his life fighting for the other side?" He takes a deep breath and, deciding it is possibly time, adds what has been his deepest hope. "If we did not let the war break us, then we can still face whatever comes our way." When he sees healing begin to reclaim the crowd, he looks at Andrew and says directly to him. "We have to forgive each other. Please, Andrew."

Andrew looks at individuals in the crowd who are now more interested in their own stories and watches them return to the private sanctuaries the shady trees offer. Robert steps off of the porch and moves towards his son. Andrew, stiff as a board, does not return his father's embrace, but Robert rests his hands on his son's shoulders, thankful to be able to at least be near him. Robert's small flicker of hope quickly fades when Andrew's eyes remain cold. The playful boy who liked to dump corn-husks on the heads of the sheep is gone. The boy who could hold his little sisters in his arms while they loved on him is gone. The boy who couldn't keep the dogs, Grady and Blue, from jumping up on him, yipping with delight when he took them up the holler to hunt was gone. A young man stands before Robert. A man he no longer recognizes. Andrew barely whispers, "Some things are unforgiveable." Robert drops his arms as Andrew abruptly turns away in disgust. Robert can do nothing but stand and watch his son disappear down the dirt road with his canvas bag slung over his shoulder.

"Seems like I was wrong." Craf's voice startles Robert. He hadn't noticed his friend's approach. Robert glances briefly at him, but doesn't speak, instead he returns his gaze to the now empty dirt road. Craf sighs and gently looks down the road as well. "Seems you did have burdens of your own to bear."

Robert nods slowly, with eyes still on the road, trying to keep his wits about him. He tells himself that he will not fall apart. Not yet. He swallows and is suddenly thankful Craf is next to him, reminding him of the depth of loss that even Robert has not experienced. It helps him push away his own pain, at least for the moment. "At least I did not lose any children to death. Not like you and Harriet."

There is silence as Robert lets the murmur of the conversations behind them remind him of the community that still believes in hope and more importantly in an unwavering unity. He swallows hard, pushing down his deep sense of failure to bring that same unity to his own family. Craf, looking up at Robert's grief-stricken face, finally responds, "Some things feel like they are worse than death."

Elizabeth Neill, August 27, 1865

I wasn't sure if I should be thankful for the soft drizzle that Sunday morning or not. I would normally welcome anything that promised to ease the heat, but that day it caused the ride in the wagon to church to be somewhat of a challenge in our Sunday-best. Lurching back and forth in the back, Jimmy, Sarah-Jane and I held a canvas over our heads, while Mammaw squeezed between Ma and Pa on the wagon's seat with the only two umbrellas we owned. Once we arrived at church, I pointed out that Viney and her whole family hadn't bothered to fight the weather, but from Ma's quick admonishing, I figured there was more to it than I knew, nor did I ask. Viney would tell me sooner or later.

Although the small church was dry, it didn't take long for the humidity to make us all wish fall would hurry up and arrive. It was clear that even Reverend English was miserable since he mercifully shortened his sermon, leaving out his usual dissection of how numerous verses can be applied to our lives. Instead, he picked only one, telling us that the Lord placed it on his heart that this was the one we all needed to hear. I silently asked the Lord to place brevity on his heart more often. As soon as the last *amen* was lifted, I skirted out of the church and nearly ran over Rachel-Emma on my way out. I quickly wrapped my arm into the crook of hers as we scurried down the steps and over to the Davidson River, giving all the parishioners plenty of room to congregate outside, especially since the morning drizzle had stopped and the noon sun was beginning to peek through the clouds.

"James-Henry is back." Rachel-Emma blurted out as soon as we could see the clear river water below us, rippling around random rocks and confidently babbling to itself.

I looked at her radiant face and clasped both of her hands in mine and squeezed them. "I am so happy for you." Jealousy began to churn deep within, but I forced the memory of James to play second fiddle at that moment. "Is he well?"

Rachel-Emma squeezed my hands in response and leaned in; I could almost feel the heat from her rosy cheeks. "Better than well.

He asked me to marry him." My stomach lurched, but I quickly harnessed my pain and turned it into a loud squeal. "Shhhhh." Rachel-Emma whispered as she turned to look if anyone heard me. "We ain't quite ready to let others know yet. With the war bein' barely over and all."

I frowned and leaned in, suddenly hoping that she wouldn't lose her man like I did to divided loyalties. "You mean your Ma and Pa don't know yet?"

She gently shook her head, "Oh no. They know and they have already given their blessin'." She nodded at the people behind us. "They reckon it will take a bit for others to be alright with me marryin' a Union sympathizer and recruiter."

I found myself genuinely befuddled. "So, not meanin' no disrespect, but how come your parents are so quick to bless you? What about your brothers that died fightin' for the Confederacy?"

"Of all people!" Rachel-Emma pushed away from me. "I thought you'd be supportin' me."

I suddenly realized that my own jealousy was tainting my joy for my friend. How could she be getting married, when people she loved actually died? It seemed a deeper level of betrayal than what James was feeling towards me. I calmed my voice and adjusted my body language by gently touching her arm. "I am sorry I upset you. I was only curious." I dropped my eyes for a moment, hesitating long enough to control the cry that wanted to escape. "I am so very happy for you."

Rachel-Emma studied me for a moment and then reciprocated my touch with placing her hand over mine. "Ma and Pa said that they are tired of the pain the war has caused, and they hope that our marriage can be a message to others in the county. A message of healin'." A gentle flush deepened the already rosy cheeks. "I ain't really interested in messages. I only want to marry my man, but if that makes Ma and Pa feel better about it then I ain't gonna argue." She managed to get a chuckle out of me, but then her eyes studied me again. "What is it Elizabeth? There is something that is ailin' you."

I welcomed my friend's concern, but I had already cried more hours than I cared to count, and I was not going to fall into despair again. So, I swallowed hard and dug deep so I could offer her a genuine smile. When it emerged, I faced her and whispered, "Not everyone is as fortunate as you. My James will not be returnin' to me. The war has torn us apart." Before

Rachel-Emma could offer me her condolences, I stopped her. "But you, Rachel-Emma, you and your family deserve all the joy that can possibly come from this marriage. This God-forsaken war owes you at least that much."

CHAPTER 27

Robert Hamilton, October 18, 1865

The only sound Robert can hear is the dozen or so men shifting in their chairs, causing the floorboards to squeak. Having shoved merchandise and supplies up against walls and into adjacent rooms, Probart Poor has transformed the trading-post's respectably sized central room into a court room, as he has done numerous times in the past, when a smaller gathering permits. He, and everyone else, had hoped that the temporary courthouse would be ready, but unfortunately heavy rains had caused delay. Everyone in the room would clearly prefer spending this Wednesday morning working and not sit once again awaiting new directives. The silence in the room is evidence of everyone's weariness and the need for these continuous directives to stop.

Although a chair next to George is empty and located close to the front, Robert chooses to lean against the back wall, finding a spot next to B.C. who acknowledges his friend with a solemn nod. Both men turn their attention to John Clayton, who is chairing this Term of Court. He stands up to face the small gathering of men and moves to the small podium, but leaves the gavel at rest, since there is clearly no need to use it to call the meeting to order. From his awkward shifting of his weight it is obvious that he is as uncertain about orders from Raleigh and Washington as are his predecessors, Overton Erwin and Leander Gash who are sitting in the two seats closest to him. Clayton clears his throat and finally begins, "Gentlemen, we have further orders from Governor Holden. We must hold another election."

B.C.'s voice startles Robert as he breaks the uncomfortable silence. "What on earth for? We are tryin' hard to get back on our feet and many have end of year crops comin' in and winter a-comin'."

Heads that have turned to listen to B.C. are nodding as they swivel back around to face Clayton. But the chairman only acknowledges the outburst with a single nod as he then decides to simply move forward by reading from the document, "We must vote to either ratify or reject the ordinance declaring null and void the ordnance of May 20, 1861, to secede from the Union. Also, one prohibiting slavery in the State of North Carolina." He looks up from the paper and nods again, indicating his task of sharing this new directive is complete. However, he is clearly surprised when he is met with silence, at least at first. Slowly, whispers between individuals begin to arise and confused looks asking for clarification are instantly met with shoulder shrugs.

Robert raises his voice above the slowly growing din. "I understand and accept votin' on the document prohibitin' slavery. But, regardin' the first directive . . . Are you sayin' that we are to vote on somethin' where we had no say about it in the first place?" He looks around at the room and then adds, "In fact, if I remember correctly, several of us in this very room pleaded with Raleigh not to secede. AND that Governor Holden was the editor who put it in his newspaper, except only much later when it was a most opportune time for him. How dare he be the one to send this directive to us!" Robert stops himself before he says something he will regret. He is suddenly aware how weary he is from traveling to all the townships in Transylvania to administer oaths of allegiance to families who are barely surviving.

Leander Gash quickly stands up next to Clayton, and nods to the chair that he has a few words. Clayton eagerly waves for him to say his piece as he retreats to his own chair behind the podium. "Now friends, let's not get all tore up about this." He addresses Robert directly. "We thank you, Bob, for all you've done in assuring allegiance is secured from all our folk." Several heads nod and glance at Robert, who suddenly is embarrassed. He did not intend this to be about him. He simply nods his appreciation. Gash dramatically runs his fingers through his hair and raises his voice in his commanding tone that makes even Robert feel at ease. "I would like to take this opportunity to say a few words. First, I want to remind you all that I am running for the North Carolina Senate seat and I ask you all to cast your votes next month. I intend to represent us fairly in Raleigh." All the men nod, familiar with Leander's political aspirations and find comfort that someone they know may have a say at the State level. Leander clears his throat as if preparing to make an even more profound statement. His clean-shaven face continues to intentionally paint a picture of a serious position. "Secondly, now, we all know that Governor Holden has no say in these matters. He is the President's puppet after all. So, the way I see it is that the lot of us should be tickled about these continued directives." He pauses for effect and Robert can already feel a lightness sweep over the room.

"And why is that?" George calls out giving Gash his desired prompting.

"Because," Gash suddenly delivers a wide mischievous grin, "it means they finally came around to the wisdom we sent in our letter from before the war and are really tryin' in a backward way to invite us back into the United States of America."

Much needed laughter suddenly fills the room, and even Robert embraces the levity as he chuckles and shakes his head at Gash, who is soaking up the moment's triumph like a mischievous school boy.

Elizabeth Neill, January 2, 1866

The fresh snow from the night before managed to clothe the Oak Grove Church in white, erasing any sign of disrepair. There could not have been a more fitting scene for Mr. Lankford and Betty's wedding. We all figured that it was only a matter of time before he wed his deceased wife's sister. She had, after all, been by his side since her death and was practically raising his girls. Still, it was a joyous occasion, full of anticipation and preparation. I had initially worried if James would be present, but Pa said that Mr. Lankford had informed him that James was going to stay in Polk County while Betty's parents came to the ceremony. I was much relieved.

We were almost the last guests to arrive and settled into the back pew, with Viney, Millie, Aunt Rhoda and Uncle Bob only two rows in front of us. I figured John-Riley was in charge of the Hamilton homestead and his younger siblings, a position I was sure he was relishing. Viney spotted me and we waved to each other, both giddy with excitement. Aunt Rhoda turned, following Viney's gaze, and smiled broadly at Ma, but then promptly nudged Viney to turn around and pay attention to the ceremony as it began.

I unbuttoned my wool coat since it was considerably warmer in the church, after all, each pew was filled with family and friends witnessing Betty and Mr. Lankford stand in front of the minister. I was in awe of the scene unfolding, not because I was surprised, but because it had been a long time since I had seen such beautiful clothes. Although Mr. Lankford appeared in a newly tailored dark brown wool jacket, with his hair neatly combed and unruly curls obedient for once, it was Betty that took my breath away. My cousin, Millie, had spent numerous hours on her loom weaving the most beautiful blue wool shawl for Betty to drape over her shoulders. But the shawl was only the final touch. Betty had sewn a new dress for herself from the Valley Store's latest arrival of dark blue wool, which she adorned with delicate lace along the sleeves and collar. Viney slowly and carefully shared with me that Millie told her that Betty confided in her that she was disappointed that B.C. had not yet managed to receive any shipments of silk. It had been great fun to hear the gossip, because, if disappointments were centered on shipments of silk, then the war was not only over, but slowly life was moving forward.

As Mr. Lankford and now the new Mrs. Lankford turned to face the guests as husband and wife, the soft hoop swivel of Betty's dress created a beautifully dramatic effect. I hoped one day I could have a hoop, but for now layered petticoats would have to do. I gently smoothed out the front of my blue-striped dress, the same one I had worn a little over four years ago at the Lankford's home, when James, unbeknownst to me, asked Pa to marry me. I had grown some since then and, although the dress was a little snug under the arms, it still fit well enough, even with me turning nineteen soon. Instead of James' blue ribbon tied in my hair, I had my auburn locks neatly tucked into my winter bonnet.

The preacher lifted one last prayer of blessing and, as soon as the newlywed couple walked down the aisle past the pews, their family members began to file in behind them to exit the sanctuary. Ma told me last week that everyone was invited to the Lankford home up the valley for a celebration instead of standing outside in the cold. I was looking forward to it, especially the Lankford's sweet cider and gingerbread. The smile, that seemed permanently plastered on my face, suddenly faltered when a red headed man fell in behind the groom. His eyes briefly met mine, clearly as shocked as I was to encounter each other unawares. James quickly averted his eyes, but not before I observed something he was trying to hide. His eyes held a longing. For me. Maybe. A familiar flame began to ignite, but I quickly extinguished it, reminding myself that I would not go through his rejection ever again.

By the time we exited the church, the bride and groom and their family's wagons were already making their way, leaving narrow, winding wheel tracks in the snow as they headed towards the warmth of the beautiful Lankford home. As I watched the familiar red-headed figure manning the reigns of his wagon filled with his kin, Pa touched my shoulder. "I promise you, B.C. said James wasn't comin'."

I looked at him and nodded, "I know, Pa. I reckon he changed his mind and decided he shouldn't miss it." I suddenly shivered, not sure if it was from the cold.

"You think he only came back to see the weddin'?" Pa asked, lifting his eyebrows.

"Pa, stop joshin'." I frowned. "That is not funny."

Pa shook his head. "I'm not joshin'. I am serious. I saw how he looked at you."

I should have realized that everyone was watching the procession and that means everyone saw James' reaction. Suddenly, my cheeks felt like they were on fire, but Pa didn't say anything and instead began to head toward our wagon. When I didn't move, he turned to me again. "Are you comin'?"

Viney and Millie climbed onto their wagon, tucking themselves under some quilts. As their wagon lurched forward Viney smiled at me again and hand signaled something, pointing towards the procession of wagons. She was clearly telling me that we would talk at the Lankford's. I had been looking forward to this celebration, but the joy had faded knowing that it would be inevitable that I would face James again. "Pa, I think I'll walk home. You head on up without me."

Pa contemplated if he should make me come with them, but instead he nodded. "Make sure you button up that jacket or else you'll catch your death." I was surprised to find my wool jacket wide open and quickly fastened the buttons as Pa jumped on the wagon with Ma and my siblings, who seemed to be confused with why I was staying behind. However, within moments all three faces turned to look at me with pity, a clear indication that Pa had explained to them what had happened.

I laughed at their looks and forced a large grin and yelled. "Stop your frettin' and bring me back some food!" Sarah-Jane smiled and nodded, clearly happy that she could do something to help my sorry state.

As the sounds of the wagons and the cheerful voices hooting and hollering faded, I finally turned to head towards home. I pulled my mittens out of one of my pockets and was thankful for the warmth they offered from the small breeze that had begun to add a new depth of cold to the already chilly day. Each step I took was met with the soft crunching of the hardening snow. As I began to move from the front of the church down the small hill, I realized there was another sound I hadn't heard before. A soft swishing, followed by rhythmic scraping, caused me to turn my head up the hill towards the back of the church. Since I had no other plans, I decided to explore who else might still be lingering after the ceremony and plodded back up the incline.

It was only a few minutes before I came right up on Amanda Lankford's grave and, to my surprise, Pink, who had his back to me and was all bundled in a wool jacket and a warm wool cap, with flaps tightly tied over his ears. He was scraping the grave stone with a small shovel. "What are you doin'?"

Startled, Pink jumped up with the shovel ready to defend himself. When he saw it was me, he shook his head. "You shore scared me, Miss Neill!" He pointed at the grave stone with his shovel. "Mister Lankford is payin' me to uncover these graves from the snow."

"Why on earth is he havin' you do that?"

"Ain't none of my business. From what I figure, it looks like the family wants to pay their respects." He swings his shovel to point at two small white mounds. "Still got the two young'uns to uncover."

Memories of the two babies who died made me wish I hadn't come back up the hill. It was easier to wallow in self-pity than face the facts that there are those who have suffered much greater tragedies in their lives than I had. But since I had already made the mistake of letting curiosity guide me, I decided I would make the most of it. After all, I wanted to hear the latest gossip from Pink, who seemed to know the business of most, at least in my neck of the woods. "So, Mr. Smith, do you have any news?"

Pink smiled as he contemplated my inquiry and then casually began to uncover the first small mound. "Well, I reckon there is news of that Thirteenth Amendment. I heard tell it was finally made an official law early in December."

Ma had told me around Christmas time that slavery was finally officially outlawed. I couldn't believe it had taken so long and was sad that President Lincoln had not lived long enough to see it actually happen. But still, I was happy that it had finally passed. "That is great news, although it took long enough."

Pink nodded as he focused on scraping the layer of frozen snow off the stone. "I ain't gonna complain. That's for shore!" I watched him finish scraping the stone until he took a step back to inspect his work. Deeming it satisfactory, he began to uncover the second small mound. After a few more minutes he stopped and looked at me. "You're awful quiet. Ain't never seen you this way. I guess there is hope for you after all!"

I laughed, knowing darn well he was making fun of me. "Hush your mouth Mr. Smith!" I teased, but my smile faded quickly.

Pink noticed and frowned slightly. "I reckon you got some heart-ache?"

I raised my eyebrows. "What are you talkin' about?"

"Come now, Miss Neill. I seen you and Mister Morris sweet on each other and then as fast as lightnin' there ain't no sign of the two of you courtin'." He shook his head. "Cain't fool me none."

"Well, confound it! You're right, but he has moved on and so have I." I suddenly rubbed my hands together, as if I was trying to warm them up, even though my mittens were doing a fine enough job. "I don't want to talk about it."

Pink nodded and then turned to continue to uncover the second small mound and then began scraping it. "Well, it ain't my business! But I got some real gossip, if you figure other people's lives are more interestin'."

I stopped rubbing my hands together. "Do tell!"

Pink stopped scraping the almost visible gravestone. "Well, it appears Harriett Steward is expectin' sometime come spring."

I was confused for a minute why this was significant since, for one, I didn't know who she was and secondly, it seemed babies were born all the time. "That is good news, like every other baby born. I am happy for her and her husband."

Pink shook his head. "You don't understand. You see, according to all the talk, Harriett will be givin' birth to the first free black person born here."

Suddenly, I felt a happiness well up inside of me. This *was* significant. "That is so wonderful! She and her husband must be very proud!" Pink's eyes suddenly dropped as he contemplated if he should say more or not. I began to frown and finally asked, "What's wrong? What are you not tellin' me?"

Pink took the shovel in his hands and turned it over a couple of times before he decided that maybe I could be trusted. "It ain't so simple, Miss Neill. You see the baby's daddy is Jackie Patton."

It took several moments before his words sunk in and I finally grasped what he was telling me. Jackie Patton was white. I thought of all the times I had been to the Patton's home and how many times Pink had spoken about the Patton's supporting their slaves as well as other slaves worshiping on their land. Pink observed me as I continued to process this phenomenon. I knew enough about babies and then figured that this baby was conceived while Miss Steward was still a slave, but the months didn't add up. It was clearly conceived after the war. I finally looked at Pink and asked, "I don't understand? How can this be?"

Pink suddenly burst out laughing. "Well, we all know how this can be!"

I reddened a little. "You know what I mean!"

Pink took a deep breath and then turned to continue scraping. "It's not the *how*? It's the *why*? Nobody knows, 'cause she ain't talkin'. Nobody is talkin' about what really happened. But when that baby is born everyone will know that somethin' did happen." I stood there with my mouth wide open and realized there was so much I didn't understand. Had this baby been willingly conceived or had nothing changed? It seemed no one knew or no one dared to say . . . either way it would be frowned upon and hidden. My heart was heavy, but one thought lifted my spirits. If this baby really was the first free black to be born in Transylvania, then regardless of the why, this baby might have a chance of never being forgotten.

Robert Hamilton, January 8, 1866

It has not snowed since B.C. and Betty's wedding and Robert is thankful for the brilliant blue sky and mid-day sun, even if the wind's ruthless chill still causes him to pull his wool scarf over his mouth and nose. It feels strange passing Probart Poor's store without stopping. He guides Mae along actual streets with actual signs, finally identifying the street's names. He follows Poor Street and wonders to himself if people will willingly move to this street, but decides it is not his worry. He turns right to head down England Street and then left onto Main Street. As he moves along Main he smiles at the sign that says "Caldwell Street." B.C., whose full name is Braxton Caldwell Lankford told him he is happy with his middle name being used, especially since others in the county who have Caldwell in their names can share in the honor. As Robert finally reaches the public square where Main meets Broad Street, he dismounts and walks into a two-story building. The new-wood smell reminds everyone gathered that the recently constructed, albeit temporary, court house is almost finished. The jail cells are still lacking some bars, but the main courtroom floor is respectable enough to gather and hold court. The winter has been harsh, so the current session is actually their continuation from the December 1865 session. No one objects to the session being titled as such and Robert is thankful that there is generally an atmosphere of cheer as the men continue to comment on their new courthouse. Some are already discussing what will need to be considered differently when the permanent brick courthouse is eventually constructed. When Robert notices George, he is slightly perplexed, since as the current sheriff, it would seem he should be conversing with the other men, but instead he is sitting in a chair, alone in thought. As Robert heads towards George to find out what is on his mind, he is stopped by the sudden calling of the court to order. Robert decides his curiosity will have to wait.

As the session begins, William A. Paxton, who is chairing, adjusts some papers as he stands behind the same well-worn podium that was carried over from Poor's Store that morning, a reminder that funding is tight and the permanent courthouse will be the one furnished with loftier and commanding furniture. In the meantime, all present are simply pleased they are no longer surrounded by food staples and farming supplies. Paxton looks up at the small group of Justices and speaks. "Well, friends, it is a new day and we are still coping with all the cantankerous orders from Raleigh and Washington. But before we move on to business, I want to announce that this job is only temporary for me. You must find another chairman by next month." Robert tries to muffle his chuckle, since it appears every session has a different chair, clearly an undesirable position. It is no surprise to anyone else in the room, since there are no objections. Without warning, Leander Gash turns around, points to Robert, and mouths the words *you're next*. Robert's face drops and he immediately regrets his earlier chuckle. Leander, now Senator Gash, will leave later this month for Raleigh and, although everyone is pleased with his election, they will miss his presence in their own court proceedings.

Paxton, clearing his throat, moves on with court business and asks, "Does the Special Committee have a report on the mental state of our dear brother, Francis Allison, down the river?"

B.C. acting as the Special Committee Chair, stands, straightens out his jacket and reads the report, "He has been found insane and unable to conduct his business. One son is appointed as his guardian." Robert had heard of Francis Allison's failing state-of mind, but was not surprised. So many of his grandsons had died during the war and his own twin sons had fought on opposite sides. With the war over and the loss of all his slaves, he was financially struggling, even with many of his former slaves still living on his land. Robert knows that Doc Allison, who changed his name to Doc Smith, is still working as a blacksmith and cobbler for the Allison family and neighbors. Times are hard for everyone, and it finally was too much for Francis. Robert is pulled out of his thoughts as B.C. continues, "Off the record, I would like to ask for prayer support for this and many other families who were so split with sons fightin' on opposite sides and the great toll it has had on the families as well as the community itself."

After everyone lifts up their words of support, Chairman Paxton calls the court back to order. "Now for even more hard work we have to deal with today. We must decide what to do with several children with no family support and how we can serve the several widows as well."

Paxton looks towards George, who continues to appear preoccupied. "Sheriff Neill, we see you have several children to be bound out to families. Is that correct?"

As if drawn out of a fog, George collects his thoughts and stands, "Yes, your honor. Some were removed from families who were unable to feed or clothe them. Others have been 'turned out' by their families when the families can no longer provide for them. They are to be bound out to different families to be taken care of and to learn a trade. Our Transylvania community is comin' forward to make the best of many bad situations." George pauses and gestures toward Robert. "Already, Robert Hamilton and his wife, Rhoda, have agreed to bind the orphan named B.M. Parker." Robert nods, but his thoughts are already racing to his conversation with Rhoda two days ago when they decided to take on this boy. Robert can't shake Rhoda's words telling him that taking on this boy won't make things right with Andrew. Robert had promised Rhoda that he was not trying to replace Andrew, but was only doing what was needed. Robert can't forget the look Rhoda shot him. Deep down, they both know Robert hoped that helping Parker would somehow fill Andrew's void.

Robert realizes that everyone is looking at him and is perplexed at first, before he realizes that Chairman Paxton is addressing him. "Yes?" Robert says quickly in hopes that he was not agreeing to something unawares.

Chairman Paxton, seemingly indifferent to Robert's inattention. "Thank you, Sheriff, uh, I mean Bob, for taking this child into your family fold." Robert nods, reluctantly accepting the gratitude. As soon as Robert thinks Paxton is going to move on to other matters not pertaining to him, he is confused when the chair continues addressing him. "Now Bob, the Court needs to ask you if you will serve as Road Commissioner as we try to rebuild. Give special attention to the Island Ford Bridge and Dunns Rock Bridge, and the damage to the Greenville Turnpike." Robert raises his eyebrows and is pleasantly surprised. Discussion over who would serve as Road Commissioner had been debated, but Robert, feeling like maybe his time serving the community was beginning to wane, had never considered that the justices would settle on him. "Yes. I'll do what I can," Robert answers eagerly, feeling honored and overwhelmed at the same time.

B.C. stands to face Robert and, after one swift swipe of his hand through his white beard he speaks, "Off the record." He pauses to make sure the court reporter acknowledges his request before he continues, "Bob, we all want you to serve as Chair of our Court." Robert can't believe that earlier, when Leander Gash mouthed *you're next*, he meant that it would be addressed so soon. Robert glances at Leander who innocently shrugs his shoulders while wearing a told-you-so look. B.C., however, is not playing around and his seriousness causes Robert to adjust his mindset. After all, B.C.'s voice commands attention. "We think you can help us bridge these big divides and family splits in Transylvania. The Court of Pleas and Quarter Sessions is about the only place we can find justice and work toward findin' peace amongst ourselves. Honestly, no one else here is willin' to take the job on because no one knows what is to happen. Ain't nobody faced the unknown like you and George durin' the war." Robert swallows as B.C. holds his gaze. A brief awkward cough from George is Robert's only clue that George also found the statement telling. But Robert pushes away his suspicions, since he detects no animosity in B.C.'s voice. In fact, his old friend continues, "We all know about your courage and leadership skills that seem to run in the Hamilton family." Robert genuinely smiles, thanking B.C. for his kind words, but continues to wonder how many really know all he did during the recent war. As the attention is drawn away from Robert, he ponders how long he will worry, but at the same moment he embraces hope in the future as the chair of Court of Pleas and Quarter Sessions and as Road Commissioner, both jobs where he can continue to prove his loyalty to the county.

As B.C. takes his seat, George, who is eager to move on with business, sees no harm in calling out informally, "Is it true that we are under military rule?" It is finally clear to Robert what George has been preoccupied with all this time.

Paxton responds, "Yep, Sheriff. We have no idea exactly what to expect, but hopefully it will stop all this bushwhacking and other fighting. We got to re-build our county as best we can, having lost so many men and so many others returning in bad shape."

George slowly stands and faces the justices gathered; his sheriff's star prominently placed for everyone to take notice. "I haven't seen any military around here doin' my job yet? And it appears that bushwhacker attacks and murders are only increasing." George waves his arm, pointing beyond the brand-new walls. He raises his voice, "All over the county I'm getting word of their treachery. John Byrd Allison, a respected citizen livin' up in Cashier's Valley came into town with word of one group that came through their home, with his sister, Margret-Nellie, deathly ill lying on her bed. Those ruthless bushwhackers came through and took everything from her home, includin' Margret-Nellie's bed frame, leaving her on a mattress on the bare floor." With every word George speaks, Robert can feel the lightness in court room change to anger. "People in the county have begun to refer to these bushwhackers as Pharaoh's Army."

"That is a fitting name!" Paxton responds, but quickly shrugs his shoulders. "Still, Sheriff, until we get military up here to help, what can we do?"

George looks at Robert, both suddenly reliving the night they confronted the bushwhackers. Robert wishes that it had been the last time they would have to deal with these merciless bands of men. George's voice is calmer, but his anger is still simmering. He slaps his sheriff's star, "I only have this badge, but I swear I will encourage every mountain man, woman and child to carry their shotguns when they open their doors. I will let each law-abidin' citizen know that they are in their legal right to defend themselves against these murderers and thieves and if the men who dare to be a part of Pharaoh's Army haven't done their dirty deeds yet, then our mountain people can shoot them for trespassin'." There is silence in the room, so George takes a deep breath and asks, "Is everyone here in support?" Slowly the men nod and find no legal issue with George's approach.

Robert finds himself nodding and almost smiling at George's plan. Robert decides to help solidify the validity and appropriateness of his approach. "Sheriff, you are simply reinforcin' our old mountain tradition of announcin' who you are and your business when you enter

415

anybody's property. Seems if this widely respected approach is not heeded, then it acts as an early warnin' for those tryin' to protect themselves!" With law on their side, Robert is pleased that George is going to make sure that every family can protect themselves.

CHAPTER 28

Elizabeth Neill, February 11, 1866

Emma-Rachel and James-Henry were sitting so close in the front pew that I thought for sure Reverend English would bop James-Henry on the head and tell him to move over at least a foot, even if they were getting married next month. But it was all too clear that the Reverend was only concerned with the condition of his very pregnant wife sitting in the other front pew across the small aisle. Naomi, who was due soon with their fourth child, was squeezed between her parents, each with a grandchild squirming in their laps. Mary-Lovenia, the oldest of the English babies, already six, had decided it best to sit a few rows back with another little girl from up the valley. She clearly wanted nothing to do with the fussy babies. I couldn't believe six years had already passed and, somewhere in the middle of those six years, war had come and gone, people had died, James had professed his love and then left me and my Union-sympathizing-self behind, and, all the while, Reverend English and Naomi kept having babies. I leaned back in my pew and sighed.

"What is it?" Viney whispered. Sitting next to me, she was so close I could smell her morning coffee and my first thought was how happy I was that we were able to get real coffee again, even if it was rationed. Clearly Viney was enjoying it too.

"Nothin' really." I smiled and then whispered. "How many babies you think that Reverend English and Naomi will have?"

Viney's eyes grew wide and she looked at the gaggle of children already demanding more attention from the congregation than the sermon. She leaned in close again. "I ain't sure . . . at this rate I reckon they'll be aimin' for the holy number seven."

"Naw!" A giggle began to rise. "I bet you they'll have no less than eight!"

"Shhhh!" Aunt Rhoda leaned over to Viney and, while trying to hold it to a whisper, fussed, "Stop this! You are both young ladies now. Not little girls."

Viney and I straightened up and as soon as Aunt Rhoda wasn't looking at us anymore Viney glanced at me enlarging her eyes and silently opening her mouth imitating her mother's stern admonition. I slapped my hands over my mouth so I wouldn't completely burst into laughter, and it took some serious effort to hold our glorious outbursts until the last amen let us run to the side of the ever-faithful Davidson River. We may have been grown women, but the war took our childhood. We were simply claiming some of what we both thought we had lost. It felt good.

Robert Hamilton, February 17, 1866

In spite of last night's fresh snow fall, the temporary courthouse is filled with more people than usual for this month's Transylvania Court of Pleas and Quarter Session. Robert finds it refreshing to see more community members come to listen to the official court proceedings, but is suddenly surprised to see Reverend Elijah Allison walk in with his half-brother Doc Smith and Doc's son, Pink. Robert had heard Elijah was not planning on returning to Brevard, but is pleased that he has changed his mind and come back to preach. Although Robert and the other justices know Doc Smith well, even though most still know him best as Doc Allison, it is still a surprise to have a black man and his son in their midst. Reverend Allison, Doc Smith and Pink move to the back of the room, nodding to those around them. Seemingly

418

unbothered by the curious looks, they settle in to observe the proceedings.

It is Robert's first time to officially chair the Transylvania Court of Pleas and Quarter Sessions. He has already been addressed several times as 'Worshipful" much to his embarrassment even though he is aware of this old English tradition. He wonders if the other justices are overusing the title to bedevil him. He decides it is best to try to conceal his embarrassment by moving on with business at hand in hopes the other justices will follow his lead. Robert easily manages to guide the court through decisions on routine matters, including listening to a report from the Commission on Town Lots for the town of Brevard who propose that the remaining lots should be sold to raise enough money for the County building needs, especially the Courthouse.

As chairman, Robert appoints several men to be the Wardens of the Poor. Perry C. Orr, Samuel Wilson, Eli Patton, and W.R. Galloway are all instructed to meet in June. Robert addresses the four men, who are all sitting in the front row, directly. "Gentlemen, please do your homework and find some solutions for the many poor and homeless. They need food and shelter, clothes and care. Both the Sheriff and the tax reports will be of help as well as the several churches who are all tryin' to meet many needs. You may have heard that many of us farmers are plantin' larger gardens this year to help out." The four men, now Wardens of the Poor, all nod and agree to take on this challenge. Robert is pleased that there is now officially a plan set in motion to address the issue, one that has always been a focus and concern of his.

At the end of the session, he observes the large crowd watching the court, and realizes there is a hand raised towards the back. It is Pink. Robert doesn't know how long his hand has been raised, but he nods towards the young man he has seen grow from a fearless and, at times reckless, young boy to what Robert guesses is a sixteen or seventeen-year-old young man. The curious look in Pink's eyes quickly prods Robert to acknowledge him. "Yes, Pink. Do you have a question?"

Of course, the heads in the room all turn, causing a curious ripple effect, leaving Pink, stumped for a moment, clearly having never had this many men staring at him waiting for him to speak, especially not white men. As his eyes grow wide and his hand remains stuck in the air, his Uncle Elijah whispers something to him, which causes him to break away from his paralysis and look at Robert again. "Yes, Sir." Pink finally drops his arm and clears his throat, avoiding looking at the see of faces between him and Robert. "What do you hear from Washington? We hear tell some news ain't too good." He pauses and glances briefly at the sea of white. "At least not for us freedmen."

Immediately the heads turn back to Robert as he takes in a deep breath. He was hoping that the news had not reached many, but he is clearly wrong. He lifts his voice, not only for everyone to hear, but also so he can sound more-matter of fact. "Basically, President Johnson is fighting with Congress over this Reconstruction business. That is why we are getting mixed messages and are not really sure what is happenin'."

"What business?" Reverend Allison's voice booms, sounding more like a preacher, demanding for Robert to stop beating around the bush.

Robert sighs and shakes his head, but continues addressing the Reverend, Doc and Pink directly. "The President seems to be against the 14th Amendment to the Constitution givin' citizenship to former slaves." He watches as the Reverend and Doc shake their heads and Pink's fists clinch. Still, Robert continues, "And when some states put old pre-civil war leaders back in office and then set out several 'Black Code' laws, congress overrode them after which the President vetoed them. Congress overrode that, and he has been fightin' them ever since, even tourin' the land to get popular support."

Reverend Allison's voice fills the room. "We had head rumor of such and hoped it was all devilment. What on earth are these Black Codes?"

At this point murmurs and talk amongst the crowd is suddenly rising, so Robert grabs the wooden gavel and, for the first time, has to call the court back to order. "As I understand, they restrict blacks in the same way that slave codes used to. The slave codes restricted votin', gettin' a public education, havin' weapons and even had guidelines for worshipin'. So, basically there was no room for any equal treatment. The Black Codes are tryin' to do the same thing. But our state did have some exceptions on voting. Basically, the laws are still about findin' ways to keep the freedmen from having equal rights with whites. But it is important to note that four or five northern states already had black codes up until the war was over. They also wanted freedmen's rights regulated."

"For the love of God, help us understand this!" Reverend Allison commands the room again. "Why on earth does this President not want to have freedmen? Was the war for nothin'? Did our brothers and sons fight each other and die to face another war?"

Everyone in the room is aware that Elijah fought on the side of the Union and even guided the Kirk's Raiders for a short time, while his twin brother and many nephews fought for the Confederates.

Robert waits for the room to settle and then he explains, "Unfortunately, it's all extremely political. You have to remember that Johnson was only Vice President six weeks when President Lincoln was killed. Lincoln chose him because he was a Southerner and a Unionist. Lincoln wanted to reunite the land and thought havin' him as a runnin' mate might do that. The problem is Johnson never wanted to free the slaves or at least never give them rights. He was for the war to keep the land together but it appears also to keep the slaves in place, as many Unionists did."

"What does this mean for us?" Doc Smith spoke for the first time. "What does this mean for my boy?"

An ominous quiet filled the room, and Robert let the silence linger as he searched within himself for an answer. "I'm not too sure, Doc. We received word from our own Senator Gash that at the state level they continue to argue about what it should look like." Robert pauses, looking for any words of encouragement. "I do know that as long as the federal government and the state government keep arguin' about the black codes and what should and should not be enforced, we all have got to keep movin' forward and do it our way for as long as we can. Maybe the arguments will die out and nothin' will come of it and one day we will all be wonderin' what all that fuss was about."

A few nods indicate that some in the crowd take Robert's explanation as a possible outcome, but most continue to shake their heads, acknowledging that it is not really the most probable. Suddenly, Pinks voice echoes across the room. "This Reconstruction business is shore messed up."

Elizabeth Neill, March 18, 1866

I didn't mind that my hands were sore from pulling the broken willow branches off the heavily-ice damaged trees. By the grace of God, the trees were still mostly standing like faithful friends in front of Mammaw's house. The winter had left its mark with forests popping and cracking, leaving paths and roads scattered with splintered branches or, in many cases, whole trees toppled over, unable to bear the weight of the heavy ice storms or the sudden accumulation of wet snow. It wasn't so much that I was hoping to clean up winter's mess, but it was simply so wonderful to be outside with the sun shining and, for the first time in a long time, not wearing anything on my head to keep-me-from-my-death, as Mammaw pointed out on more than one occasion. Even though I still wore my winter jacket, I left it unbuttoned and let it and my hair blow haphazardly in the cool breeze that would sneak up on me. I found myself, in those moments, turning to face the wind, close my eyes, and welcome it by breathing in as deeply as possible, letting the promise of spring flood all my senses.

It was in one of those moments, with my eyes closed, my jacket and hair flailing about and each of my hands grasping a willow branch, that I failed to hear the footsteps come up from behind the farthest Willow tree, closest to the road and the large watering trough, which was beginning to fill again with slowly trickling water. A familiar voice interrupted my moment of tranquility. "The wind sure looks good on you."

My eyes shot open and I stood still as stone as James appeared in front of me. He wore a wide brimmed hat, which he quickly pulled off and held in front of his chest, anxiously rolling its edges. He stared at me for a minute, waiting for a reply, but as I continued to stare in disbelief, he lifted one hand up to shove his ever-falling red hair out of his face.

I frowned and was genuinely confused to see him. I had worked hard to keep any flutter from surfacing when I thought of him, and had been quite pleased with my success, until that moment. The familiar flutter burst forth quicker than two shakes of a lamb's tail. "Mr. Morris?" I finally found my voice. "Why are you here?" I was not going to pretend that it was okay for him to drop by and neither was I going to give any hint of the resurgence of old feelings.

James began to walk closer and with each step, I stepped back one step. Finally, he stopped and frowned. "What are you doin'?"

I held up my two hands and waved the willow branches at him. "I'm cleanin' up the broken branches."

James gave me an exasperated look. "No! You know what I mean! Why are you backin' up?"

I threw the willow branches on the ground next to me and wiped my hands on my jacket, before dramatically thrusting my hands on my hips. "Well mister, you still didn't answer *my* question. As long as I don't know why you are here and what your intentions are then I have no desire to be closer to you than I would any wild snake that would sneak up unbeknownst to me."

James' mouth opened and then remained open in shock for a moment. He took in my defiant stance, my chin that was jutting out and my hair that continued to flap in my face. The free-flowing hair that had been a joy only moments ago became a sudden nuisance, causing me to shake my head to the side to get it out of my face, without using my hands that I was determined to keep on my hips. I was attempting to make a point. Suddenly James' face transformed and a huge grin emerged followed by a large guffaw. "Oh, Elizabeth. I have really missed you!"

I felt heat rise and I was not sure if it was anger or embarrassment. He was not taking me seriously and I was very serious, even though I lacked a convincing execution. "You can call me Miss Neill, if you please. And I have not missed you." I lied. I felt tears welling up and I began to reach back down to find the willow branches I had discarded. I didn't want him to see me cry. But it was useless. I miscalculated my step and stumbled to the ground catching myself, hands first, in the soggy soil. I quickly jumped up and looked at the dirt on my hands, ignoring the wet mud splotches on the front of my skirt, where my knees had managed to make two perfectly round imprints. "Look what you've done!" I fussed at him, but didn't look at him as I began to walk towards him, and then right past him towards the large water trough. Once I reached the trough, I straddled the side of it and I reached out my hands to let the trickle of cold spring water slowly wash away the dirt. The lump in my throat hurt so badly that I couldn't hold it any longer and I gave into real sobs.

"I'm sorry, Elizabeth." James had eased himself onto the edge of the trough right next to me, leaving his hat on a stump nearby. He reached up and removed my hands from the water. They were clean, but cold as ice. He wiped them on his own blue-linen jacket and then held them between his own hands. I let him. "I am sorry I was so angry and left you."

I felt my sobs subside enough for me to look at him. I took one of my cold hands from him, leaving the other one still in his warm grip, and wiped by face and nose on the sleeve of my jacket. "You really hurt me."

James' eyes dropped for a moment, and I could see he was trying to control what he was about to say. When he lifted them again, he looked at me with a seriousness that scared me. He looked almost desperate. He squeezed my one hand he was still holding. "In the last ten months I have been doin' a lot of thinkin'. It ain't been easy. Every day I think of you and what I thought we'd have one day. I thought I could work so hard on my parent's homestead in Polk County and I would forget about you, but seein' you at the weddin' just about killed me. I knew at that moment that I cain't live without you, Elizabeth." He paused waiting for me to react, but I wasn't sure how I should react. It was everything I ever wanted to hear, but I felt like there was something that was missing, something that he was not saying. And then, just as I expected, my suspicions were confirmed. James' voice was too calm as he continued, "There is one thing that I need from you before we get married. I need you to apologize to me for your treasonous actions behind my back."

I yanked my hand out of his grip so fast that he almost fell into the trough, but instead managed to save himself grabbing the edge with both of his hands. I jumped up and shook my head with disbelief. "Really?" He looked at me bewildered. I went over to the small stump and snatched up his wide brimmed hat. I straightened out the edges and then handed it to him in a matter-of-fact gesture. "Thank you for your visit. Have a good day." As he reluctantly took the hat, I turned to head towards my scattered willow branches.

James scurried to his feet and ran towards me, grabbing me by one shoulder and spun me to face him. "What in tarnation are you doin'?"

Anger welled up inside of me, but one that felt calm, collected and clear. One that I could control and had no room for childish blubbering or romantic notions of unwavering love.

"Pickin' up these damn sticks, *James*!" I practically spat his name. Every blasphemous word that I had tucked away found its way to the surface, calling James names I did not know were even inside of me. When I felt some satisfaction in the shock on his face, I waved one stick at him. "This is what it is about, James. Pickin' up the mess that has been left us. This tree didn't do anything to deserve to be broken and I sure as hell didn't do anything to deserve to pick up its broken pieces. But I am not askin' this tree or the winter to apologize to me for the burden they put on me."

"This ain't trees and weather we're talkin' about!" James was raising his voice now and he was clinching the brim of his hat again.

I flung my one empty hand into the air and let out a loud sarcastic laugh. "Oh yes, that *is* right. I'm so happy you pointed that out to me." I rubbed my chin dramatically in mock contemplation. Then I stopped and looked at him straight in the eye, walked in close as possible and pointed my finger into his chest. "You want to hear it straight? Then let me educate you. None of us wanted to be pulled into the man-made dividin' that had nothin' to do with the essence of who we really are. We're farmers, bee-keepers, millers, blacksmiths, midwives, preachers, mothers, fathers and brothers and sisters. And we for sure aren't the North or the South." My eyes grew wide with something I had just remembered, and I lifted my finger off his chest and held it up in front of me. "First of all, *before* the war even started, we watched out for our Cherokee neighbors and kin. Ain't nobody over the last fifteen years or even now talkin' about who they are. Ain't nobody even thinkin' of turnin' them in to be forced out west." I pointed my finger down the road in no particular direction. "Even durin' this damn war between the Union and Confederates, we were mountain first! That is all I was doin' ... takin' care of home, family and neighbors first. If you can't see that and accept that then get out of these mountains! Don't get me wrong, it will take years for the hurt from the divided loyalties and the deaths from the war to heal. But at some point, pride has to get out of the way of humanity and reality, and true honor... so we can continue to do what it right, helpful, and good. But by God, if we can't heal as Mountain people... divided people, who even with divided loyalties stuck together and created a new county *during* the war . . . then there is no hope for the nation."

"Elizabeth." James tried to speak.

"I'm not finished!" I dropped my finger and moved in so I could feel his breath. "I'll tell you about hurt and pickin' up pieces." All I had ever heard Pink tell me came flooding back. "Just two days ago the first black baby was born in this county since slavery was abolished. Her name is Mary-Jane Patton." It didn't take James but a moment to make the Patton connection and his eyes widened as I continued. "Yes, she is half white. Many here have given birth to children of their white masters, and then raised the children as their own, with no rights at all. These folks have a real good reason to haul themselves out of here! These folks have a right to be angry! But no. What do they do? They choose to stay here to build their life. They claim their right to these mountains! They take care of each other as mountain folks. They aren't runnin' away!" I stepped back from James and I felt as if the greatest weight was lifted off me. I looked at him one last time and I felt a tenderness I hadn't felt in a long time towards the pitiful, red-haired, dumbfounded man standing in front of me.

"James, it *should* make you think a little about what in tarnation makes you so mad at me for takin' care of people!"

Robert Hamilton, March 21, 1866

Robert's boots crunch on the stiff mud, which has been transformed by last night's hard freeze from a mushy mess, difficult to traverse without strategically placed wooden planks, into a carpet of rocky ridges. He notices the frozen footprints in front of the Valley Store reveal that hogs and cattle have begun to be driven through the valley again, a rarity during the war. One horse is already tied up at the hitching post, but instead of focusing on the horse, Robert suddenly turns as he hears a wagon filled with lumber heading into town, the driver, George Clayton, only glances at Robert long enough to throw up a friendly wave.

Although Robert has already enjoyed a morning cup of coffee with Rhoda, he hopes that B.C. has some fresh coffee brewing on his wood burning stove. As he walks inside, he is not surprised to find Fletcher already leaning against the counter and talking with B.C., both holding a mug. "Look what the cat drug in!" Fletcher teases and B.C. laughs, but Robert shakes his head feigning concern.

"Now, that's not very preacher-like, is it?" Robert teases.

Fletcher laughs even louder, "I think I've never been accused of being preacher-like."

"That's for sure!" Robert smiles and then asks, "Since you are sittin' here jawin' I guess you don't have a new-born baby yet?"

Fletcher beams, "Any day now! Naomi has been cleaning house and fussing over every little thing being perfect before the baby is born."

B.C. puts his coffee down on the counter and asks, "So why are you here? You should be home with her and the young'uns."

Fletcher nods at the aisle of supplies behind him while he pulls a list out of his jacket pocket. "Oh, trust me, I am helping. Got me a list here of what I need to bring on home." Then he tucks the list back in his pocket. "Just thought I'd catch up a bit first and enjoy this coffee."

"Speakin' of coffee." Robert interrupts. "Any left for me?"

B.C. reaches under the counter and pulls out a mug and tosses it at Robert who then heads to the wood-fired stove to serve himself.

From the warmth of the stove he can hear Fletcher continue talking with B.C. "Besides, a little coffee is due since tomorrow I'm officiating the Cagle-Young wedding. That will be something else."

B.C. strokes his beard, "That sure is somethin' else. So soon after the war Emma-Rachel and James-Henry gettin' hitched. Have only heard whispers, though, and no one out-right goin' against their union. Seems if Strawbridge and Martha are fine with their daughter marryin' a former Union soldier then it ain't nobody else's business."

"True!" Robert jumps into the conversation as he emerges with his coffee. "It sure hasn't been easy on Strawbridge and Martha, but they are determined to move on." The talk in the store, for once, moves away from the war and its aftermath. Instead, B.C. talks of his girls and how Betty is doing wonderfully, and that he and Betty are expecting a child in October. After the men congratulate B.C. on the news, Fletcher steers the conversation towards the construction of new buildings in Brevard and asks if there has been any talk of bringing the railroad through town yet.

The sound of a wagon pulling up outside, causes B.C. to take a last sip of his coffee and place it under the counter. "Reckon it's time to tend to business."

As Robert and Fletcher move towards the woodstove to top off their cooling coffee with some more that is hot, the door swings open and James Deavor walks in looking somewhat befuddled. He sees B.C. first and asks, "You got someone to help me unload these crates?"

"Well, good mornin' to you too, Captain!" B.C. reaches under his counter, pulling out his mug, deciding maybe he can take another sip of his coffee after all. Robert is taken aback by the interchange since Deavor has not been visiting the mountains much since the war. The word is that he is living in Georgia and is wooing a young woman.

Deavor is suddenly aware of his own abruptness and his shoulders deflate. "Sorry, B.C. I'm only here for a short time and I just cain't quite get used to not havin' my colored help."

"You mean your slaves?" Fletcher appears next to Deavor and fixes his eyes intensely on the former captain. Robert scurries up next to Fletcher in hopes that he can defuse the conversation before the two get into their never-ending political feud.

Deavor, surprised by the two men's sudden appearance, looks at Fletcher and indignantly answers, "Yes, I miss my slaves and the money they cost me. But more than that I cain't stand figurin' out how to help my family when I'm not around and hirin' people has been costly."

Robert watches Fletcher's ears turn red and hopes his friend will not completely lose his temper. Fletcher does manage to keep his voice calm, although his fuming anger still seeps through his punctuation of targeted words. "So, you are *saying* . . . that you'd *prefer* . . . to keep these *humans* . . . as *slaves* . . . for *YOUR convenience*?"

"Oh, damn it all! Shut up Fletcher!" Deavor sighs and shakes his head. "You always make me out to be the devil!"

Fletcher, surprised by Deavor's response simple raises his eyebrows and shoulders and says, "Well, if the shoe fits!"

Deavor, exasperated, leans on the counter and places one hand on the countertop and rubs it along the surface as if smoothing out a crease. Staring at his hand he offers up the only plea he can muster. "All I'm sayin' is that times are hard for all of us. I ain't gonna head up into these mountains much til there's more time passed. Ma's afraid them bushwhackers that shot Pa will head back to finish the job since the bushwhackers don't seem to care none that the war is over."

Robert looks at Fletcher and silently begs him to be merciful, since he knows Fletcher will continue to point out how far behind the captain still is in his thinking. Both men also feel a glimmer of guilt having only informed Mrs. Deavor that the bushwhackers were not going to bother her, but never told her that they were, in fact, dead. Although their deaths are officially in the public record, it is unlikely anyone would look closely at the numerous coroner reports. With all the instability surrounding the county, it is still too early to share. Fletcher acknowledges Robert's glance with a gentle nod and then walks up to Deavor and, practically leaning over him, hands him his coffee. "Here. I think you need this more than I do right now. It can warm up that cold heart of yours some!"

The levity in his voice is not lost on Deavor and he takes the mug in his hands. "I'll take that as a truce?" Deavor dares to look up at Fletcher, who is still standing next to him.

"I reckon. For now." Fletcher teases and then a mischievous smile crosses his face. "See how I'm helpin' you now? You were cold. I gave you a cup of coffee."

"Excuse me, I think it's my coffee you gave." B.C. laughs.

Fletcher waves his hand dismissively, "Don't mess up my mini-sermon."

Deavor rolls his eyes, "Oh, is that what you're doin'? Preachin'?"

Robert, shaking his head, joins in the banter, "You better brace yourself! B.C., you better put on another pot of coffee." B.C. and Deavor laugh as Fletcher shakes his head, his turn to feign concern.

"Gentlemen. If you are done tormenting me, I will be mightily grateful to continue with God's word." Fletcher smiles gently, and the men can see he seriously does want to say something.

But Robert can't help himself and adds, "As long as it's God's word and not your word!"

Fletcher doesn't respond immediately and scratches his beard as if contemplating Robert's heeding. Then he abruptly nods, "Yes, they are God's words. Not mine."

"Well, get on with it then." Deavor is the only one to be sincerely interested and his curiosity is not lost on Fletcher.

Fletcher leans in onto the counter next to Deavor and in all earnestness says, "We were commanded to love one another. Even our neighbors." There is silence. Deavor nods slowly and just as he looks at the preacher with a deeper understanding and appreciation, Fletcher can't help himself. He slaps Deavor's shoulder and laughs, "But you sure make it hard!"

The captain chuckles and adds, "You ain't no saint yourself!"

"That's the shortest sermon you've ever preached." Robert points out. "You think some Sundays you can follow today's example?"

"Robert, God tells me that you need more than a sentence or two." Fletcher shoots back.

Deavor's laugh is genuine. "Seems like I lucked out!"

"You sure did." Fletcher agreed. "You see, there are times I'm looking out for you."

Deavor, enjoying the banter, responds, "Not been much of an inclination of yours!"

Fletcher scratches his beard again, "I do remember a time during the war when you called out for me to come to your side when you thought you were dying."

Shaking his head and chuckling Deavor responds, "Well, I wasn't in my right mind."

Robert smiles as he observes the two men who will, once they leave the Valley Store, continue to disagree and find ways to undermine each other, out of principle, in spite of this moment of truce.

Elizabeth Neill, March 22, 1866

Wearing my blue-striped dress and blue bow, now cut in two, at the ends of my two braids, I found that I was very attentive to Emma-Rachel's and James-Henry's wedding, in fact the most attentive I had ever been to Reverend English. As I watched the two exchange vows, I remembered years ago when Emma-Rachel and I cooled our feet in the Davidson River. She, although older than me, used me as an appropriate chaperone to go to the Cagle-mill, so she could get a chance to be with James-Henry. Unfortunately, the memory was also filled with hate, hurt and a full-on fist fight. But still, the memory was one of passion. I was happy their story ended at the altar and wondered if I had lost my chance at reconciliation with my James. I could still see his face from four days ago, dumbfounded from my rant, remaining in shock as he awkwardly placed his hat on his head. The wide brim of the hat, which was heavily warped from his rolling and clenching it so tightly, made him look even more befuddled. Although

I felt sorry for him, I still let him go. He had some thinking to do and a turnaround of heart wasn't likely to happen at that moment.

I kissed Emma-Rachel's cheek after the wedding telling her how happy I was for her. Instead of her moving on to the next friendly face filled with words of congratulations, Emma-Rachel flung her arms around me and pulled me in close. She whispered, "You still have your chance."

I held her embrace and whispered back, "Not likely. He hates me. I'm sure of it."

She pulled my face into her hands and looked me straight in the eyes, still whispering. "I think you are very wrong!" I frowned at how she could say that with such conviction and was almost angry with her for toying with this romantic notion that it would all work out. But, before I could say a word, she turned my head to face the cluster of trees along the path on the other side of the church. There, shifting awkwardly, stood James, in his best Sunday clothes. Emma-Rachel kissed my cheek and whispered one last time, "I know he did *not* come to our weddin'. He's clearly been waitin' for you to come out of the church." She nudged me a little with her shoulder. "Go get him!"

I found myself beginning to walk towards James as he eagerly waited for me to come to him, rather than be seen at James-Henry Cagle's wedding. I stopped half-way and found my father in the cluster of men standing close to the river. He was watching me. He glanced at James and then back at me before he nodded. I didn't know how much I needed Pa to give me permission, but I felt a weight lift as I resumed my walk, with a little more urgency.

As I reached James, I stood before him and didn't say a word. He was the one who sought me out, so I figured he knew what he wanted to say. Clearly having left his ruined hat at home, he shoved his hair out of his eyes and looked at me without anger or disgust. I welcomed his gaze, but still I did not fully embrace what it might mean. He cleared his throat and looked around at the people who were beginning to notice the odd meeting set apart from the festivity. "Can we, uh you, walk with me . . . and talk . . . where there ain't so many folk watchin'?"

I nodded and let him lead me along the dirt road that followed the Davidson River. We didn't speak for a few minutes, not until we were standing in the wide meadow where the apple tree saplings were taller than I remembered. Their empty branches stood ready to absorb spring's warmth, but the chill continued to suppress any signs of budding. Some broken branches were strewn about from freeze damage, but very few. The orchard had not suffered like other trees with larger branches, or the evergreens whose full branches could not bear the weight of excess snow and ice.

He gently touched my arm so I would stop walking and then let go immediately. I turned to face him and quizzically studied his features. He was getting older and the lines in his face were deepening, but his eyes held a youthfulness that continued to tug at my innards. "Elizabeth, how are you?"

Baffled, I blinked a few times before I found a fitting answer that wouldn't chase him away. "Well. James, I am fine. How are you?"

"I've been downtrodden." James responded as if we were talking about the weather or a common cold.

Since I had already told him all that I had to say, I continued this courteous exchange, "Is that so?" I paused and when he didn't answer, I couldn't help but goad him, "And why might that be?"

Without hesitation, and in the same civilized tone, he answered, "Well, it seems I have been quite wrong." He paused and then walked over to one of the apple trees. He inspected one of the branches for any signs of budding.

I followed him and watched him run his rough fingers over the closest branch. "Is that so?"

"Yes, it is." He seemed particularly fascinated with the end of one small branch that jutted out between us. I was happy to see no buds had begun to poke through, since the cold would ruin any chance of the small growth surviving. It would likely be another month or two before the trees would begin to come alive with growth. James' eyes suddenly focused on me, the branch between us forgotten. "It seems that my sister, Betty, and B.C. think I'm a stubborn ass and I'll be totally lost if I don't get my thinkin' right and marry you."

Taken aback by his sudden brash language, I stared a minute and took in what he was saying. Since I had recently unloaded my own share of language on him, I really was not shocked by his profanity. It was his message that gave me pause. "James, are you askin' to marry me?"

James dropped his eyes for a moment, as if he needed a moment to respond. When he looked back at me, I realized he was trying to keep from crying. He thought he was controlling it, but the crack in his voice gave him away. "Is that wrong of me?"

I took in a deep breath and stepped in closer to the man who I had never stopped loving. The branch found itself dangerously enclosed. "I don't think so. It depends what strings you're attachin'."

James' eyes widened and a gentle smile emerged. He let a few tears escape as he reached out to touch my face, as if for the first time. "No strings. I swear." I didn't know if I should believe him, and he immediately saw my disbelief. His voice was suddenly urgent, "Please, Elizabeth. I promise you I won't ask you to apologize for somethin' you had to do. I swear it!"

"Why?" I whispered. "Why now?" I felt my own throat tighten and eyes burn as my own tears revealed my inner longing for him mixed with a hurt that seemed to keep pulling me away from believing any word he said.

He reached out and moved one of my braids in front of my shoulder and took the blue bow in his fingers, feeling its soft texture. "Because you are the only person who can make me see the world anew. I saw it anew when I first met you. I saw no joy in my everyday life and then all-of-a sudden you brought me hope. I saw it anew during the war when you were waitin' for me, even when there was no assurance of me comin' home alive. And I saw the world anew when you opened my eyes, only days ago to a world of hurt and healin' beyond my own." His face became a blur as my tears welled up and, at the same time, a smile emerged from deep within, spreading across my whole being. James took in my visible change and hesitated only a moment, looking for one last second to confirm that he had indeed broken through my wall. He closed the small gap between us, flattening the apple branch without care, and kissed me. And I kissed back. Willing. Wanting. Without hesitation.

After several minutes of rediscovering each other's tenderness and touch I pulled away and took in his complete vulnerability and hunger. I smiled at him and teased, "I do have one string attached."

He took my bait. "And what might that be, Miss Neill?"

"Well, Mr. Morris." I reached out and gently moved his one strand of red hair out of his face. "I don't ever want to leave these mountains."

"We will never leave these mountains!" James promised and came in for another kiss.

CHAPTER 29

Robert Hamilton, December 24, 1866

The afternoon sun is beginning to disappear behind the mountain ridge that rises behind the Hamilton homestead. The snow on the evergreens has melted some during the day, leaving patches of dark green to break up the sheet of white. Robert is sitting in his favorite rocker on the front porch patching up corn-shuck stars in preparation for another Christmas celebration without fear of being discovered or the constant bracing for that unexpected and weary knock on the door. He hears a squeal as Emily, now nine, manages to keep up, in spite of her club foot, with her little sister, Rachel, who is a rambunctious seven-year-old, throwing clumps of soggy snow at each other. Robert smiles at the scene and is thankful at least a few of his children will remember their childhood more fondly than his older ones.

"Pa?" John-Riley interrupts Roberts's thoughts. "Can you help me with haulin' some of the fire wood to the porch so we got plenty for tonight and tomorrow?" John-Riley nods his head towards the front door behind him and adds, "Ma said we better or else it'll be a sorry Christmas!"

Robert laughs at John-Riley's imitation of Rhoda's words and carefully puts down his repaired star and stands up, stretching his stiff legs. "Well, we better listen to your Ma!"

John-Riley and Robert head up to the barn and grab a flat-bed wooden wheelbarrow. The wooden wheel creaks as John-Riley places it close to the large woodpile that is stacked along one side of the barn.

Robert and John-Riley begin to load the wheelbarrow, one log at a time. As soon as the wheelbarrow is full, John-Riley lifts the handles and begins to haul the load over to the front porch, with Robert following behind him. The wooden wheel leaves a single muddy track as it churns up the mud under the packed snow. Watching his son, Robert realizes, for the first time, how similar John-Riley is to Andrew. At eighteen he is the same age Andrew was when the war started. Robert has not thought of Andrew in some time and he tries to push away the onset of his somber mood before John-Riley notices, but it is too late. John-Riley has already brought the wheelbarrow to a halt and is looking at his father.

"I ain't Andrew, you know?" John-Riley says as a matter of fact before he jumps up on the porch.

"I know that!" Robert answers defensively. He reaches for a log and hands it up to his son who places it on the dwindling log pile that reaches only a few feet across the front porch.

"I ain't so sure you do." John-Riley holds out his hand to receive another log.

Robert hands the log to him but does not reach down to pick up the next one. When his son comes back to him ready for the next hand off, he realizes his father is staring at him, quite confused. "What do you mean?" Robert asks and will not continue until his son is forthcoming.

John-Riley plops down on the edge of the porch, dangling his legs over the side. He is not quite eye-to eye with his father, but close enough. "Pa, you been avoidin' any talk of war since it's been over. You talked about it all the time, keepin' us all filled in and we always knew what you were thinkin'. Then, when Andrew came by and left us all behind, you stopped talkin' about anything that has to do with the war, like it never happened."

Robert frowns and lets his son's words sink in for a few moments. "You are right. I thought maybe you all had given up enough of your childhood to the war, and I didn't want to burden you anymore."

John-Riley's laugh draws attention from the girls, but only for a fleeting moment before they decide nothing interesting is really happening at the woodpile. "Pa, that war stole my youth. Not you. I never blamed you, and I will never blame you. But I can't have you pushin' me away because you are tryin' to make sure I don't have to bear the woes of the war anymore. Well, that's a pile of horse shit."

"John-Riley!" Robert interrupts. "The girls!"

"Oh, please. They've heard worse." Ignoring his father's parental admonishment, John-Riley continues, "All of us followed you proudly, Pa. We ain't done talkin' about the war and we will, by God, never forget Yankee Holler. You may never talk to outsiders about it, but you better keep talkin' to us about it, 'cause it is somethin' we were a part of and it will always be a part of us."

His son's words sink in, and surprisingly seem to lift a weight that Robert did not know he was carrying. He glances over at the little girls and asks, "Are you talkin' on behalf of all of you children?"

John-Riley smiles. "Yes. I know for sure Millie, Viney, Matilda and Joel all feel the same way." He points a finger towards the squealing noises. "When it comes to those two I ain't so sure. But they need to be reminded, at least that's my two cent's worth. We are all still in this, Pa. Somethin' bein' over don't mean it never happened."

Robert nods and reaches for the next log. As John-Riley stands back up and reaches for the log, Robert holds onto the log for a moment to draw his son's attention and smiles. "John-Riley. How did I get such a wise son?"

John-Riley grins. "I get it from Ma's side." Robert doubles over in laughter.

* * *

With the woodpile satisfactorily stacked, the Hamiltons are all gathering around the fire as they wait for the cornbread to finish baking. Robert observes each of his children and begins to realize that he cannot let his loss of Andrew keep him from proudly raising the rest of his children. Suddenly, a knock on the door causes the whole family to freeze. Even the two youngest respond to the learned behavior, but aren't quite sure why. Rhoda, who appears from the kitchen, is first to speak. "Now, who in tarnation would be visitin' us on Christmas eve?" She forces a smile looking at the children first and then raises her eyes to Robert. "Maybe Pa can go find out who it is."

Robert, who is surprised by his own stupor, quickly jumps up and, out of habit, grabs the colt still hanging in its spot. The children gather closer to Rhoda who has taken Robert's seat. As much as they are all trying to be calm, Robert realizes it will take time before they cannot react suspiciously to every unexpected knock. As soon as Robert has his belt secured, he hears a voice call out, "Hello? Is anybody home? It's the Filmores. Don't mean to sceer you none." Robert and Rhoda look at each other perplexed. A second voice is suddenly heard through the door, but this time a female. "Miss Rhoda? It's Annie. Remember me? Ya'll helped us with our young'uns."

Rhoda's hand reaches her mouth in disbelief at the same time Robert's mouth drops. They can hardly believe it. Robert flings the door open just as Rhoda jumps out of her chair and hurries to greet the Filmores. "Lordy!" Rhoda cries as she embraces a young woman who, although still very thin, is clearly in better health than the last time they saw them while they hid in the Hamilton's root-cellar. "Do come in!" Rhoda practically pulls Annie and then notices a little boy holding his ma's skirt. "This must be little Benny." Rhoda doesn't give the boy a chance to protest and swoops him up in her arms. "You're about five now, right?" She tickles his belly with her finger as he nods.

Robert extends his hand to Tommy, who also looks healthier than when he was a pale deserter hiding under his bed. "Well, hello, Tommy. It warms my heart to see you alive and well." Robert also extends his hand to a young boy Robert estimates is about ten now. Robert recognizes his fierce white hair, the same tuft of hair that kept watch through the small log cabin window. "Still tow-headed as ever!"

The boy smiles shyly, so Tommy reintroduces his son. "This here is our boy Otto. He's growed up a bit."

"More than a bit!" Robert smiles and waves Tommy and his oldest son to follow the other two into the warmth of the living room and the excited greetings the rest of the family is offering.

Tommy lets Otto walk in front of him and, as Robert begins to close the door, Tommy is suddenly aware of Robert's Colt strapped around his waist. Frowning, he quietly asks, "Who you expectin'?"

Robert glances down at his gun and then quickly begins to unbuckle the belt. "Tommy, lots of sheep have been sheared since you been here."

Tommy opens his eyes widely and nods solemnly, "I cain't believe you done right by more folk than us."

Robert realizes that he has suddenly shared too much with Tommy. Just because he helped the Filmores doesn't mean that the Filmores knew he has helped others. Robert wishes he could take back his last words, but he can't so he thinks it best to say nothing and direct Tommy over to the fire where Viney already has Benny in her lap. She holds up a rough-looking small corn-husk doll swaddled in a soft green rag and waves it at Robert. "Look, Pa. They still have the doll I made." Viney's joy makes Robert push away his fretting over his choice of words and begins to rejoice again in this small reunion.

Annie reaches out and touches Robert's arm, getting his attention. "We'd a not lived if'n it hadn't been for you. We made it to Tommy's family in Tennessee, although we almost froze, but our boys were warm 'nough from them jackets you spared."

Robert is genuinely delighted that their seemingly impossible plan had worked. "Happy to hear it."

Tommy, standing on the other side of Robert, continues the narration while Joel invites Otto to toss some pebbles into a can in the corner. "Once we were safe, I found there was a real hurtin' for rebuildin' roads and, such and since I am learned in layin' rock and masonry, I was able to provide a little for my family. We came on back here 'cause we still got our land and Annie's family lives here. She missed them somethin' awful. I done fixed the old log home up real nice."

"We are really happy for you!" Rhoda smiles and reaches over to tussle the five-year-old's hair. Still happy to play with Viney, the young boy pays Rhoda no attention. "I can't tell you what a Christmas gift this is to see you all survived the journey."

Annie reaches over to Rhoda and squeezes her hand. "We are forever beholden to you. I've done told all my family and friends!"

Rhoda's smile falters as she looks at Robert. He struggles to keep his smile on his face as he realizes that it is likely only a matter of time before word spreads. With the Filmore family home, as glorious as it is, the sudden reality of their spreading "the good news" only reignites fears that had begun to dwindle.

Elizabeth Neill, December 26, 1866

I felt things were quite out of whack when we arrived at Reverend Allison's home for the marriage of Pink's parents. I found myself surrounded by several families whose skin colors ranged from dark and light browns to pink and bronze-skinned whites. Many freedmen had decided to stay. In fact, they had already built a church community, and last I had heard, they were meeting in Doc Smith's blacksmith shop and called themselves the French Broad Baptist Church. At that moment, all folks were dressed in their Sunday best. At least two dresses looked like they had been recently made from linsey-woolsey and I wondered if the Allisons had managed to obtain several yards of the material before the Confederate army seized the rest for their soldiers. A few men were still wearing their jackets made from blanket cloth and I wondered if it was in place of well-worn shirts. In any case, they all wore leather shoes, some more worn than others, but with Doc and Pink doing the cobbler work for the Allisons, I was sure that no one would go without, especially not in the frigid cold.

Pa brought our whole family along, and Jimmy and Sarah-Jane were already standing near the fireplace pestering Pink, who was soaking up the attention. The wooden floorboards creaked under the weight of the number of people moving between the larger living room area and some back rooms, which I had not dared to go into yet, for fear of being too nosey. I couldn't see Ma anywhere and figured she had managed to slip into one of the back rooms with the notion of helping the women folk. Pa was near the front door and was busy talking with Reverend Allison, both men's arms were waving in heated discussion, so I turned my attention to the bride and groom, Pink's ma and pa. I could still clearly hear Reverend Allison's precise enunciation of their full names, "In front of God and country, Doc Allison Smith and Maryann Thankful Gaskins are hereby pronounced husband and wife." I felt so ignorant when Pa told me we were going to their wedding. It was one more reminder of how little I knew about what it meant to be a slave. Pa explained that many former slaves who were husband and wife were not going to go through the legal marriage process since they felt that they were married in God's eyes, even if they had done it their own way. Some jumped over a broom, others created their own rituals. But in this case, since Doc's brother was a minister, they had been more than delighted to have him officially and legally marry them.

I had kept my wool jacket on, since I was still cold from the long ride through the valley, even though the trip had been over an hour ago. I did, finally, manage to unbutton it as I moved through the tight space. I heard names of the black families that were gathered and celebrating this moment. There were McJunkins, Hemphills, Browns, Stewarts and a Gash family. I didn't ask any of them all the questions that were shooting through my head for fear of seeming rude, but my curiosity was physically visible on my face. "They're all foundin' members of our church." Pink's voice startled me. I hadn't seen him come up next to me, and I was embarrassed that I had clearly been staring.

"Was I that obvious?" I whispered.

"I'm shore if our Revered Walker could have a word with you, he would." He teased. He pretended to straighten out his already stiff collar and I noticed his shirt was also new, even though his denim pants, with his knees wearing thin, had seen better days. "Ain't you been taught it ain't fittin' to stare?"

"I'm sorry. I just don't know these people." I looked up at Pink who was quite a bit taller than me now. "Why aren't you meetin' at your church in your Pa's shop?"

Pink frowned and I could see I was, once again, asking something that should maybe be left alone, although I wasn't sure why. "It burned down."

My eyes grew wide. "I'm sorry, I didn't know. What happened?"

Pink shrugged and was trying to be light about it, but he had practically grown up in that workshop. "Ain't nobody quite shore. We figure the woodstove caught somethin' ablaze." I really hoped that that was what it was, but since he didn't offer any suspicious speculating, I decided not to ask any other questions. Suddenly, Pink's face lit up and he pointed at a large white man that looked an awful lot like Reverend Allison. This man, however, had a much whiter beard and he seemed to be a little more reserved. "My Uncle Lish said we can rebuild the church on some of his property just up the hill." I realized his Uncle Lish was Reverend Allison's twin brother Elisha Allison, who had fought in the war on the side of the Confederacy. I found myself suddenly staring at the well-groomed white man in the corner, carefully sipping a cup of coffee. "Are you starin' again?"

I jerked my head quickly to look at Pink again. "Dang it! Sorry, Pink. I am just surprised." I quickly realized I hadn't expressed my happiness over the news, and I had reverted to calling him Pink. "I mean, Mr. Smith, I think it is mighty fine that you will have some land to build a real church buildin'. I only said I'm surprised because. . ."

". . . he was a Confederate?" Pink finished my sentence and then shook his head. "Of all people, Miss Neill, you should know about movin' on. Ain't you and Mr. Morris getting' hitched next month?"

Suddenly, the heat in my cheeks announced both my embarrassment and personal bliss, causing Pink to chuckle. "Stop laughin'!" I fussed and was suddenly so warm that I took off my jacket and held it across my arms in front of me. "I don't want people lookin' at me!"

Pink crossed his arms and his grin grew wide. "Oh, so you can stare at these people, but they ain't got no business starin' at you?"

"That's not what I meant, and you know it!" I was doing the best I could to move my back to most of the bodies in the room. My blue and white striped dress had finally grown too small and had been transformed into a skirt, which I wore with one of Ma's white blouses. It wouldn't be long before I would need to put my jacket on again, but, at that moment, I welcomed the cool airiness the blouse offered.

Pink sighed and then looked at the room filled with family and friends, both black and white, and then he looked back at me and his smile softened. "You think, Miss Neill, this is the beginnin' of a new way? You think colored folk and white folk will be figurin' out we're all on the same side?"

I turned myself back around and took in the unusual sight. Although the space was mostly filled with the French Broad Baptist's congregation and Pink's Allison relatives, along with my family's very out-of-place presence, there was some familiar talk between all folk, even if it was clearly strained at times. Several children and teens, along with Jimmy and Sarah-Jane, seemed to line the walls and stared rudely at everyone, as I had, but no one paid them much attention.

I turned back around and faced my old friend. "What do you think?"

Pink's eyes suddenly became serious and the little boy was gone. "I think it's still just a dream. Got too many people in high places fightin' to keep us down."

"But that doesn't mean it will change this." I waved my hand at the festivity. "Or us!"

Pink sighed. "I ain't so shore, Miss Neill." He found his mischievous smile again and stood up as straight as possible. "But I shore will live like I'm free. Even if I'm told otherwise. I'll have my Uncle Elijah marry me and my wife one day, regardless if it's allowed and he'll shore be up for it, he's done told me already." I smiled at his defiance, but he was not finished. "I'll teach my children and their children what matters and about bein' good and kind and doin' what's right in God's eyes. Could be, one day, maybe years from now, their white kin will reckon it's time to remember that we're all kin." Pink looked straight at me, and I saw hope. "Miss Neill, when that happens, then I reckon we can get on with buildin' a county that won't let what divides us be greater than what unites us."

Robert Hamilton, January 31, 1867

The gently falling snow is not a hindrance for family and friends as they gather mid-day at the Oak Grove church. Even Strawbridge and Martha Young, along with Fletcher and his wife, Naomi, are setting foot in a neighboring church for this joyous occasion. Standing in the back, Robert is aware that Rachel-Emma and James-Henry are not present, but understands that James is not quite ready for James-Henry to be in attendance on this special day. Robert feels honored that he, himself, is at least allowed to witness this union, and has already experienced James' attempt to muster up some fondness for this old former-Union-sympathizing sheriff. It was only last Sunday that James came up Lambs Creek and asked Robert to instruct him about raising sheep. Being a farmer now, James wants to have his own flock one day. Robert, realizing that Elizabeth was probably behind this, still whole-heartedly welcomed the dialogue.

Viney, who is standing at the front next to Elizabeth, is beaming at the bride and groom while the rest of Elizabeth's cousins and siblings are sitting in the front two pews. The familiar back of George's head stands out with a growing bald spot shining conspicuously. His wife Sarah can be seen for a moment when her head leans into whisper something to George and then, once he smiles at her, her profile disappears again behind a large woman sitting behind her. Everyone is taking in the cherished moment. There is a beautiful simplicity in Elizabeth's choice of wearing her mother's old wedding dress. At first, it looks like a simple white linen shift, but its intricate embroidery along the edges of her long sleeves reveal it is more than an undergarment. Millie's beautiful weaving is once again displayed in a light-blue woolen shawl that rests gently on the edge of Elizabeth's shoulders. A simple blue ribbon is intricately woven through her carefully braided auburn hair. James can't stop smiling at his beautiful bride and is clearly enjoying her absorption of his own smart get-up he did borrow from B.C, clearly modified considerably to fit his slight frame. Robert feels a moment of contentment, something he has not felt in a long while. Elizabeth is clearly no longer a child and Robert believes she hasn't been for a long time. He smiles at the memory of her stubborn words that she practically spit at him when he was forcing her to choose sides, only to be lectured by her that *she* would *not* choose sides. Instead, she had argued that it was up to *him* to decide to choose her side: that of family and protecting these mountains. This was something he had always believed he was doing, but she made him see the hypocrisy in his own actions. At that moment he knew she would survive whatever God and war threw at her.

The Morris and Lankford families are tightly squeezed into four pews, except James' brother, B.T., stands at the front next to the smitten groom. The former Confederate captain of the 64th Regiment is clearly pleased with not having to command more than his unruly children, who, with one look from their father, quickly stop their bantering in the front row.

B.C. has invited all to gather at his home after the wedding for a celebration; wagons are already stocked with baskets of pies, cornbread, dried meats and jars of green-beans and corn. Robert feels his stomach grumble as he pictures the potential spread of food, still a rarity. He feels a little guilty when he realizes his hunger causes him to wish the ceremony would hurry along. It is only moments, though, before he forgets his hunger and is beaming at the official announcement of Mr. and Mrs. James Morris.

As Elizabeth and James walk down the aisle, they begin to pass Robert, but Elizabeth stops for a moment and throws her arms around Robert. Surprised, it takes a moment for him to return the embrace. As he holds her, he hears Elizabeth speak softly into his ear. "Uncle Bob. I didn't have to lose him after all. Maybe we *can* have it both ways!"

Robert knows she is trying to give him hope about one day reconciling with Andrew, a hope onto which he no longer holds. As she begins to pull away, he stops her for a moment to look straight in her radiant blue eyes. "Elizabeth, you have your all. Don't let anybody else's grief or loss take away from your joy." Robert chuckles and whispers in her ear, "Because, one thing is for sure... you sure fought for it, and won."

Elizabeth Neill Morris, April 21, 1867

"Come here!" James whispered in my ear, as he grabbed my hand pulling me away from the front of the very same church we were married in only four months earlier. The snow was finally gone and spring was showing off her beauty. Trees and flowers were in full color, and I couldn't keep track of how many different hues of red, yellow, orange, blue and purple there were outlined by the fresh green grass and clear blue sky.

"James! I'm talkin'." I tugged his arm back towards me and fussed at him. "We can't be rude!"

James whispered in my ear, "You're always talkin'. Ain't rude to stop talkin'."

"James!" I fussed, but I immediately felt a soft touch on my hand. It was Susan Lankford who, standing right in front of me, had been observing our banter.

"It's okay, Elizabeth, you and Uncle James go on now." Susan grinned and waved for us to move. I nodded at her, thankful that she was fifteen and could handle James' behavior. She had not started calling me Aunt Elizabeth and, being only five years older than her, I was not in any hurry. Susan quickly turned and headed over to her father, B.C, and her step-mother Betty, who were beaming as others patted the arms and squeezed the tiny hands of their eight-month-old daughter, Arabella. It was Betty's first baby. I lifted a silent prayer of thanks to God that her child was born healthy.

"What in tarnation are you up to?" I teased James as he pulled me around to the side of the Oak Grove Church and then stopped at our favorite spot a little way down the bank.

He moved in behind me and wrapped his arms around me as we both faced the rolling mountains in front of us, and the Valley Store off a little way to the right. His chin was right above my shoulder and his breath tickled my ear as he asked. "Do you see it?"

447

I took in a deep breath and absorbed the view, the bright colors looked like brilliant splatters fighting to be seen as the green leaves began to fill in and absorb their intensity. A gentle warm breeze blew my hair into James' face and he flattened it down again. He waited patiently as I searched for what he was hoping I could discover on my own. In spite of the view's magnificence, I furrowed my eyebrows, because I wanted to see the special surprise without his help. I finally sighed and began to turn my head to the right ever so slowly to tell him that I gave up, but I suddenly stopped. I saw it. To my right flourished a brilliant white. Yes, I forgot the white, its own beauty in the midst of the hodgepodge of colors. The dogwood tree. Our dogwood tree, in full bloom. Each white flower in the shape of a perfect cross. I was in such awe of its beauty, but instead of commenting on its overwhelming enchantment, I simply said, "I still have it!"

James didn't expect those to be the first words out of my mouth. "Have what?"

I turned around to face him and wrap my arms around his shoulders. "I have the small dogwood bloom you gave me after the war started . . . remember? That Fourth of July when you promised to come back and court me. I pressed it and kept it." James opened his mouth, but had no words, since he found himself befuddled. I laughed watching him trying to make sense of why I would hold on to the little bloom. "What? Cat got your tongue?"

James grinned and pulled me in close. "No, I reckon you always figured we'd get hitched."

I held his gaze. "I sure did. But you sure put up a fuss!"

James laughed and leaned in for a gentle kiss before he responded, "I promise not to be so ornery in the future!"

I suddenly felt mischievous and pulled away a bit in mock concern. "But what if one of our young'uns wants to marry one of James-Henry and Rachel-Emma Cagle's young'uns? Are you sure you won't be madder than a wet hen?"

James guffawed and teased, "When Hell freezes over!"

"James!" I fussed.

He pulled me into him again and his breath was warm on my bare skin, "Ain't likely to happen."

"And why is that?" I felt the one strand of red hair, falling into his face, tickle my cheek.

James paused and then kissed my cheek and then my ear before he whispered, "Because we ain't got no young'uns." He kissed my ear one more time. "Yet."

As my face turned red, I hoped, but only for Ma and Pa's sake, that no-one from church had decided to come around the side to take in the mountain-view. In any case, I wouldn't have heard them, or, frankly, cared. This was our time. I would have given anything to stand on that gentle slope, with his arms wrapped around me forever.

CHAPTER 30

Robert Hamilton, November 6, 1870

Blue and Grady's hearty attempts at sending out warning barks, quickly subside as George and Sarah appear around the final bend of Lambs Creek, walking towards the Hamilton homestead. They welcome the two aging hounds with some table scraps that Sarah had tucked away the night before for today's visit. Although the trees have long surrendered their brilliant display of reds, oranges and yellows, to winter's unforgiving barren-branches, the frigid cold has not quite yet come to roost. The sun's rays warm anything it can reach, leaving only the shade's chill as a vivid reminder of the cold.

"Mighty fine day for a Sunday afternoon visit!" Rhoda greets the two as they climb the front porch steps. Robert is bundled up with his wool jacket and one of Millie's beautifully creative wool scarves wrapped around his neck. He is contently rocking and smoking his pipe. Rhoda looks at the empty rockers and contemplates if they should join her husband for a moment before she adds. "Come on inside. Got the fire nice and toasty. Reckon it's too much of a chill on the porch." She eyes Robert. "Are you comin'?"

Robert nods and just as he begins to stand up, George protests, "Why don't Robert and I sit a spell out here and catch up a bit while the two of you go on in. We'll be in shortly."

Robert pauses and looks at his wife if she is in agreement. Rhoda smiles at first, clearly eager to talk with Sarah some on her own, but quickly puts on her best stern face. "I reckon it'll be fine. But don't you two go a talkin' about important stuff without us. You hear?"

Robert settles back in his rocker and takes his pipe out of his mouth to respond with an equally stern grimace. "Same goes for the two of you!"

As the women laugh at what on earth Robert might think he would miss, George walks over and stands near Robert and waits for the women to disappear into the house. Robert looks up at his friend and raises his eyebrows, "What news makes you want to visit out in the cold without the women?"

"Let's head into the sun. No need to freeze in the shade." George is already headed down the steps before Robert has a chance to respond. It is only moments before Robert follows George all the way up to the wooden fence around the pasture, where some sheep begin to move towards them, falsely thinking it is time to be fed. Both men lean against the wooden fence and let the sun hit their leathering faces.

"Well?" Robert prods.

George takes a deep breath and finally starts. "B.C. handed me several copies of the *Raleigh Standard* that he'd been savin' and I thought you'd be very interested in the unfolding of some of the events."

Robert turns away from the sun to face George. "What news would I be interested in that causes you to be frettin' like this?" Robert likes to think he stays on top of the news, but he realizes that several years of taking care of building roads, looking for land to set up a poor house for the aged and infirmed, along with farming, have more than taken his time away from keeping up with the latest news. Over the last several months, B.C. has shouted out and shared key headlines with him when Robert has afforded a few moments to sit a spell at the store, but other than that, he is almost embarrassed with his lack of insight on the latest. George has spent some recent years in the public as Superior Court Clerk and is more likely to keep up with news, so Robert is thankful at least one of them is staying informed.

George shakes his head as he watches Robert take a long draw on his pipe as if preparing himself. "Bob, I've been a-tellin' you about all that trouble east of here with the Ku Klux Klan and Governor Holden's attempts to stop their violence they are inflicting on freedmen and whites who support them."

Robert nods gravely, "Yes, I remember you talkin' about the KKK and how our Governor put out a militia led by that cutthroat Colonel Kirk who wreaked such havoc during the recent war."

George nods. "Unfortunately, yes. I can't believe Holden was able to suspend *habeus corpus* and throw folks in jail without trial or even a hearin'. He has let Kirk use similar tactics as the KKK use in the process of fightin' them. Each side is burnin' and hangin' people . . . murdering as they see fit." George shakes his head. "It's like a whole other war has started."

George nods and both men suddenly turn their attention over the fence to a scuffle between to ewes over a small pile of hay that had been missed at the morning's feeding. Even after the largest ewe triumphs and runs off, the two men lean on the fence in silence.

Robert is not sure how to respond since he wants to believe that there has to be an end to each side's continuous desire to justify evil deeds. He final says, "I can only pray that healthy reasoning and peace soon take hold."

George looks away from Robert at the remaining sheep who are now eagerly searching the ground for any other remnants of fresh hay, but to no avail. George turns to face Robert again, leaving the sheep, who have settled for a drink of water from the small creek still bubbling along the edge of the pasture. George removes his wide brimmed hat for a moment and runs his hand through his thinning hair before replacing the hat. "I hope it happens soon. I'm afraid we have a long way to go."

"Robert? George?" Rhoda's voice, calling from the front porch, suddenly interrupts their focus. "Are you comin'?"

Robert waves at his wife indicating they are indeed on their way. As they head back towards the house Robert extinguishes his pipe and tucks it in his jacket. "I never thought that the war's end would ignite new local and national problems for folks to get all tore up about. It seems there is always an extreme response that sets off another extreme response. It's hard to know what is right and wrong anymore." As they begin up the steps he stops and looks at George, who looks downtrodden. "Well, that is not really true. I will stick with Elizabeth's notion that family and mountain come first. Hopefully that will help us keep some sense of direction."

* * *

Inside, after having shed their winter jackets, both men are greeted with a warm cup of coffee by the fireplace and sit in two empty rockers. "What did we miss?" George teases as Sarah settles in the rocker next to him.

Sarah smiles broadly. "I told Rhoda how Elizabeth and James are farin' well livin' at your Ma's house with their little girl Sarah-Leoline already a year and a half old. AND a second young'un is on the way, due springtime." Robert smiles at the news and enjoys the change in conversation. He is happy to hear Elizabeth and James finally moved in to live with her grandmother, after having lived and worked on a farm further down the valley for a spell. James is already beginning to build his own flock of sheep and the central location of the Boylston Turnpike will help him build a reputable farm of his own.

It's Rhoda, rocking a little more vigorously than the others, who decides it's been enough talk of babies and such, and looks straight at George and asks, "What do you reckon is behind all the crazy county court stuff?"

George takes a sip of his coffee as he mulls over Rhoda's question. "Well, it has been a strange two months and I reckon I am still puttin' together the pieces."

Robert nods and sips his coffee as he listens to George recap their strange encounters, leaving them both befuddled. George scratches his beard and looks at Robert as he reflects, "You know, I thought we were doin' well when, during the September board meeting, they settled all your former sheriff debts, then appointed you as County Road Commissioner. Then in October they gave you that big job of examinin' the road from Mill Hill and the Dunns Rock Hotel to the township line with no time limit." George shakes his head as he adds, "But then, out of the blue, one week later they told Adolphus Garren to do the same thing!"

Scratching his beard, Robert replies, "Well yes. I knew somethin' was comin' and was not surprised when they rescinded my appointment and gave it to Garren. But you were hit much harder and crazier than I was, when, in the October 11th meetin', they declared the office of Superior Court Clerk vacant- your office! Never heard such nonsense."

George interrupts to explain, "They claimed I had not renewed my bond on time, knowin' full well I always did and how it took time to get all the required signatures. However, my office was only vacant barely a month since Judge Cannon approved my bond and my continuing to serve as Court of Clerk." George places his coffee cup down on the hardwood floor at the foot of his rocker and looks at Robert clearly confused. "Bob, you just said that you knew somethin' was comin'. What do you figure is really goin' on? How come they seem to be doin' such little things? To embarrass us? To punish us?"

"The Filmores?" Rhoda's sudden interjection of the family they hid during the war surprises George and Sarah, but not Robert. She watches her husband nod his head, so she continues, "You reckon after all this time, word that Tommy and Annie Filmore spread when they first came back has finally reached enough folk?"

"That's my guess." Robert takes another sip of coffee. "I know it seems long, but I'm sure there were a lot of people who didn't believe it at first . . . but we *did* help an awful lot of people, not only the Filmore family. Seems the further away we are from the war, the more willin' people are to share their secrets."

George scratches his beard and clears his throat. "So then why are you not furious?"

"As I figure it, it is not really so personal." Robert begins to rock again. "We all know each other. Our families go way back, and most are tied together in marriage. But do take note that two of the four justices on the board that tried to boot you served in the Confederate army, and the chairman was actually a prisoner of war with the Union. They suffered things we don't know and many of their buddies and kin did not come back. Those who did are surely puttin' pressure on them to do somethin', anything to show they have some power. We all did what we did out of convictions and now we are all tryin' to rebuild this community and county together. I had expected far worse comeuppance for what we did, but this is not only understandable but what they need to do to show us that they know our secret." A small mischievous smile grows, and Roberts's eyes reveal that there is a flip side. "You see, they have their retribution, but no one else really knows, since they are still lettin' me work for the needs of the county poor house." Robert finds himself snickering. "Wouldn't reflect too well on them if they completely ruined the reputation I rightly earned after the war."

George considers his closest friend's perspective and finds himself a little more at peace with the awkward, yet brief, loss of his job. He leans back in his chair, resting his head in his hands behind his neck and smiles. "I guess if losin' your job, and fear of losing my job is the worst fate we will suffer then I'll take it."

"Besides there have been greater losses than our jobs." Robert reaches out and squeezes Rhoda's hand, both remembering Andrew. "But, in spite of it all, I would do it over again. Our names may not be on a street plaque, but maybe we will have left an even greater legacy." Robert looks at Rhoda, Sarah and then George, who are all sitting up a little straighter and find themselves drawn to the familiar flicker of the warm fire.

EPILOGUE

Robert Hamilton and George Neill's secret never became wide-spread knowledge, until recent times. The valley behind the Hamilton house, however, was and still is known to many of their descendants as "Yankee-Holler".

Robert Hamilton died November 12, 1904 and only five months later George Neill died April 21, 1905.

Two escaped Union soldiers, Daniel Avery Langworthy and Harold B. Birch, recorded their experiences about separate journeys as Union POW's including their escapes, and events leading them to Transylvania County and being saved by the "High Sheriff," Robert Hamilton. Langworthy's book is entitled *Reminiscences of a Prisoner of War and His Escape* and includes pictures. Birch's work is entitled *The 101st Pennsylvania in the Civil War, Its Capture and POW Experience*.

Elizabeth and James Morris inherited Sarah Clayton Neill's home (Elizabeth's Mammaw) where they raised their children. The home was known as the "The Morris House" for many years until it burned in 1953. Although there is nothing left of the home, a small road nearby bears the Morris name. Today, thousands of people drive on the Boylston Road (Asheville Highway or NC 280), a four-lane highway now in place of the "The Morris House". The Transylvania County

Sheriff's Office and jail are located on the hill above Morris Road where George Neill, former Deputy, former Sheriff, and former Clerk of Court, pastured his sheep.

Elizabeth and James Morris had nine children. Their first son, was named Wavery Lenoir Morris who, on April 9, 1895, married Mary Lucretia Ann Cagle, the daughter of Rachel-Emma Young Cagel and James Henry Cagle.

B.C. (Braxton Caldwell) Lankford, held many public offices including, but not limited to, postmaster, Chairman of County Commissioners, Justice of the Peace and became Mayor of Brevard in 1892. Today Caldwell Street still bears his name.

"General" John Calloway Duckworth was born 28 December 1829 and died 25 February 1872. He married Louisa A. Duckworth, his cousin. After he led the Transylvania County Home Guard during the Civil War, he was elected as a representative to the North Carolina General Assembly and died during this political service. His gravestone identifies him as "General Duckworth," although any documented reference to the titled rank is a mystery.

Alex Fletcher English and wife Naomi Young English did indeed have eight children and their fourth child, Edwin Strawbridge English practiced medicine in Transylvania County and, according to oral history, was the first to have an automobile in the county. The English Chapel, along the Davidson River, was eventually named after Alex Fletcher English.

Captain James Deavor did not return to live in Transylvania County until 1871, after he met and married Emma Louise Combs in Ringgold, Georgia. After his return to North Carolina, he was elected as a North Carolina State Representative. His home is still standing today and is known as the Allison-Deavor House, a cherished historical site and tourist destination.

Pink Smith married Emmaline Hunt at the French Broad Baptist Church May 27, 1875. His white Uncle, Rev. Elijah Allison performed the ceremony. The Church officially began in 1865 at the end of the war, and the graveyard contains the remains of many former slaves.

Pink Smith and Emmaline Hunt had four children. Their daughter, Mary Smith, married Jim Aiken (born bi-racial in 1861). Jim Aiken was considered a successful businessman in Brevard at the turn of the century and was even the Brevard Fire Chief. Their daughter, Loretta Mary Aiken, became a famous entertainer under the stage name Jackie Moms Mabley.

When Pink was an old man, after 1915, his white cousin Andrew Fuller Allison died. So, Pink helped Fuller's widow and children by making sure they had enough firewood and he would stay with them as needed.

After the first generation of relatives passed, the racial divide within Transylvania County deepened as segregation and Jim Crow Laws swept the South and blood relatives across races were no longer recognized or acknowledged. Transylvania County was not immune to hate-crimes. Yet, in the midst of the ongoing turmoil many families continued to rise above it all and hand down their stories so not all would be forgotten. As the nation began to push for desegregation, Brevard High School took the leap in the 1962-63 school year by integrating a few students. The following year, the High School was fully integrated and its 1963-64 football team was one of the first in North Carolina to integrate. In spite of fighting prejudice and racism, they were North Carolina High School Co-Champions that year.

To be "from here" carries heavy weight and honor, whether born or adopted into the mountain culture. There is an unspoken connection between all who know their roots run deep. A connection, which despite differences, and spoken or unspoken secrets, remains remarkably unbroken.

APPENDIX A: Obituaries

SYLVAN VALLEY NEWS
MORTUARY
Hon. Robert Hamilton Dead.

It becomes the sad duty of the News to record the death of this aged and highly respected citizen, which occurred at his home two miles from Brevard on Sunday morning last, aged about 85 years.

Robert Hamilton was one of the best-known citizens of the county. When Transylvania county was organized, he was prominent in the council and, we are informed, was elected its first sheriff. He was for many years a county commissioner and helped to build up its financial standing to a foremost place among the counties of the state. We are informed that he has served the people in both branches of the state legislature with honor to himself and the county.

"Uncle Bob Hamilton" as he was familiarly known, was a companionable and instructive entertainer, and no one ever went about him, be it stranger or neighbor, without feeling that he was better for the visit. His door was always open to all, and in the early history of the county the poor always found him their friend. He was a kind and considerate husband and father, and his children have mostly settled around him. He was good citizen in all that the word implies, and leaves behind him a nice home which his industry and frugality had built. He is one man of whom we have never heard a harmful word spoken.

During the last few years he has been a great sufferer from cancer of the face, and his death was not unlooked for. His life and public services are worthy (of) a more extended notice, but we have no historical data at hand.

(Page 7, November 18, 1904)

SYLVAN VALLEY NEWS
Death of a Pioneer Citizen
George C. Neill, an Old, Well Known and
Highly Respected Resident, Dies at a
Ripe Old Age

George C. Neill, one of the oldest and best-known citizens of Transylvania County, died at his home two miles north of Brevard on Friday and was buried with Masonic honors the following day, aged 82 years.

Mr. Neill had in many ways endeared himself to our people. He was born and had spent all of the years of his life within a short distance of the beautiful vine-clad cottage which he has occupied during the lattes (r) years of his life. He was born in Buncombe county, lived many years in Henderson, and then when Transylvania was formed, he became a citizen of it without having moved his residence from the farm where he first saw the light.

Mr. Neill has been prominent and a leader among our people, having held the county offices of sheriff and clerk of the court, both depending on the votes of an intelligent citizenship. For the last quarter of a century he has been United States commissioner, which office he only relinquished about three years ago.

Mr. Neill was a good citizen in all that the word implies. He was a good neighbor, ever ready to assist the needy; a good churchman and for many years a member of Davidson River Presbyterian church, and was a kind and considerate husband and father.

A large gathering of friends and relatives were at the funeral, which was conducted by Rev. C.B. Currie, assisted by Rev. C.P. Moore and the Masonic fraternity, and the internment was at the Davidson River cemetery. He lived a pure and blameless life and died in the full hope of a blessed immortality.

RESOLUTIONS OF RESPECT.

Whereas, it has pleased the Great Architect of the universe to remove from our midst our Brother and Past Master George C. Neill. Therefore be it resolved.

That in the death of our Brother each member of Dunns Rock Lodge No.267 has lost a faithful friend and brother, and that as long as our feeble senses perceive the light of the sun by day and moon and stars by night, we shall cherish his memory, for we believe that he has gone to that celestial city not made with hands, eternal in the heavens, where there is no need of the sun by day nor of the moon and stars by night, for there shall be no night there.

That in the death of Brother Neill Masonry at large has lost a faithful expositor of the tenets of our noble order and one worthy of the emulation of every member of this Lodge.

That the heartfelt sympathy of every member of this Lodge is hereby tendered to the members of the family of our deceased brother, that a page be inscribed in our minute book sacred to his memory, and that a copy of these resolutions be sent to the family, ta(o) the Sylvan Valley News and Orphan's Friend for publication.

W.M. Henry
T.D. England
Z.W. Nichols
Committee

(Page 7, April 28, 1905)

POSTSCRIPT TO APPENDIX A

Announcements of the deaths of the two Lambs Creek friends in the local *Sylvan Valley News,* shown above, were only five months apart, with Robert Hamilton passing at 85 years and George Neill at 82 years.

Both were described as "highly respected" citizens, and well known. Their service to Transylvania County was detailed in terms of not only their service as sheriffs and, for Robert, as "commissioner" and, for George, as clerk of court. (Actually, the writer may have confused Robert's service on the Court of Pleas and Quarter Sessions with the County Board of Commissioners which replaced the former during Reconstruction.) Both men are described as dedicated family men, good husbands and dedicated to helping others, especially those in need.

Robert Hamilton's warm, welcoming personality and open home is underlined, but no reference is made for him, or George, as to what they did up Lambs Creek during the Civil War, except what might be implied by the "open door" comment. Robert suffered from cancer of the face, perhaps as indicated by his blurred picture, the only one found. No pictures of George Neill have been found. A bit of caution by the obituary writer is noted in the use of the term "We are informed" in reference to Hamilton's supposed service in "both branches of the state legislature." Recent research into the state archive list of all members of the state legislature did not indicate he served in either. This may be based on mis-reading the early county records where local representatives served on various local committees to choose state representatives. His name, however, was clearly on the early Transylvania letter asking for a vote by all citizens about ceding from the Union, as shown in Appendix F.

Two related factors discovered during research for this story raise some questions about the causes for the passing of Robert Hamilton: First, the note in his obituary that "During the last few years he has been a great sufferer from cancer of the face, and his death was not unlooked for" and secondly, the only known picture of him shows a blurred lower face, not unlike those of Sigmund Freud and others who suffered from such cancer. Most notable in the United States was President Ulysses S. Grant who suffered years and "treated" his disease with whisky and by smoking up to 12 cigars a day.

The research into connections of smoking tobacco and cancer were not made until a century or more later. This story indicates use of pipe smoking and other tobacco use (snuff, chewing tobacco) as fairly common in the era, although some churches preached against such use. Growing tobacco was also a common, profitable practice and North Carolina was one of the leaders in production and marketing. Extensive use in the armies of both the South and North are documented, even rationed.

Hamilton likely was treated by Transylvania County's "saddlebag doc" A.J. Lyday and his son, Dr. Elliot Lyday. Both studied medicine in Charleston and Elliot trained also in dentistry. The log cabin office in Penrose was used for simple exams and most work was done in home visits. The likely exam by the son, "Ell" would have been a tactile feeling in the mouth of the cancer tumor tissue, quite different from the other mouth tissue, according to former Brevard ENT physician Fred Bahnson.

He might have used carbolic spray to fight infection, the new discovery from Scotland by an English physician, Joseph Lister. This could have stimulated a discussion about infections and the very controversial issue of that day, the "germ theory." Most schools and homes taught that infections come from "bad air," and not from anything you could not see, other than bad air. Thus, ventilation was crucial, even in cold weather. A normal microscope exam could not have shown the cancer cells without the technical skills of an advanced lab. The physical exam itself may have been different between the father and son in that the modern stethoscope was slowly being developed. The father may have used a rolled up stiff paper or a slender monaural stethoscope which was a hollowed-out tube of wood looking like a horn. It is probable that a more modern scope was used by the son.

In any case, Robert Hamilton lived to a relatively old age for his day (85 years) since the average life expectancy in the United States at his death was about forty-seven years.

George C. Neill's death notice is more colorful and includes the old, popular image about having lived in three counties and never moving, from birth to death. His activity in the Dunns Rock Masonic Lodge is underlined. The Masonic Resolution of Respect speaks for itself. His active participation in the Davidson River Presbyterian Church is also noted. What is not widely known is the note that he served as a United

States Commissioner for a quarter of a century. This service would have been during a difficult period of Transylvania history when the Reconstruction policies had finished with military rule no longer present.

We have no record of how many cases he handled during this period or who appointed him to this important judicial role. His record as Transylvania sheriff and clerk of court is well documented, however. The United States Commissioner system goes back to the early days of the country, established in 1793 to try many petty cases and lighten the load of federal courts. The U.S. Commissioners could also issue search warrants and arrest warrants, as well as determine bail for federal cases. Prior to the era of prohibition, the revenue agents would have taken some cases of not paying correct taxes on whisky produced in federally approved distilleries, such as the two in Transylvania County, one in Dunn's Rock, the other on what is now Country Club Road. More noteworthy, before and after prohibition, were the many illegal "moonshine" private distilleries where revenue agents arrested the operators. Commissioner Neill would have dealt with the predecessors of Agent V.B. McGaha, the former sheriff and revenuer from our previous book, *Sons of Mercy and Justice.*

Also, Commissioner Neill or his predecessor, would have issued the federal warrant for the notorious Transylvania outlaw, Lewis Redmond, who killed the U.S. Marshall Al Duckworth near the Walnut Hollow and East Fork section of the county. That story is also integrated in the former book. The U.S. Commissioners served in Transylvania County until 1968 when that job title became "magistrate" as replaced by the Federal Magistrates Acts; Congress finally changed the title in 1990 to "Magistrate Judges."

APPENDIX B: REQUESTS FOR PARDON

Requests for Pardon by Three Transylvania Leaders

Taken from *North Carolina Civil War Amnesty Papers*, Vol. 12, by Sandra Lee Almasy, 1999

BACKGROUND: On December 8, 1863 and March 26, 1864, President Abraham Lincoln, as an attempt to suppress the rebellion and to induce persons to return their loyalty to the authority of the United States, offered amnesty and pardon to anyone who swore the following oath: *I, _____ _____, do solemnly swear, (or affirm,) in presence of Almighty God, that I will henceforth faithfully support, protect, and defend the Constitution of the United States, and the union of the States thereunder; and that I will, in like manner, I abide by, and faithfully support all laws and proclamations which have been made during the existing rebellion with reference to the emancipation of slaves. So help me God.*

On May 29, 1865, after the assassination of President Lincoln, President Andrew Johnson proposed the above oath with certain limits (such as slaves were not property to be returned) and a list of fourteen exceptions for certain classes of persons. These three Transylvania leaders were in the first category of "pretended civil or diplomatic officers . . . of the pretended Confederate government." Gash and Duckworth served as postmasters and Lankford as tax assessor.

The three texts show several misspelled words, most obviously that of President Andrew Johnson in the first two. Likewise, the first name of Leander S. Gash is produced as 'Landen' and several words are

465

incorrect. The turmoil within the North Carolina governor's office is noted in that W.W. Holden, provisional governor appointed by the President, is replaced by Jonathan Worth by the last pardon request. The reader may also notice that the ending of all three contain the promise "to ever pray," a phrase seemingly indicating a strong loyalty to United States, similar to an oath or the phrase "So help me God."

Most significant is the fact that the general oath of amnesty and pardon (above) was administered to Transylvania Justices of the Peace on July 20, 1865 as recorded in the Minutes of The Court of Pleas and Quarterly Sessions, Transylvania County. Robert Hamilton is on that list of participants. By the August 26, 1865 Special Court Session Governor Holden had ordered that the above general oath be administered to the citizens of the County. Robert Hamilton is one of the eight justices selected to do that. The debatable issue is why he was not required to be included in that first exception of "pretended civil officers . . .of the pretended Confederate government." It appears that the local sheriff would have been included, but, as this story indicates, there is no record that either Robert Hamilton or George Neill was required to swear an oath of allegiance to the Confederacy. Word on the North Carolina secession was only reaching the county during the days of Transylvania's formation. Hamilton clearly saw his loyalty to the people of Transylvania.

L.S. Gash-of-Transylvania Co. N.C. – Applies for pardon – Rebel Postmaster 1st exception – Sept 8, 65 – Executive Office N.C. – Raleigh Aug 28th 1865 – An immediate pardon is respectfully recommended in this case. – W.W. Holden, Prov. Governor – in the matter of – Landen S. Gash- P for Pardon

To his Excellency, Andrew Johnston, President of the United States:

The petition of Landen S. Gash of the County of Transylvania in the State of North Carolina, respectfully represents unto your Excellency, that he opposed the pretended secession action of the State of North Carolina and the other Southern States by all legitimate means in his power and never yielded a voluntary assent to the rebelious action of said States, on the contrary, he always opposed such action and frequently during the rebelion xposed himself to great personal peril by a free and open expression of opinion in opposition to rebelion; that nevertheless, the price of uncontrollable circumstances, committed him in point of action to the rebelion, and he held the office of <u>Post Master</u> at Claytonville in said County under the pretended Confederate States Government, voted at most of the popular elections and paid such taxes as were required of him, that he never voluntarily assented to any act of hostility to the Federal Government; that on the contrary, he was friendly to it and this good will was not concealed; that he is rejoiced at the termination of the war and desires the immediate restoration of the government and ardently desires the perpetuation of the Union; that he has truly ans sincerely returned his allegiance to the Government of the United States, if indeed, he has ever abandoned the same, and intends hence forth to be a true, and loyal citizen thereof.

Your petitioner is advised that he is xcluded from the benefits of your Excellency's Amnesty Proclamation, dated the 29th of May 1865, & hence, he prays your Excellency to grant unto him special pardon for such participation in said rebellion And you petitioner will ever pray & C

At Claytonville N.C.
July 18th A.D. 1865

John C. Duckworth-of- Transylvania Co N.C.- Rebel Postmaster- Applies for pardon-1sr exception-P. Nov 7th 65- Executive Office- Raleigh Oct 20th 1865-Pardon respectfully recommended- W.W. Holden

To His Excellency Andrew Johnston
President of the United States

The petition of John C. Duckworth of Transylvania Co N.C. respectfully represents unto your Excellency that possessing little political knowledge was to a small extent influenced by the trill of succession at the commencement of the late rebelion and accepted the office of Post Master at Catheys Creek in said county under the pretended authority of the so called Confederate States government but I now seeing the impropriety of the relution returned to the union party and has promptly acted with it ever since that he has truly and sincerely returned to is allegiance to the government of the United States and intends hence forth to be a true and loyal Citizen thereof

Your petitioner is aware that he is excluded from the benefit of your Excellencys amnesty Proclamation dated the 29th of May A D 1865 and hence he prays your Excellency to grant unto him a special pardon for such participation in said rebelion And your petitioner will ever pray & C at Catheys Creek NC

August 8th 1865   John C. Duckworth

<Nov 9, 1865 Recommended for pardon by Govr. Holden>

In the Matter of – B. C. Lankford- Transylvania Co. N.C.- Pet. For Pardon – 1st Exception- Tax Assessor- P. Feb 1/66- Executive Office N.C. Raleigh Jany 5 1866 – Pardon respectfully recommended- Jonathan Worth -Gov of N.C.

State of North Carolina}

Transylvania County}

To his Excellency Andrew Johnson, President of the United States. Your petitioner having held the Office of <u>Tax Assessor</u> for a time during the rebellion and according to your proclimation I am not allowed the benefit of the Amnesty Oath without Special pardon and being desirous to take the oath in <u>good</u> <u>faith</u> that I may be entitled to the privileges and protection in common with my fellow citizens. Your petitioner being a civil officer of the State was not forced to take up arms during the rebellion.

You will See the accompany oath that I willingly Subscribe to, and by granting the above request Your petitioner as in duty bound will ever pray

5th Sept. 1865   B.C. Lankford

APPENDIX C: LETTER

Letter from Brother John Hamilton 1869

Papers Related to Crimes Committed by the Ku Klux Klan in Alabama, 1969-1879

Hamilton, John
Statement in regard to outrages committed by Ku Klux on Geo. Moore & Robert Roundtree (colored) also on himself &c.
Broomtown, Alabama
August 29th, 1869

Lieutenant- Sir

I learn through my friend J.S. Smith that you wanted to see me concerning the way the Ku Klux had been cutting up. All the information I can give you is what I got from the blacks Tuesday after they was abused on Saturday night. I had a conversation with Reaner, she told me that some disguised men came a way in the nite ordered them to open the door and before she could get her son George awake they burst down the door and some came in and others surrounded the house and they tuck out George and gave him some wher from 24 to 30 lashes and one came into bed where she and a neighbor woman was sleeping and wanted in bed with them and they refused him but he said if they girl that was not in bed with Reaner did not submit to him he would shoot her and had a gun in his hand, the girl commenced crying and said she did not want to dy and then he set his gun down by the bed and stript off the cover and got on the girl in the bead with Reaner and some of the rest tried to get George's wife out doors to some of the other men and let them have to doo with her, they would whip her nearly to death she told them that she had just miscarid and couldn't. they then tuck one of George's children up by the heals and druget over the floor bumpin its head and said it would make a good pot of soop and then noct George down and left and went some 3 or 4 hundred yards to Robert Roundtree's and broak down his door and ordered him up, it fritened him til he broke to run, they shot some 15 or 20 round slightly wounding him in the thigh then tuck off his gun and a fine hat. This was all at J.L. Belots or his lands on Saturday nigh before the Congressional Election. On Monday night there was some fifty or sixty at the foundry and shot one colered man thare the doctors said he would be bound to dy, but he is yet a live the ball is lodgd against his neck vain, now this is about all the information I can give you. I got my information from Reaner Rarry col'd then but i learn she has sence married Aston Belot- also from George Moore her son that they whipt and nockt down.

I learn from Squair Alexander that he went and investigated the case but when I saw Reaner and George and some other colored folks I told them not to tell anything unless it was to one of the Republican party and they told me they would not. I told them if they told what had tuck place they would kill some any boddy of them I also told Reaner she had better not tell any boddy else, for the most of the people if they don't belong to the party they seem to favoret if they have not stated to you just as I have I have no dobt but what it is from the caution I gave them as a friend.

They was a meeting in the settlement of wher I live the verry day this develment was don at night and several of my neighbors was gon, but whether that was what the meeting was for I ant able to say, now sir, having all confidence in my friend Smith I write this to you in confidence that you will not reveal my nam. I have been cald all the hard things that any poor man ever did hear, and has been nearly murder by a crowd holding me and cutting me with their nives. I would have come to see you before now but I would be in danger of my life if it was nown.

You will do me the favor to not let anyone no that I wrote you, if they is anything more you wish to no from me at any time please send me J.S. Smith for he is a tride friend.

I would live verry much to see you if I could.

Your truly

Ever more

(signed) John Hamilton

a true copy

James Miller   1st Lieut. 2nd Infantry Post Adjutant

National Archives Microfilm Publications

Microcopy No. 666

Letters received by the office of the Adjutant General

(Record Group 94) (Main series) 1871-1880 Roll 67, 1872

COMMENTARY ON WAR'S END AND APPENDIX C

At the conclusion of the Civil War confusion and chaos reigned. By May 1865 there were a million soldiers in the Union Army and reduced by the following January to almost eighty-eight thousand troops in the South for occupation and peacekeeping. By October 1, 1867 there were only about twenty thousand. Southern States began using "Black Codes" to restrict activities of blacks, including voting, gathering and having firearms. Vagrancy and other minor infractions of rules placed them in jails and into involuntary labor, similar to slavery. Some Northern states had limited black codes prior to the war.

Various groups such as the "Regulators" began to form, basically as outlaws, attacking both Unionists and blacks. Some, as the Ku Klux Klan and Red Shirts, clearly carried out deeds of murder, harassment and intimidation. In 1865, the Freedmen's Bureau was formed to educate and protect the freed slaves, but it was disbanded by 1869. The U.S. Army was the basic occupation force as the South was divided into five military districts. North and South Carolina made up Military District 2 and Alabama was in District 3, along with Georgia and Florida.

471

The commanders sought to protect polling sites and to keep peace, with wide authority, even over governors and legislatures. Their protection of blacks and white supporters included research into Klan and other unlawful acts. This letter from Robert Hamilton's brother, John, who had moved to Alabama, is one record of such crimes. Different Hamilton family members had moved to Alabama with some staying on, others returning. Their support of the freed blacks is captured in this document requested by the federal authorities, as well as showing the danger to their lives for doing so.

The increasing activities of the KKK precipitated the use of the 7th US Calvary from South Carolina to put down riots in Rutherford County, N.C. and to arrest 40 men, including the leader, Randolph Shotwell. Likewise, the so-called Kirk-Holden war in North Carolina, told in this story, was part of the attempt to control the violent acts of the Klan.

During the later months of the Reconstruction era, the Army assisted the Internal Revenue Bureau attempts to control the runaway moonshining across the South, especially in the Appalachian Mountains. The end of Reconstruction, and removal of the Army, occurred in 1877, when President Rutherford B. Hayes made a compromise with Southern Democratic leaders. That did not stop the illegal activities of bootlegging or violent Klan activity. White southerners took control of each southern state and Klan activities slowed and became focused on race rather than politics.

For further information, see "The Army and Reconstruction" a pamphlet by Mark Bradley at the Center of Military History (CMH).

APPENDIX D: Bushwhackers

Although the account in this story of the attempt to capture the bushwhackers is fictional, it does capture some of the recorded violent actions of the bushwhackers in Western North Carolina during the Civil War. The existence of these so-called guerilla bands was, at best, outside the law, both civilian and military. In different accounts they were called "outliers," "outlaws" or deserters from the Confederates, or from the Union. In some notable military actions, such as the Shelton Laurel massacre in Madison County and the Big Creek execution in Haywood County, the supposed bushwhackers were disposed of, ignoring any military rules of order. Those actions supposedly justified the vicious guerilla responses of the notorious "Kirk's Raiders" who played a role in this story.

The violence of the bushwhackers against citizens was sometimes matched by violence by those capturing them, such as hanging them and leaving the bodies to decay on the ropes. In some cases, during a raid, the bushwhackers forced the victims to feed them, and in one case, play a fiddle for them, before shooting them down. The most famous bushwhacking family trauma, where the family did get some limited justice, was in nearby Flat Rock at the home of wealthy low-country rice planter Andrew Johnstone. One afternoon six armed men, claiming to be Confederate scouts and aware he was a strong Confederate, asked for food. The staff made a fine meal, and the bushwhackers talked and played the piano with the girls. After the meal Johnstone offered bread for their trip and his son slipped into another room, loading a pistol. The men were told to shoot the family and did hit the father, although he was able to shoot back. His eleven-year old son shot four of them as they fled. The father died, as did two of the bushwhackers. The story goes that the bushwhacker who died on the lawn was buried with a devil's head on a stone marker.

In the story above, and in others, the lack of any identity is to be noted. When stories about being forced to feed the men or face-to-face encounters happened, no recognition was ever reported. Likewise, no identification was found on bodies. This fit their need for anonymity while doing the dirty deeds. When the Hume Dunns Rock Hotel was burned by bushwhackers, Mrs. Hume was forewarned by one, but she did not know who he might have been.

Many attempts were made to curtail or stop the bushwhackers both by military units and home guard. Captain B.T. Morris of the 64th North Carolina Regiment, assigned to track down bushwhackers, wrote about the task as a "lost cause" since they knew the mountains so much better. Ten men of his unit were ambushed in Transylvania County from a "great slab of granite with an overhang over the trail." This appears to describe Dunns Rock overhanging the main trail/road up the mountain (crossing Dunns Creek) and close to the burned Hume Hotel. Several firearms were used: shotguns, pistols and rifles. One soldier was killed, and all others were hit several times.

Morris gave details of a few successful anti-bushwhacker hunts, one in Green River Cove, not far from Transylvania County. A known bushwhacker had shot his neighbor, who was at home on leave and who identified the perpetrator, a renowned "vile" man. They set up an ambush for this ambusher, in the woods above a house of ill-repute that he frequented. The ladies tried to warn him, as did his dog, but they were able to shoot and kill him before he got his gun out to return fire. This is one of the very few identified bushwhackers, an opportunist who lost.

It should be noted that bushwhackers were "irregular soldiers" on both sides, sometimes even authorized by a chain of command. Their lack of uniforms and identity marks magnified their clandestine methods. The Confederates occasionally authorized them as "partisan rangers," not to be confused with the local rangers authorized by the fledgling Transylvania County Court. The local rangers' job was to help keep some order as best they could with so many men away during the war. They often were men too old, or unable to fight and tried to be eyes and ears for the sheriff. After the end of the war many bushwhackers continued in the violent, lawless actions across the country, ennobled by the wartime experiences. Such men as Jesse James, Bill Quantrill, Cole Younger and others who carried out atrocities further west during the war, continued as outlaw bands.

The reader is encouraged to read the book by William R. Trotter entitled *Bushwhackers the Civil War in North Carolina the Mountains* (John F. Blair Publisher, 1988) for further details.

APPENDIX E: ARBITRARY DATE?

Transylvania County's North Carolina Date

May 20, 1861 was not an arbitrary date approved by the state legislators in their February approval of the new county in 1861, but chosen because of historical reverence for May 20. It was so special that it was also chosen as the day the State ceded from the Union when delegates from the counties voted on May 1st. Significant dates are noted on the North Carolina state flag and the Great Seal of North Carolina. Such dates are as follows:

May 20, 1775 is the date given for the Mecklenburg Declaration of Independence, a text supposedly written in Charlotte, Mecklenburg County predating the United States Declaration of Independence by more than a year. The date, May 20, was significant in the minds of the state leaders to their choice to cede on that day. Confederate leader Jefferson Davis spoke to a Charlotte audience in 1864 saying that the Carolinians were "the first to defy British authority and declare themselves free." Thus, the motto "first in freedom" became a popular North Carolina slogan. The authenticity of the actual text has been questioned in relation to the textual closeness to the U.S. Declaration and which one might have been first. It was published shortly after the Revolutionary War.

May 31, 1775 the Mecklenburg Resolves were passed and published later, from memory, but some confusions exist as to whether the Resolves actually called for independence. This document is sometimes confused with the Mecklenburg Declaration noted above.

April 12, 1776 The Halifax Resolves was adopted by North Carolina calling for independence from Great Britain, some three months ahead of the U.S. Declaration. The delegates of the Fourth Provincial Congress of North Carolina met in Halifax and passed it unanimously, encouraging the Continental Congress to push for independence.

The 1861 North Carolina Flag carried two dates, May 20, 1775 and May 20, 1861 the day for ceding from the Union. However, by 1885 the second date was replaced by that of the Halifax Resolves, April 12, 1776.

APPENDIX F: *THE NORTH CAROLINA STANDARD*

Public Meeting in Transylvania County as Reported in *The North Carolina Standard*, Wednesday Feb. 10, 1864

At a public meeting held in the town of Brevard, on the 30th January,1861, Maj. Samuel Wilson was called to the Chair, and Rev. J.H. Duckworth requested to act as Secretary. On motion, the Chair appointed the following gentlemen as a committee to prepare a preamble and resolutions for the action of the meeting, viz: O.L.Erwin, L.S.Gash, James Hamblin, Robert Hamilton, and Squire Morgan, who retired a short time and reported the following preamble and resolutions, which were unanimously adopted by the whole meeting.

WHEREAS, The fundamental principles of our government recognize the right of our people to assemble together and discuss the principles of the same, together with the laws already passed, as well as those in contemplation of being passed; and further, to inaugurate such measures as we may think necessary to amend the whole in a peaceable and Constitutional way. And whereas, this country is dreadfully distressed and being devastated with one of the most dreadful civil wars known to man, with no propositions nor prospects, that we see, for peace, short of utter ruin and starvation, and we, being beyond the reach of railroad and steamboat navigation (without the means at our command to reach them) must starve if the present state of things is to continue for another year. And, whereas, the present system of conscription, tithing and impressment law is unsuited to a free people, whilst the financial scheme of forced loans- the universal conscribing of all our male population, whereby making them liable to military court martial, together with the suspension of the writ of *habeas corpus* as now proposed by

Congress can but foist upon us a military despotism such as never can nor never has been submitted to by a free people who remained free.

Resolved, That we are in favor of calling a Convention of the State for the purpose of acting with the other States of the Confederacy, each acting in its sovereign capacity, with the view and for the purpose of trying, at least, to conclude a treaty of peace with the federal government or the respective States of the federal Union.

Resolved, That if the other States of the Confederacy refuse to take such action after being requested to do so, the State of North Carolina will proceed to business in her sovereign capacity, and take such steps and make such overtures of peace for herself as the Convention may deem best for the State, subject, however, to a ratification of the people at the ballot box.

Resolved, That his excellency Z.B. Vance, Governor of North Carolina, be requested to call the Legislature together as early as may suit his convenience, with the view and for the purpose of calling a Convention of the State; or, sat least, to submit the proposition to a vote of the people- to vote "Convention" or "No Convention."

Resolved, That in the event of a majority of the votes cast in the State be favorable to a Convention, his Excellency the Governor, be directed to order and election for members to said Convention as soon as practicable, to assemble as early thereafter as he in his wisdom may think best.

Resolved, That the Senate and House members from this district be requested to vote for such Convention of the State.

Resolved, That a copy of these proceedings be furnished to the Standard and the Times, with a request that they publish the same, and that the other papers of the State be requested to copy.

Dr. Love, of Henderson County, offered two other resolutions indicating the terms on which we are willing to make peace. But the meeting preferred leaving the Convention to act without any dictation as to terms, etc. Failing to get a second to either resolution, there was no vote to act on them. The Doctor, however, admitted that he himself would not have voted for one of the resolutions.

The attendance was large and all walked off quietly without noise or disturbance. The greater portion of them also signed a petition to be sent to the Governor, asking for the call of a Convention.

SAM'L WILSON, Pres't   J.H. Duckworth, Sec'y

APPENDIX G: THE KIRK-HOLDEN WAR

The Kirk-Holden War: February 1870 to September 1870

Technically, this brief violent struggle may not have been a "war", but it was a significant historical event in Caswell and Alamance County, North Carolina during the Reconstruction and affecting the entire State. During that tense time, the State of North Carolina experienced the very aggressive rise of the Ku Klux Klan (KKK) using violence and intimidation against recently freed slaves to prevent their voting or serving in any capacity. Also, any whites who supported the rights of freedmen were in danger, especially the Republicans who were in power after the election of 1868 when most Democrats lost their seats. More than 40,000 KKK members across the state resisted Reconstruction efforts. In February 1870, a beloved black town councilman and constable, Wyatt Outlaw, was lynched by the KKK in Alamance County. In May 1870, a white Republican state senator, John W. Stephens, was murdered by the KKK in the Caswell County Courthouse. In July that year, Governor Holden declared an insurrection and called for a militia to put it down, suspending *habeas corpus,* and inviting the controversial Col. George W. Kirk to put together that militia of volunteers.

George Washington Kirk was from Greene County, Tennessee, just over the state line from Western North Carolina. He deserted from the Confederate army and first worked as a guide for the Union because he knew the Appalachian mountain area well. He also assisted escaped Union soldiers, slaves and refugees as well as recruiting men for guides and part-time guerrillas. By 1865 he was a notorious Union Colonel leading violent and ruthless raids into Western North Carolina with part-time fighters, including many deserters. One raid was to a church meeting near Mars Hill and another against Warm Springs. With money and goods stolen, he provided Spencer repeating rifles. He and his 600 men pillaged Waynesville, killing and capturing several as well as burning the home of Revolutionary War hero Col. Robert Love. His was a war of terror; he was greatly feared and hated.

William Woods Holden was a native of North Carolina, studied law, was admitted to the bar in 1841, and was in the Whig Party, changing to the Democratic Party two years later. He became the owner and editor of the *North Carolina Standard*, perhaps the most influential newspaper in the state. As a Democrat in the 1840s and 1850s, he supported slavery and secession. When the war began, he became increasingly critical of Confederate government and became active in the peace movement, running unsuccessfully for governor against Zebulon Vance in 1864. When the war ended in May, 1865, U.S. President Andrew Johnson appointed him as Governor. Holden helped organize the state Republican Party in 1866-67.

In early July 1870, Kirk and his 300 volunteers marched into Yanceyville and began arresting men around the area including respected citizens such as an ex-congressman, lawyers, an Army Captain and one sheriff. Within a short time, he had arrested over 100 men. The KKK retaliated and marched on Pittsboro with about 30 men to take it over. Kirk's forces pursued them into forests around Chatham County resulting in a bloody battle. After a few skirmishes, the battles ended with about two dozen casualties, half on each side.

By September, Governor Holden disbanded Kirk's militia, and by November ended the state of insurrection in the two counties. Several men arrested and imprisoned by Kirk demanded that Kirk be arrested for false imprisonment. A U.S. Marshall arrested him, and took him to Raleigh. Kirk was either released or escaped and slipped back home to East Tennessee. Democrats took back control of the State Legislature in the August 1870 election. Holden was later impeached, tried, convicted (along party lines) and removed from office, the first Governor in the United States to be removed from office.

The North Carolina Senate voted unanimously on April 11, 2011 to pardon Governor Holden posthumously. Holden, ever the newspaperman and writer, had once written "you can't be pardoned for a crime you didn't commit."

APPENDIX H: FACT OR FICTION

It is very possible that readers may be curious about the accuracy of some of the events that unfold within the plot, some seemingly improbable at times. It was very much an eye-opening journey for us as we dove deeper and deeper into official historical court records as well as written and oral history. We hope the following will help the reader separate fact from fiction and deepen their understanding of the story.

For the most part, all the main characters are based on real people and their real lives, but there are several fictional characters that have been woven in to allow for the plot to build and move along. Most antagonists are fictional: the bushwhackers, hostile confederate soldiers, certain county folk, and guests from South Carolina. In addition, some slaves/freedmen are fictional, and others are not: Pink Smith, Doc Smith, Tony Bowman, Jessie, Reily, Ben Gash and Harriett Steward are based on real people and most of the rest of the slaves/freedmen are loosely based on general information from historical records. However, there is a brief encounter with William Deavor's slave, Mary, whose name was directly pulled from a handwritten bill of sale. Finally, the Filmore family is fictional, although it needs to be noted that the actual event of how the sheriff helped initially hide Tommy Filmore is loosely based on a real account handed down by the Hamilton family.

Although Elizabeth and Pink lived during the same time period, their friendship and conversations are completely fictional.

Conversations are all fictional, although court sessions that are intertwined lean heavily on actual court records. The establishing of the county and the onset of war are all well documented as well as the official petition written to Raleigh before North Carolina seceded.

Marriages (even the most unlikely), births, deaths, enlistment dates, loyalties and divisions are all based on real events and accounts.

Oral history offers interesting twists, for example the love-hate relationship between Fletcher English and James Deavor and its strange unfolding. The story of Deavor calling for Fletcher after having been shot by Kuykendall is one passed down through oral history. The actual timing is vague, but the request he makes of Fletcher is based on the oral history.

Other oral and written historical accounts help paint clearer pictures of the time and the people such as John Byrd's accounts of war and its aftermath, the role of Elizabeth's grandmother's house along the Boylston Turnpike. The story of Robert F. Hamilton and his unique Civil War experience and the roles of the Young, English, Cagle, Mackey and Orr families along the Davidson River as well as other families, are well documented and shared. The physical descriptions of individuals are also enriched, including Pink's grey/green eyes, James' bright red hair and the notion of Cagle-blue eyes. Photographs help add additional characteristics.

Conflicts between oral and written: There are two occasions where there are conflicting stories and evidences. The initial one is the long-recognized belief that the Lankford House was built in 1854. However, two letters give rise to the likelihood that the Lankford family did not build or at least did not complete/move into the house until after the war started. One letter written from Amanda Lankford sent to her brother James discussing the death of her child and places her across from the Oak Grove Church. Another letter was written by Sue Clingman (Lankford's daughter) where she shares her memories of the days at the store and remembers coming home and wondering why people were gathered to discuss the new county that was just founded and where to have the county seat. We chose, for the sake of the plot and based on the two letters, to have the Lankford House built after the start of the war. Another question is where Henry Mackey was actually shot. Some accounts have him shot at the Red House (Probart Poor's Store), but oral history passed down to several Mackey descendants tells a detailed version of him being shot on his porch as he held a lantern. We chose to use the oral history version.

Letters, wills, and obituaries played a role too: the Lankford Family and their store and deaths of babies, Leander Gash's opinions and actions, Robert Hamilton and George Neill's life and death (including a level of distance between Andrew and his father), and Gertrude Orr Gash's death certificate revealed the name of the mother of the celebrated first free black child born in the county.

The establishing of the French Broad Baptist is heavily drawn from Nathanial Hall's work and led to several exciting discoveries about Pink's family and the role they played as well as the Allison's role in the establishing of this church. Relationships and experiences between Pink, Doc and the Allison family is heavily drawn from historical accounts passed down on both the Allison side and the Smith side.

The Union soldiers' time with the Hamilton's is based on two of the Union soldiers' accounts of their experiences.

Bushwhackers indeed wreaked havoc across the county. The Wilson Campground indeed burned, although who did it remains speculation. However, the bushwhackers were credited with not only the burning of the hotel and the murder of Captain William Deavor, but many other folks were robbed and murdered in cold blood during these times. However, the incident in the forest between the bushwhackers and the sheriff and his men is fictional.

APPENDIX I: MAPS

For the curious, who wish to see how the past and present locations and highways align, we have included a few clarifying maps. We hope these additions, although minimal, will paint a more accurate picture for those who need a clearer orientation.

Please understand that we provide this information as a visual courtesy only. We do not in any way suggest there is unilateral public access to these sites. While some locations are indeed open to the public, others constitute private property and, thus, are not. Please be sure to know and respect all boundaries and thereby avoid any trespass issues.

Thank you!

Although both maps are designed by Paul Parker at the request of the authors, the Wilson Campground overlay has been inserted courtesy of Gene Baker.

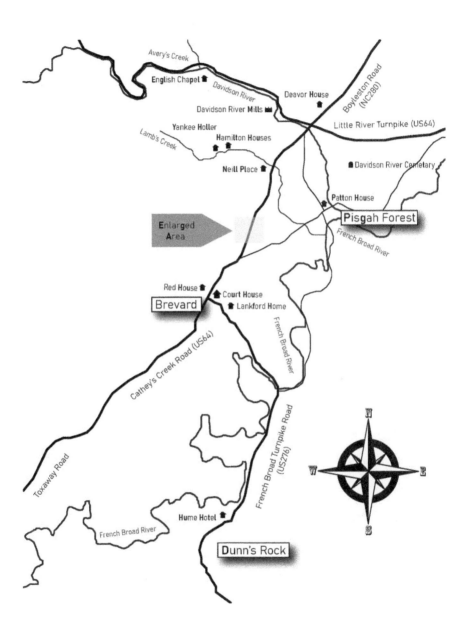

APPENDIX J: PHOTO GALLERY

The following pictures give only a limited glimpse into the faces of a few individuals in the story, mostly taken in their later years. Notably missing, and not found anywhere, is an image of George Clayton Neill.

Robert Hamilton   Rhoda Hamilton

Courtesy of the Rowell Bosse North Carolina Room, Transylvania County Library

Elizabeth Neill
Courtesy of Mary Galyon

Martha Gash Young &
Strawbridge Young
Courtesy of Mary Galyon

Pink
Smith
(left)
Courtesy
of
Kimberly S.
Howell

James
Morris
(right)

Courtesy
of Mary
Galyon

| Leander and Margaret Gash | Braxton Caldwell (B.C.) Lankford | Probart Poor |

Leander and
Margaret Gash

Braxton Caldwell
(B.C.) Lankford

Probart Poor

Courtesy of the Rowell Bosse North Carolina Room, Transylvania County Library

James-Henry Cagle

Rachel-Emma Young

Courtesy of Mary Galyon

Hume Hotel's remains

Courtesy of the Rowell Bosse North Carolina
Room, Transylvania County Library

As They Appeared After Reaching the Union Lines
(From left to right)
Lieut. J. E. Terwilliger, 85th N. Y.
Capt. C. S. Aldrich, 85th N. Y.
Capt. D. A. Langworthy, 85th N. Y.
Lieut. G. S. Hastings, 24th N. Y. Batt.
Capt. George H. Starr, 104th N. Y.

Union Soldiers

(left & right)

From Langworthy's *Reminiscences of a Prisoner of War and His Escape* by Daniel Avery, 1915

The Other Five Escaped Officers

Confederate Soldier Reunion 1910 (right)

Courtesy of the Rowell Bosse North Carolina Room, Transylvania County Library

English Chapel (left)

Courtesy of the Rowell Bosse North Carolina Room, Transylvania County Library

Oak Grove Church (right)

Courtesy of the Rowell Bosse North Carolina Room, Transylvania County Library

491

G. Keith Parker and Leslie Parker Borhaug

SPECIAL THANKS AND ACKNOWLEDGEMENTS

So many people have been a great help in this endeavor, both in their writing, conversations, and willingness to share. We mention some in deep appreciation for their help, still with the fear we may miss some in the many months and years of research and writing. First and foremost, special thanks need to be given to Mary Galyon, a direct descendent of several characters in the story. Her wealth of knowledge and genealogical research that she has compiled and so generously shared with us, brings her ancestors to life once again. Also, our thanks to Jonlyn Parker for her willingness to be part of the early editing process and walk through the tedious work with us with great excitement and unending enthusiasm as the story unfolded. To Tore Borhaug goes our appreciation for making the years of writing possible with his unwavering support and encouragement.

Likewise, the tremendous research support of Marcy Thompson, Local History Librarian for the Transylvania County Library, and her excitement in rediscovering the past was crucial. We thank Nioca Robinson, great-granddaughter of Pink Smith in the story, for her support and friendship during the entire process. Thanks to Paul Parker for assistance with map creation and site locations and Kimberly Sebranek for spending countless hours editing and providing feedback, integral to the flow of the story. Thanks to Ben Onachila, who meticulously journeyed through the manuscript and provided

493

invaluable feedback. Also, thanks to Diane Supinski who copy-edited the manuscript in preparation for publication, her expertise and time are greatly appreciated.

The cover would not have happened without the help of Maya Borhaug and the photography and editing skills of Sarah Borhaug. Thanks to you both! And Amy Borhaug, thanks for your continued support and honest feedback! Scharme Price, thanks for the time you put into working on the historical photos, so they can be viewed, void of scratches, tears and damages. Your expertise is much appreciated!

Much gratitude to Lewis Whiteside, great-grandson of Pink Smith, who was willing to spend his time reading and offering critique and support of the manuscript. A special thanks to Hattie Sanders, Ian Sanders and Kimberly S. Howell, who helped locate and then shared the only known picture of Pink Smith, Hattie Sanders' grandfather.

Numerous individuals shared information or gave feedback that allowed for depth of story, development of plot, or helped us make crucial contacts. We thank you Jewel and Wayne Allison, Michael Allison, Tim Ballard, Diane Brewton, Dr. Fred Bahnson, Rachel Cathey Daniel, Edith Darity, Deputy Eddie Gunter, Barbara Hawk, Dr. Paula Denise Hutchinson, Peter and Dawn Johnson, Rev. Spencer Jones, Richard Jones, Don Jordan, Elizabeth Jones Leff, Linda Gash Locks, David Mackey, Sheriff David Mahoney, Charles Moore, Amanda Mosser, Graham and Edward Neuhaus, Carroll and Kae Parker, Guy Payne, Mary Lou Hamilton Rhodes, Alfred Thompson, Tracie and Daniel Trusler, and Paul Williams. We would also like to thank Karen Smith and colleagues in the County Deed office, as well as Camp Carolina, located on that historic site of the Hamilton family in the story. Likewise, early research into the Hamilton history by Mark Valsame, from the State Archives of North Carolina, played an important role in the research.

Special thanks also go to Keith's colleagues on the Transylvania County Historical Society Board of Directors for their ongoing support and sharing of helpful information and even letting us look at the ancient Gash family flintlock rifle and Navy Colt pistol (on the back cover) from the same time and neighborhood. Gene Baker's long-term and detailed work on the founding of the county has been invaluable, especially the location and sketch of the Wilson Campground.

Finally, we thank the families of Transylvania County who took time to record their family stories and shared them in the three Transylvania County Heritage Volumes (Which can be found at the Transylvania County Library's Rowell Bosse North Carolina Room).We barely broke the surface on all that happened during this time in Transylvania County. The numerous stories that are not covered in this work are worthy to be read again and again.

We would like to acknowledge and honor the following works from which we referred to in the process of writing the historical fiction novel:

Almasy, Sandra Lee. (1999). *North Carolina Civil War Amnesty Papers, Vol. 12.* Raleigh: State of North Carolina Division of Historical Resources, Civil War Collection.

Barrett, John G. (1963). *The Civil War in North Carolina.* Chapel Hill: The University of North Carolina Press.

Brewer, Sue Dempsey. (1999) *Minutes of the Court of Pleas and Quarter Sessions of Transylvania County, N.C. 1861-1867.* Anderson, S.C.: Self Published.

Bumgarner, Matthew. (2000). *Kirk's Raiders: A Notorious Band of Scoundrels and Thieves.* Hickory: Tarheel Press.

Birch, Harold B. (2007). *The 101st Pennsylvania in the Civil War, Its Capture and POW Experience: The Saga of a Lucky Bedford, PA, Lieutenant and his Unlucky Regiment.* Bloomington: Author House.

Catton, Bruce. (2005). *The Civil War.* Boston: Houghton Mifflin.

Galyon, Mary Ann Daniels. (n.d.) Research Papers: Family BibleTreasures, How We Descended from John Morris, James Neill's Hattery Shop, James Wesley Morris, Life as a Union Recruiter, Preliminary Notes on the Churchwell Morris Family, Robert A. Hamilton Family, Some Neill (Nail) Ancestors of North Carolina, The Gentle Custodian, Young Family: Facts, Fiction, Speculation, Myth and Possible Mistakes. (Brevard: personal communication, 2016-2020).

Gash, Leander Sams. (1863). Letter to His Excellency Z.B. Vance, Governor of North Carolina. Raleigh: Vance Papers, Department of Archives and History.

Gash, Leander Sams. (1983). Prelude to the Reconstruction: The Correspondence of State Senator Leander Sams Gash, 1866-1867, Part I (Otto H. Olsen, and Ellen Z. McGrew, Ed.). *North Carolina Historical Review*, volume LX, Number 1. Raleigh: North Carolina Historical Commission.

Gash, Leander Sams. (1983). Prelude to the Reconstruction: The Correspondence of State Senator Leander Sams Gash, 1866-1867, Part II (Otto H. Olsen, and Ellen Z. McGrew, Ed.). *North Carolina Historical Review*, volume LX, Number 2. Raleigh: North Carolina Historical Commission.

Hall, Nathaniel B. (1961). *The Colored People of Transylvania County, 1861-1961*. Washington: The Catholic University of America.

Hamilton, John. (1869). Statement in Regard to Outrages Committed by Ku Klux on Geo. Moore & Robert Roundtree (colored) also on himself &c. (From) Broomtown, Alabama. Washington: National Archives Microfilm Publications, Microcopy No. 666.

Hutchison, Paula Denise. (2017). *A Family of Trees: Hunt, Hutchison, Mills, Sharp,Smith, Whiteside.* Charlotte: Self-Published. holysalt@yahoo.com

Langworthy, Daniel Avery. (1915*). Reminiscences of a Prisoner of War and His Escape*. Delhi: Facsimili Publisher, 2016.

McCrary, Mary Jane. (1984). *Transylvania Beginnings: A History*. Easley Southern Historical Press.

Minutes of the Court of Pleas and Quarter Sessions of Transylvania County, NorthCarolina County, N.C. (1861-1867). Microfilm in Archives of Transylvania County Library, Rowell Bosse North Carolina Room.

The Heritage of Transylvania County North Carolina Volume III, Commemorating the150ᵗʰ Anniversary of The Founding of Transylvania County in 1861. (2012). Waynesville: Walsworth Publishing and The Transylvania Genealogy Group and County Heritage.

Transylvania County Heritage North Carolina. (1995). Waynesville: Walsworth Publishing and Transylvania County Heritage Book Committee.

Transylvania County Heritage North Carolina Vol.2. (2008) Waynesville: Walsworth Publishing and The Transylvania Genealogy Group and County Heritage.

Trotter, William R. (1988). *Bushwhackers, The Civil War in North Carolina in theMountains*. Winston Salem: John F. Blair Publisher.

Wineapple, Brenda. (2019). *The Impeachers: The Trial of Andrew Johnson and theDream of a Just Nation*. New York: Random House.

ABOUT THE AUTHORS

Leslie Parker Borhaug is the award-winning author of a Silver 2012 Independent Book Publisher Award for her novel, *Unchained (2012)*, which she penned under the name LB Tillit. Combining her passion for teaching, North Carolina history, and writing, she also wrote three award winning books, with her students, about Transylvania County's local history: *Behind Closed Doors of the Allison-Deaver House* (2003), *Lake Toxaway... Back in the Day* (2004), and *Brevard Standing Alone, North Carolina's First Integrated Football Team, The Untold Story* (2005). Borhaug lives in Brevard, North Carolina with her family. For more information on Borhaug's other works as LB Tillit, please visit lbtillit.com.

G. Keith Parker, Ph.D., has published articles and books in the U.S. and Europe in history, theology and depth (Jungian) psychology, including the award-winning *Seven Cherokee Myths: Creation, Fire, the Primordial Parents, the Nature of Evil, the Family, Universal Suffering and Communal Obligation* (2006). Parker is Past President of the Transylvania County Historical Society Board of Directors and he lectures at college, church and community events on local and Cherokee history. He resides in the Dunn's Rock Community, south of Brevard, N.C. where his family has lived for over two-hundred years.

Borhaug and Parker previously published *Sons of Mercy and Justice: A Transylvania Story,*(2012) which won an award from North Carolina Society of Historians (2013). The father and daughter team are descendants of the Hamiltons.